The Price of Fame

By

Diana Grazier

"The Price of Fame," by Diana Grazier. ISBN 1-58939-462-3

Published 2003 by Virtualbookworm.com Publishing Inc., P.O. Box 9949, College Station, TX, 77842, US. ©2003 Diana Grazier. All rights reserved. No part of this publication may be reproduced, stored in a retrieval system, or transmitted in any form or by any means, electronic, mechanical, recording or otherwise, without the prior written permission of Diana Grazier.

Manufactured in the United States of America.

This is for Jim, who believed in me, and for Judy, who helped me believe in myself.

Prologue

I paused at the top of the stairs. As I did so, the skirt of my dress got caught up in the wind. It billowed out and swished around in front of me, sweeping slightly to the right in the direction of the wind. I could barely see my feet because of the thick fog, and I could only see the outline of my shoes. I was afraid of falling, but I ran down the stairs as fast as I could. I had one hand on the railing for support, but the other was outstretched, and I heard my own voice calling out in the wind. I called out, but I knew in my heart that he would be there at the bottom of the stairs. He always was. I had seen it happen this way so many times before in my dream, and there was no reason to believe that it would be any different now.

-1-

I never lived an ordinary life. That's the bane of being a child star. It didn't bother me until I reached adulthood, and then I began to wonder about all of the things that I missed. Some say they would trade places with me at any time, but I'm not so sure. We all pay a price for everything we do. In the few split seconds that I flew down the stairs, my life shuffled before me and became a neatly stacked deck of cards. For the first time in my life, I knew exactly what I wanted. I only hoped it would be there when I got down the stairs.

Most deep seeded puzzlements of the conscious mind have roots deeply embedded in childhood. For almost as long as I can remember, my mother dragged my sister Carolyn and me to every audition available to mankind. Fame was something that she wanted for herself, but she never achieved it, so she tried to pass this desire on to her daughters. She was a very domineering and controlling person, and Carolyn and I often spent our time together staying out of her way. Producers and directors can spot a stage mother ten blocks away, so for the first few years or so, we got absolutely nowhere because they stayed out of her way, too.

I remember showing up once at an audition, and someone who seemed to be the boss began screaming with colorful expletives to "Get that stage mother out of here!" I looked around to see whose mother was deserving of such language, and it turned out to be mine. After that, she saw the wisdom of hiring an agent to do the legwork and help keep her under some kind of control. Andrew Carver entered my life when I was four years old. He became my agent, publicist, and confidante. He was a father figure to me because I never knew my own father. I decided that everyone else's father must be like Andrew.

One day, with Andrew's help, Carolyn was cast in a cereal commercial. My mother threw a fit about the dress that Carolyn was supposed to wear. "Dark-haired girls don't look good in orange!" she said. "Can't she wear something pink or navy?"

The director patiently explained that the dress accentuated the color of the cereal box, but she continued to complain loudly from the sidelines.

Andrew took my mother aside, grabbed her by the shoulders, and said, "Look, Irene, the purpose of this commercial is to sell the cereal, not Carolyn. All they want is a cute little kid to take a mouthful of cereal and make people think it's the best thing in the world since *Sugar Smacks.* It's their product. It's their money. If they want her to wear an ugly dress, she'll wear an ugly dress. And if they want her to eat the box, *she'll eat the box!* Either she'll do what they want, or they'll get someone else. It's as simple as that! Do you understand?"

My mother made a waving gesture with her hand and rolled her eyes at him, but she never said another word. Later we saw the finished product. I had to admit that my mother was right; it was an ugly dress, but boy, oh boy, the box sure looked good!

Carolyn and I looked so much alike that we were often mistaken for twins, even though she was taller from being two years older. We had long, thick, black hair, which was probably our greatest asset. We also had very fine features with large, dark eyes and cute, turned-up noses. We were of average height, slender of build, and we learned to walk with grace. Our mother saw to that. She was always telling us to stand up straight and be proud of any height that we might attain.

With Andrew's help, and with less and less interference on my mother's part, Carolyn was cast in a few more commercials. My mother was domineering and controlling, but she wasn't stupid. As soon as it was evident that parts were coming in more without her help, she began to stay at home and usually asked Andrew to take us. One day, Andrew called and said there was an audition going on in which they were looking for a little girl to star in the lead role on a new television series. They wanted to look at six-year-old girls, and they were willing to cast an unknown for the part. Andrew took both of us, but since I wasn't six, I didn't get the chance to audition.

About a week later, we were notified that Carolyn was on the "call-back" list. This time my mother came, too. We sat in a stuffy little waiting room with hard-backed straight chairs. There was nothing to read, nothing to look at, and nothing to do. I got out of my chair and wandered around the room. My mother told me a few times to sit down, but I couldn't sit still; I was so bored. I began to play a little game with myself. The floor was made up of little tile squares, and I was trying to walk inside of them without stepping on the cracks. A man carrying a stack of files entered from a side door. I was busy not stepping on cracks, so I didn't move out of the way fast enough. I bumped right into him, and his papers went flying.

My mother jumped out of her seat. "I'm terribly sorry," she said to him, and then she shook her finger at me and said in a stern voice, "What did I tell you about behaving yourself today?"

"Word for word?" I asked.

"Word for word," answered my mother, who was obviously very angry.

I wanted to cool her anger, so I launched part of the tirade that she had said earlier. "You said, 'Now, Joyce, I want you to sit quietly and speak only when spoken to. We don't want people thinking that Carolyn's family doesn't know how to behave or that we have no couth at all. Maybe we don't, but no one has to know that.'"

My mother was mortified. She hadn't meant for me to remember all that, let alone tell some producer that we might not have any couth.

The producer just smiled. "Was that word for word?" he asked.

Before my mother could answer, I piped up, "Yep. Word for word."

Still smiling, he stooped down in front of me so we could look at each other from my eye level and said, "I'll bet you're good at remembering lines."

"I could if you told me what to remember," I said.

"How old are you?"

"Four," I answered, holding up four little fingers.

I had just given the wrong answer. He stood up, stuffed his papers back into the folders, and began to walk away. It intuitively came to me in a flash why six-year-old girls like Carolyn were wanted, and not four-year-old ones like me. To this day, I haven't figured out what gave me this kind of insight at such an early age, but I said to him, "Hey, mister! I can read!"

The next thing I knew, I was auditioning. First they asked me to make a happy face. Then they asked me to make a mad face, and then a sad face. Next they tried a few scenes. At first I was reluctant because, as I tried to explain, my mother told me never to make a scene. They thought that this was hilarious, but then they explained that all of the scenes they were going to do were make believe and pretend, so my mother wouldn't mind about that. I was told what to say and how to say it. In return, I just regurgitated what I had been told. It was that easy. They seemed to like me, and for some reason, they laughed at almost everything I said or did. I heard Richard Larson, who was going to be the director, tell Michael Parks, the producer, that I was perfect. They actually liked the fact that I was four. It gave me two years longer to be a kid if for some reason the show had a long run. It would run for fourteen seasons. My unusual life was about to begin.

M y character's name was Jenny Johnson. I played an orphan growing up in a children's home. I always wondered if the Broadway musical, *Annie,* was the inspiration for the show, but no one ever said that to me. Annie was eventually adopted; Jenny was not. If she had been, the premise of the show would have been gone. The cast was made up of other young actors and actresses who played children in the home. There were a few regulars, but I was the star.

I was very unprepared for the problems of being a television star. First of all, they changed my name. I was born Joyce Lynn Bryantelli on June 26, 1960.

"It's too big of a name for a little girl," explained Michael, as we sat around the table to discuss the final terms of my contract. "Joyce sounds too grown up, and Bryantelli–well, it's too Italian."

"That's what she is!" exclaimed my mother.

Michael heaved a tired sigh. "Irene, the name of the game is marketing. We need the public to embrace her. We want her to belong to everyone."

"What name do you have in mind?" asked my mother.

Michael shrugged his shoulders. "I don't know. How about Debbie or Donna?"

My mother stared at him incredulously. "Oh, come on! Does she look like a Debbie or a Donna?"

"What about her middle name?" asked Richard. "We can change it to Lynn or Linda."

I jumped out of my chair. "No!" I shouted, almost in tears. "I hate my middle name!" I looked pitifully over at Andrew, and I watched his heart melt.

"Don't cry, honey," he said. "We won't change your name to something you don't like." He cast a baleful look in Michael's direction. "Call her Joy Bryant. It's not so big, not so Italian, and it won't change her identity completely."

The next big problem that we had to deal with was where we would live. Because of the traffic, the studio in New York City was a two-hour drive. The hours I would have to put in at the studio were long enough for a small child. We couldn't add four or five more to each day. We would have to move to Manhattan.

Carolyn and I created our own little world. We played games and sang songs, but Carolyn was moody, and there were times when she just kept to herself. I was used to that, but she had been giving me the cold shoulder lately. It seemed more than just a mood. I was afraid to push the issue because she might tell me that I couldn't sleep in her room. I had a terrible fear of being in the dark alone. I never liked the dark, but being alone in it made it much worse. All of the ghosts and gremlins in my imagination came to life in the dark, and I stayed wide-awake for hours. My mother was very unsympathetic to the problem, so Carolyn graciously allowed me to share a space in her bedroom to sleep. I had a bed in one corner of her room, but I didn't keep any of my things there. I had my own room; I just never slept in it. After several days of getting the cold shoulder, I decided to ask why.

"It's not fair. If we move from Kensington, I'll have to change schools, have a new teacher, and make all new friends. You're not in school yet. You don't understand. We'll be separated from Leisel, too."

"Do you think we'll have to sell the house?" I asked.

"Of course not. The house has been in our family for years. You know the story. Mom will never sell the house."

Yes, I knew the story. We lived in an exclusively wealthy suburban neighborhood near New York City. The residents called a few square miles near the center of town, Kensington; however, it wasn't written that way on a map. There was an unspoken and generally well-adhered-to rule that when someone died, the property was either left to the family, sold to the nearest neighboring estate, or sold to an already existing resident or family. Outsiders weren't welcome, although they never really knew it because there was never anything for sale. Therefore, we were made up of very old families and very old money.

That night, long after I went to bed, I heard Andrew's voice downstairs. It was unusual for him to be at our house so late. I crept out of bed and sat on the stairs, carefully keeping myself out of their field of vision.

"I'm worried about her, Andrew," my mother said.

It wasn't like my mother to worry about us at all. Other than trying to launch us into stardom, she paid very little attention to us. I'm not saying that it was an easy job; it was tremendously time-consuming on her part, but we could never sit and talk to her, or take our problems to her, or ever have any fun with her. Aunt Ellie, my father's sister, was much the same way, and I think that's why our cousin Leisel tried to spend as much time with us as possible. I thought they were talking about me, but they were discussing Carolyn.

"She won't eat; she won't sleep, and she's angry all the time," said my mother.

"Do you think she's jealous?" asked Andrew.

"No. She's more upset with Joy over creating a situation in which she has to change schools than she is with the fact that she had a good chance of getting the role herself. Just how close did she come to getting it?"

"Richard said they really liked Carolyn, and they narrowed it down to just two girls. Carolyn was prettier than the other girl, and they liked that about her, but the other girl was more spontaneous. When Joy bumped into Michael by chance, he saw the best of both worlds. She's just as pretty as Carolyn and even more spontaneous than the other girl. Look, Irene, it's none of my business; they're your girls, but I have a suggestion. The girls might look alike, but they're as different as night and day. Carolyn is shy and reserved. She doesn't like changes and she doesn't adjust well to new situations. Joy is outgoing and effervescent. She can go with the flow. Stay here with Carolyn and get a guardian for Joy in New York."

I crawled back into bed and pulled the covers over my head to shut out residual gremlins. I trusted Andrew. If he wouldn't let them change my name to something I didn't like, he certainly wouldn't make me live with someone who wasn't nice.

The biggest problem, which didn't manifest itself until much later, was that there was never time to be a little kid. All of my time was mapped out for me. Most of it was taken up with things associated with the series, such as learning my lines, rehearsals, and the taping of the show. Then I had what I considered to be extracurricular activities designed to turn me into a superstar. My mother's long-range plans later became my long-range plans. I was going to succeed in doing what many other actors and actresses failed to do, and make the transition from television to the big silver screen.

Acting came naturally to me because I was basically uninhibited to begin with, and most four-year-olds are natural hams, anyway. I took to singing like a duck takes to water, but dancing was more difficult. My mother tried to take me to Bordeaux, a famous dance instructor in New

York City, to learn dance. I had difficulty learning the steps, and I couldn't seem to get my right foot straight from my left. It was very frustrating, and the French instructor had no patience.

One day, I saw a young woman watching us. She had a very sympathetic expression on her face. She watched us for quite some time, and then she took my mother aside. "Dancing should be fun, not a chore," she told my mother. "Bordeaux is a good instructor, one of the very best, but he doesn't know how to teach a small girl who wasn't necessarily born to dance."

"You don't have to be a born dancer to learn," my mother told her.

"No, but what Bordeaux does best is teach people that have raw talent to become top dancers. These people live, eat, and breathe dancing. Your daughter breathes other things, and I believe your ultimate goal is different. Do you want a professional dancer, or do you want a well-rounded actress? Those are different aspirations altogether. She can be taught, but she'll need patience. Let *me* teach your little girl. Within a year or so, if you aren't happy with me, she can come back to Bordeaux, and they'll be able to work together very well."

I prayed that my mother would agree, and for once, this prayer was granted. Katherine O'Shaunessey was beautiful. She had red hair, a slight Irish brogue, and she also lived in Kensington. She said that she had four sons, and they liked living there, so it was better for her to commute to New York City every day to teach dancing.

I had lessons with Kate for one hour, three times a week, for over five years. She started over again with basic steps, and then she waited for me to learn them well before going on. She said that I would be a jack-of-all-trades and a master of none, unless I really wanted to master one. I learned ballet, tap, jazz, and modern dance steps. My favorite dance was the waltz. I felt like I was gliding across the floor on clouds.

My mother took Andrew's advice and left me in the care of a paid guardian. Her name was Della, and I adored her. She was soft where my mother was hard. I could tell her secrets, and we made up stories and laughed every night before we went to bed. I returned home occasionally on weekends, and also for a portion of the show's summer hiatus, but most of the time, I stayed in a Greenwich Village apartment in New York City.

-3-

The days continued to flow into weeks, and the weeks into years. I never had a close relationship with my mother, so I didn't miss her. I missed Carolyn, but I adapted to our separation after awhile. I supposed that she did the same. It was mostly her choice to stay in Kensington, anyway.

I had an innate ability to converse with just about anybody, but a friendship from the heart where I could share secrets and dreams was a foreign concept to me. Sure, I told Della many things, but I longed to have a friend my own age. There are certain things that you just don't tell a mother figure. I always had to wait until the summer, and then I could come home and share things with Carolyn and Leisel.

One day, when I was almost twelve, we decided to go horseback riding. Carolyn and Leisel had been there several times, but I had never been on a horse before in my life. I asked them to get me the gentlest nag the stable had. I was introduced to Tessie, a tall, strange colored horse they called a roan. The horse was very gentle. In fact, she was too gentle. She didn't want to move very much at all. I didn't want to cantor, gallop, or even trot, for that matter, but a slow, continuous walk would have been nice. She just moseyed on down the path, occasionally stopping to nibble at grass along the way. It took me forever to catch up with the others at the end of the path.

Leisel said, "Maybe you'd like to use my horse to go back. It's just as gentle as yours, and at least it moves a little bit."

I was afraid that she'd do something to the horse if I changed places with her. I had visions of her making it rear up on its hind legs as soon as I climbed on. Leisel liked to play jokes, so I was a little suspicious.

"No, that's all right," I answered. "I asked for a nag, and I got a nag."

I finally got Tessie to the end of the path. As soon as I turned her around to go back to the stable, she broke into a dead run. I tried my best to hang on. I dug my knees inward, and as I did so, I lost my footing in the stirrups. They swung freely at her sides, and I was too scared to put my feet down to feel about for them. I hung onto the reins and to the horn of the saddle for dear life. We ran headlong through the path, and she even tried to brush me off by veering off course and getting too close to some of the trees. I ducked under limbs, and branches slapped my face. I felt my hair flying behind me in the breeze. I was terrified, and I didn't know what to do except scream and hang on.

Leisel and Carolyn galloped behind me. Out of the corner of my eye, I saw Leisel's red hair flying in the wind, and I heard Carolyn screaming, too. What seemed odd was that it was easier to keep my balance in the saddle when the horse was running than it was when we were walking. It was a nice, even run rather than an awkward walk. I was sure that I was going to fall off and break my neck, but as soon as we neared the stable, Tessie stopped running. The stable boy came out.

"I thought she was a gentle nag," I snapped.

"She is, but some of these horses know that after they take someone out, they get to come back inside the stable and get fed. She wanted to get home, get you off of her back, and get fed. You really can't blame her for that."

I had to blame somebody, so I said, "Then you shouldn't promote her as a gentle nag. I've never been on a horse before in my life, and she could have killed me."

He had a puzzled look on his face. "When they asked for horses, no one told me that you couldn't ride. As a matter of fact, I think one of those girls rode her once before, and she did the same thing."

About a week after the horseback riding incident, we went to an amusement park. I was upset because the strap that held me in on the roller coaster broke. I was terrified that I would fall out, but my momentum held me in place. I told Carolyn and Leisel that I would never go to an amusement park again.

I also came home for Carolyn and Leisel's graduation from junior high. As we ascended the unusually long flight of stairs, I was in awe. I had never been inside a real school before. I went up and down the hallways, gawking inside all of the empty rooms. I looked at all of the desks, books, and blackboards. I passed a sixth grade room. I went inside and sat down at one of the desks.

It was strange to sit there, knowing that was where I would have been if I hadn't done my series. I wondered what it would have been like, but I couldn't ask anyone because they would never understand that I didn't know anything about school. It probably would have sounded very odd to Carolyn and Leisel, too, even though they were well aware of my situation. I had a private tutor. I never sat in a formal classroom, read aloud to any classmates, played a game in a schoolyard, or made any school friends.

Leisel poked her head inside and broke my train of thought. "Hey, are you coming?" she asked.

I reluctantly pulled myself away from the desk and walked out into the hallway.

"We have to go downstairs to the gymnasium. That's where graduation will be," she explained. When we reached the stairs, she suddenly jumped up on the banister and slid all the way down in a matter of a few seconds. "Still as slick as snot," she remarked. "I'd tell you to try it, but it's kind of dangerous, and we really aren't supposed to do it. Some of us do it anyway. I'm surprised that they haven't removed them and put something in that's not so tempting to slide on. I figured I deserved at least one last slide."

The night of the graduation, we decided to go to the movies. There was a new actor that I had never seen before, named Brandon DeLorrier. He was from Great Britain, and he had an English accent. I loved accents. He took my breath away just looking at him. Carolyn and Leisel were affected the same way, and they talked about nothing else on the way home.

In the movie, a famous person was assassinated, and one of the characters was put in a mental hospital for the criminally insane. Leisel said, "You know, people get put in those places and they never get out." She said it in a very serious tone, which was very uncharacteristic of her.

"Maybe they shouldn't get out," I said.

"Maybe they shouldn't be there in the first place," she said. "You can't tell me that a person can be that crazy, and no one notices it. Maybe someone who noticed it should have told someone so that they could get help before everything got out of hand. Or maybe that person should have asked for some help. Now it's too late; they're stuck in there, and they'll never get out."

"You're taking the movie way too seriously," said Carolyn.

"I guess I am," she agreed with a short laugh, and then she changed the subject to something else.

-4-

When I was thirteen, I met another young actress named Marilyn Brigham. She was a year older than I was. She was tall, with long, blonde hair, and she was extremely pretty. She had long, shapely legs, and she liked to wear a lot of make-up even when she wasn't working. I met her on the set of *Jenny Johnson,* and we became instant friends.

Marilyn lived in the same apartment complex as I did. Her guardian happened to be Michael Parks. At one time she actually lived in a children's home. She never knew her parents or her family. Her mother dropped her off at the children's home when she was less than a year old, stating that she could no longer care for her. She went in and out of foster homes until she met Michael. He took one look at her, saw a pretty face and some acting potential, and brought her home to be part of his family. He cast her in some pictures, and she was given some parts in my series. There was an air of sadness about her that I thought she tried to conceal. At first, she never talked much about her life except to say that she would give anything to know something about her parents and learn why they didn't want her.

Whenever we had any free time, we would get together and talk. She was wise to worldly things. Her entire life didn't consist of television, and by now, I couldn't remember a time when mine didn't. We talked about all of the things that thirteen and fourteen-year-old girls talked about: clothes, movies, boys, and sex, and not necessarily in that order.

"What kind of person would you like to marry?" she asked one day.

I shrugged my shoulders. "You'll laugh if I tell you."

"No, I won't," she protested. "I have dreams, too."

"Well," I said, looking up at the ceiling, "I can't put a name or a face to this person, but I know that I want someone that just not anyone can have. I want someone who could choose anyone in the whole world, but he chooses me because he loves me." I waited for her to laugh and tell me that was ridiculous, but she didn't. I looked at her. "What kind of person do you want?" I asked.

"Someone rich and famous," she said.

We loved the nineteen-year-old actor, Brandon DeLorrier. Marilyn said that he looked like a blonde Adonis, and I couldn't have agreed more. I had just started going to parties and benefits, and I always hoped he would be at one, but he never was. He occasionally came to New York City, but he spent most of his time in Hollywood.

"Do you think he has a girlfriend?" I asked Marilyn.

"Sure. Several of them," she said. "He probably gets more ass than a toilet seat. I wouldn't mind if he had mine." She loved to say things that would shock me.

"Have you ever done it before?" I asked.

"Promise not to tell anyone?"

"Cross my heart," I said, making a crossing motion against my chest with my finger.

She leaned forward and said almost in a whisper, "I've done it a few times."

"Did you like it?" I whispered back. I didn't know why we were whispering; there was no one else around.

"Sometimes I did, and sometimes I didn't. You just don't dwell on the times you don't like it."

"Why wouldn't you like it?"

She shrugged her shoulders. "It depends upon who you're with."

"Who were you with that you didn't like?"

"If I answer that question, you must never tell. Never. If you do, they might take me away from you, and I couldn't stand that. You're the best friend I ever had."

"I promise," I said.

"Michael," she whispered. "But he put me in television, and he knows I'll never do anything about it; otherwise it might jeopardize any future career I have. I'm going to be just as famous as you one day."

I almost fell out of my chair. Michael? How could that be? He never, not once, did or said anything inappropriate to me. "Does his wife know?" I asked.

"She doesn't like me very much, so I'm assuming that she knows. It's not that bad. He's really good looking, you know, and I'm not afraid of him. He's very nice, and he doesn't force me. It's just that I'd feel better about it if he were single, that's all."

I was in shock. I was very well aware of the show business circuit, and what some actors and actresses sometimes did to get parts, but I was never affected by any of it. Andrew sheltered me from most of it, and I was lucky because Richard and Michael always looked out for me.

"Remember, Joy," warned Marilyn. "You promised. If you love me, you'll never breathe a word. I don't mind- really, I don't. I have plans, and I need Michael right now even more than he needs me; he just doesn't know it yet."

"What if you get pregnant?"

"I won't get pregnant. He always uses protection."

We were silent for a long time, and I was trying to let this horrible revelation sink in, when she said, "There's another reason you can never tell, Joy. If you do, it'll jeopardize your career, too. It could put some bad publicity on your show, and it'll ultimately affect you. At the very least, they might cancel the show."

There's a streak of selfishness and self-preservation in all actors and actresses. I would never tell. I knew it, and she knew it. I would also never look at Michael again in the same light.

I also made friends with an up-and-coming actor named Tony Milano. He was cast in a few of my shows, but he was not a "regular." He had no problems getting regular work, though, because he was always hired to do shows and bit parts.

"You're going to be stereotyped," he told me. "In fact, you already are. You'll have difficulty getting another series after you leave this one, and you'll probably never get to the big-screen. That's why I've turned down several offers to do my own series. I'm not going to jeopardize my chances."

"Maybe you already have," I said. "You haven't had your own series, but you've certainly been seen on television. You're still a television actor."

He got mad and walked away. We had become friends, and I knew that it would take more than that to make us quit speaking to each other. There would come a day, however, when we would stop speaking.

-5-

I was glad that I had Marilyn to share my problems with. When I was fourteen, Michael told Andrew to tell me that I was too fat to wear shorts and tank tops. I was astounded.

"I'm not fat," I said to Andrew. "Look at me. I grew a lot this year; of course I put on weight, but I'm not fat."

"Well, you know that the camera adds weight to you. They're just worried that things will get out of hand."

"They're telling me things are already out of hand if I can't wear shorts and tank tops." I threw my hands up in the air with exaggerated frustration. "Okay, you did the dirty deed. I won't wear them," I said, as I walked away from him. I was acting like it was his idea in the first place. I was often guilty of shooting the messenger lately. I was still upset later, and I spoke to Marilyn about it.

"Oh," she said, waiving her hand in disgust, "that's the oldest complaint in the business."

"What am I going to do?"

"Don't wear shorts."

"Marilyn, that won't solve the problem. They're saying I'm too fat."

"You only have a few options, Joy. Don't wear shorts; go on a diet; take diet pills, or do what I do."

"What do you do?"

"I eat whatever I want, and then I stick my finger down my throat and throw it all up later."

I wrinkled up my nose. "That's gross," I said. "I hate vomiting."

"Then just go on a diet. It's not that hard."

"So why are there twenty-million obese people in the world?"

"I'll tell you what," said Marilyn, ignoring my question. "Let's go out and eat everything we're not supposed to eat, like ice cream, potato chips, and candy. We'll have a farewell party, and tomorrow you can start watching what you eat."

So, that's what we did. We gorged ourselves sick on junk food. I probably gained another five pounds, and Marilyn probably just solved the problem by sticking her finger down her throat.

I said something to Richard, and he told me that there was a right way and a wrong way to lose weight. He was always willing to drop whatever he was doing and sit down and talk to me if something was bothering me. He said, "Quit eating all of the junk food and start eating more fruits, salads, and vegetables, and you'll eventually lose whatever weight you need to lose. Then you have to make those foods a way of life. I've seen them give actresses diet pills, and all it does is pep them up and make them feel lousy later. Promise me you won't do that." I nodded my head, and he continued, "I'd rather see you wearing baggy clothes for the rest of your life than doing that. And do not - I repeat: *do not* - do what Marilyn does. It's called bingeing and purging, and that can cause serious health problems. I've seen people die from doing that."

I solved the problem by taking Richard's advice. I also had to add another program to my already busy schedule: working out on exercise equipment every day. Within six months, I was wearing shorts and tank tops again. This was the hardest program for me to do because I had to get up an hour earlier every day to fit it into my schedule. I later became known for having a great figure, but it didn't come naturally or overnight. It took a tremendous amount of hard work, sweat, and determination to keep going with it. Sometimes I hear people say that actors and actresses have all of the time in the world to work out. They can afford their own personal trainers and their own exercise equipment, so it's no wonder that they have great bodies. I beg to differ with that. If it were that easy, no one in show business would have a weight problem. A person still has to be motivated to do an exercise program, and they have to find the time to do it. In my case, I didn't have all of the time in the world. I just sacrificed an extra hour of sleep every night and got up earlier.

September 1, 1975. If I had a diary, I would certainly have written this date down. I met Brandon DeLorrier at long last. I was invited to attend a benefit and also to be on Jerry Lewis' telethon for muscular dystrophy in Las Vegas, Nevada. I didn't want to make the trip by myself, so I invited Carolyn and Leisel to go with me. Carolyn never liked to venture far from home, so she declined, citing our mother's health as an excuse. Leisel liked adventure, and she wasn't about to turn it down. I let her borrow a dress from my wardrobe so she wouldn't feel out of place. She had beautiful and expensive clothes, but these benefits were like fashion shows, and everyone wore the newest and latest designs. Sometimes the designers talked us into wearing their clothes just to give them more publicity.

My gown was made of white chiffon, with thin spaghetti straps. It showed a small amount of cleavage, and it clung tightly to my torso. The dress hugged my hips provocatively, and it flared out elegantly when I walked. I thought it would look beautiful on the dance floor if anyone asked me to dance.

We entered the large ballroom, beautifully decorated with heavy red velvet draperies, golden ornaments, and large crystal chandeliers. Small round tables with red silk tablecloths and white silk napkins were scattered throughout the room. Champagne flowed from fountains, and every gourmet food imaginable was served on silver platters.

We were in the middle of eating dinner when Brandon DeLorrier walked in. He took my breath away. Right after the initial shock of seeing him, I noticed a beautiful girl with long blonde hair, large breasts, and shapely legs hanging on his arm. I was extremely envious. She reminded me of Marilyn; only this girl was older- probably about nineteen or twenty. She had on a long chiffon gown with a slit up the side, showing her leg all the way to her mid-thigh, but what I noticed most about the dress was that it was a very unusual shade of orange. It was almost a burnt orange, and I had never seen anything quite like it in chiffon. Not only was I envious of her, I was envious of that gown, too. I watched her receive many compliments on it. I told myself that my mother said long ago that dark haired girls don't look good in orange, so that stunning dress wouldn't have the same effect on me, but it didn't help much; I would have died for that dress. My food suddenly tasted like rubber, and I felt peculiarly unsettled. Usually I was unruffled in any social setting.

Tony Milano came over to the table. I had no idea he would be there. He was always one of the few boys around my age that didn't fall all over me when I walked into the room. We were friends, so I was no novelty to him. I was somewhat attracted to him, so I always wished that he would pay more attention to me.

"Mind if I join you?" he asked.

"Sure, go ahead," I said.

For once, Leisel was quiet. I decided it was because she was sitting in silent awe of her surroundings. Tony and I chatted awhile, and then he offered to introduce me to Brandon. He had a bit part in Brandon's last movie. He took me by the hand, and we walked over to the table.

"I'd like to introduce you to a friend of mine," Tony said. "She happens to be a fan of yours."

Brandon set his drink down and stood up. "And she, mine," he said with a smile. He held out his hand. "How do you do, Miss Bryant?"

I was shocked that he actually knew me, and Tony seemed to be, too. I shook Brandon's hand.

He turned to the blonde girl at the table. "This is Miss Julie Bishop," he said. "Julie, may I present Miss Joy Bryant."

The girl just simpered at me, and I wanted to slap her face. I turned my attention to Brandon. I wanted to be able to say something that would make him remember me after that night, and not just as another celebrity.

"What are you doing for the telethon?" I asked.

He smiled. "I know this sounds sort of crude, but I'm selling myself off to the highest bidder. The one who pledges the most money will get a date with me."

"What if the highest pledge comes from a man?"

He threw his head back and laughed. He had a nice laugh. "I meant the highest *lady* pledging money."

"I hope she's ninety years old," I said. "That would serve you right." He laughed again. I was enjoying myself immensely, and he didn't appear to be in any hurry to terminate our conversation.

"What are you doing at the telethon?" he asked.

"I plan to sing a couple of songs - nothing really earth shattering."

"I've heard you sing before," he said. "You have the voice of an angel."

Before I could respond to that wonderful compliment, Julie stood up, pulled at his sleeve, and asked him to dance. She shot me a baleful look as she walked past. Having been successfully snubbed by this girl, I returned to my seat. Leisel was still in shock and had nothing to say.

Tony asked me to dance. We didn't talk much while we danced, but it felt good to be held by him. I would have been on cloud nine, except that I kept looking over at Brandon. He was holding Julie tightly in his arms, and they were whispering into each other's ears while they danced. Jealousy stabbed at my heart like a knife.

When the dance finished, I went back and sat by Leisel, and Tony began roaming through the crowd. I knew that he was networking, and that I should be too, but I was very unsettled after meeting Brandon. Leisel saw me stealing looks at Brandon, and she suddenly became her old self. She got out of her chair, walked straight over to him, and whispered something in his ear. Cold fear gripped my heart because Leisel was capable of doing and saying anything. He laughed and smiled at her, and then he stood up and walked over to my table.

I heard the magic words, "May I have this dance, Miss Bryant?" He held out his hand to me, and I placed mine in his as I rose from the table. I thought I could feel sparks of electricity from his body move into mine. I never dreamed that I would one day touch his hand, let alone be asked to dance. It was a very magical feeling.

"What did my cousin say to you?" I asked, as he held me in his arms while we danced.

"It's not polite to tattle," he said.

He was a wonderful dancer. It was a waltz, my most favorite dance in the whole world. I thanked Kate O'Shaunessey, Bordeaux, and everyone else who made it possible to have wings on my feet for this one night.

Halfway through the dance he said, "I'm glad I came here tonight. I almost didn't come."

"Why not?"

"Don't get me wrong, but most of the people here are small screen, not big screen."

I stopped dancing abruptly. "Oh, I see," I said, rather coldly. "You are big, and I am small. I suppose you have to watch the company that you keep. Well, you shouldn't be seen with me. It might hurt your big screen reputation."

I walked off the dance floor and left him standing there with a puzzled expression on his face while other couples floated by. I was positive that no one had ever snubbed Brandon DeLorrier since he first burst onto the Hollywood scene, and I had just done so in public.

"What happened?" asked Leisel.

"Nothing," I answered, feeling very pleased with myself. "He'll remember me now."

With Leisel's help, I got even with that blonde snit that he was with, too. I waited until she went to the restroom, and we followed her in. We had to time it perfectly, so that she was already in the stall, and that way it would seem like we wandered in there after her and didn't know she was there. I also didn't want her to know who we were. I waited half of the night before she went into the restroom. I was beginning to think that she was part camel with a bladder the size of a drum.

"Someone is wearing the ugliest dress that I have *ever* seen," I began.

"I know which one- that blonde, with a sort of burnt orange dress," said Leisel.

"Yes! I guess she doesn't know that orange is considered tacky in Hollywood. Nobody wears orange these days. As you can see, she's the only one wearing it."

"Maybe she thinks she's starting a new trend," said Leisel. "We're famous for new trends every few years."

"I don't think she's that sophisticated," I said. "She probably doesn't know she's committing a social gaffe. She's obviously not from Hollywood's inner circle, but no one will be rude to her because of Brandon. They'll just smile at her and tell her how beautiful she looks and how lovely the dress is, and in reality, they just want to gag."

We didn't want to hang around too long in the restroom and have her come flying out of the stall at us, so we exited as quickly as we could and returned to our table. When she came out, she was obviously distressed. She seemed to be looking around the room in agitation, probably trying to determine who had been talking about her, so Leisel and I stopped following her with our eyes. We had seen enough anyway. Out of the corner of my eye, I saw her pulling at Brandon's arm and whispering in his ear. A few moments later, he ushered her out the door. I wondered what excuse she used to get him to take her home.

Maybe she told him that she was suddenly ill. I seriously doubted that she told the truth. We were doubled over with laughter.

Leisel said, "I didn't think that you had it in you."

"I've had a good teacher," I said.

A bout four months after the telethon, I got a strange call from Carolyn. She hardly ever called to talk to me when I was in New York City, so I knew this had to have been important. I gasped at the news. Leisel was pregnant! I decided to come home and get the whole scoop. When I got there, I found Leisel uncharacteristically aloof. Carolyn told me that she didn't want to discuss it with anyone, not even her. Leisel never told anyone. It just became apparent to the naked eye that she was pregnant. Aunt Ellie was extremely upset, and Leisel didn't like being hounded every moment of every day, so she moved into our house. My mother just ignored the situation.

I tried to get her to tell me something- anything- but she never would. If I asked her a question, she either pretended not to hear, or she started a conversation about something entirely different, as though I had never asked anything in the first place. I tried everything. I tried to get her to talk about it; I kept quiet about it; I purposely ignored it, but nothing worked.

One day, when she was about eight-and-a-half months along, I could stand no more. "I want you to know something," I told her. "I'm absolutely at my wit's end. I don't understand why you won't talk about it."

"Talk about what?"

"The baby."

"What baby?"

"Don't start that crap with me. I've had enough of it, and it's almost to the point that I'm ready to wash my hands of you. Look at you, Leisel; you're pregnant!" I felt stupid pointing out such an obvious fact to her eight-and-a-half-month pregnant self.

"I am?" she asked, incredulously.

I slapped my forehead with both of my hands. "Oh, forget it!" I said. "And forget you!"

I stormed out of the room and returned to my Greenwich apartment. She showed up at my doorstep a week later and asked if she could spend the night.

"I've got a long day tomorrow," I said, as I stood in the doorway. I was tired of playing games.

"Please, I'd really like to stay," she begged. "I don't like having you mad at me."

"Okay," I said, determined not to bring it up, because I could take this nonsense no more. I opened the door wider and invited her in.

I had a king sized bed in my room. I graduated from having Della share the same room with me, but I never got over the dark. I knew it was silly for a fifteen-year-old girl, but I slept with a nightlight on. I let Leisel share the bed with me, and she finally broached the subject that night.

"I've figured out what I'm going to do," she said, while we were lying in bed.

"About what?"

"About the baby."

"What baby?" I asked.

"You know what baby. Look, you don't understand how it has been," she said, staring up at the ceiling.

"Then make me understand."

"This baby can't be real to me. I just can't let it be real. I've spent the better part of almost nine months trying to convince myself that it doesn't exist."

I pulled myself up slightly in bed on one elbow and looked at her. "Why would you do something like that?" I asked.

"If I didn't, I'd never be able to give it up."

"So you've decided not to keep it?"

She sat up in bed and looked back at me. "You know me as well as anybody, Joy. Can you imagine *me* being somebody's mother? What do I know about being a mother? What do *you* know, for that matter? We never had anyone to show us how. I don't think I'm ready to be a mother, or that I'll ever be a good one."

"You won't know until the time comes. Look at it this way: At least you know how not to be a bad mother."

"That's not enough," she said. "And there's more to the story than I'll ever be able to tell."

"How does Bill feel about it?"

"He doesn't know."

"He doesn't know!" I exclaimed. "How can he not know?"

"He doesn't. I told everyone that I want to spend my senior year in Europe. I have a friend in Europe. I send her letters addressed to Bill, and she mails them back to him from England. He has no idea. Except for today, I haven't ventured out of your house for the past three months."

"Don't you think that he has a right to know?"

"I have a right to do what I want to with my own body, and the baby's body, too. I decided to have the baby, but I can't keep it. I might have gotten an abortion, but I waited too long." She paused for a long time, and then she said, "I want to get married some day, but not right now. Bill's parents will never accept that this happened. Look how long it took for them to even let him take me out on a date. This is his first year of college. He needs to graduate before he takes on a family. I care about Bill, and I can't do this to him."

"Can you really give the baby up to a perfect stranger?"

"I never said it was a perfect stranger," she said.

"You're going to give it to someone you know?"

"I don't want to talk about it," she said. "I'll never talk about it. If you love me, you'll never ask me about it. Never."

From the finality in her voice, I knew that she would never talk about it. Asking more questions would be utterly fruitless. She lay back down in the bed and turned her back to me. The discussion was over - almost.

"I don't mean to throw a damper on this whole thing," I said to her back, "but aren't you afraid that Bill will find another girl in the meantime?"

"It's a calculated risk that I have to take," she said, without turning around.

"And you plan to keep this secret for the rest of your life?"

"If anyone can do it, I can," she said. And I knew it was true.

Two weeks later, in the middle of a snowy March night, Leisel left the house unnoticed. She gave birth in an unknown hospital in New York City, and she gave the baby up for adoption. She never told us if it was a girl or a boy, and Carolyn and I never brought the subject up again.

-8-

My mother's health rapidly declined. She was hospitalized, but I seldom got a chance to see her because of my schedule. I didn't have an ordinary job where I could take a leave of absence. I had obligations to fulfill. When I finally did see her, I was shocked at what I saw. She was skin and bones. Her cheeks were hollow, her eyes were sunken, and she had no hair because of chemotherapy. She didn't look like my mother. She must have noticed the shocked expression on my face.

"Gorgeous, aren't I?" she asked.

"I wouldn't want to look like you," I said, trying to make light of the situation, but then I was sorry because it didn't sound quite so funny afterwards.

"Nobody should look like me." She was silent for a few moments, and then said, "Look, I don't have much time, and I know it. I have to get my house in order."

"Don't talk like that, Mom," I said, not quite knowing what else to say. "You can beat this."

She shook her head. "No. Not this time. I'm too tired, and we have to face this thing." She reached for my hand. "I wasn't the best mother in the world. I didn't know how to be a mother."

"You did the best you could," I said. "I wouldn't be where I am today without you."

"That's true," she agreed. "Look, Joyce," she said. She hadn't called me Joyce in almost a dozen years. "I signed the papers to make you an emancipated minor. You and Carolyn will be responsible for yourselves. I need you to promise me that you'll take care of her."

"Carolyn?" I asked, somewhat astonished.

"Yes. She's not as strong as you. She never has been. You haven't been home much, but I've watched her. She's just as pretty as you, but it takes more than beauty to be successful. She finds life harder than you do, and I suspect that she always will. She'll have plenty of money, just like you, but she'll need some emotional support. Promise me that you'll look out for her."

I nodded my head. I couldn't speak because there was a huge lump in my throat. It was now clear to me that my mother was going to die. She was saying goodbye. Ever since she was diagnosed with cancer, I was afraid that she would die and that I wouldn't get a chance to say goodbye, and now I realized that this *was* the goodbye, and that I would most likely never see her again.

"I promise," I said.

We were silent for a bit, and then I jumped out of my chair and began to pace back and forth in the room. "I don't know what to do," I said, feeling very frustrated. "I have to go back to Manhattan, and you're so sick. I think I should stay here, but I don't know how. They'll never let me."

"I know how it is," she said, reaching for my hand. "I want you to go back to New York City. I want you to go back and break a leg."

I didn't cry until I left the room, and then it took me a long time to stop. I went back to Greenwich Village, and I was notified a week later that my mother died peacefully in her sleep with Carolyn and Leisel at her side. I had to make special arrangements to attend the funeral because we were in the middle of a shoot, and the writers had to revise the script. They weren't happy about doing this at the last minute, but it was done.

Photographers were at my mother's funeral. I was being watched, and stories would be printed about my demeanor. I didn't know if I should just be myself, and cry because I felt like it, or if I should remain calm and stoic. I opted for calm and stoic. The next day, tabloids made a reference to my coldness, and they chose the most fitting picture they could to prove it. I was looking off in the other direction when they placed my mother's casket into the ground. I looked away so I wouldn't cry, but it was reported that I was cold and detached.

The night after the funeral, I was very agitated. I still had some unresolved feelings about my relationship with my mother. I decided that she must have loved us in her own way. I knew that I loved her because she was my mother, but I hated her, too. She wasn't like other mothers who played games with their children, and who told stories and baked cookies. I decided to get out of the house and get some air. I went into the garage and climbed into my new BMW. I never had much of a chance to drive it, anyway.

Leisel came out of the house and jumped into the passenger side. "Where do you think you're going?" she asked.

"Out."

"Out where?"

"I don't know. Anywhere–just away from here. Everything in the house looks like my mother. I can't stand it."

"You don't have your license to drive that car yet."

"So what?"

"Well, you better hope you don't get stopped. Don't speed or anything."

We ended up at a movie theater, and we saw Brandon DeLorrier's latest film. I went away from the picture feeling better, and Leisel and I laughed as we remembered fixing him and his girlfriend at Caesar's Palace. As I drove home, a middle-aged man, maybe in his late forties or early fifties, stepped off of the curb as I turned the corner, and I hit him. I saw him roll up onto my windshield and off the right side of my car. I was so scared that I kept on driving. Out of my rear view mirror, I saw him get up, and I prayed that he wasn't hurt.

"You should have stopped," Leisel said.

"I know, but I was scared. Everything went through my mind all at once. He'll sue me even if he's not hurt, and the papers will be printing all kinds of hateful things about me. Do you think we should go back and see if he's okay?" I began to cry, and my hands and legs were shaking.

"Absolutely not. Look, pull over and let me drive. If we get stopped, I was driving, okay?"

"You can't take the blame for this."

"I probably won't have to. We're driving home and staying put. Pull over."

I pulled over to the curb and exchanged places with Leisel. "What if I killed him?" I asked.

"Then a dead man just got up and walked. Come on, Joy, we both saw him walking."

I was almost faint with fear, but something else was bothering me, too. I could have killed another human being, yet I was so concerned for my own welfare that I left the man laying there. He got up, but even if he hadn't, I might have left him there, anyway. That knowledge was very disturbing.

"I'm so scared! What are we going to do?" I asked.

Leisel's eyes were peeled on the road, and there was a very determined expression on her face. "We're going home; that's what we're going to do. This never happened. We'll never mention it again, not even to Carolyn. It never happened, starting right now. No more talk about it, not ever."

"But-"

"Ever!"

There was a report on the news about a hit and run on the corner of First and Central. The victim had minor injuries, and he was treated and released at a local hospital. The police were on the lookout for a young woman driving a dark colored BMW. Leisel and I sat in silence as we listened to the report, and we didn't even turn to meet each other's eyes.

The next day, I checked my car to see if any damage could point a finger at me as being the driver, but I didn't see any, and then I returned to my apartment. I felt sick inside, and I was fearful that someone would find out, but no one ever did. Leisel and I never spoke about the incident.

-9-

In the late spring of 1978, we were notified that the network was not going to pick up our show for the fall season. So at the end of our fourteenth season, at the ripe old age of seventeen, when most people my age were just getting started in the work force, I was unemployed. That fall, when the new season would have ordinarily started, I decided to go back to Kensington.

It felt strange to be home. Carolyn wasn't used to me being home, and I wasn't used to it, either. It was a big house for two teenaged girls. Leisel came over quite often and broke the monotony. She was in the same boat we were. Her father had died long ago, and Aunt Ellie recently died of cirrhosis of the liver. So now Leisel was rattling around in a big house of her own, just like we were.

Andrew looked for new parts, but no one wanted to hire Jenny Johnson. It wasn't Joy Bryant that they didn't want to hire; they just didn't want Jenny Johnson. You would think that people in the business would understand that I was just playing a role. I wasn't Jenny; I was Joy. If I made Jenny that believable, then I was a good actress, but it never works that way. Producers and directors are the first ones to stereotype you.

"Everywhere we go, people flock to you. You're still loved and remembered. I don't know what you're worrying about. Something will open up for you," said Leisel.

"I don't know," I said. "I guess I'm just used to having lots to do."

"You need to go out and meet new people and do new things-things that you never had the chance to do before."

"I'm so out of synch that I don't know what people do. You know, I've never had a date. Not a real date, anyway."

A recent fiasco with Tony didn't count. We went to a party together, and he left with someone else. I vowed never to speak to him again.

"You've never had a date?" asked Leisel. Her eyes were wide with wonder.

"No. When have I had the time?"

She laughed. "We can fix that. I know tons of people who'd love to go out with you."

"Oh, I don't think so."

"Yes, I do," she insisted. "I have the most wonderful person in mind right now. Let me fix it for you."

"No," I protested. I knew all about Leisel and her jokes at other peoples' expense. She'd set me up, all right, and I'd never live it down. "I don't trust you," I said.

"Why not? Have I ever steered you wrong?"

"Many times. I'm not about to be the butt of one of your jokes."

"I don't intend to make it a joke. I know people who'd love to take you out. You'll have a wonderful time."

Like a fool, I let her set me up with someone. "He better not have bucked teeth and be a half of a foot shorter than me," I warned.

"Trust me," she said.

I knew better than to trust her, but I was so starved for male attention that I allowed it.

"It's all set," she told me a few days later. "A guy by the name of Gary Shawn will take you out this Saturday."

I knew that it was shallow to ask this question, but I couldn't help it. "What does he look like?"

"He's very handsome. Unusually handsome."

Oh, sure, I thought. What had I gotten myself into?

I received a phone call the following Friday. A young man's voice came through the receiver confirming our date. It was a very pleasant, masculine voice, but I knew that the most pleasant voice in the world could often distort reality. "Is this Joy Bryant?" he asked.

"Yes, it is," I said.

"My name is Gary Shawn. Leisel has arranged a sort of blind date for us tomorrow night."

"Oh, yes," I said, feeling uneasy. There had to be a catch with Leisel involved.

"I was told that you want to know what the average all-American girl does on a date."

"I suppose I'm not up on those things," I said.

"Well, a date for an all-American girl consists of bowling, a movie, and pizza, not necessarily in that order."

"That sounds good to me."

"I have family obligations every night until about 8:30, so I hope you won't mind getting started a little late."

I had all of the time in the world, but to him I just said, "No, not at all. I'll see you after 8:30."

There was a slight pause, and then he said, "I know that blind dates are a little bit awkward, and I usually won't do this."

"Yes, they are," I agreed. I thought that his voice sounded pleasant enough, but there still had to be a catch.

"I guess it's really half of a blind date, because at least I have the advantage of knowing what you look like."

"Tell me the truth," I said. "If you didn't know what I looked like, would you be doing this?"

"*No way,*" he said, emphatically. "Considering the source, which is Leisel, I don't think I'd dare. You have a lot of guts."

I laughed. At least he had a sense of humor.

When the next day came, I had butterflies in my stomach all day long. Would he like me? What did he look like? I had visions of a "bucky beaver," someone with two major bucked teeth, horned rimed glasses, and a whole foot shorter than me, coming to my house to pick me up. I decided that I would have to handle it with grace and go through with it. My paranoia got worse as the day went on. As I dressed for the date, I threatened Leisel, "If this is a joke, I'll kill you! I'll never speak to you again!"

"It isn't a joke. Believe me, he's a very nice guy. I know him very well. He's a complete gentleman."

To me, that was the same as telling some guy that a woman has a nice personality, while everyone knows that she's as ugly as a mud fence.

Leisel was saying, "Bill and I could have doubled with you, but I thought you might like to get to know each other."

Her assurances gave me very little comfort. I was too used to her practical jokes. I was even nervous about what to wear, and Carolyn had to help me pick something out.

"Your designer jeans will be fine, and wear this white silk blouse," she said, as she rummaged through my closet. "Just don't order spaghetti."

When I heard the doorbell ring, the butterflies fluttered around in my stomach and my heart pounded wildly. Carolyn answered the door and called out to me. I came out of my room and slowly walked down the winding staircase. I was very unprepared for the tall, thin, and very handsome young man waiting for me at the bottom of the stairs. He had light brown hair and beautiful green eyes.

"Hi, I'm Joy," I said.

He smiled and shook my outstretched hand. "I'm Gary."

As we walked out to his car, he said, "I'm sorry that I can't get here earlier. Have you eaten dinner yet?"

I shook my head. Who could eat after being filled with such anxiety all day?

Gary walked me over to the passenger side of his Jaguar and opened the door for me. He said, "This certainly isn't my first date, but I've never been out with a celebrity before. I have to admit that it makes me a little nervous."

"I put my jeans on one leg at a time, just like everybody else," I said.

"Sure, I put my underwear on that way, too," he said, and I laughed, relaxing somewhat. "I thought we'd go to Guiseppi's," he said, as he slid into the driver's seat, "unless you have a place in mind that you'd rather go."

My mind raced. *Italian,* I thought. Did he choose an Italian place because I was Italian? I must remember not to order spaghetti. "Guiseppi's is fine," I said.

Even though he said that he was nervous, he didn't seem to be. He walked straight and tall, and he ushered me into the restaurant with an air of confidence. He opened the door for me, and he put his arm lightly around my waist as we were led to our table. People stared, but they did that anyway whenever I walked into a room.

"How long have you known Leisel?" I asked, as soon as we were seated at the table.

"Since kindergarten. We have mostly the same friends. I guess you can call it a clique. I knew that she was your cousin. She was always very proud of the fact that she was related to Joy Bryant."

I hadn't known that. I knew that she loved me, and Carolyn, too, but she was never overly affected by the fact that I was a celebrity. She treated us the same; she never gave me preferential treatment because I was a celebrity and Carolyn wasn't. I was reflecting on this when flashbulbs popped. People came over and asked for autographs. Even the waiter wanted one. This always happened whenever I ventured out in public, but it was new to Gary.

"Does this happen all the time?"

"Most of the time. I don't mind unless I'm eating, and then I think it's downright rude, but I really can't say so because I end up being the one that looks like the idiot."

We talked about all kinds of things, such as what it was like to be a celebrity, growing up without knowing what everyday people do, never having any free time for myself, having every moment of every day mapped out for me, and now dealing with the cancellation of my show. I suddenly realized that we were talking mostly about me.

"Tell me about yourself," I said.

"I'm the youngest of four boys, all born one year apart, one right after the other."

"Your poor mother."

"Yes, well, she had plenty of assistance from my father, and also from some hired help. She owned her own business in Manhattan, so she didn't spend all of her time dealing with us. She died less than a year ago from some rare kidney disease. Zachary's the eldest; he's twenty-three, and then Francis- we call him Frank- is twenty-two; Patrick is twenty-one, and I just turned twenty. Zachary was basically raised to run the estate, and it'll ultimately go to him one day. He also helps out in my dad's newspaper business. Frank is interested in computer programming, and Patrick is fascinated with photography. He's always running through the house with a camera on his shoulder. We have reels and reels of family pictures, and sometimes it feels like we have no privacy."

"What newspaper does your father write for?"

"The Kensington Chronicles. You might not have seen it. You probably haven't been in Kensington very much."

"Why did they nickname our small section of town Kensington? I've never figured it out," I said.

"I've heard different stories, but the one that I tend to believe is that it was named after one of the Royal Palaces in England. Our section of town is considered elite. How much more elite can you get than being in a royal family? You have to admit that we're all made up of old families and old money. Do you know how far your family goes back?"

"The first Dutch colony in the 1620's, I've been told. How about you?"

"The Mayflower; they were Dutch, too. We're probably related to each other from way back, maybe from twenty generations ago. We're probably two blue-bloods who could only produce hemophiliacs."

I was enjoying myself immensely. He was poised and confident, with a subtle air of cynicism. I found myself becoming very drawn to him. All too soon, we were finished with dinner.

"How do you feel about bowling?" he asked.

"I'm game, but I have to admit that I've never been bowling before."

"You're kidding! Never?"

I shook my head.

"We'll have to do something about that," he said.

Heads turned again as we walked into the bowling alley. People nudged each other with their elbows, and I saw some of the boys give the "thumbs up" sign to Gary, but he ignored them. He helped me pick out a bowling ball because I had no idea what I was doing. He chose a ten-pound ball and said that I should be able to lift it well enough to throw it.

"I hope you won't mind me making a fool out of myself," I said. I wasn't afraid of looking like an idiot, but I wasn't sure how he would feel. After all, I was his date. Some people take these things very seriously.

"I have enough problems worrying about myself to ever worry about someone else," he told me.

I was having a wonderful time, and yes, I probably did make a fool out of myself with the whole room watching, but I didn't care. I attacked bowling with the same exuberance that I attacked everything else. I watched Gary as he went first. I watched him hold the ball and set it under his chin. Then he walked calmly down the walkway to the start of the lane and threw it. *No sweat,* I thought.

Then it was my turn. I didn't know that my fingers were supposed to go into the ball a certain way. I put my index finger and my third finger into the two upper holes, and I put my thumb into the lower hole. I awkwardly marched up to the start of the lane and threw the ball. I had no rhythm and no grace. It literally bounced down the lane. I knew that I must have looked like the cartoon character, Fred Flintstone, when he went bowling. The crazy part was that I knocked all of the pins down.

Gary closed his eyes and slapped the sides of his head with both of his hands. He laughed so hard, that he could hardly stop. "What in the world was that?" he asked.

"A strike," I announced proudly. Other people were grinning at my Fred Flintstone-like presentation.

"I'm sorry I neglected to show you how to hold the ball," said Gary, still laughing. "You have to put your third and fourth fingers in the first two holes, like this," he said, showing me. "And your thumb goes in the lower hole. Then you stand at the second line of dots here and walk slowly, you don't have to run, about four steps to the start of the lane. If your foot crosses the line where the lane starts, it'll buzz, so you have to make sure your feet don't cross the line."

I nodded, trying to take it all in.

"And keep your thumb out in front of you when you throw the ball. Look, I'll show you."

As he took his turn, he walked me through it. I tried to duplicate what he did, but I couldn't do it very well. I threw gutter ball after gutter ball. "I liked Fred Flintstone's way better," I finally said. "At least I got a score."

"Maybe what you should do is go up to the lane, stand backwards, and throw it between your legs. Maybe then, your ball will go straight."

He was joking, I knew, but to his amazement, I said, "Fine, I'll try it."

I marched down to the start of the lane, turned around backwards, and stuck my tongue out at Gary in defiance. I viewed the pins by bending over and looking between my legs. I set the ball down between my feet, aimed, and pushed with enough force to make it go down the lane. We watched the ball go halfway down the lane straight, and then it dropped off into the gutter at the very last moment.

"So much for that idea," I said. "It didn't help much."

"It usually helps six-year-olds," said Gary, still laughing.

Gary got me a lighter ball. It was easier to throw, and I knocked a few pins down with it, but I ended up with a dismal score of thirty-five.

"Well," said Gary, "are you totally humiliated, or do you want to try it again?"

"Again, of course," I said. "You'll find that it's hard to humiliate me. People can stare all they want. It can't possibly be as hard as learning how to dance at Bordeaux's." I shook my finger at him. "I'll get it down one day, and I'll eventually beat you." I threw another gutter ball. "But not today," I added.

It was almost midnight when we left the bowling alley. "It's so late that maybe you'd like to make the movie another night," Gary said.

I had a good time, and Gary seemed to also, but I wasn't completely sure how he felt until he suggested going out with me again. "I'd love to go to the movies with you," I said.

"We can make a nine o'clock show tomorrow night if you'd like, and then we can get a pizza afterwards, if you like pizza."

"I'm Italian," I said. "I like pizza."

Gary escorted me to my front porch. We chatted for a moment, and then I let myself into the house. He didn't try to kiss me goodnight.

I was mildly disappointed, but maybe he felt that it was too soon to make a move.

"I'll see you tomorrow night," he said, and then he stepped off the porch and turned toward his car.

I walked up the stairs to my bedroom still smiling.

-10-

Leisel wanted to know the whole scoop the next day, and she called me on the telephone to find out.

"How did it go?" she asked.

"I had a good time. I wasn't sure that I would, but I really did. Thank you."

"Are you going out again?"

"Yes, we're going out tonight. You know, I thought that you were pulling some kind of joke on me."

"How did he act?"

"Like a complete gentleman," I said.

"I knew he would."

I couldn't wait for the evening to come. I kept looking at my watch, and I found myself singing all day. I was so happy.

We went to see the latest movie starring Brandon DeLorrier. He had made about six motion pictures by this time. I sat there, enthralled. *A blonde Adonis,* I thought. His character died in the movie, and I found myself crying in the end.

"You should have told me," said Gary.

"Told you what?"

"That I needed to bring a handkerchief."

This made me laugh. "Next time you'll know."

We went to get a pizza after the show. "All of this Italian food is going to make me fat," I said.

"You can go on a diet for the rest of the week," Gary said. "I won't be free until next weekend, so I won't be guilty of corrupting your diet during the week."

He was suggesting that he'd like to see me again, so I was happy. I smiled and asked, "What kind of work do you do?"

"I work for my father's paper, but I'm in the process of trying to get hired with a New York City newspaper in Manhattan. I've been offered a job, and I'll probably take it. I want to be a serious reporter, but sometimes you have to take whatever jobs are available and start from there."

"What will you be doing?"

"Running a kind of gossip column."

"A gossip columnist!" I gasped.

"I have to start somewhere."

"Yes, but a gossip columnist!" I literally shrank from him. We ate in silence for a few minutes, and then I couldn't help myself; I had to ask, "Am I going to be fodder for your first column?"

"I never thought about it, but now that you mention it, it wouldn't be a bad idea."

I could tell by his voice that he was just being facetious; he didn't mean it. I made him angry, and I knew it. I liked Gary; I liked him a lot, but one could not be in show business without being suspicious. I felt like I was giving him an inside scoop that I didn't wish to give to anyone.

"It's a job, Joy," he said quietly. "You can either deal with it or you can't. I'll let that choice be yours." I said nothing, so he continued, "I have to start somewhere professionally, and it's a good job. I don't want to work for my father for the rest of my life. I want to be known for my own work as much as you want to be known for yours. Surely, you can understand that."

I just shrugged my shoulders at him and said nothing.

I thought that this might be my second and final date with Gary, but he kept calling, and I kept seeing him. I was drawn to him in a strange way. He was very complex. He could be cold and detached, and he could be warm and feeling. I eventually learned to anticipate his moods and understand his ways. Most importantly, he seemed to genuinely enjoy my company. He never tried anything physical with me; not even so much as a kiss, which sometimes puzzled me. He was very much a gentleman, and I considered myself to be too much of a lady to make the first move. Besides, I didn't know how. We seemed to have an unspoken understanding between us, and we just didn't discuss his professional aspirations.

-11-

One night, Gary asked me to attend a college dance. I had never been to a prom in my life, so I was excited about going. Gary told me that I might be disappointed because I was used to going to benefits and charity balls and rubbing elbows with celebrities. I didn't care about that. I had a date for a dance!

I picked out my dress carefully. I didn't want to be overdressed, but on the other hand, I didn't want to be underdressed. Many of the people attending the dance were affluent, so choosing an expensive gown to wear wasn't a major consideration. I just wanted something that fit the occasion. I picked out a long, white evening gown with a pink sash that showed off my small waistline, and the skirt flared out slightly when I walked. I wanted a dress that swished prettily with each spin or twirl. I've always thought that watching the movement of the dress is as nice as watching the dancer. My dark hair and dark complexion contrasted the whiteness of the gown, and as I looked into the mirror, I was satisfied with what I saw.

Most women who have beauty know it. They might feign modesty, but that's all it is. I knew I was pretty, and prettier than most girls my age, but I tried to consider it a gift from God, just as much as someone with a very high I.Q. or someone with an extraordinary talent could be blessed with a similar gift. I saw the look on Gary's face when he saw me, and I knew that he was pleased with my appearance.

The dance was already in progress because we didn't arrive until almost nine. As we walked into the ballroom, heads turned. Again, I saw whispers and elbow nudging and thumbs-up signs. Gary pretended not to notice, but he seemed proud to be with me. He put his arm lightly around my waist and led me across the floor to an empty table. He got me something cold to drink, and we sat at our own table, quietly chatting. People slowly started to come over to the table. It was like everyone was waiting for some brave soul to make the first move, and then everyone was lining up. Gary introduced me to countless people. Some were getting ready to ask for autographs when Gary excused us from the congregating crowd and led me out onto the dance floor.

The band was versed in all kinds of music. They played a good mixture of fast and slow dances from the 50's, 60's, and 70's. I was pleasantly surprised to find that Gary was very easy to dance with. "You're a wonderful dancer," I told him, during one of the slow songs. He had his arm snugly around me, and I felt my heart beating wildly.

"You're not so bad yourself."

"I shouldn't be. I put a lot of time, effort, and tears into learning how. It didn't come easily for me."

"Some of the best things in life don't come easy," he said.

I closed my eyes and let myself enjoy being held by him as we slowly swayed to the music. I was aware of many eyes watching us. Several pictures were being snapped, but I tried not to dwell on that.

"Is this music anything like they have at the dances you're used to going to?" he asked.

"Yes, and no. I love a good waltz, but I'm sure that kind of dancing wouldn't be popular with this crowd."

"Well, that isn't a dance that everyone learns, but I'm sure there are several people here who can do it fairly well."

I excused myself to go to the restroom. I heard people talking about me, saying how pretty my dress was, and wondering how Gary ever got to know me. No one said anything negative, but I was reminded of the time that Leisel and I sabotaged Brandon DeLorrier's date in the restroom. The very same thing could happen to me if someone were inclined to be spiteful. I felt a sudden pang of remorse for what I did almost four years ago.

As I walked out of the restroom, I noticed for the first time a small, petite, blonde girl of about nineteen or twenty sitting in one of the chairs along the wall. She seemed more of a spectator than a participant. When we made eye contact, I knew something was wrong. She looked very pretty, but she also looked extremely sad. Those sad eyes haunted me. Off and on throughout the evening I found myself looking around, and I frequently saw her eyes following Gary and me. People that came over to sit by her seemed to be comforting her in some way. They talked to her, and then they turned their heads to us and back again to her. I didn't want to ask Gary about her, so I decided to ask Leisel later. When I did ask, Leisel told me that there had to have been hundreds of pretty blonde girls there, so unless I knew a name, she couldn't answer, but she couldn't imagine one person that would have a problem with Gary and I being out together.

When I returned to the dance floor, the band struck up a waltz. Gary was grinning at me. As I looked around the room, I noticed that there were a few couples gamely attempting to do it, and some were genuinely proficient at it. Gary held his hand out to me. "May I have this dance, Miss Bryant?"

I smiled and took his proffered hand in a rather formal way, and he led me out onto the floor. I knew that Gary was a good dancer because I had been dancing with him all night, but this was different. He glided me across the floor in the most graceful way. I had danced with professional people who didn't do it nearly as well as he did. He didn't adhere to the basic one, two, three step of a waltz. He swung me out at times, and I twirled under his arm and back again.

People began to stare. Other couples walked off of the floor just to watch us. I felt like Cinderella at the ball dancing with Prince Charming. We looked at each other as we danced about the room in perfect unison. Gary had a slight smile on his face as he looked at me, and as I returned his gaze, a feeling of elation came over me that I had never experienced before. It was a very long waltz, but it could have gone on forever as far as I was concerned. His dancing style was decidedly professional. When the last note of the music sounded, Gary, who was still holding my right hand in his, made a formal bow to me. I curtseyed, and he kissed my hand. People clapped and cheered.

I was astonished. "I had no idea that you could do this," I said, as we walked back to our table. "From the look on everyone's face, I don't think even your closest friends knew that you had this in you. Where in the world did you learn to dance like that?"

"My mother was a professional dancer, and she made sure that all of her boys could dance. I didn't like learning at the time because I was just a young boy, but I have certainly appreciated it since junior high. You never went to school, but before junior high, doing things with girls isn't appealing to most boys, and I had to put up with an occasional joke or two. But when my friends were struggling to learn, I already knew how. Zachary is probably the best dancer of the four of us, but I'm not too bad."

"You certainly aren't. What studio did your mother teach at?"

"O'Shaunesseys in Manhattan. Our name was shortened to Shawn a few generations back, probably in an attempt to make us seem less Irish, but she liked the sound of it and used the name professionally."

"O'Shaunesseys! Kate?"

He nodded.

"What a small world! Your mother taught me for five years."

Gary smiled. The band was playing another slow song. He stood up and offered me his hand. I could still feel the excitement of that waltz as we danced.

"I came here expecting to be like everyone else," I said.

"I'm sorry," said Gary. "Maybe it was selfish of me, but for once in my life, I didn't want to be like everyone else." He held me tighter, and we glided across the floor.

-12-

Gary and I began to see each other every weekend. It was always a late date because he never came any earlier than 8:30. We went to movies, bowling, dinner, and once we even went ice-skating. I had never been skating before, and I could barely stand up on them. He had to hold me upright as I tried to maneuver around the rink. I fell so many times that my tailbone hurt. We laughed hysterically about my clumsiness.

"Maybe you should pretend like you're dancing, and then it'll be easier for you to glide across the ice," said Gary.

"At least when I'm dancing, both of my feet are solidly on the ground. What's with this tiny little blade, anyway?"

Gary still never tried to make a pass at me. He wouldn't even kiss me. Once in a blue moon he would give me a quick kiss on the cheek, but that was the extent of it.

"You know, I've been going out with Gary for almost a year. Doesn't it seem odd to you that he has never once tried to make a pass at me, and that he has never tried to kiss me?" I asked Leisel one day.

"No," she said. "I didn't think he would."

"Why?"

She became very evasive, and said, "Gary doesn't go around kissing girls, that's all."

"We're not talking about someone making the rounds with everybody kissing on them. I think it's strange that he hasn't tried it with me just once."

She became even more evasive, and I knew that I'd get no further with her. It wouldn't have bothered me so much, but Leisel was the keeper of many secrets, and I knew that she had to have known the reason. Another thing I noticed about Gary was that he never drank alcohol, even though he was twenty-one. Leisel always had a few drinks at parties, and occasionally, so did I, even though I wasn't twenty-one. One day I asked him why.

"I've had alcohol before, but I don't like the effect. I like to be in control of my senses. Even a little bit seems to affect me adversely, so I just stay away from it all together."

Somehow, that didn't surprise me. Gary was a person who liked to be in control. I understood, because I also liked control. We never tried to manipulate each other, however, probably because we knew it would be futile. We would have to share, or we would never get along. One day, when I could stand it no more, I asked Gary why he never tried to kiss me.

"Most young men my age are only out for one thing," he said, in answer to my question. "I guess I don't want you to think that I'm like that."

"Gary," I said, "by now I certainly know that you're *not* like that."

He leaned over and kissed me fully on the lips. It was so full of feeling and passion, that it took my breath away.

-13-

Andrew was working on trying to get me cast somewhere, but it was still the same old thing; they didn't want Jenny Johnson. I began to experience mixed emotions about returning to work. I wasn't sure how Gary would react. We certainly wouldn't be able to see each other as frequently as we had been.

"You seem to be getting awfully serious about Gary," Leisel told me one day, while we were eating breakfast at her house.

"Why shouldn't I be? We like each other's company."

"Are you in love with him?"

"That's none of your business," I said, as I buttered my toast.

"I just don't think it's a good idea to set your heart upon him, that's all."

"And why not? You're the one who set us up in the first place. Why would you have misgivings now?"

"I never expected it to get this far. You know that I don't like to talk about people, but I'm going to say this just once because I love you. I think that he's using you. In fact, I know he is."

I set my butter knife down across my plate, and it made a clanking sound. "How would you know?" I asked, coldly.

She shrugged her shoulders.

"Leisel," I said, as patiently as I could, "if you're going to start something, the very least you can do is finish it. I asked you a question, and I want an answer."

"Because Gary doesn't like *girls,*" she spat at me. "Do I have to spell it out for you any more than this?"

She turned her face away from me. It took a while for this bombshell to sink in. When I finally found my tongue again, I said, "Are you out of your mind?"

"I knew you wouldn't believe me. That's why I didn't say anything earlier."

I threw my napkin down and got up from the table. "I've had enough of this conversation. I'm going to ask Gary why you would say something like that."

"Why would he tell you? You're his meal ticket."

"Gary is wealthy, too. He doesn't need a meal."

"I mean his ticket to fame. Look at his job. He writes a celebrity column, and they're a dime a dozen. Through you, his career could really take off."

"You still haven't answered me. Why did you set me up with him in the first place?"

"Look," she said, getting up from the table and standing squarely in front of me, "I wanted to pick out somebody that I knew you'd be safe with. You said there had to be a catch; well, there was. I didn't want you to go out with someone who'd take advantage of you. You were totally naive in the world of dating. You would have been a great trophy for most of the college boys that I knew. I knew that you'd be absolutely safe if you went out with Gary."

"What are you up to, Leisel?"

"You don't believe me."

"I don't believe you!" I shouted, almost in tears.

She seemed to be thinking hard about something. I could almost see wheels turning around in her head. "What if I said I could prove it?" she said.

"How in the world are you going to do that?"

"I want you to meet me for breakfast at a place called Tiffany's. I'll tell you where to sit. Go in the back entrance at seven o'clock and ask the waiter for table five. If it's taken, you'll have to come back another day."

"Why table five?"

"Because Gary sits at table four every morning. He meets his friend there every day. Don't show yourself to Gary. Just sit in the booth and listen to them."

"What if he sees me?"

"There are partitions for privacy there. He won't see you unless you run into him while he's being seated. Get there at seven, and that won't happen. I might be a little late, but I'll join you."

I went through the rest of the day with my mind in a depressed fog. I kept telling myself that it couldn't be true. Gary loved me. Before today, I would have staked my life on it. I wasn't a naive fool. Yes, I was inexperienced with normal, everyday things that everyday people did, but I wasn't stupid when it came to relationships. I was an eyewitness to celebrity romances all of the time. I knew what it was like when people used each other, and I knew what some people did to get to the top. I knew all about the morals of the business I was in, and of the casting couches that everyone talked about. I knew that Marilyn participated in those things to further her career, and she was even making some headway now in Hollywood. So even though I was lucky to have avoided many of the pitfalls, I was still not blind to what went on. I barely slept that night, and I counted the hours until dawn. *I'll go tomorrow and see that it isn't true,* I told myself.

I walked into Tiffany's and asked the waiter for table five. I prayed that it would be empty, and it was. I was on pins and needles waiting for Leisel to join me. Gary showed up before Leisel did, and he sat down at table four. About ten minutes later, a man who appeared to be in his early twenties walked in. As I watched him make his way across the room, I noticed that he had a very feminine walk.

"Sorry I'm late," I heard him tell Gary. "I was detained." He also had a feminine accent to his voice, which I had heard before. This person was obviously gay.

"What detained you?" asked Gary, who seemed upset about it.

"An old friend," he said. There was a pause, and I heard the man say, "What are you getting so bent out of shape for, anyway? It isn't as though you haven't been having diversions of your own."

"You mean Joy?"

"Yes, I mean Joy. You've been spending an awful lot of time around her. One might think that you're getting pretty serious. I don't suppose that you've ever told her your little secret."

"No, not yet."

"Well, what are you waiting for? Don't you think she'll understand?"

"How could she *possibly* understand, Brian?"

"Well, she's in show business. She has probably seen and heard it all. But I can certainly understand why you'd want to tread carefully. After all, if you play your cards just right, and if you were to marry her, it certainly wouldn't hurt your career any, would it?"

"No," said Gary. I heard a slight ironic laugh in his voice. "It wouldn't hurt."

I got up from the table and ran out of the room undetected by them. I didn't stop running until I got home. I forgot that Leisel was supposed to meet me.

I couldn't sit still. I paced up and down in the house, and I felt sick inside. I wondered if it was possible for my heart to physically hurt, or if it was just my imagination. That evening, Gary came over to my house. He immediately saw that something was wrong and asked me about it.

I decided to put on my best acting face. "It's nothing," I said. "I guess I'm just a little tired."

"We don't have to go out anywhere," he said.

I was trying to find a way to broach the subject, but I couldn't figure out how. For the first time in my life, I was at a loss for words.

Gary took my hand. "Do you know what today is?"

I shook my head.

"It's the first anniversary of the night we met. I thought women kept up on those things."

I smiled at him, but the smile felt wooden. My whole body felt wooden.

"I want you to know that I've never felt this way about a woman before. I know that I'm only twenty-one, but I also know that I can look for the rest of my life and never find anyone quite like you. I want you to be in my life–always." He brought my hand to his lips and kissed it. "Joy, will you consider marrying me?"

My thoughts raced. He was asking me to marry him, and he was keeping his big secret to himself. Leisel must have been right. *If you had only asked me yesterday, the answer might have been different,* I thought. Out loud I said, "I'm terribly sorry, Gary, but I can't marry you."

I said it matter-of-factly, but in reality, I had to summon by best acting skills to say it with any composure. He had a stunned look upon his face, and I could tell by looking into his eyes that he honestly believed that I would accept.

I suddenly felt the need to explain. "You're a social climber and an opportunist, and I can't marry you."

"Why would you even think that, Joy?"

"Because I know, Gary; I *know!*" I said, and I burst into tears. "You are only using me to further your career."

He dropped my hand as though it were a hot potato. "You really believe this?"

"Yes, I do."

The hurt expression left his face, and his eyes blazed with anger. He stood up and towered over me. "I want to make one thing perfectly clear: I don't need to marry you to give myself a name. I can be just as famous without you at my side as with you, and maybe even more."

"What do you mean?"

"You'll see," he said, and he stalked out of the room. A few moments later, I heard the door slam.

I couldn't believe what had just happened. I sat in confused and stoned silence. How was I going to put my life back together again now? I was concentrating on this very problem when the phone rang. It was Andrew. "How would you like to go back to work?" He sounded excited.

"What do you have in mind? Another series?" I asked, as I wiped tears from my face.

"No, how about Broadway?"

"Broadway?" I was genuinely surprised.

"Why not? You can sing and dance, just like everyone else they hire to do those plays. You might find that you like having a live audience. Your singing talents have been showcased in the past, so you won't have to prove anything more than you already have."

I thought about it for a few moments. I knew several actors that said they preferred Broadway to television. They all described a rush of exhilaration during performances, which I assumed was due to adrenalin. They said that there was nothing like connecting with a live audience and hearing the applause.

"What show do you have in mind?"

"What has always been your very favorite musical, ever since you were a little girl?"

"Oh, it couldn't be my favorite musical," I said.

"You're thinking that I don't remember what your favorite one is," said Andrew, reading my mind, "but, I do. We had to get you a special tape of the television broadcast because you'd get so mad if they aired it and you didn't get a chance to see it."

"*Rogers and Hammerstein's Cinderella!* Are you serious? Are they planning a revival of that?" I was almost jumping up and down with excitement.

"The one and only," he said. "I convinced them that you're perfect for the part. You're beautiful and talented; you can dance, and you can sing like nobody's business. What do you say, Joy?"

"I say that I need a change, and I need something to do right now, or I'll go crazy. Thank God for you, Andrew!"

-14-

I moved back to Greenwich Village. Della hadn't lived with me since my mother signed the papers to make me an emancipated minor, but I still saw her every now and then. She kept in touch with Marilyn and told me from time to time how she was.

I ran into Marilyn late one evening, and we went to a restaurant together. We hadn't seen each other in over a year and a half, but it was as if there had never been any time or distance between us. She had just returned from Hollywood, where she had been cast in a bit part with Brandon DeLorrier. She even dated him a few times.

"What's he like?" I asked.

"He's arrogant, conceited, and very adorable. I enjoyed every wicked moment of it."

"Are you still seeing him?"

She sighed and shrugged her shoulders. "I see him once in a while. He spends some of his time in New York, but I think he sees lots of women."

"More ass than a toilet seat," I said, as I remembered back to when we were two precocious teenaged girls. We shared a laugh over that memory.

"Yes, and I said that he could have mine."

"Does it bother you that he sees other people?"

"It does, but I can't do anything about it. He'd just stop seeing me altogether if I made a fuss about it. What about you? I knew that you had some kind of a romance going on. What happened to it?"

"It unraveled and fell apart," I said. "I don't want to talk about it."

There was no point in going into the whole thing. I had been so busy that I didn't have much time to dwell on it, anyway. I had always heard that time is a great healer, but I decided that *work* is a greater remedy. Load yourself up on work so you can't even think about it, and before long, *time,* the ultimate healer, will pass and there will be no more pain. I was proud of myself for being so philosophical.

Marilyn sighed. "It's not easy to be in love," she said.

This was none of my business, but I couldn't help it. I said, "Whatever finally happened between you and Michael?"

"His wife didn't like me. She knew, and she was pressuring him to send me back into foster care. It wouldn't have been good publicity for him. After all, he made a fortune producing a series about children living in an orphanage who needed parents. How would it look if he sent his foster child back into the system? Della bailed me out. She offered to take me off of his hands, and I haven't seen him since. I never told her the whole story. I don't think I'll ever tell anyone but you. Even now, it could be professional suicide. I think Della knew something was funny, but she never pushed the issue. I only had to stay with her for a few months because I turned eighteen soon after, but I stayed with her a little bit longer until I went to Hollywood."

I changed the subject. "Marilyn, I've never seen you looking so thin. Are you still bingeing and purging?" Her cheeks were hollow, and her clothes seemed to hang on her.

"No, I haven't done that in a couple of years. Lately, I've been able to eat almost anything I want, and I'm still losing weight. It must be my hectic schedule."

We decided to share the apartment, and Marilyn moved in with me. We went everywhere together in our spare time. We window-shopped up and down Fifth Avenue, and other times, we went on actual shopping binges. Manhattan was full of stores that catered to the wealthy. We tried on ridiculous hats and wigs and laughed like crazy. I think we sometimes infuriated some of the snooty salespeople.

It was a well-known fact that if you had to ask the price of a magnificent gown, you couldn't afford to buy it. There were times when I felt guilty about spending tens of thousands of dollars just on clothes, jewelry, and accessories. Marilyn had a different philosophy.

"When I didn't like my food, the house mother would tell me how lucky I was to even have food, and to think about all those poor starving people in China who would love to have my food. I was told that I should appreciate what I had, and that I should eat it. Well, shouldn't it work the same way with everything else? I should be happy that I have all of these nice things, and appreciate them because of all of the poor starving people in the world that can't afford them. I should appreciate what I have, and I should wear them."

Marilyn tended to be more cynical than I was, but then, I had a tendency to be drawn to cynical people, like Gary. He had said things that shocked me, but if I really thought about it, I was able to understand where he was coming from. It was just a different perspective, which usually had a ring of truth. Marilyn had a harder road in life to climb than I did, and Gary just had a reporter's nose and an uncanny ability to look at human nature with a cold, calculating eye. He wouldn't be caught dead with rose-colored glasses on, and I wouldn't know if they were sitting right on my face.

I loved being around Marilyn. We talked of all our hopes and dreams and aspirations. I still sensed a feeling of sadness about her at times. One day she told me why.

"I really hate not knowing where I came from," she said. "I used to lie in bed at night and wonder if someone out there looked like me. I even wondered if my parents would notice me when I had parts in television and movies and decide to come and get me."

"I used to think that about my own father," I said. "I believed that he'd return home one day to see his famous daughter, and then he'd be able to brag about being my father. It never happened."

"I know this might sound silly," Marilyn said, "but I used to look at everyone walking down the street, and I'd try to see if anyone at all might look like me. Only, I could never picture a man looking like this," she said, pointing to herself. "You know, a masculine form of me."

"I can't imagine a masculine form of you either," I said. "But, Carolyn and I do sort of look like our father. I've seen a few pictures of him, and it's strange. He was masculine, but we look like him, and we're definitely feminine."

One day, Marilyn showed me a poem that she wrote, and it touched my heart. I could feel all of the hurt and the pain of being abandoned and of never really knowing where she came from. It was just a few simple words:

I wish I could have known you
I know I would have loved you
One day we will meet in eternity
Dear God, please let it be.

-15-

Opening night was coming up soon. I was nervous, but I loved the play so much, that I felt very confident in my ability to assimilate the part. I know it sounds silly for a nineteen-year-old girl, but I believed in the story of Cinderella. I *was* Cinderella!

Rehearsals for the play were in full swing. There were a few changes that I had to get used to. I found the stage lights to be brighter and more colorful than the lights on the set of a television shoot. I also had to remember to make broader, more sweeping gestures. The director kept telling me that a camera can pick up subtle facial expressions and convey them to the television audience, but the audience in a theater cannot pick up on those things. Because of this, an actor has to bring the audience to him with the use of more body language. I studied these techniques when I took lessons, but studying them was not the same as the actual practical experience of doing it.

One week before the opening, my co-star, who was playing Prince Charming, got into a minor car accident. It was minor in the sense that he wasn't seriously injured, but it was major in the sense that he wouldn't be able to dance. It's usually customary for the understudy to step in, except the understudy was in the car with him. He sustained a few more injuries, and although none of them were life threatening, he was also unable to dance. I thought that they were going to close it down, and I was terribly disappointed. The director said that he had a friend who was going to be starring in some Shakespearian plays soon on Broadway, and maybe he would be willing to come early and help us put on this play.

When the director asked me to meet the new Prince Charming, I literally backed up a few steps. I couldn't believe my eyes.

"We have met before," Brandon DeLorrier said, with his charming British accent. "Joy is perfect for the part. Not only is she beautiful, but she, like Cinderella, has a tendency to run off."

The director looked at him strangely because he didn't fully understand, but I certainly did. I felt my cheeks redden.

The director said, "I was afraid that this wouldn't be your forte. It's light and whimsical."

Brandon shook his head in disagreement. "It's a lovely story. Everyone adores it. I've been accused of being shallow and unfeeling to other aspects of entertainment other than movies, but I can assure you that it's a misrepresentation of what I actually feel. I know that this may be hard for *some* people to imagine, but I prefer theater to the big screen."

My cheeks reddened some more.

I knew that Brandon could act, but I had never seen him dance professionally or even sing a song. These fears were completely set aside when we rehearsed our first song, *Ten Minutes Ago.* Our voices blended together in melodious harmony. Everyone cheered and clapped.

"I never knew you could sing like that," I remarked.

"Hollywood almost never showcases an actor's full potential, and neither does television, as far as I can see. An absolute perfect role almost never comes around. That's why the theater holds a special charm. I performed in the musical theater in London. I have always been a fan of William Shakespeare, so I perform his plays whenever I get some free time between movies."

When rehearsals were over, he surprised me by asking me to have dinner with him. The very idea frightened me, but I knew that this opportunity might never come again. "I'd love to have dinner with you," I heard myself saying.

As we were seated at the table in a wonderful, romantic French restaurant, he said, "I've thought a lot about you in the past few years."

"Good, bad, or indifferent?" I asked.

"All three, I guess." He pointed his fork directly at me. "You know, you were pretty hard on me at that benefit."

I feigned surprise. "*I* was hard on you? As I recall, you insulted *me.*"

"It wasn't intended to be an insult. As I recall, I was in the process of telling you that I was having a very good time. You misinterpreted what I meant when I said the benefit was comprised primarily of television celebrities. I wasn't implying that I thought I was better than anyone else."

I said nothing, because I didn't know what to say.

He took a sip of his wine and continued, "Haven't you ever gone to a party and felt utterly out of place, even though you knew everyone in the room? Maybe everyone else is dressed differently, or talks differently, or knows how to do different things. I was only commenting on the fact that I was afraid before I got there that I might be out of place; people might be looking at *me* and thinking that I didn't belong there, but you never gave me the courtesy of finishing my statement. You see, Joy, I was pleasantly surprised to find that I wasn't out of place. Everyone made me feel at home, until you walked off the dance floor. How would you feel if I got up from this table right now?"

For a moment, I thought that he would, and it would have been the ultimate payback, but I calmly said, "I suppose I wouldn't like it, especially if you stuck me with the bill."

He threw his head back and laughed. He had such a nice laugh. I remembered that we had an easy way of being able to converse with each other at the benefit too, until his girlfriend dragged him away.

"I know that I should be ashamed of myself, Brandon, but I'm really not. You see, if I hadn't done just that very thing, we wouldn't be sitting here having this conversation, and I'm truly enjoying myself." He smiled at me again, and I felt my heart melt.

After that, I found myself caught up in a whirlwind romance. He came over to see me every night. He showered gifts, flowers, and his undivided attention upon me. I only had one problem: Marilyn. She was still in love with him, even though she knew that he saw other women. She just never expected one of those other women to be her best friend.

I was afraid that our friendship wouldn't withstand the storm. But I also knew, beyond everything else, Marilyn loved me. I believed in my heart that she would forgive me. She was extremely angry at first. She shouted and even threw things at me. Later, I had to laugh, because I realized that all of the things that she threw were unbreakable objects like pillows and cushions. But at the time, it was quite serious.

"How can you do this to me? You, my best friend!"

I tried to reason with her calmly and quietly, but she was beyond reason. Finally, I just got angry with her, grabbed her by the shoulders, and said, "Look, Marilyn, I didn't take him away from you. If he still has the need to see other women than you, then either you're not what he was looking for, or he'll never be what you ultimately want."

"How can you be so sure he won't be that way with you?"

"I'm not. Maybe I'll find out that he's just a selfish, egotistical, narcissistic little pig. If he is, then he doesn't deserve either one of us."

"I know you're right. I just don't want you to be right." She started to cry, and I put my arms around her until she stopped.

"I want us to stay friends," I said. "I couldn't bear it if we weren't friends."

"I'm pregnant," she said. Her face was wet with tears. "How can our friendship survive that?"

I stared at her blankly, as though I hadn't heard her correctly. It was a shocking revelation. I silently hoped that Brandon wasn't the father, but I knew from looking into her eyes that he was. "Does Brandon know?" I finally asked.

"Yes, and he said that he will support any decision I make, but he won't marry me. He likes me, but he doesn't love me. I asked if he had ever been in love before, and he told me that he hadn't been, and maybe he didn't know how to love. Is this really someone you want to get involved with?"

"I'm already involved," I said.

I spoke to Brandon about it. "Why didn't you tell me?" I asked.

"I was waiting to see how I felt about you. If you meant nothing to me, then the baby would be none of your business. If you meant something to me, the baby would become everyone's business." His eyes searched my face. "It looks like this baby is going to become everyone's business. For the first time in my life, I feel like I'm in love."

He pulled me close to him and kissed me. I could feel the warmth of his body against mine, and I never felt so happy in all of my life. "You've probably said that to all of your girlfriends," I said.

Carolyn and Leisel were happy for me because I was dating Brandon. Leisel was talkative as usual, but there was something different about her that I couldn't quite put my finger on. She seemed to have difficulty conversing one on one with me. Carolyn hardly spoke at all, but that was normal behavior for her. It was unusual for her to visit me in Manhattan in the first place, and I believed that Leisel must have dragged her along that day.

"You and your sister look very much alike," Brandon observed.

"Yes, we do. Sometimes people mistake her for me and ask for autographs. When she tries to tell them that she's my sister, and not me, some have actually gotten mad. Maybe that's why she seldom leaves the house anymore."

"You look alike, but you don't act alike," he said. "She doesn't seem very comfortable in her own skin. Not like you are, anyway."

"Well, that has always been a problem, but she thinks that I'm free and easy because I've been thrust into more social situations. It might be partially true, I don't know."

-16-

It was opening night. As I waited for my cue, I was filled with mixed emotions. The elation of the play, and a romance with Brandon, against the deflation of hurting my best friend, and having my best friend pregnant with Brandon's child, was emotionally draining. I had to tell myself to concentrate. I needed to let my mind clear of all outside things and just concentrate. I was no longer Joy Bryant, friend of Marilyn, girlfriend of Brandon. I was Cinderella, who wanted to go to the ball.

When the curtain opened, I looked out and saw the largest audience that I had ever performed in front of. I thought I could hear them breathing. In the opening act, I started singing, *My Own Little Corner,* and I felt the adrenalin rush that other theatrical actors told me about. I knew that I was hooked. There was truly something special about a live audience. The rest of the night went by in a pleasant blur. The highlight of my night was the dance at the ball with Brandon and the two duets we sang together. *Ten Minutes Ago,* however, was my personal favorite.

There was someone in the audience whose presence would have been of great interest to me if I had known, but I didn't find out about it until the next day. I read rave reviews in the paper following my performance. Then, I ran across this very negative review:

I happen to have had the pleasure of getting to know Miss Bryant personally. Cinderella was a lowly person who wanted to go to the ball and become royalty. Joy Bryant is royalty who always wanted to be a lowly person. Talent aside, one might wonder why Joy Bryant, of all people, was chosen for the part of Cinderella.

I showed it to Marilyn. "That's so mean!" she said. "Who wrote that?"

"Gary Shawn," I answered, and I threw the paper into the trashcan.

-17-

The Broadway presentation of *Rogers and Hammerstein's Cinderella* lasted six weeks. We played to a full house every night. It probably could have been extended due to popular demand, but it was time for the rehearsals of Brandon's Shakespearian play. He was playing the lead role in *Hamlet.* His days were completely full, but I saw him almost every evening.

Marilyn seemed to accept that we were dating, although we seldom talked about it. One day I got up enough courage to ask a question. I simply had to know if he was seeing other women, while at the same time expressing his undying affection for me. "Does he seem different around me?"

Her eyes fell on a bouquet of roses, and she looked at me with a sad, wistful smile. "He never sent me flowers, said he loved me, or made any promises. If he has with you, then he's different. He probably isn't seeing anyone else."

Marilyn seemed sick all of the time. At first, we thought it was morning sickness, but when the nausea went away, she was still prostrate with weakness. She was losing weight instead of gaining it, and I was becoming concerned. I insisted that she see a medical doctor.

Initial lab work was done, and then the doctor came in to talk to us. He seemed young, probably in his late twenties or early thirties. He wore wire-rimmed glasses, a crisp white lab coat, and he reminded me of a nerd. *He was probably the class nerd with big brains,* I thought, *so he has to be good at what he does.* My mind rambled on with nonsense because I was filled with anxiety. I forced myself to concentrate. He was saying that she had an abnormally high sedrate, and the white blood cell count's differential showed that she had a condition called lymphocytopenia.

"What can I take for it?" asked Marilyn.

"Lymphocytopenia is not a disease in itself," said the doctor. "There is a cause for it, and we have to determine the cause. The cause is most likely another disease process."

The doctor explained that a high sedrate indicates that some inflammatory process is going on in the body. He also explained that the CBC showed some abnormalities with the white cells, and that Marilyn had a low count of lymphocytes.

He began to ask other questions, and Marilyn confirmed that she had been getting night sweats, experiencing fatigue, weight loss, and an occasional unexplained low-grade fever. She blamed all of it on the pregnancy, but if she thought about it, she was probably feeling that way prior to her pregnancy.

The doctor examined her neck, under her arms, palpated her abdomen, and then palpated near her groin. He took a biopsy out of one of Marilyn's lymph nodes in her neck, and then we went home to await the results.

"I'm really scared," Marilyn told me.

I was scared too, but I tried to downplay it. "It's probably nothing. Your immune system is probably just weak from being pregnant." It sounded stupid, even to my ears, but Marilyn just nodded her head and seemed to go along with that explanation.

After about three days, we got the call from the doctor to come in and discuss the results of the tests. It seemed like an eternity before they called her name to go in.

"You have non-Hodgkins lymphoma," the doctor said calmly.

I knew that Hodgkin's was fatal, but this was non-Hodgkins. I breathed a sigh of relief. "Non-Hodgkins," I said. "So, this is not a fatal disease."

"On the contrary," he said, looking at me. "Hodgkins and non-Hodgkins are cancers of the lymphatic system. Non-Hodgkins can be more aggressive, and it's often more difficult to treat. There are two types, which are classified as aggressive and indolent. Indolent is very slow growing, but I'm afraid that this is an aggressive form." He turned to Marilyn, whose face had gone completely white, and said, "You must decide what to do about your pregnancy."

"What about my pregnancy?"

"You must have chemotherapy as soon as possible. You are four months pregnant. The baby cannot possibly withstand the chemo, and we cannot wait five more months to start it. If we do, you'll surely die."

"You're telling me that I have to abort the baby?"

"I'm telling you that if you want to improve your odds of survival, you must waste no time in getting started on chemotherapy. You must sacrifice the pregnancy."

"Sacrifice? You mean abort it, don't you?"

The doctor nodded.

"If I abort this baby, can you give me a guarantee that I won't die anyway?"

"No, there are no real guarantees in life, except that your odds of survival increase with each day of earlier intervention."

I didn't like the doctor's bedside manner. He seemed cold and unfeeling, like a computer answering questions. There are no guarantees in life. Well, you didn't have to be a brain surgeon to know that.

"I have to go home and think about it," she said, and left the office. As soon as we got outside, she broke down and cried in my arms. "I can't be dying! I can't! Not now!"

She was so distraught that I had difficulty keeping her on the sidewalk. I held onto her arm and tried to pull her to me. I was afraid that she was going to walk out in front of a car.

"Oh, why does it have to be right now? I want this baby! I have to have this baby! I want to have children, grandchildren, and great-grandchildren."

"Maybe you still can," I said softly, "only not this one."

Marilyn went to the library, checked out a stack of books, and retreated to her room. She wouldn't come out, not even for me, for four days. Finally she emerged from her room. "I've made up my mind." She pointed her finger at me and said, "And you're going to accept it. I'm *not* aborting my baby."

I was aghast. "Are you insane? Do you know what the ramifications are if you don't get an abortion?"

"I think I know what they are. I've thought of nothing else for the last four days."

She paced back and forth, and then she finally sat down beside me. "The prognosis even with chemotherapy and radiation is rather grim. I never knew where I came from. My lineage, unlike yours, can't be traced backwards, even though I know it goes back to the beginning of time. I don't even know the people who are in the generation next to me. To me, my family tree begins and ends with me. If I die childless, my lineage stops right here. I don't want that. I want to know that my life will go on. I want to know that I was here for some purpose, not just to live in an orphanage and make a few movies."

This line of thinking was way too heavy for me to grasp. I just wanted my best friend to stay alive. "Your life could go on- with proper treatment. You could have children and grandchildren. What's more, you could *know* your children and grandchildren."

"Joy, this is a very fatal disease. I'm going to die with or without the chemotherapy. I've read all about it. All I'll be doing is buying more time."

"If you have this baby, and you die, who's going to take care of it?"

"I've thought of that, too," she said. "The answer to that question is you."

I almost gagged on my own spit. "Me! Are you crazy? I'm nineteen years old. I'm not ready to be a mother, and what's more, I don't know how to be a mother. How in the world can you consider giving your baby to me when I barely know how to direct my own steps? I'm ambitious and selfish and arrogant. Just ask Gary Shawn; he tells the public that all of the time in his columns. What kind of a mother do you think I'd be? I'd most likely put my own career first. My career has always come first, even to the detriment of myself."

"Yes, you *are* all of those things, plus more. You're kind, generous, and forgiving to a fault. You have a great capacity for love, even though you sometimes have difficulty showing it. You'll be a good mother. People balance careers and families all the time."

"A good mother has love for her baby," I mumbled to the floor.

"You'll love the baby."

My head jerked up involuntarily. I studied her face, and I realized that she was serious. "How can I possibly love this baby when it's killing you?"

"The baby isn't killing me. Non-hodgkin's lymphoma is killing me. You'll be a good mother, and you'll love the baby."

"How can you be so sure?"

"I'm sure of one thing. You'll be good to my baby because you love me."

I started to cry. I walked across the room, put my arms around her, and buried my head in her neck. "I do love you. I can't imagine my life without you. Please don't make me live without you. Please reconsider this decision."

"You're getting tears all over my neck," she said, but she was crying, too.

-18-

My life was bittersweet. I was in love with Brandon, and I was sure by this time that he was in love with me, but my best friend was dying. Brandon came over as often as his schedule would allow. I was offered other parts, but I didn't want to leave Marilyn alone. She had good days, but she had bad ones, too. Carolyn moved in with us temporarily to help me take care of her. It was a big sacrifice for Carolyn because she never was one to venture far from home.

I still had not consented to have sex with Brandon. I wasn't sure why. Looking back, I believe I was secretly afraid that if I had sex with him, he would finish the conquest and see other women. It was certainly possible that he would start seeing other women because I *didn't* have sex with him, but it was a risk I had to take. My mother used to say, "Why buy the cow, if you give away the milk for free?" I decided that I would not be free. Brandon never made an issue out of it, so I just stuck to my resolve.

I began to see articles printed about me in newspapers and tabloids, especially since my Broadway debut. Some things were true, and other things were out and out lies. Gary Shawn was making a name for himself by covering several celebrities, but his favorite celebrity seemed to be me. He was always making some kind of negative remark about me. I thought that I had known him well; I never dreamed that he could be so vindictive, and I never understood why. Leisel visited once in a while, but it was rare. When I asked what she thought about Gary's vindictiveness and the things that he wrote about me, she was very evasive. I noticed a real change in her demeanor. She wasn't the same fun-loving person anymore. She seemed more serious and somewhat sad.

When Marilyn reached her seventh month of pregnancy, she was told that the baby was viable. It could be born now and still live. She said that she didn't care that it was viable; she wanted to be sure that it would live. She might have sacrificed some precious time out of her own life, and it would be all for naught if this baby wasn't born healthy. I resented this baby. I considered it a parasite, living off of Marilyn and sucking whatever time she had left dry.

She finally went into labor about a month earlier than her due date. I called Brandon and told him that his baby was about to be born, but I knew he wouldn't come. His play was still running, and he felt awkward about the baby, anyway. He was the father of his girlfriend's best friend's baby, and his girlfriend would soon be the mother of his child. It was odd, and I didn't blame him for feeling awkward about it. I thought that he might express a desire to adopt the baby since it was his child, but he never mentioned it.

At four in the morning on October 12, 1980, Jo Dell Marilyn Bryant entered into the world. She weighed five pounds, two ounces, and she had brown eyes, blonde hair, and a wrinkled up red face. She was the ugliest baby I had ever seen, but Marilyn was overjoyed. She wanted to name the baby before giving it to me to be adopted. I really didn't care about naming it, but I thought the name sounded rather stupid.

"I never knew anyone by that name," I said, as I visited her in the hospital. "Are you sure you want the baby to go through life with an odd name like that?"

"You and Della are the two most important people in the world to me. I have to name her that."

"Why don't you just name her Joy Della Bryant?"

"There's only one Joy Bryant. We can't do that to her."

"Well, what about Della Joy Bryant?"

"I don't like the name Della all by itself. Jo Dell is much prettier, and then I can give her my name as the middle name."

I quit arguing. As Marilyn held the baby in her arms, I could see how happy she was. A lawyer came to her bedside that day, and the adoption papers were signed. I was suddenly the mother of a brand new baby girl. I would have been happier if I had been the owner of a brand new car.

By the time Marilyn gave birth, her cancer was very advanced. She had two choices. She could opt for hospice, in which nurses would come to the house and help her get though the dying process with as little pain and suffering as possible, or she could opt for chemotherapy and hope that it would buy her more time.

She decided to take the chemotherapy in the hopes of having more time with the baby, but she became violently ill. I stayed up with her all night and held her head while she vomited. The next day she announced, "I've decided I don't want any more chemo. I'd be sick all of the time. I can see right now that I'd have no quality time, and I don't want my last days to be miserable. I just don't want to hurt."

She seemed okay during the day, but at night, she was anxious and afraid, and sometimes she had irrational anxiety attacks. One night I heard a loud shriek, and Carolyn and I ran into the room. We found Marilyn sitting upright in bed, gasping for air.

"Oh, Joy! Help me! They're going to put me in a coffin, and there's no air in there!"

We sat on the bed, and finally, with a lot of effort, we calmed her down. We discussed the possibility of cremation, but she didn't like that idea, either. It seemed to me that those were the only two options, so I let the subject drop.

We called the hospice nurses the next day, since they would be more skilled at making her feel comfortable. She was hooked up to an I.V. so that she could have Morphine for the pain when she needed it, and she also had some Ativan for her anxiety attacks. The nurses came by to check on her, but Carolyn and I assumed most of her care.

"I'm not as afraid as I was," Marilyn told me.

I assumed that the medication was helping her with that because she was pumped full of Morphine and Ativan, but I had to admit that she seemed more comfortable. "I'm glad," I told her.

"I just need you to hold my hand when the time comes and walk me through it."

"Okay," I said, but I wasn't sure how much more I could take. It was terrible seeing my best friend slipping away more and more each day. Up until that time, I didn't think that it would ever be possible to wish for the death of someone I loved so much, but I began to realize that it would be more merciful.

About three weeks later, I walked into the room where Marilyn was resting. I thought she was asleep, so I started to slip quietly out of the room. She opened her eyes. "You don't have to leave," she said. "There's something that I want to talk to you about." I sat down on the side of her bed, and she made an effort to sit up. "I'm a little worried because you don't seem to be bonding very well with the baby."

"What do you mean by, 'bonding with the baby?'"

"You don't seem very interested in her, that's all. Carolyn takes care of her more than you do."

"Yes, and I've had my hands full taking care of you." I was extremely uncomfortable talking about all of this.

"I want you to stop blaming the baby for this, Joy; I would have died anyway. The baby didn't ask to be born; I just made the decision that she would be born. I know that you'd love her if you'd just let yourself. Soon, all that will be left of me will be her. If you love me, you'll love her."

I squeezed her hand and said nothing.

"I have something that I'd like you to give to Jo Dell for me when she's old enough to understand it. It's in my top drawer in a small box."

I walked over to her dresser and pulled out a small box. When I opened it, I saw that it was a plaque with a gold inscription engraved on it. It said:

> *I wish I could have known you*
> *I know I would have loved you*
> *One day we will meet in eternity*
> *Dear God, please let it be.*

My hand covered my mouth, but I couldn't choke back the silent tears that spilled out over my hand. When I regained enough composure to speak, I said, "I'll take care of her. I'll be a good mother."

Marilyn smiled, sank down in the bed, and drifted off to sleep.
She drifted in and out for the next two days. Sometimes she awakened confused. Her breathing seemed shallow, and I could tell it wasn't going to be much longer. Della stopped by for a brief visit almost every day.

"Do you think she's dying right now?" I asked.

"It sure seems so," said Della.

We brought the baby with us and sat in the room in case she woke up and wanted something. A slight rattling noise sounded like it was coming from the back of her throat. When it seemed like she would no longer wake up again, she opened her eyes and startled me.

"I've forgiven my mother for giving me up," she said. "Maybe she had to. Maybe she was sick and had to, you know, like me."

I held her hand. "Maybe so," I said softly.

"Soon we'll meet in eternity."

As soon as she said it, I saw that she was unconscious again. As I leaned closer, I realized that her breathing had stopped. I was still holding her hand. "Dear God," I said. "Please let it be."

-19-

Rain poured down on the day of Marilyn's funeral. It was a slightly chilly mid-November day. I was afraid to take the baby out in that kind of weather, but it cleared up and got warmer. I realized then that I had just felt my first maternal instinct toward the baby. I dressed her warmly in a coat and hat, and put several blankets in the baby carrier to keep her warm. If I had been going to anyone else's funeral, I probably would have found a sitter, but after all, this funeral was for the baby's mother. I still found it hard to consider myself a mother, but I was determined to do the best I could for her. Besides, this was Brandon's child. He came by to take us to the funeral.

I stood there like a stone statue, but I didn't cry. I had cried myself out over the past few months, and especially during the last few days. There were just no more tears left. Flashbulbs popped at all of the different celebrities showing up for the funeral. I had to remind myself to put on a pleasant face, and I thought that I did until I saw a tabloid months later. The tabloid depicted problems between Brandon and me. I realized from looking at my morose face that this was shot during Marilyn's funeral; only they used this picture as fuel for the later story.

-20-

All celebrities get fan mail, and fans follow them from place to place. The real question is the degree. I started getting fan mail with the debut of *Jenny Johnson* when I was four years old. Sometimes the volume was several hundred to over a thousand a week. Most of the mail I received over the years was upbeat, amusing, and encouraging. But some of it was downright ugly, and it upset me. Richard told me to set aside any mail that didn't have a return address, and someone else could open it. If the letter had something in it that might upset me, they would just throw it away. I finally agreed to this method.

In 1978, after my show was cancelled, I still received mail. It was sent in care of the studio, and I picked it up every couple of weeks. Because I was no longer doing a weekly show, the mail slacked off somewhat, but because of syndication, I was still being seen, often by a younger batch of fans who were not even born when the original episodes aired. I no longer had a dressing room at the studio, and I didn't have anyone to read my mail for me unless I employed someone myself, so I just brought it home. I had more time to answer mail since I was no longer doing the show. I was again dealing with some nice mail and some not so nice mail. One author, in particular, wrote to me over a span of about three months. The first one I noticed was around the end of December in 1980.

Dear Joy,
I have never written to a star before. You are so beautiful that I wish I could reach out and touch you. I have watched you come and go into your house, and sometimes I wanted to show myself to you, but I can't do that just yet.

The letter frightened me because it sounded like someone was watching me. After what recently happened to John Lennon, everyone was more than a little spooked. I showed the letter to Andrew, and he seemed very concerned. He wanted to keep the letter, and he showed it to the police. He made me promise to give him any more letters like this one.

Carolyn was aghast that someone might be watching us and ordered a new security system for our home. It cost us over a thousand dollars a month to pay for maintenance of it. The police basically told us that these were just words, and since no one actually tried to hurt me, there was nothing they could do. Even if they knew who was sending the letters, they could do absolutely nothing except issue a restraining order unless this person tried to cause me harm.

"You mean they'll do nothing until he comes to slit my throat?"

"The laws protect the rights of the criminal," said Andrew.

A few more letters followed:

Dear Joy,
I enjoy seeing you undress. I wonder what your naked skin will feel like next to mine. Some day I intend to find out.

After Marilyn died, I moved out of my apartment and returned to Kensington. I was nervous with this nut out there, apparently looking over my shoulder, so I decided to go back to Manhattan. Upper Central Park had some very beautiful and expensive houses, penthouses, and apartments, especially between 59th and 96th streets, but I still felt more at home in Greenwich Village, even though some people said it was over-run with beatniks. Two days later, on March 30, 1981, I received this letter:

Dear Joy,
Why did you move away? It is harder for me to find the time to see you, but good things are worth waiting for. Maybe I will move to Manhattan, too.

I showed the letter to Carolyn and Leisel. I was almost in a panicked state. "He knows where I am," I gasped. "I can't hide from this person. His eyes must be on us all of the time."

"Maybe we should start looking for the boogey man under the bed again," said Carolyn, with an uncharacteristic stab at humor.

Later that day, we heard the news that John Hinkley, Jr. shot President Reagan and was taken into police custody. "He'll never get out," Leisel said. "They lock those people up and throw away the key. Somebody should have noticed that he was nuts before this happened."

I vaguely remembered that she had said something like that several years before. From the look on Carolyn's face, she remembered it too, but we just exchanged glances and said nothing.

After that last letter, I didn't hear from this person again for several months. *Maybe he forgot about me,* I thought, but I was wrong. He would surface again at a later time.

-21-

I felt safer in the apartment because there were more people around, but I still went back and forth between the apartment and my home. I asked Brandon if he thought I was being irrational, and he said that he didn't think so. He got letters all of the time from women asking to sleep with him, but never anything threatening. I could have hired someone to guard us, but I was leery of doing that. I had some bad experiences with security guards while I was working on the set of *Jenny Johnson.* The studio hired people to protect us, and sometimes the guards spied on us just as much as the people they were supposed to be protecting us from. Some of them were downright spooky. Michael had to intervene with a few of them.

Brandon came over fairly often to see us, and he started showing more interest in Jo Dell. He held her and rocked her, and sometimes if he thought no one was looking, he sang to her. One day, when he thought I wasn't near the room, I heard him say, "Do you know who I am? I'm your daddy."

Out of the blue, I received a call from Andrew asking me if I was ready to go back to work. Due to popular demand, the network wanted to bring back my show. The only problem was that Jenny Johnson would be too old to be living in a children's home. They decided to send her off to college, and then bring in a love interest for her. Because I was being brought back by popular demand, Andrew said that I would have more leverage than ever before. I could come back on my own terms.

"What kind of terms?"

"If you had the chance to change things from your last show, what changes would you make?"

"A bigger dressing room, shorter hours, better pay, creative control, and some say over who I work with, for starters," I said.

"That's fair enough. We can negotiate those things."

I was very excited, and I spoke to Brandon about it. I was afraid that he would be against it and say I was falling back into the same old stereotypical role, or that I was a mother who should be caring for her child, but he never did. He seemed genuinely happy for me.

Andrew and I met with network executives to negotiate my contract. The next problem was who my co-star would be. Several names were thrown around, including Tony Milano. I never told Andrew that we had a falling out. All anyone ever knew was that we were friends, and we always had a good chemistry on camera. I decided that I could bury the hatchet, if I had to, for the sake of my career. A big problem was that Tony was always afraid of being stereotyped. Andrew said that Tony may never have been offered his own series, and that it was just a lot of big talk from him. Also, some big-screen stars were starting to migrate to television, and it was thought that working in television might not always have a stigma attached to it for stars that do television and would like to do movies.

Then, Andrew, who was also my publicist, came up with a brilliant idea. "Let's do what they did for the role of Scarlett O'Hara in *Gone With the Wind*," he said. "In *Gone With the Wind*, they already had their Rhett Butler. They just needed a Scarlett. They agreed to audition as many actresses as necessary to fill the part, and they weren't afraid to try an unknown. It was a public relations dream. It helped promote the movie almost as much as the book did. Here, we have our Jenny Johnson. All we have to do is find our John Doe, for the lack of a better name."

The producers loved the idea. The public was anticipating the return of Jenny Johnson, and casting calls were coming in from all over the country. I was told that I would have a major say in the hiring of my co-star. As Andrew eloquently put it to the major executives, I had to agree to work with this person, and the whole series could depend upon just the right chemistry.

I was unprepared for the barrage of over six thousand actors who stormed the studio looking for a chance to audition. It was organized chaos. They were sorted by casting directors looking for certain qualities, such as looks, charm, and someone who could literally burst forth onto the screen. It seemed like a tall order. In the looks department, they couldn't get someone who was too short or too tall for me because we had to look pleasant together on screen. But even the most handsome person in the world might not have enough talent. This person would need to have a certain charisma, be able to read and memorize lines, and he would also have to be able to sing and dance just a little in order to please me.

One day, I happened to be walking through the building where several men were waiting to be called for auditions. I saw two men in their early or middle twenties, standing closely together, and they seemed to be having a disagreement. One man was tall, dark, and very good-looking. He was the sort of person that could make everyone do a "double take" if he walked into the room. The other man was of average height, with average looks, and he wore glasses. Being very nosy, I walked closer to them. I wanted to hear what was going on.

The tall, dark one said, "I don't know why you want to do this. This is all a publicity stunt."

"What makes you think that this a publicity stunt?" the other man asked.

"She wants a more celebrated actor, like Tony Milano. They're going to audition all of us, say they found no talent, and choose him anyway. In the meantime, they've whetted everyone's appetite for the return of this show. Believe me, she doesn't want two jug heads like us. Come on, let's get out of here." He started to pull the other man toward the door.

I was somewhat hurt to have people talk behind my back in this way, which was amazing because I endured tabloids that talked behind my back to the entire world for most of my life. I was also upset because this man had read my motives completely. I *had* decided if no exceptional talent was found that we would try to get Tony, even though I had no desire to see him again.

I stopped them before they reached the door. "Are you on your way out?" I asked.

"Yes," said the taller man, "I think we're probably out of our league."

"You'll never know unless you try. That's what this audition is for," I said with a smile. I escorted them personally to a casting director and said, "Try these two jug heads next." The looks on their faces were priceless.

The candidates were narrowed down to about twenty by the time these two men showed up. The casting directors decided to take the best ten or fifteen and give them special screen tests. I went up to Mary Jo, the casting director, to ask about my two jug heads. I meant to apologize to them before they left and explain that I had feelings, too. Mary Jo was very excited. One of them had absolutely no potential, but the tall, dark, handsome one was exceptional. I couldn't believe it. I stood there, stunned.

"I had him read, and then I put him on film. I have a screen test that I'd like you to see. Actually, I have ten screen tests that I'd like you to see, but this man is magnificent!" said Mary Jo.

I followed her into the film room and looked at the screen test footage. She was right; I was totally blown away by this person. "What's his name?" I asked.

"Grant Carlton."

"Has he studied acting before?"

"Musical theater in college, but that's all. I think that he's a natural. Most importantly, I think you two would look good just standing next to each other. I think you should do a screen test with him, and even with some of the other finalists, if you wish. My personal feeling is that this Grant Carlton is a gold mine."

I did a few screen tests with what I considered to be the top five candidates for the role. On film, I had an unmistakable chemistry with this man, even more so than with Tony. I asked to see him.

"We haven't officially met," I said. "I'm Joy."

He smiled, stepped forward, and stretched out his hand. "I'm Grant," he said.

"I wanted to talk to you because I have to make sure that we can really work together. I guess we didn't start out very well. I didn't mean to embarrass you by calling you a jug head, but I wanted you to know that I heard what you said."

"I'm sorry," he said. "It wasn't right to pin a motive on you, but I did think that it was a publicity stunt." He looked me right in the eye and didn't fumble around for words. He wasn't intimidated at all by me.

"It *was* a publicity stunt," I admitted. "You saw right through me, and that's what hurt most of all. I did want Tony for this role with all of my heart, but after seeing you, I'd like to work with you even more."

He smiled broadly. He had a wonderful smile, and his dark eyes danced. I noticed that he had a presence that most people didn't have. I never asked a man out on a date before in my life, but I asked if he would mind joining me for dinner so we could talk about the possibility of him taking the role.

"Do you live in New York?" I asked, as soon as we were seated at the table.

"No, I was only visiting New York with my friend when we heard about the auditions. I'm from Xenia, Ohio. I've lived there all of my life."

"Do you have a big family?"

"No, just my parents and my fiancée."

"How are they going to feel about you pulling up stakes and making a move to New York?"

"I'm sure it'll come as a big surprise, but I've made up my mind. I'll make arrangements for Sally to join me as soon as I get settled."

"Did you ever dream that one day you would be an actor on prime time television?"

"No," he said, with an ironic laugh, "I can't say that I have. I've always enjoyed acting, but I've been studying to become a psychologist. I only have one more semester to finish."

"Are you sure that you want to give it up after getting so far?"

Grant smiled. "I can finish that semester anytime. I really want to do this. An opportunity like this might never come up again."

"The casting director said that you had no formal training. She said you must be a natural."

"I took dance lessons for seven years, and I can sing well enough to get leading roles at college, but I never had any formal acting lessons. I hope it *will* come naturally."

"Oh, it will; I can tell. Your screen tests were fantastic. One thing that you might want to think about is hiring a manager and a publicist. I don't know what I would have done without Andrew. You can try to manage yourself, but many actors find it more trouble than what it's worth."

"I can see that I have a lot of things to do in the next few weeks."

"Well, a few of the scripts are written, but the actual rehearsals aren't ready to start for a few months, so that'll give you time to get your house in order."

The waiter came over to take our order. I don't even remember what I ate. All I know is that I was having a wonderful time. I was busy marveling over the chemistry that we had between us, and how open we could be with each other. This chemistry would be noted both on and off the screen, and I didn't know it at the time, but this man would replace Marilyn as my best friend. I would be able to tell him anything, and he would be as helpful and as unassuming as anyone could ever hope a friend would be. I went home feeling very light and happy, as though my heart were singing.

-22-

Gary Shawn was moving up in the world of journalism. He was still doing light and breezy columns on celebrities, but his popularity was growing. He had a cynical, almost caustic air about him at times, and he was certainly amusing to listen to. I would have been even more amused if some of that cynicism weren't pointed directly at me. He was seen occasionally on morning news shows, like *Good Morning America,* and I noticed that he took potshots at me as often as he could. If there were any articles written about me in magazines or tabloids, invariably, there would be some kind of witty and unflattering quote that came from Gary. He told me that he would be just as famous without me, and it seems as though he spoke the truth. He worked tirelessly at it. One day, on prime time television, he was asked what he thought about my imminent return to television and to the role of Jenny Johnson.

He said that he was very surprised I agreed to reprise the role, but it was probably the only one I could get after letting myself get stereotyped into it in the first place. He said that he supposed I was doing the best I could do for myself, and that I had no choice but to accept it. He was speaking the truth, but the way he said it made it sound horrible. He made it sound like I had no talent to do other roles, and that I was taking what I could get. He had a gift of taking a morsel of truth out of a situation, and then stretching and embellishing it so that it would hurt.

Brandon, on the other hand, was very happy about my return to television, and he told me that he wanted to take me out on the town to celebrate. Carolyn agreed to baby-sit, and he took me to one of my favorite restaurants. It was in a large, circular skyscraper that overlooked the city. The floor of the room moved very slowly around in a circle, so that one could eventually get a full view of every side of the city. It was such a beautiful evening. Stars twinkled outside the window, and a full moon could be seen in one corner of the sky. We were in a private, romantic booth next to a window so we could stargaze if we wished to do so, and for this short time, I thought we were free from the adoring gazes and whispering lips of fans and the insensitive prying eyes of paparazzi.

"I still don't understand why he hates me so much," I said to Brandon. "Gary Shawn is like a pit bull. He takes a morsel of truth and hangs on to it like a dog with a bone. His attacks on me are downright brutal. I can't even defend myself. If I do, he makes it seem like I'm the one who's stupid."

Brandon smiled. "That's just part of the job, Joy. You're a public person. You have fame and celebrity, and you have to take whatever unpleasantness comes with it."

"It's just hard, you know. Most people have only one or two people talking behind their back at once. I can have half of the country. That's why I don't want to give interviews anymore. They take a half-truth and then plaster it all over for the world to see. If I become known as someone who doesn't give interviews, maybe people will understand that things written about me aren't necessarily true. Don't people know that I have feelings, just like everyone else?"

"You could do that, but it would only have a limited value. People are going to believe what they want to believe. If they read something negative about you, even though you have a reputation of not speaking to the media, if they want to believe it, they will. No amount of denial on your part will make any difference. If you have a goal not to give interviews anymore, let yourself get back on track with your career, and then think about that move. Don't cut yourself off from the media now, because now is when you need them the most. You need all of the publicity you can get right now in preparation for your return to television, good and bad. You must give interviews."

He reached across the table and took one of my hands into both of his. "Besides," he said, "I have one more role that I want you to play, and the publicity is going to be enormous. You won't be able to avoid the media no matter how hard you try."

"What role is that?" I asked.

As he held my left wrist with one hand, he slipped an engagement ring on my finger with the other. My eyes widened with surprise and wonder. This was the happiest moment in my entire life. Nothing thus far had ever been so monumental. I could feel the spirit within my heart swell and soar like the wings of an eagle over the highest mountain peak. Suddenly, a flashbulb went off and totally destroyed the moment.

My spirit came back from the mountain, and my heart was no longer soaring. As I turned in surprise and in irritation, within the face of the loveliest moment in my life being broken, I saw that I was staring directly into the face of Gary Shawn.

"I'm sorry to interrupt what appears to be a particularly intimate moment," he said, "but I saw the ring flash from the moonlight, and I couldn't resist."

Brandon thought that this was amusing, but I was extremely irate. "You were spying on me, you son-of-a-bitch!" I spat at him with uncharacteristic profanity. "You have your tabloid picture, and you'll conjure up a story. Now get out of here, and let us be!"

He didn't answer. Instead, he grinned and snapped another picture, this time of my irate face. This was the picture I later saw in a magazine, and not the one of Brandon's proposal. It was extremely unflattering, as was the caption that was printed underneath it. I vaguely thought of Richard, who always waved those unflattering pictures in my face. Since he was going to direct the new show, I wondered if he would have something to say about this one, too.

Later on, it didn't matter. I was engaged to Brandon DeLorrier, and the whole world could go fly a kite, as far as I was concerned. He could have had his pick of any woman in New York or Hollywood, or the whole entire world for that matter, but he chose me.

-23-

The news of our engagement was news, big news, even bigger than I dreamed it would be. Newspapers, tabloids, and talk shows made it sound like the prince of Hollywood, Brandon DeLorrier, chose his bride out of all of the fairest women in the kingdom, and he chose Joy Bryant of New York City, known as one of the fairest in all of the land. The news that we were to be married reached far and wide to people of all circles. One person that it reached was someone I would rather have not known about it at all, and of whom I hadn't thought of in several months: my unwanted pen pal of unknown origin.

I was more frightened this time because I was receiving phone calls instead of letters. He told me what I had been doing the day before, what I was wearing, and how he could have reached out and touched me if he had wanted to. The voice was difficult to make out. It was high pitched and obviously disguised, and it reminded me of a voice that a ventriloquist would use for a marionette.

I didn't say anything because I didn't want to frighten anyone. I tried to tell myself that this person was harmless, and that he just got his kicks out of scaring me. I found myself becoming very paranoid. I didn't want to leave the apartment unaccompanied by someone, and I almost fell to pieces if I found myself in the house alone. Brandon noticed a change in my behavior, and I heard him discussing it with Carolyn. I was staying in Kensington at that time while preparations were underway for my new show. I would be staying in Manhattan very soon, and I wanted to spend some time with Carolyn before I got completely caught up in the daily grind of the series.

"Maybe she's stressed out over the upcoming marriage and the plans for her new show," he said.

"I don't know," said Carolyn. "She has always been able to handle enormous amounts of stress. I think it's more serious than what she wants us to believe. She's a good actress, and she's covering something up."

I was incensed because they were talking about me, and I came out of my room in a fit of rage. I accused them of saying things that weren't true, and I told them that they were no better than the tabloids. I refused to go out with Brandon that night, so he left the house in a foul mood.

"I wish you'd tell one of us what's going on," Carolyn said. "You're acting like you're losing your mind. Everyone is noticing it."

I am losing my mind, I thought.

Sometimes he called to tell me that he knew I was in the house alone. Then I started getting calls that he would be making his move soon. I could never engage him in a conversation; he just said what he had to say and hung up. Carolyn and I kept a gun in the house for protection, and I took it from our usual place and moved it up to my room.

One day, Carolyn said that she was going shopping. I wanted to go too, but Jo Dell was taking a nap, and I never liked to disturb her from her nap because then she would be cranky, and I disliked dealing with a cranky baby. The phone rang again. I had recently become afraid of answering the phone, and I knew who was on the other end of the line before I reached for the receiver, but I picked it up anyway. It was like an itch I had to scratch.

"I know that you are alone right now," he said, "and I have decided to kill you. As a matter of fact, I am in your house right now. There is no escape."

I slammed down the receiver and quickly moved Jo Dell under my bed. I ran to get the gun, and I saw the doorknob turn. In my haste to save my baby first, I neglected to lock the bedroom door. I was shaking, and I barely had the chance to load the gun and aim it when the door opened.

"Joy, what are you doing?" yelled Brandon, and he fell down to the ground to avoid my aim.

I slowly put the gun down. My eyes were wide with terror. I started crying and screaming that someone was trying to kill me, and that he was in the house right now. It took Brandon a long time to convince me that there was no one there. He gently took the gun from my shaking hands and pulled me to him. "Tell me what's going on," he insisted, and I did.

"How did you bypass my security system?" I asked.

"Carolyn was on her way out the door, just as I was about to ring the bell. She said that she was going shopping, and that you were upstairs in your room with Jo Dell."

"Yes, that's right; she left to go shopping."

"I'm calling the police," said Brandon.

"It won't do any good," I insisted. "They told me that unless he makes a move, they can do nothing to him. He can walk in and kill me, and then they can arrest him. I thought that I'd have to protect myself, but I almost shot you."

The police came and questioned me. They called Andrew, and he brought in all of the letters that we thought had come from him. It was difficult to tell if the same person wrote all of those letters. Detectives looked through all of my unread fan mail, as well as any that had been opened but not thrown away. I explained that the letters stopped a few months ago, and now I was getting phone calls.

The detective thought that the stops and starts coincided with surges in my popularity. I began receiving letters around the time it was announced that I was going to reprise my role. Then I started getting phone calls as soon as my engagement was announced.

Brandon was extremely angry that I kept this information from him, and he even voiced his opinion that I was stupid for not calling the police. I explained again to Brandon, this time in front of the detective, that I was told that the police were unable to protect me unless this person made a move against me, and so far, he had not. Brandon's anger calmed toward me when the detective confirmed this, and then his anger was directed at the detective.

"She's a public figure," explained the detective. "If she's in the public eye, then she may be the target of a few nuts out there. She has to decide if she is going to be frightened into living her life as a recluse, or get on with her life, which may be flying in the face of real danger. I don't want to say that it's nothing because in the case of John Lennon, and even our President of the United States, we know that there are a few real nuts out there. The only consolation is that most of them are really harmless, and they get their satisfaction just by scaring someone half to death."

He questioned everyone in the household. He talked to Carolyn and asked if she ever received any phone calls. Actually, she had never seen me take any of those calls. The maids, the cooks, and Jo Dell's occasional babysitters were questioned, but nothing definitive surfaced. They asked me if I had any enemies, or anyone who had caused me even a little bit of trouble. The only one I could come up with was Gary Shawn.

The police pulled Gary in for questioning. I found this little piece of information out because he called and told me. "I like to be a thorn in your side, Joy, but I'd never intentionally hurt you."

"You intentionally hurt me all of the time."

"I've never caused you any physical harm. I would never throw sticks and stones to break your bones, but names are a different story. I *am* guilty of that. But really, Joy, I'm extremely concerned about your welfare."

His voice sounded sincere, but I still had my hackles up. I retorted in a jeering, accusing voice, "Since when were you ever concerned about anyone but yourself, Gary Shawn?"

His voice changed from concerned to sarcastic as he said, "Oh, I don't know. Maybe you're right. I guess it suddenly occurred to me that if something were to happen to you, it wouldn't do my career much good. I've done well for myself being your villain, and I hope it never stops. Therefore, I sincerely hope you'll take care of yourself for me."

I hung up on him.

Oddly enough, the phone calls stopped after that. I figured that this person knew that the police had a presence in my house, and that they were working on an open case now in an attempt to find him.

-24-

The first rehearsals were beginning for the return of my show. I could tell that Grant was somewhat nervous, but then, so was I. We memorized and practiced our lines, and then it was time to do the actual filming. Richard told us that he wanted us to start on opposite ends of the set, walk toward each other as though both of us were not paying much attention to what we were doing, and then bump into each other. I needed to spill the contents of my purse on the floor, and Grant was to bend down and help me pick them up.

"Action!" yelled Richard.

I walked toward Grant, but as soon as we were to bump into each other, he moved his shoulder away to soften the impact.

"Cut!" yelled Richard. "She won't break," he said to Grant. "Keep your shoulder where it is, and let her do the bumping if you want, only it has to look like a real bump. You can't move out of the way, or it'll look fake."

It took two more takes before we got it right for Richard. Then, when we did get it right, the contents of my purse didn't spill out, so we had to do it again.

"Cut," said Richard. "Try it again."

"That's how it goes sometimes," I whispered to Grant. "This is normal."

"This is harder than I thought it would be," he said.

"It'll get better once you know what's going on, but really, this is normal."

It wasn't long before I realized that Mary Jo was right; Grant was a natural. He looked wonderful on screen, and he exuded masculine sexuality. I knew that he was going to be our next heartthrob.

Grant and I were also becoming friends. We had to promote our show, so we attended several benefits, motion picture premieres, and public appearances on the talk-show circuit. Grant was outgoing, effervescent, and very natural in front of the camera. He always answered an interviewer honestly and candidly, and he had a wonderful sense of humor. He had the gift of gab, just as I did, so we made an amusing couple wherever we went.

One interviewer asked us about our first impressions of each other. We looked at each other funny, and the interviewer picked up on it. "Are you going to keep it to yourselves?" he asked.

"We probably should," said Grant, "but since this is such a nice audience, we can share our secret, can't we?" he asked me.

I nodded, pretending by using body language that I was reluctant, but if he really wanted to, he could share it with the audience.

Grant played off my response and leaned in closer to the interviewer as though he were disclosing a powerful secret. "She called me a jug head," he said. The audience roared with laughter.

I opened my mouth wide in surprise and said, "You called *yourself* a jug head. I only agreed with you." The audience was still laughing.

"So that's how it was," said the interviewer. "What made you decide that you could work together?"

"Chemistry," I answered. "We look good together on film, and we decided after our first meeting that we could be friends as well."

"And before anyone gets the idea that this chemistry goes any further than what's on the screen, I need to point out that you are both engaged to other people."

We nodded.

"Joy is engaged to actor Brandon DeLorrier."

Another nod.

"And when will the wedding be?"

"We've finally made plans for sometime in the fall. We have to wait for his current movie to finish filming, and it should be around that time."

"So, you're in the process of conducting a cross-country romance."

"Yes, but we still get the chance to see each other fairly often."

"And you," said the interviewer to Grant. "When will we hear wedding bells for you?"

"We originally set the date for the fall, but it will most likely be sometime in the spring. Everything changed overnight. We lived in Ohio all of our lives, and to make a move to this big city was a monumental change. I came here on a vacation, and we never expected this to happen in a million years. We're still in the process of trying to digest it all and get our bearings straight."

Grant was right; they had to get their bearings straight. His girlfriend wasn't particularly overjoyed by all of the changes in their lives. She was petite, and rather pretty, even if she was somewhat pale. Her hair was blonde, almost yellow, and her skin was a translucent white. She seemed very shy, and I observed fairly quickly that she wasn't comfortable being thrust out in the limelight when she was with us. She didn't like having her picture taken, and since no one is ever safe from the paparazzi, it was taken quite often when she was out with Grant. The camera misses nothing, and most of her pictures were somewhat unflattering. When we went to benefits and parties, she often stayed at home, leaving Grant and I to attend alone.

Grant was a wonderful dancer, even better than Brandon, and I enjoyed dancing with him at most of the functions that we attended. Our pictures were plastered all over the papers, tabloids, and magazines. Brandon was used to publicity, and he knew that most of the pictures were set up for promotional purposes, but Sally didn't. She and Grant fought bitterly about it, and she even accused him of being in love with me.

On Grant's twenty-fourth birthday, we all got together for a party. Brandon was able to attend, and we had a wonderful time. Sally looked like she would rather have been in the dentist's office having her teeth pulled, but I tried not to notice because it was Grant's problem.

Brandon ordered strawberry cheesecake for dessert. "It's your favorite," he said to me in a very playful mood. He fed me a scoop of it from his fork. "In a few more months, we'll be feeding each other wedding cake." He put his arm affectionately around me.

Grant had a very wistful look on his face as he watched us, and my heart went out to him. I was extremely happy, and I wished that Grant could be, too. A few weeks later, Grant told me that he and Sally called off their engagement, and that she had returned to Ohio. She told him that she loved him and always would, but they would only move farther and farther apart, and there would come a time when he would resent her.

I was surprised but not surprised at the same time. "How are you feeling about all of this?" I asked.

"I'm okay. She hated every minute of New York. She felt out of place, and she always believed that people were looking down on her. Some of the newspapers did, of course, and I tried to tell her not to let it bother her, but it did. She was also terribly jealous of you. I think she expected me to beg her to stay or to go back to Ohio with her, but all of a sudden, I knew that this was right for both of us. Our lives did change, and it's better that we accept it now."

"She must not have loved you very much," I said.

"On the contrary," disagreed Grant. "She gave up her own happiness in exchange for me to be able to find my own. There can be no greater love than that."

I reflected on that different perspective. Maybe he was right. Maybe she did love him in a way that I would never understand. I would fight for Brandon with my very last breath, and I could never walk away hoping that he would find greater happiness. I would make sure there was no greater happiness than me. I knew Sally was jealous of me. Women get vibes from each other all of the time, but I just ignored the whole thing because it was irrational and irrelevant. I was marrying Brandon in the fall. Grant was my best friend, and if she couldn't handle that, then too bad for her. I just never put her shoe on my foot, because if the roles were reversed, I certainly wouldn't have wanted Brandon to be the best friend of any woman.

"Well, we have a day off," I announced, changing the subject. "What do you want to do today?"

"I want to take a walk in the park," he said.

"I haven't done that in years."

We walked arm and arm through Central Park. A gentle breeze blew our hair about, and we shared all kinds of hopes and dreams. My dreams were filled with being the wife of Brandon DeLorrier, and his were the dreams of a man who recently found that his star had begun to rise, just a tiny bit, in the sky.

-25-

Grant started dating again. He was seen in the company of a few up and coming actresses, but he told me that he wasn't ready to get serious about anyone. Then, I became very surprised when he began dating Carolyn. I had never seen her so happy. Her demeanor changed, and she became more animated and less withdrawn. Her entire face lit up whenever Grant entered the room.

I wasn't sure if they suited each other, but I was happy for her. Sometimes I found that I had no one to talk to when they were with each other. I had become used to Grant's company, and I missed him when he wasn't around. I slipped one day and expressed this feeling to Carolyn.

"You're jealous!" she exclaimed.

"I'm not jealous," I protested. "Grant's only my friend. I love Brandon with my whole heart, and I'm looking forward to our marriage."

She still had a skeptical expression on her face. I didn't think that I convinced her very much, but she said no more about it. I saw a tabloid in which Grant had given her a kiss, and since Carolyn had a close physical resemblance to me, they printed it as if it were me that he was kissing. I was very upset and called Brandon, but he assured me that he could tell the difference.

"Most people can't, though."

"The people that know you can, and that's the most important factor to consider."

After about two months, Grant stopped coming around to see Carolyn. She was devastated. I had seen her devastated before when boyfriends left, but it was as though a beautiful blossom had fallen off and left only a stem. She seemed more depressed than before. She wouldn't eat and wouldn't even talk to me. I was so worried about her that I asked Grant what was going on, even though I knew it was none of my business.

"I'm sorry that she's taking it so hard, but I realized that she's not what I'm looking for. It's not fair to keep her hanging by a string simply because I can't have the person I really want."

"And who do you really want?"

"She's just a dream," he said. "Everyone I meet, I wonder if they can fill the dream. Carolyn can't, and it's not fair to either one of us. Don't you believe in dreams?"

"I've always been a believer in dreams. You know that. I've seen too many come true."

"Mine won't," he said morosely, and then he changed the subject and became his usual, entertaining self.

-26-

Grant and I were invited to perform on the stage of the Schubert Theater in Chicago. It was a song and dance extravaganza. Andrew agreed it would be a good publicity move. It would give Grant more exposure, and I would get a chance to break from Jenny Johnson. I was afraid to travel by plane, so we decided to drive there.

First, Grant wanted to show me Xenia, where he grew up, and then take me out to the farmhouse where his parents were now living. His parents were on a vacation, but they were expected to return on the day that we would be traveling through Ohio. It was decided that we would spend the night at his parents' home before moving on to Illinois. We would have only two days once we got to Chicago to get ready for the show, but Grant and I weren't worried. We practiced the songs and the dances that we were going to do before we left, so we didn't foresee any problems.

Grant told me that the Midwest, which I had never seen before, was the flatlands. New York, away from the big cities, was filled with beautiful rolling green hills and meadows. The Midwest was full of farmlands, cornfields, and tornados. Ohio was very close to the Midwest and the tornado belt, and occasionally some of the bad weather spilled over into it. He told me that a tornado tore through Xenia in 1974 and leveled parts of the town. His home was untouched, but it made an impression upon his mother.

"She keeps a storm cellar that's out of this world," he told me. "It's like a mini-hotel. There's water that she changes out regularly, candles, books, mattresses, blankets, sheets, canned food, a radio, and everything else you'd need. She got stuck in a bare cellar once for over twenty-four hours because storms raged all night long, and she swore that if she ever had to spend the night in one again, it would at least be in comfort. Personally, I think that it's overkill, but what do I know? I wasn't the one stuck in that cellar all night."

It had been raining ever since we entered Ohio, and the sky seemed to be getting darker and darker. I turned to Grant and asked, "Why have you become so quiet all of a sudden? And why do you keep looking at the sky?"

"This is a tornado sky," he said.

"Are you trying to scare me after all of this talk we had about tornados?"

"No, although I'll be glad when we get to my parents' house."

I watched the sky too, and as we entered onto the road leading to his parents' farmhouse, the sky turned very dark, almost black. The clouds were made up of strange shades of green and gray. As we turned into his parents' driveway, the rain changed to hail. We sat in the car, not wanting golf ball sized hail to fall on our heads. When the hail finally stopped, it became unusually calm. Grant got out of the car and started to lead me up to the porch, when he turned back to look at the sky again.

"There it is," he said, pointing to the sky, and I literally froze. A large, black funnel cloud with a long, snake-like tail descended out of the sky, and it was coming in our direction. The calm we had just experienced when the hail stopped quickly turned into violent winds, and I could barely stand up. "Come on!" yelled Grant, as he yanked on my arm. He pulled me toward the back of the house and down into the storm cellar.

I heard a loud, roaring noise, almost like a train approaching at full speed, and it seemed directly overhead. I heard things falling on the ground above the storm cellar, which I assumed were parts of trees and fences. I prayed that the house would be spared, but I couldn't imagine how. It sounded like the tornado was directly above us. With the exception of the moment I almost shot Brandon with my gun, I had never been so scared. I buried my head in Grant's chest and prayed for it to be over. I was terrified that the hatch of the storm cellar would be blown off, and that we would get sucked right out of there and meet certain death.

As soon as it sounded like the tornado had passed us by, Grant lit a candle and found the radio. A class four tornado had just ripped a path outside of Xenia, and the residents of Xenia were being warned to take cover.

"Will it come back?" I asked.

"That one probably won't backtrack. It was on a roll in one direction. The only other concern that we might have is there could be more than one. We need to stay put down here and listen to the radio."

We listened to the radio for about an hour before deciding it must be safe.

"I'm afraid to look," said Grant. "I don't know what we'll find. The house is probably gone." He climbed up the ladder of the storm cellar and attempted to lift the hatch, but it wouldn't budge. "Something must have landed right on the lid," he said. "I hope it wasn't the house."

I began to panic. "What are we going to do if we can't get out of here?"

"We'll get out of here. My parents are due back tonight or tomorrow. They'll find us. I know they weren't home because the car wasn't there. They were most likely detained because of the bad weather."

"Are we going to suffocate down here?"

"No. There's enough air that comes down through the rafters. I can see some light, so we'll get enough air. Something is just lying across the top, and I can't open it."

We listened to the radio until it got dark. We were extremely grateful for his mother's wisdom because we did get hungry down there.

"It's just stuff like sardines, Spam in a can, and crackers," said Grant, "but it'll do."

"No caviar in a can?" I asked, trying to muster some of my old dry humor.

"Nope."

We continued to listen to the radio by candlelight, and we tried to amuse ourselves by telling stories and rehearsing some of the songs we would be singing at the Schubert Theater. It was almost ten o'clock by the time we decided that we wouldn't be rescued that night, and Grant said that we needed to conserve the candles.

"How long do you think we'll be down here?" I asked.

"Someone will find us tomorrow. Even if they don't, we certainly won't die down here. We have enough food and water to last three months, although it might get awfully ripe down here. If you have to go to the bathroom, you can use that bucket with a lid on it."

"That bucket will overflow in three days," I muttered, even though I also believed that we wouldn't be there that long.

There were two twin mattresses on the floor, and we pulled out the sheets and blankets. Grant blew out the candles after I crawled onto my mattress and pulled up the covers. I was hot, so I threw off the blanket and just used the sheet. I laid in silence for about ten minutes, but I couldn't sleep, and I knew why. As crazy as it seemed, I was afraid of the dark. I knew no boogey man could get me down there, but fear is often irrational.

"Grant?" I asked.

"Hum?" he said, sleepily.

"I know this sounds terribly childish, but I'm scared."

"Of what?"

"Of the dark. I have been my whole life. Even now, I sleep with the light on."

"What will Brandon have to say about sleeping with a light on once you're married?"

"I'm not afraid if someone sleeps with me."

"I'm sleeping with you."

"I know, but I'm still scared. I know how stupid this sounds."

"We can't waste the candles, and we can't risk a fire down here, either."

"I know."

"Here," he said. "Hold my hand."

I reached for his hand, but I couldn't touch it, so I pushed my mattress closer so I could hold his hand. "Grant?" I asked, a few minutes later.

"Yes?"

"Do you mind holding me just a little?"

"Are you still scared?"

"I know it sounds stupid, but yes."

"No, it doesn't. Come on over here."

I pushed my mattress so it touched his, and he put his arms around me. I began to feel safe and warm, and I relaxed. He stroked my hair and rubbed my back, and I felt even more relaxed. I pulled my arms around him tighter, and he kissed my forehead.

"Better?" he asked.

"Much better," I whispered.

I couldn't see his face in the dark, but I could feel the warmth of his body against mine. It was a very pleasant feeling, especially since I was literally scared out of my wits a few hours before. I nestled my head on Grant's shoulder and turned to look up at him, although I couldn't see him. Our lips met, and we suddenly found ourselves caught up in the moment of sharing a kiss. We had kissed each other before on screen, but this was different. I found myself kissing him back again and again, each time with greater urgency. Our arms wrapped around each other tighter. He touched my face and hair with his hands, and an electrical excitement sizzled throughout my entire body. I couldn't stop kissing him or from wrapping my body around his. His hand reached out and touched my breast, and I felt my body rise to meet his touch.

"Don't stop," I heard myself say.

Grant made love to me gently and passionately at the same time. "I love you," I heard him whisper. "I've loved you since the day we met."

I wasn't necessarily surprised to hear him say it, but I thought he was caught up in the moment, too. I couldn't have stopped myself any more than I could have stopped a speeding locomotive or an oncoming tornado, and neither could Grant. We made love for what seemed like hours, and finally we slept, wrapped in each other's arms.

-27-

Rays of light filtered through the rafters as I awoke. Grant was already out of bed, sitting in a chair. I was somewhat embarrassed when I looked down at my naked body. The memory of last night's unbridled passion came flooding back to me. I quickly wrapped a sheet around me and tried to put my clothes on from beneath the sheets. It seemed foolish since Grant and I explored each other's bodies in the most intimate of ways for what seemed to be half of the night, but I couldn't help it. Things appeared different in the light of day. Grant must have thought so too, because he just sat there, lost in thought.

Morning passed into afternoon, and still no one had come. I hated doing nothing. I believed there was a solution to every problem, no matter what it was, so there was always something a person could do. I grabbed the broom and wrapped a pair of my white underwear around it with a message in red lipstick that said, "HELP," and forced it in between an opening in the rafters. Grant laughed hysterically at me, but I didn't care. The funny thing was that an airplane flying overhead noticed my white flag flying in the breeze and summoned help. The news media also learned of the story of someone trapped below that set out a white flag, and reporters were sent to the site.

One of the local reporters knew that this house belonged to the parents of Grant Carlton. He never dreamed that he would see Grant pulled out of the storm cellar, and never, in wildest imagination, would he have thought that Joy Bryant would be there, too.

Grant was elated to find the house still standing. It had major wind damage to the roof, and several fences and trees were destroyed, but that was about all. A tree had fallen, or was dropped by the tornado onto our storm cellar, and that's why we couldn't get out.

We found ourselves in a major story on national television, especially since we survived a major tornado and were trapped below for almost twenty-four hours. They also reported far and wide my unusual S.O.S. What seemed a good idea at the time ended up being a national joke because talk show hosts like Johnny Carson and David Letterman got a hold of the story and went to town. I had to admit that it was funny.

Unbelievably, reporters pushed their way into the cellar itself. They took pictures of where we had food and water, and even of the mattresses that we had pushed together. Tabloids promoted the story of a secret love nest and how we had shared a night of passion in the face of turbulent danger. They would have said that even if it wasn't true, but the fact that it was true made it seem even more sordid.

Gary Shawn was the only one who didn't have anything derogatory to say. Someone asked him on prime time television about it, and he turned all of his venom onto the interviewer. He said, "They certainly couldn't have predicted a tornado. They didn't go down there to have a good time. They went down there to save their lives, and they're lucky to be alive. Any responsible journalist will take this point of view, and I don't believe this line of questioning is responsible."

I was extremely surprised. I thought, of all people, he would have made a major production out of it. My warm thoughts toward him didn't last long, though. He smiled at the interviewer and said, "Maybe you'd like to ask me something else. I'd be happy to tell you what I think about her underwear stuck up there on that broom."

I met Grant's parents for the first time. His mother was warm and friendly, and his father seemed somewhat shy. I saw all kinds of pictures of Grant because his mother got out the photo albums, and I saw that she was making a scrapbook to follow his career. He was an only child, and it was very obvious that they doted upon him.

As much as I hated to fly, we had to take an airplane from Ohio to Chicago in order to get to the Schubert Theater on time. Also, our car had been severely damaged in the storm. We landed at O'Hare airport just in time to be whisked into a limousine and taken to the performance.

We performed to a sold-out audience who must have been aware of the problems that we had to get there. I never bowed to so many standing ovations in my life. Brandon called from Hollywood to tell me that he was relieved to hear I was fine, and that he would be in New York around the time that Grant and I were due to return home. I didn't notice anything different in his voice, but he knew all about tabloid news, so I figured that he must have taken it all with a grain of salt. I was unaware that he wanted to look into my face for the answers, so he was just reserving judgment.

Grant and I didn't discuss what happened until our return. We went about our business as usual. We performed at the theater as though nothing had ever been out of the ordinary. We stood on stage and sang and danced with all of our might and vital forces.

I don't know how to describe performing for an audience except to say that I can feel the music deep within me when I sing. Grant is the same way with dance. He never described his feelings to me, but it comes across dynamically, so I know that he feels the music, too. Some actors and actresses can hit the right notes and make the right moves, but what makes a performer great is being able to feel it and express it at the same time.

Our performances were hailed with great critical acclaim. They said that we performed with perfect harmony, melody, and unison, and insinuated that we were wasting our talent on a weekly television series. Grant, in particular, was hailed as a largely unknown and under-appreciated artist with unlimited potential.

I assumed correctly that when we got home, we might talk about it, but I had difficulty bringing it up myself. Grant came over to my house as usual on the evening of our return, and we went to work as usual the very next morning. Later that night, he brought the subject up.

"I'm only going to say this once because it's hanging over our heads like a thick cloud of smoke. I wouldn't change anything that happened for the world, but I hope that we didn't do anything to hurt our friendship."

"I'm just as responsible for it as you are. You're my best friend, and nothing's going to change."

"I didn't know that you were a virgin, or I might not have done it."

I shook my head. "You would have done it. Nothing in this world could have stopped it once we got going. It all started very innocently. I had no idea how naïve I was, and I had no idea of the powerful force of sexual attraction."

"I thought that you and Brandon must-" He didn't finish his sentence because he saw the look on my face.

"I know it sounds stupid, but I was saving myself," I said, but then I turned my back to him because tears were burning my eyes. I didn't want him to see me cry.

He put his arms around my shoulders, and instead of shrugging him off I turned toward his chest and buried my face under his chin. He held me and stroked my hair.

"I love Brandon," I said. "I've loved him for so long, that I don't know what I'm going to do when he tells me it's all over."

"Maybe he won't," said Grant. "He doesn't have to know. You should keep it a secret. Don't tell him, not ever."

"He's not stupid," I said. "He'll know. I just need to know that you'll still be my friend, because I can't bear to lose you both."

He smoothed the hair away from my face and looked directly into my eyes. I could see my reflection staring back at me in his dark eyes. "You won't ever lose me," he said, very gently. "I know you weren't meant for me, and the best I can hope for is that we'll always be friends. We don't ever have to talk about it again. Good friends are always aware of how the other feels." He kissed me on the forehead and said goodnight.

I don't know how Brandon knew; he just knew. I don't know if my face gave it all away, or if he just believed the reporters, but he knew. Our wedding, which was only a month away, would be cancelled, and the whole world would know why. It would be public humiliation on top of the most devastating moment of my life. I took the ring off my finger and handed it to him.

His face looked incredibly sad. "All I could think of when I was coming here was taking this ring back, but I don't want to."

I looked at him in a state of shock.

"I know that people do things that they ordinarily wouldn't do in times of great stress. You were scared, and you thought that you might die. You turned to each other out of comfort, not love."

I was suddenly suspicious. "Why are you being so understanding? There's a catch; I know there is."

"As long as we're laying our cards out on the table, I need to let you know that I've been no angel myself," he said. "I've been with other women once or twice."

I stood stock-still. I could have been knocked over with a feather. "While you were engaged to me!" I raged at him. "How could you do such a thing?" I felt sick inside.

"Things just happen, Joy. I'm telling you that I understand how it happened with you. I don't blame either you or Grant."

"Well, that's chivalrous of you! What kind of marriage can we expect to have when we're cheating on each other already? I might have had a reason for it. I was scared and lonely and frightened out of my wits. What kind of excuse do you have? How many people knew about your dalliances and have been secretly whispering behind my back?"

"It takes two to cause a problem, Joy. You've had a share in this from the very beginning."

"Oh, no! You are *not* going to blame me for your sleeping with other women."

"When are you going to grow up?" he yelled at me, pacing around the room with agitation. "I am a man of flesh and blood, with needs and wants and desires. Do you know what blue balls are? Well, I've had them- from waiting on you! I've wanted you more than I've wanted anyone. Ever. I still do."

I was at a loss for words, so I just stood there limp, like a rag doll, as he exploded in frustration and anger. Then his voice softened.

"Look, Joy, affairs are not about love. They're all about not getting what you need from the other person."

"Then why didn't you tell me? Why didn't you make more of an issue about it than you did?"

"It wouldn't have done any good. You've been keeping yourself from me while entertaining little girl notions that you can save yourself for marriage, and I let you keep your little girl notions because I can plainly see what's going on. You can't break yourself from being Jenny Johnson even when you're supposed to be Joy Bryant. Do you think that Jenny would ever have sex before marriage? No! And, therefore, neither will you. You are trying to maintain an image, even when nobody else would ever believe it at this point."

He was right; I knew it. And he knew that I knew it. He pulled me into his arms and ran his fingers through my hair.

"I love you, Joy. I know that you have doubts, but it's true. We can forgive. I'm willing to try. Are you?" He held me tighter. "We can make our marriage a love so rare; a love that most people never know can exist; one that most people never live to see."

I looked into his face. His eyes were pleading with mine. I nodded.

"Don't withhold yourself from me anymore, okay?"

I nodded again, and he kissed me deeply and passionately.

"We need to lighten up. Let's go out on the town. Put on a lovely dress. I want to take out the most beautiful woman in the world."

I put on a dress, Carolyn agreed to baby-sit for us, and Brandon took me out on the town. I felt the tension between us ebbing away, and soon we were acting like our old selves. That night, when Brandon escorted me home, he went with me up to my bedroom, and we began to make love. His kisses were pleasant and tender, but something felt wrong. I was expecting the warmth and passion that occurs with spontaneity, and this didn't feel quite the same. Brandon must have known because he suddenly stopped kissing me.

"It's okay, Joy. The time isn't right tonight, but it will be very soon. I can wait a little while longer."

He stayed with me and held me all night long, and I knew that we had survived this crisis.

-28-

Brandon was true to his word. He never spoke of my night in the storm cellar again, and when he was around Grant, he was as pleasant with him as he had always been. One week before our wedding, which was to take place on October sixteenth, I ran around with last minute details. Brandon was in Hollywood, finishing up the last few scenes in his latest picture. My dress was made, flowers were ordered, and invitations had been delivered. We were expecting a gala celebration with over 1,000 people, as well as those who might walk in uninvited. Reporters would only make our day more miserable if we tried to exclude them, so we decided that, as long as no one was particularly obnoxious, we would allow them to attend.

Brandon's family was scheduled to fly into New York later in the week. I wish I could say they were overjoyed, but clearly, they were not. They never approved of his move to Hollywood. They had their hearts set on him returning home, marrying the daughter of a family friend, taking up the family yachting business, and living happily ever after. Marrying me almost assured this would never happen. His brother, Reginald, was most vocal about it. At first he refused to attend, but Brandon talked him into it. He had one brother and two sisters, but he seldom spoke of them, and I never saw any pictures.

October tenth started out just like any other day. I noticed a tear in my wedding dress and called the dressmaker to repair it. Carolyn and Leisel were going to be my bridesmaids, so I asked them to come over and try their dresses on for one final fitting. Leisel remained somewhat distant from me, but she readily agreed to be a bridesmaid. Her relationship with her boyfriend, Bill, had deteriorated. He met someone else in college and was getting married very soon. I wondered if she was jealous because I was getting married and had a baby, especially since those were the very things she had given up. She still never discussed anything with us, so Carolyn and I just let the subject be.

I was singing the song, *Ten Minutes Ago,* when someone knocked on the door. Leisel answered the door, and I heard her make a strange noise, almost like a muffled scream, but not quite. When I entered the room, the first thing that I noticed was her face. Her head turned slowly to me, and she looked like she had just seen a ghost. Grant was standing in the doorway. His face looked terrible, too.

"What's wrong?" I asked.

Grant walked over to me and took my hand. "Joy, he said, pointing to the couch, "come sit with me."

I felt cold fear rise from the pit of my stomach into my chest. I could barely breathe, but I allowed him to lead me over to the couch.

"I didn't want you to find out from the news media because the story is just starting to break," Grant said, "but there has been a terrible accident. Brandon was killed this morning in a head-on collision in Los Angeles."

I don't remember the rest of his words. They seemed to be growing farther and farther away, as though he were talking to me at the end of a tunnel. I strained to hear, but soon I could hear no more.

I woke up in a hospital room two days later. The doctor told everyone that I was suffering from a condition called hysteria, which is caused when a great shock happens to the body. The body cannot accept what happened, so it just shuts down. I was told that I was very lucky. There have been rare but documented cases of people staying that way for five, ten, and even fifteen years. They go to sleep, and then awaken years later. I had been aware of some activity in my room, but voices seemed so far away, and I had no desire to open my eyes. I could hear Carolyn's voice and Grant's voice, and once I could have sworn that I heard Gary's voice.

Grant and Carolyn were at my bedside when I woke up. I remembered what happened immediately, and I began to cry uncontrollably. Grant sat on the bed and held me while I cried. When I finally had no more tears left to cry, I asked him what had been going on for the last two days.

Brandon's family had come to claim his body. They took him back to the Isle of Wright, an island just off the southern coast of England, to be buried. I never had a chance to say goodbye, and now his grave would be somewhere across the Atlantic. Hollywood was planning a memorial service for him in three days. The doctor had a few misgivings, but I convinced him that I was fine to attend.

I barely remember the trip to California. Reporters were everywhere. I knew that the world was looking at me, so I tried to put on the bravest face that I could. I brought Jo Dell with me because I thought that, even though she was just a year old, she had the right to be at her father's memorial service. It occurred to me that she had missed her first birthday party, so I would have to plan one later when we got back home. I would get Carolyn to help me. Grant was at my side the entire time, and I don't think I could have managed without him.

Our filming schedule was about two weeks behind, but I made myself move though the motions. I was numb. Carolyn packed my wedding dress away and took out everything that might remind me that I missed my own wedding. I still had the baby to care for, and I was suddenly glad that I had Brandon's child. I was filled with guilt and remorse about the things I could have done and should have done while he was alive. I regretted the night that I spent with Grant in the storm cellar, and most of all, I regretted the fact that Brandon and I never made love. For the first time in my life, I hated Jenny Johnson, whose image I had steadfastly upheld and maintained. Brandon and I never made love because of her.

It took about three months before the first feelings of normalcy started to return and before I could even mention Brandon's name without becoming teary-eyed. Grant was absolutely wonderful. We fulfilled our filming schedule, and in between, he was always over at the house or my apartment helping me do whatever good friends do for each other. We started networking again, attending parties and premieres. The first time I went to a theater, I saw a preview of Brandon's last movie that he had finished just before he died. Grant held my hand and told me how wonderful I was doing. We went out to dinner and went dancing once in a while, and soon Brandon's death was no longer at the forefront of my thoughts. I successfully put him on the back burner, but he still smoldered in my memory.

-29-

It had now been six months since Brandon died. I was feeling more and more like my old self, and my sense of humor was beginning to return. I could talk about Brandon without becoming visibly upset, and I thought that things in general were going as well as could be expected. Life goes on, and I told myself that Brandon would have wanted it that way. I still had moments when I was alone that I felt down in the dumps, but I was seldom alone. I worked twelve to fourteen hours a day, and Grant helped keep me occupied the rest of the time. We never spoke about the night we made love in the storm cellar. It was like it had never happened.

On this day, Grant and I took a walk through the park. I loved the park. It was over 800 acres of sprawling green grass and azure sky. It was like old times, walking arm in arm through the park with Grant, with the wind blowing through our hair. It was spring, and I felt the first touches of spring fever. We were talking about just things in general, when Grant looked at me and said out of the blue, "Why don't we get married?"

I stopped walking and looked at him. "Why?" I asked.

"What do you mean, 'why'? I love you- *that's* why. We're together all the time. The only thing that we don't share is our bed as man and wife. We're well suited for each other. Why shouldn't we get married?"

"I can't marry you. Not right now. My heart is still caught up in the past. I need a little more time."

"Maybe I should have thought of a more romantic proposal," said Grant. His voice sounded very disappointed.

"Oh, Grant! It wasn't the proposal! I just need more time." We held each other's hands and continued our walk.

Our lives went on just as they did before. We went to work, saw each other after work, and went out on the town once in a while. One day, Gary Shawn decided to break the monotony.

Carolyn, who was not prone to drinking, got totally smashed one night in a local bar in our hometown. It was right after I had turned down Grant's proposal. The police called me to come and get her, and when I finally got there from driving in from New York City, she was crying and starting to sober up. She was charged with being drunk and disorderly, and also for lewdness in public. I was aghast. Carolyn was prim and proper; she had never been lewd in all of her life. Clearly, there had to have been some mistake.

The officer shook his head. She was on the roof of a one-story building dancing with no clothes on. A crowd had gathered, and then I learned something that shocked me out of my shoes. While she was dancing in the nude, she told everyone that she was Joy Bryant! Me! People had gathered around to see Joy Bryant dancing on the roof of a bar in the nude. I was so shocked and mad that I could have slapped her, but she looked so pathetic.

"I'm sorry, Joy. I just didn't know what I was doing."

"What made you get so smashed, anyway?"

"I don't know. I was out with Leisel, and then she left with someone else. She does that, you know. I had a few more drinks, and by that time, I no longer knew exactly what I was doing."

"Were there any reporters there?"

"Only one, I think."

"One is enough." I paid her bail and helped her to her feet. "You're going to feel terrible in the morning- in more ways than one."

The next day, when I picked up the morning paper from our front porch, there was a story in the Kensington Chronicle that I was dancing in the nude on the roof of the bar. The author was Gary Shawn. I was irate. He could certainly tell the difference between us. He knew Carolyn, and he knew me. I called him on the phone.

"You sleazy slime ball! You knew it was Carolyn and not me!"

"I printed the facts, Joy. There was a drunken lady that said she was Joy Bryant, and that's what I printed. From the picture, one can easily discern that it's most likely you."

"But you knew it wasn't me!"

"Prove it."

"I *will* prove it. I'll see you in court." I hung up on him.

I hired a lawyer to pull Gary into court. My lawyer and I were scheduled to meet Gary and his lawyer before the case went to trial. I was suing for a sum of one million dollars. I knew there would be publicity about the case, but I wanted to exonerate myself from these accusations. Besides, I was sick of Gary printing truths and half-truths at my expense.

"You have no case," said Gary, as he sat across the table from me with his lawyer.

"We have a perfect case of libel and slander," I said. "You knew the difference between us, and you printed that story anyway."

"There's no way that you could ever prove if I knew the difference between you. If we were to pass the picture to the jurors, will they honestly say that it isn't you beyond a reasonable doubt?"

He knew that I wouldn't want that picture passed around, not even to a jury who might be inclined to be on my side. With as much composure as I could, I said, "You knew me. I think we can pull in several people who are able to tell us apart. You haven't exactly been a complete stranger."

He rocked back in his chair and grinned at me, and I was so mad that I wanted to slap that grin right off of his face.

"I printed a story, but it was never circulated. You cannot sue me for an un-circulated story."

"What do you mean by saying, 'it was never circulated?' I have the copy right here," I said, and I pulled it out.

"The one and only copy," he said.

My lawyer leaned forward and said to his, "Are we to understand that this is the only print of this particular paper?"

"The one and only," Gary's lawyer concurred. "Just try to find another copy. There won't be one. He printed it from his father's press, changed the typesetting on one paper only, and set it out on Joy's front steps. No one else has ever received it."

I was stunned. I had to drop the charges because it seemed as though I had no case. If I did sue over the one copy that I had, it would just call attention to the nature of the contents of that one paper that no one else had ever seen, and it would be stupid to do so.

On the talk-show circuit, Gary was asked about the charges that I had leveled against him. He explained that I did indeed accuse him of libel and slander, but I dropped all charges due to lack of evidence. He wrote something similar in his column. He made me sound like a total idiot.

-30-

Two years passed since Grant first asked me to marry him. He asked again, several times, but I still refused to make any commitment, citing that I wasn't ready to consider marriage again. Once, I even told him that I didn't feel like I loved him in the same way as I had Brandon, so it really wouldn't be fair to him. He told me that he had enough love in his heart for the both of us. I just laughed and said I still wasn't ready.

Recently, however, I began to notice a slight change in Grant's demeanor. He seemed quieter, less energetic and vivacious. It was as though he had a great weight on his mind. He stopped coming over as much, and I was beginning to miss his company. If I called him to take me out somewhere, he had an excuse as to why he couldn't go. His contract with our show was coming due, but he hadn't signed a new one, and I was beginning to wonder. One night, he decided to tell me why.

"I love you, Joy. It hurts me to see you every day and to be so close to you, yet so far. You keep saying that you need more time, but it has been two-and-a- half years, for God's sake. I'm competing with a dead person, and I can't take it much longer. That's why I've stopped seeing you so much. I think that I might return to Ohio."

I was at a loss for words. I had nothing to say because I knew that he was speaking the truth. He was going to walk away from the show, and that's why he hadn't signed a new contract.

I talked to Carolyn about it, and she proceeded to tell me how stupid I was. "Brandon is dead," she said. "Nothing is going to bring him back. If Grant leaves, your show will be canceled, and no one else will ever be able to take his place. You need to seriously think about that fact. What would be so awful about marrying him, anyway? You're together all the time."

Two more days passed. Grant hadn't called, and it was being said that he didn't intend to renegotiate, even though he was offered a substantial raise in the next contractual agreement. I asked Della to watch Jo Dell for me. I needed some air. I felt like I was suffocating.

I walked through the streets of Greenwich in a daze. I didn't think that I was going anywhere in particular. It began to rain, but I didn't realize it. I found myself on the front steps of Grant's brownstone apartment. I rang the bell, and Grant came to the door. He looked at my wet hair and bedraggled appearance. It was obvious that I had been out in it for a while.

"What on earth are you doing out there in the rain?" he asked.

"I don't know why I'm here," I said.

He opened the door wider and motioned for me to come inside. "You must have come here to tell me something," he said, "or was it just to get out of the rain?"

"I'm glad you're here. I was afraid you wouldn't be."

His eyes searched my face, and it was as though he had read my thoughts. He knew the reason, but he had the need to force me into saying to him out loud why I was there. "What did you come here to say?"

I just looked into his eyes, and I didn't answer.

"Let me go first," he said. "I love you, Joy. I always will."

I put my arms around his neck, and as I did so, I saw by looking over his shoulder that some of his bags were packed. "I love you, too," I heard myself say.

The engagement of Joy Bryant to Grant Carlton was big news. It seemed even bigger than it was when I became engaged to Brandon. Grant signed his contract, and we were in the process of planning our wedding.

"I don't want to wait," said Grant. "I keep pinching myself, and I'm so afraid that you're going to back out at any moment."

"I won't back out," I said.

"Let's make it a week from next Sunday," said Grant, looking at a calendar. "I guess that will be April sixteenth."

"No!" I said, somewhat louder and more defiantly than I meant to.

Grant looked at me strangely.

"Not the sixteenth," I insisted. He was still looking at me strangely, and I felt the need to cover up exactly why the sixteenth was so distasteful to me, so I added quickly, "Let's get married next week. That will be April ninth. Is that okay?"

"Sure," said Grant, with a wide smile spread across his handsome face. "The sooner the better."

One week passed with excessive speed. Neither Grant nor I had any particular religious affiliation. We wanted a non-denominational wedding with a simple address from the minister, vows, rings, and "I do's." The chapel had to be large enough to accommodate the few hundred people who were expected to attend, as well as others who might walk in uninvited. We knew that reporters and photographers would spoil our own wedding pictures, so we were able to successfully keep them outside during the ceremony, and then they were allowed in to take a few pictures of their own.

My gown was of white satin and lace, studded with a few pearls, and it had a scooped neck and three-quarter length sleeves. The scooped neck showed a faint outline of my breasts, and it tapered down snugly against my sides to accentuate my small waistline. A very long train trailed behind me as I walked down the aisle, and I carried a bouquet of red and white roses. Carolyn and Leisel were dressed in red and white, and Grant had on a black Tuxedo with a white buttoned down shirt. His friend from Ohio, the one who auditioned with him the first day we met, was his best man. I believe his name was Theodore, but Grant called him Thor. I had no father, so I asked Andrew to give me away.

As I walked up the aisle on Andrew's arm, I experienced a surreal feeling inside. *I am being married,* I thought. Grant's face was beaming. When Andrew and I reached the end of the aisle, Andrew took my hand and placed it in Grant's. I could feel energy from Grant surging into me. The only thing that I would remember later from what the minister said was that we should treat each other well and respect each other's feelings.

"Do you take this man to be your lawfully wedded husband?" the minister said to me.

My voice was strong and clear as I answered, "I do."

"Do you take this woman to be your lawfully wedded wife?"

"I do!" I heard Grant say with great exuberance, and I could hear people laughing slightly because they were touched, like I was, at his enthusiasm. He squeezed my hand. When it was his turn to repeat his vows, his voice faltered, and I saw tears in his eyes. Then he recovered and was able to get through the rest of his vows. My heart was touched deeply. I reached up and touched his face with my hand.

We exchanged rings while photographers snapped rounds of pictures, and then the minister told Grant that he could kiss his bride. His kiss was warm and passionate, and I felt a zing that I had experienced before. I clearly and involuntarily remembered the night that we spent in the storm cellar. With a growing excitement, I realized that he would make love to me that night, and I longed to feel his touch once again.

The minister asked us to turn around, and he addressed the audience with the words, "May I present Mr. and Mrs. Grant Carlton!"

Applause broke out all around. I almost felt like I was playing a role on stage, but this was for real. Grant and I were married.

The reception was in full swing. We had hired a caterer, who provided the finest of gourmet foods. The cake was beautifully decorated with white frosting and red roses all around it. A band played in the background. Grant almost never left my side, holding onto my hand all evening and dragging me about the room while he talked to friends and family. I had never seen a man so happy. He loved me, and since he wore his emotions on the surface, it was obvious for all to see.

I had to excuse myself from him to go to the restroom. As I walked into the room, I saw my reflection in the mirror. My eyes were wide and sparkled with the excitement of the day. I had been told that all brides are beautiful on their wedding day, even if they weren't particularly attractive, and that they seldom look prettier than on their special day. It must be the excitement. Excitement must enhance beauty. I looked into the mirror, and what I saw was a beautiful bride. Then an unwanted thought crept into my mind. I would have been a bride two-and-a-half years ago if circumstances hadn't prevented it from happening.

I rejoined Grant in the reception area, and it was time to cut the cake. As we held onto the knife together and cut a slice out of the cake, I said, "You better not shove this in my face."

Grant looked at me in mock surprise. "I wouldn't dare mess up your face," he said, "unless you entertain the impulse to shove it in mine."

I laughed and decided that it would be inappropriate to do so, especially since I had applied my makeup very carefully that day.

Flashbulbs popped. People cheered. Champagne flowed. It was a beautiful day. The band struck up a romantic waltz, and the lights were turned down low. "That's our cue," said Grant. "Mrs. Carlton, may I have this dance?"

I smiled and took his hand, and he led me out onto the floor. People clapped and cheered, and more flashbulbs popped. I looked over Grant's shoulder and noticed that Carolyn appeared to be upset about something. I saw Leisel talking to her animatedly, and I vaguely wondered what it was all about. I would have been more interested if I had known the exact conversation, but I wouldn't find out for years. When I saw Carolyn again, she seemed to be her old self. She was caring for Jo Dell, and she would also take care of her while Grant and I went on our honeymoon.

Jo Dell was an intelligent and quiet little girl, who seemed very sedate and reflective. She didn't remember her father, but she had pictures of him in her room, and she referred to him as her daddy. She wasn't especially happy to have a new daddy, even though she had known Grant almost all of her life. I told her that she was adopted and that I wasn't her real mother because I thought she had a right to know, and also because I thought that it would be easier if she knew at an early age. She called me Mommy, even though she also had pictures of

Marilyn. I assumed it would be a short matter of time before she would call Grant "Daddy," but I was wrong.

I slipped away from Grant while he was dancing with his mother, and as I passed the open bar, I noticed Gary Shawn. He walked over to me and extended his hand in a rather formal way. "I sincerely hope that you'll be very happy, Joy," he said.

"Since when have you ever been sincere about anything in your life, Gary Shawn?"

"Oh, I don't know," he said, "but I really do mean it. Be happy, Joy."

He turned around and began to walk away, and I was instantly ashamed of myself for being so rude. "Dance with the bride?" I asked his back as he walked toward the door.

He stopped and turned around, and we stared at each other in silence for a few awkward moments. I couldn't read the look on his face. Then he smiled. "I'd love to dance with you. It has been a long time."

The band struck up another waltz, and Gary led me out onto the dance floor. I suddenly remembered his formal dancing style. We were taught our skills from the same person, so we matched perfectly. The room was full of performers, but Gary was an exceptional dancer, professionally trained, and it was obvious to all. People stopped dancing, and heads turned to watch. We floated instead of danced about the room. Gary kept his eyes on my face, just as he had almost five years before at his college dance. I looked into his eyes, and I saw my own reflection staring back at me. My face felt hot, as though it were flushed. When we finished, I curtsied, Gary bowed, and he kissed my hand. People were still clapping as he exited the reception hall door and left the party.

"What was he doing here?" Grant asked.

"Getting a scoop, just like the rest of them, I suppose."

"How in the world did he learn to dance like that?" Grant was still staring at the exit door, even though Gary was long gone.

"His mother was a professional dance instructor. He learned from her. That's why his style is near perfect and he has a somewhat formal presence while executing a waltz."

"He's wasting his talent as a reporter when he can dance like that."

I nodded my head in agreement, but Gary was still moving forward with his career in journalism. He was now assigned to cover stories of some national attention, but he still threw barbs in my direction whenever he got the chance.

As this was a celebrity wedding, Grant and I chose a song to sing to each other, but it was also for the benefit of the audience. I loved the song, "Fantasy," by *Earth Wind and Fire.* Grant and I spent the past week learning the lines and working out some choreography.

I threw my bouquet, Grant removed my garter and tossed it, and soon it was time to leave. I hugged Carolyn, Jo Dell, and Leisel, and then it was time to leave with Grant for our honeymoon. The evening was full of magic, and it seemed very much like a dream.

Grant and I had reservations in a New York City hotel suite, which we disclosed to no one. He carried me across the threshold and gently laid me on the bed. He lay down next to me and began to kiss and undress me very gently and slowly. I felt myself melting in his arms. I remembered his touch from before. He had a way of touching my face and hair so that I could feel it all over. I always wondered if my response to him while we were in the storm cellar had been heightened by fear, but I could feel my body responding in exactly the same way. He was slow and deliberate, and he touched and kissed my body until I felt as though I were on fire. When I thought I could stand it no more, Grant joined me in a passionate embrace, and we rolled and rocked in each other's arms as though we were one.

I had a dream that night. I had it before, and I tried to remember exactly when it started, but I couldn't. I believe it was shortly after Brandon's death. I was standing at the top of a stairway. I turned a certain way, and my dress swished in the breeze. I began to run down the stairs, and I woke up. It didn't scare me; I was only curious about it because I had it before, but I was beginning to get frustrated as to why I was running down the stairs.

-32-

Marriage seemed to suit us. Grant acted like he was the happiest man in the world. I was happy too, but there were times when a dark mood overshadowed me. Brandon still smoldered in my heart, and as much as I tried not to show it, I believed that Grant had become aware.

There was also a downside to our marriage. Our public personas overshadowed our characters, and after five seasons, we were notified that the network was not renewing our show in the fall. They decided to have a series finale by having Jenny marry John. So once again, I put on a white dress and walked up the aisle toward Grant, this time for the cameras, while Jenny and John were joined in marriage.

"I hope they'll be as happy as we are," said Grant.

We certainly didn't have to worry about money. We had enough money so that we would never have to work again if we didn't want to, but that's not how it is in this business. There's a power and an emotion behind performing. Excitement builds up in the blood, and it has to be released by giving an awesome performance. That is what's missed when an actor does not work for a while, and this is what compels him to find more work, even if it's not the type of work that he really wishes to do. We still accepted appearances on variety shows and occasional talk shows, and we still went to parties for networking purposes, but the hectic pace of doing a weekly series had come to an end. Grant was getting calls for Broadway, and although he hadn't accepted any roles at this point, I encouraged him to look into them.

I used the cancellation of the show to have a chance to spend more time with Jo Dell. She would be five years old in October and starting school in the fall. I wanted her to attend the school that I would have attended if life hadn't turned out differently for me, so I talked Grant into moving into my Kensington home. We decided to remodel the home into something that we would both like because each room reminded me of my mother.

Carolyn didn't want to live with us, even though it was her house as much as it was ours, so she moved in with Leisel. She was worried about Leisel, who tended to drink too much and was prone to finding one-night stands. After Carolyn moved in with her, Leisel became more sedate, and there was a new activity that she had gotten hooked on, which was attending little league games. Leisel had always been a little eccentric, so it didn't surprise me.

Gary wrote something in his column about the cancellation of our show and how loyal fans needn't worry because they might bring Jenny back at a later date, this time playing a mother, or even a grandmother. Grant laughed, but I saw no humor in it at all. Grant told me that I misunderstood Gary's intentions all of the time, but I told him that he was seldom the target of Gary's poisoned pen. Gary was cold, calculating, and uncompassionate. One day, however, I got to see a side of Gary that I had never seen before, and I came away believing that there could be great compassion in his heart after all.

-33-

It was the beginning of the school year, and Jo Dell had just started kindergarten. I received a phone call from the school nurse, who told me that she had hurt her ankle by jumping out of a swing on the playground. The nurse didn't believe it was broken, but Jo Dell would have to stay off of it for a few days.

When I got to the school, I was told that they sent someone to the drugstore to get an Ace wrap to put on her ankle to control the swelling. Jo Dell tended to be somewhat dramatic when she was hurt. It was probably from being the biological daughter of two actors, and then living in a household with two more. The nurse had just calmed her down, and she thought if Jo Dell saw me, she might start making a huge fuss all over again. I was asked to wait in the teacher's lounge, and they would call me when she was ready.

It was about 1:30 in the afternoon when I walked into the lounge. All of the teachers were in their classrooms at that time. Straight-backed chairs were lined up against the walls, all the way around the room. I chose a chair on the side of the wall farthest from the door, picked up a magazine, and began to read.

I don't know if I heard his voice, or if I sensed his presence, but I knew who it was as soon as the door opened and even before I saw his face. It was Gary Shawn. For some reason, I wasn't surprised to see him, but what did surprise me was that he was holding onto the hand of a young boy. He looked like he was about eight or nine years old. I could tell by their faces that they were upset about something. The boy looked up at Gary and said, "Are you going to spank me, Gary?"

"I don't know," Gary answered, "but we certainly need to talk about it."

He sat down in a chair along the wall nearest the door, pulled another chair out of line so that it faced his, and then motioned for the boy to sit down.

"You know," said Gary, "I've always been very proud of your behavior. But recently, you've been disruptive in class, disrespectful to your teacher, and now today, you hit one of the boys in your class. This isn't like you, and I'd like to know why you're acting this way all of a sudden."

The boy looked down at the floor and shrugged his shoulders.

"Are you having problems getting along with any of your classmates?"

"No."

"Is anyone making fun of you or picking on you?"

"No."

"Does your teacher treat you differently from the other students?"

The boy shook his head.

"Is there any reason that you would like to tell me as to why you've been acting this way?"

I saw another shake of the head.

Gary's voice sharpened. "You have to help me out here. You're not giving me much choice."

"I know." The boy's voice sounded very vulnerable and small, and he was still looking down at the floor.

"Well, what reason can there be?"

The boy shrugged his shoulders again.

I knew Gary was frustrated from not getting anywhere with him, but he maintained remarkable patience. "Are you suggesting that you did it for no reason? You did it just because you felt like it? Is that what you're telling me?"

"I guess so."

Gary sighed loudly. "Okay, come over here to me." He grasped the boy's wrist and gently but firmly guided him out of the chair. He pointed to a nearby doorway. "Maybe we should go into that restroom over there so we can have some privacy."

Gary never once looked my way, but he obviously knew that they weren't alone in the room. He stood up and started to guide the boy over to the restroom, when he stopped and stooped down beside him. He gently tilted the boy's chin upward with his hand to get the child to look him in the eye.

"You know that I get absolutely no pleasure in doing this, don't you?"

The boy nodded and said, "It's okay, Gary."

I was extremely surprised. I never thought I would live to see the day when a young child would tell someone that it was okay. Gary must have been touched too, because he drew the boy to him and hugged him. His face looked incredibly sad. "I just don't want to do this without knowing why," he said, while still embracing the boy.

"I don't know why, Gary."

Gary looked the boy squarely in the eyes again and studied his face. "Maybe you don't know why," he said. "But, I do know something that you can tell me. Let's sit back down for a second. I have one more question, and I want you to try very hard to answer me, okay?"

"Okay."

They sat down in their chairs, and Gary took one of the boy's hands and held it between both of his own. "I want you to tell me what you were feeling when you hit that boy."

"I was mad. I was just so mad, but I don't know why. He played a practical joke on me. We do that all the time, but this time I got so mad that I hit him. I didn't plan on hitting him; I just did, and then it scared me because I got so mad."

Gary nodded. "What were you feeling when you talked back to your teacher?"

"It's hard to explain, but I've had this weird feeling right here." He pointed to an area between his heart and his stomach. "It comes and goes like waves. I was feeling this way when she said something to me, and I felt that if someone said one more thing to me that day, that I was going to explode."

"I know what it is," said Gary.

The boy's eyes widened with wonder. "You do?"

Gary nodded. "You're stressed out. The feeling you're describing is anxiety. You'll be feeling that more and more as you get older and start handling bigger problems in life, but once you recognize what it is, you can take steps to deal with it more effectively."

"What causes it?"

"It usually happens when someone has to deal with a major change. I've seen books that list the fifteen to twenty most stressful events that can occur in someone's life, and most of them have to do with dealing with a loss, like moving away, losing your friends, losing a pet you love, getting divorced, and the most stressful event of all is losing a family member that you love."

The boy looked down at the floor again.

Gary said, "How have you been feeling about Dad's death?"

The boy was still looking at the floor. He shrugged his shoulders, but his lips were quivering.

Gary continued, "Maybe we did the wrong thing by keeping you from going to the funeral. I listened to Zachary and Patrick and agreed to have you stay home against my own better judgment. You never had a chance to say goodbye."

The boy looked up at him and asked, "Why did he have to die, Gary?" His voice was so full of hurt and pain that it tore my heart. He suddenly burst into uncontrollable sobs.

Gary quickly stood up and scooped the boy into his arms. "I knew it," he said softly, "I knew there was a reason."

The boy wrapped his arms around Gary's neck and sobbed like his heart was going to break.

Gary held him and stroked his hair, and he patted him on the back. He spoke to him softly in a soothing voice. "He had a bad heart. It was nobody's fault; it just happened." He held him until the sobs ebbed away and finally subsided. Gary sat back down in his chair and balanced the boy against one knee. "Wow," he said. "Do you feel better?" He reached into his suit pocket and pulled out a handkerchief.

The boy nodded and said, "I'm s-sorry, G-Gary." The words were coming out in shudders. "I know that big boys d-don't cry."

"Who told you that?" asked Gary, in a gentle voice.

"Zachary."

"Well, I've seen Zachary cry."

The boy's head jerked up, and his eyes widened in interest. "You have?" he asked.

Gary nodded. "Uh-huh, and he was a bigger boy than you are." Gary wiped a stray tear from the child's face with his hand and said, "I'll tell you something else, too. When Dad died, Zachary cried too, only he did it while he was alone in his room; just like I did."

"Really?"

"Sure. There's nothing wrong with crying when you have something to cry about." Gary motioned for him to sit back down in his chair. He reached out and took the boy's hand in his again. "Now, let's talk about your behavior. You know that I cannot tolerate you hitting your classmates and talking back to your teacher, don't you?"

"Yes, sir."

"Why do you go to school in the first place?"

"To learn."

"That's right. That's your job; to learn what they teach you to the best of your ability. It's as much your job to go to school and learn, as it is mine to go to the office to work. Do you think that I can go around hitting my co-workers and talking back to my boss?"

"No."

"No, it just isn't done, so you can't go around hitting your classmates and talking back to your teacher, either." Gary patted his hand. "I do understand why you did it. You were feeling stressed out and upset. You didn't know why, and you didn't even feel like you could cry. Do you think it might have helped if you had told me what you were feeling a little bit earlier? Do you think that I might have been able to help you understand what you were feeling before it got so bad that you were striking out at others?"

The boy nodded his head.

"Does it surprise you that I figured it out?"

"Yes."

"Well, it wasn't that long ago that I was a boy. I know what it's like to be a young boy, and most importantly, I know what it *feels* like to be a young boy. You can always tell me what you feel, and I'll always do my very best to help you; that's my job. I'm not saying that I'm perfect, and that I'll never make any mistakes, but I'll always try to do my best for you. I'll tell you what we'll do. Why don't we skip work and school for the rest of the day? We can go by Dad's grave, and you can talk to him and tell him goodbye. We'll always miss him, but little by little the pain that you feel right now will fade away. It won't happen overnight, but one day, maybe six months or a year from now, you'll suddenly find that you can think about him and it won't hurt so much anymore. You'll be able to remember him, and it'll feel good, not bad. Is there anything else that you'd like to tell me or ask me?"

He nodded. "Do you really have to work so much? You're never home when I come home from school anymore, so I never have the chance to talk to you."

Gary at first looked surprised, and then he looked like he had just been punched in the stomach. He pulled the boy onto his lap and wrapped his arms around him. "You know," he said, "when someone dies, everyone reacts to it differently. What I did was I started working late so that I wouldn't have to go home and think about it. That was how I was dealing with it. I never thought about the fact that you might need me at home. I didn't do it on purpose. I'm very sorry, Alan. I'll start coming home earlier, and I promise I'll be there when you get home from school. If I have to go out, I won't go until you go to bed at night, okay?"

"Okay."

"I have one more promise, and I want you to listen carefully. If I get called down here one more time because you have been misbehaving, I *will* spank you. Do you understand?"

"Yes, sir."

"And you understand that I'll have to keep this promise, don't you?"

"Yes, sir."

Gary pointed to the restroom and said, "Why don't you go in there and wash your face so nobody can tell that you've been crying, and then we'll go tell the office that we're leaving for the day, okay?"

"Okay."

Alan went into the restroom, and Gary heaved a heavy sigh and held his head in his hands. Without even looking up at first, I heard him say to me, "Hello, Joy." He never once looked in my direction, but like me, he must have sensed my presence.

"Hello, Gary."

"What brings you here?"

"Jo Dell hurt her ankle. I'm waiting for them to put an Ace wrap on it, but it seems like they're taking forever. You know, I was really sorry to hear about your father."

"Thank you. I still get up every morning believing that it didn't happen, but then reality takes a hold of me."

"It's hard to lose someone you love," I said.

"Yes. You know a little something about that."

"I didn't know that you had a younger brother," I said, changing the subject. "For some reason, I thought that you were the youngest in your family."

"Well, I guess there's a lot about each other that we don't know," he said. "I believe that I told you I was the youngest of four brothers, all born one year apart. I never said I was the youngest in the family."

Just then, the school nurse poked her head inside the teacher's lounge and told me that Jo Dell was ready to go home. Her ankle was wrapped, but she was having difficulty standing on it without pain. I tried to help her as she hopped on one leg, but it wasn't working. I was about to pick her up and carry her, when Gary scooped her up in his arms.

"Come here, honey," he said to her. "Let me help you and your Momma out to the car."

Gary's brother came out of the bathroom, and we left the school building together. Gary helped me put Jo Dell in the car and said goodbye to me. He took Alan by the hand and I heard him ask, "Do you remember Dad's favorite song?"

Alan nodded, and I watched as they walked to their car, hand in hand, swinging their arms, and singing the lyrics to, *Who Threw the Overalls in Mrs. Murphy's Chowder?*

I thought a lot about what I witnessed that day. I'm afraid that I wouldn't have taken the chance to delve that deeply if Jo Dell had been misbehaving. My mother would have disciplined me for the misbehavior, and she would have expected me not to do it again by holding the threat of further punishment over my head, rather than trying to find and eliminate the cause. I probably would have handled the situation the same way with Jo Dell. That I should learn something about parenting from someone that I always accused of being cold and uncompassionate, and who wasn't even a parent, was rather unsettling.

-34-

It was time to prepare for Jo Dell's birthday, but I wasn't feeling well. I wasn't exactly sick; I had no fever, cough, or cold, but I felt like doing nothing- sort of like what happens when you get the flu. Jo Dell sat next to me on the couch and read stories to me, but I didn't pay much attention. I just sat on the couch and stared out the window. At first, Grant said nothing, but as it got closer to her birthday, he finally asked what I had planned.

"I haven't felt well enough to think about it. Maybe Carolyn can help me."

"She helped you last year, and the year before that, too. Do you ever remember feeling well on Jo Dell's birthday?"

I was somewhat irritated with this conversation, and I knew that he really didn't want to get into an argument, so I said nothing, and he just walked away without expecting an answer. I made an effort to order a cake and get some presents delivered on short notice. Carolyn came over and helped me get a list of some of Jo Dell's friends from school. We made some phone calls, but it was too late to send out invitations.

Two days before her birthday, I had a severe headache, and I stayed in bed most of the day. Toward evening, Grant sat beside me on the bed and held my hand. "I'm sure that it's just a tension headache, and you'll be feeling better in a few days, but you have to try not to let this ruin Jo Dell's birthday."

"Do you think I'm doing this on purpose so that I won't have to give my little girl a party?"

"No, honey, it's not that, but I've noticed that you get this way every year around this time. I think you have to recognize it for what it is."

"Well, you're the psychology major," I said. I removed my hand from his and turned my back to him by rolling over in bed. A few moments later, I heard him quietly get up and leave, and the door softly shut behind him.

The day of the party, I forced myself to act like I was having a good time. Jo Dell was clearly happy with her presents. Grant had stayed up half of the night putting a bicycle and a doll's house together for her.

"Couldn't you have bought things that were already put together?" I asked.

"Sure, but part of being a father is staying up late to put toys together."

"I wouldn't know," I said. "I never had a father."

Grant took fatherhood seriously, but Jo Dell openly snubbed him much of the time. She tended to address only me if we were in the room together. Grant always said that she would grow out of it, but after a year and a half, I thought she was growing rather slowly. He told me that she was used to my attention and didn't want to share me, but I disagreed. Jo Dell never had me to herself. Brandon was always around when she was a baby, and after that, Grant was always around. Sure, we weren't married, but he was always around. She called me Mommy, and she called him Grant, even though he adopted her. She kept a picture of Brandon on the desk in her room, and she even kissed the picture goodnight. Grant never said anything to her, but sometimes I saw a hurt expression cast a shadow across his face.

I noticed that I wasn't feeling very well the following year when Jo Dell had her next birthday. I had the same non-specific flu symptoms, but I forced myself to go through the motions of creating a nice party, and Grant said nothing.

Scripts were coming in for Grant and I to do occasional guest starring roles on established television series. I noticed that parts for him were coming in two to three times faster than they were for me, but I tried not to let it bother me. If it was an exceptionally good script, we would always do it, but often we had to travel to Los Angeles to do the filming, and I liked to stay in New York, especially if Jo Dell was in school. I didn't want her to miss out on the same things that I had, so I tried to give her as much of a normal home life as possible.

One day, I got a call from Andrew, who was very excited because there was going to be a Broadway revival of Rogers and Hammerstein's musical, *Oklahoma!* He was certain that I would be excited as well because I always loved their music, and I considered my work in *Cinderella* to be one of the highlights of my career.

Grant never dreamed that I would turn it down. "I don't understand," he said.

"I'm just not interested, that's all. I'd rather do something else."

"It's not like the offers are pouring in anymore, Joy. You know just as well as anyone that you have to make yourself seen."

"I know you've been getting more offers than I have. You don't have to rub it in."

"That isn't what I mean, and you know it."

"I'd rather do something else."

"Well, let's not argue about it." He walked out of the room, but he poked his head back through the door. "Let's do something different for a change," he said. "We haven't been out on the town for a while now. Let's go out to dinner and go dancing afterwards."

I decided that would be a good idea because it would keep Grant from bothering me about doing the play. I put on a nice evening dress, and I sat down at the vanity to put on my makeup.

"You look pretty, Mommy," said Jo Dell, as she sat on the bed and watched me get dressed. "I wish I were as pretty as you. Why couldn't I have looked like you?"

"That would have been impossible, wouldn't it?"

"I guess so. Sometimes I forget that you're not my real mother."

"I *am* your mother; I'm just not your biological mother. That's really the only reason that you can't look like me, but as far as I'm concerned, you're my real daughter."

She beamed. She wasn't a beautiful child. She had Brandon's rugged features, and although those features made him look like a blonde Adonis, I found that they seemed awkward in a feminine face. She wasn't homely; she just wasn't exactly pretty, and at seven years old, she was starting to notice.

"When you get older, I'll show you how to put on makeup, and I think you'll like what you see. Makeup makes the most of a person's best features, and it downplays the worst. That's what I do."

"You look pretty without any makeup, Mommy."

"Thank you, honey." I kissed her on her forehead and continued to dress for the evening. I was happy when I saw Grant's appraising look when I entered the room.

"The most beautiful woman in the world," he said, holding his arms out to me. I felt my breath catch because Brandon used to call me that. Jo Dell made a face at his comment, but I didn't put any great significance to it, and I forgot about it almost immediately.

We had a wonderful evening. We danced out on a terrace under a moon lit sky. The breeze was light and gentle, and the stars stood out plainly, like a dark blanket filled with shimmering diamonds. We were offered coffee and dessert out on the terrace.

"You order for me," I told Grant, as I excused myself to go to the restroom.

When I came back, he was sipping his coffee, and he reached over and handed me a dessert plate. It was strawberry cheesecake. I gasped involuntarily when I saw it, but Grant seemed not to notice.

"I remember you once said that it's your favorite."

"Not anymore." I set the plate down on the table. I had no intentions of eating it. The very thought of eating it made me sick. I picked up my coffee cup and took a sip out of it.

Grant looked momentarily surprised, and then he motioned for the waiter to come back over and asked him to bring me something else. We ate our dessert in silence, and then the band started playing again.

"That's a beautiful song, Grant. Let's dance."

Grant stood up from the table and held his hand out to me. I noticed as we walked onto the dance floor that Grant's demeanor had changed. He wasn't quite as bubbly and effervescent as he had been earlier. It was as though the champagne had gone flat. After a few more songs, he said that he thought we should get back home.

Grant and I enjoyed a very satisfying sex life from the very beginning of our marriage. I still wondered at times what it would have been like with Brandon. Somehow I always assumed that it would have been just as good, or maybe even better. I halfway expected after such a romantic evening that Grant would want to make love to me, but he just rolled over and turned out the light.

-36-

Grant was getting more and more roles requiring him to travel to Hollywood. Sometimes I went with him, and other times I just stayed at home. One time when he was away, I received an answer to a question that had haunted me my entire life. What had become of my father?

Carolyn and I hardly knew anything about our father because my mother never talked about him. We couldn't ask questions because she wouldn't answer them. She just evaded the subject by telling us that some things are better not to be brought to mind at all, and he was one of them. She never told us that he was dead, and she never mentioned a divorce. My mother wasn't inclined to tell out and out lies; she was just a master at evading a subject altogether. Carolyn and I decided between us that our father must have run off and deserted us. After all, who would want to live the rest of their lives with our mother? We sure didn't. We loved her, and we missed her, but that wasn't the same thing as living with her. Now that my mother and aunt had passed away, I believed that we would never know the answer. I was wrong.

Grant was in Hollywood filming a variety show with a list of other well-known personalities. I expected him to be gone at least another week. They were busy working out last minute changes to the scripts and the choreography, and then they had to do the actual filming. I could have gone with him, but I decided at the last minute not to. I wasn't asked to be a part of the show. I wasn't sure if that bothered me or not, but I didn't want to be hanging around the set.

I found myself missing Grant terribly, and I was entertaining the idea of going up there anyway, when I got an unexpected phone call from Gary Shawn, of all people. He wanted to see me. He had uncovered some important information that he was sure I'd like to know. I was sure it was an exceptionally mean piece that he was going to tease me with, and I almost told him that I'd read about it in his column as I always did, but there was a different ring to his voice. I decided to go against my better judgment and see him.

I invited him into my sitting room. I noticed that he seemed somewhat ill at ease. "What news have you unearthed about me now?" I asked. "Maybe you saw me carried away in an alien ship, and that I've finally given birth to little green lizards because, as you recently pointed out, I've never given birth to anything else."

"You know that's not my style, Joy. I didn't mean to insinuate that there was anything wrong with the fact that you and Grant haven't had any children together yet. But, I must have struck a nerve somewhere."

He *had* struck a nerve. I had been disappointed that Grant and I had been married for over three years, and that I hadn't become pregnant yet. I enjoyed raising Jo Dell, and the thought of having another child, especially a biological one, was very appealing to me. I considered going to a fertility specialist, but I didn't want the publicity, and I knew stories like that tended to leak out. That piece he wrote had hurt me deeply, but I didn't want him to know. "You always strike a nerve," I said. "It's what you live for these days."

"I came over to call a truce, just this once, if you'll accept my little white flag."

"Why should I?"

"Look, I'm not the monster that you think I am. I like to cause you some mild anxiety, but I'm not malicious."

"That's debatable."

"Do you want the truce or don't you?"

"Sure, what did you come here to say?"

"I found out that your father is alive."

"What!" I exclaimed. I was glad that I was sitting down, but then I got suspicious. "How would you know?"

"I remember you told me once, when we were on better terms, that you would give anything to know what happened to him. I decided to do a little investigative reporting, and I came up with the answer."

"Well, where is he? Why aren't I reading about it in your column? Is he the Unabomber or something?"

"No, it's nothing like that. He has been in a mental institution all of these years. Your mother must have felt that it would hurt your career if that juicy piece of information ever leaked out."

"Has he been kept there against his will all of this time? Is he well enough to get out, and just hasn't been allowed to?"

Gary shook his head. "No, Joy; he evidently has a problem with multiple personalities."

"I want to see him." I could tell by the look on his face that he didn't think it was a good idea. "I don't care what you say," I told him. "I want to see him. I want you to tell me right this minute where he is."

Gary reached up and rested both of his hands on my shoulders. "Joy, you're thinking with your heart and not with your head. Can't you see? If you appear up there, people will put two and two together, and it'll be all over the tabloids. Professional people are supposed to maintain confidentiality, but this is too juicy of a story not to leak out. Someone will recognize you, and they'll put the names together: Bryant and Bryantelli. Some forms of mental illnesses are thought to be hereditary, and soon the tabloids will be writing that you've become mentally ill. You know that I'm speaking the truth."

Yes, he was speaking the truth, but I had to know. I had to see him. "I know it, Gary," I said, "but that's a risk I'm going to have to take. Can't you get me in there somehow? I can disguise myself. You don't know what it's like to always have questions and never really know."

"But now you do know. Isn't that enough?"

"No. Would it be enough for you? I want to know what he looks like. I want to know if he remembers me, and if he has any idea who I am. How would you feel if you had never known your father?"

"That's an unfair 'what if' question. The fact is, I *did* know my father, so looking back with that kind of hindsight, I'd have to say that I wouldn't have liked it very much. He was a major force in my life. That's not the same situation that you're in because, in reality, your father wasn't a factor in your life. Even if you were to meet him now, he'll never be a major influence on your adult life as he might have been in your childhood. You never know, if he had been around, he might have prevented you from becoming Joy Bryant. Your life might have been totally different. You can't play games with 'what if' questions."

I didn't want to start crying in front of him, but I couldn't help it. I was horrified that I couldn't hold the tears back.

"Okay," said Gary, in a voice full of resignation. "You win. I'll figure out a way to get you there somehow. I'll speak to the attending physician and explain a need for utmost secrecy."

"Where is he, Gary?"

"I'm not telling you that, unless I speak to Grant. You're not going to make that drive without someone with you. It has some nasty, winding roads; you'll be unusually anxious, and it's in the middle of nowhere. Your mother chose the spot well."

"How far of a drive is it?"

"Probably about ten or twelve hours."

"Would you be willing to take me?"

"Sure, unless Grant would rather do it."

"He's in Los Angeles, and he won't be back for about a week. I don't want to wait that long. He won't mind if I go; he'll understand." I held out my hand. "Truce?" I asked.

"Truce," said Gary, as he shook my hand. "I'll pick you up tomorrow morning around nine."

It occurred to me that I was being a very rude hostess. "Since we have a truce, can I offer you a drink? Coffee, tea, bourbon, or do you still not drink alcohol?"

"I still don't drink alcohol. It's important to me to keep my senses."

"You mean control, don't you? You always have to be in control."

He looked at me with disdain. "I thought we had a truce."

I clamped my hand over my mouth. "Yes, we do. I suppose we'll have to keep reminding each other."

Gary stood up to leave. "Well," he said, "I should go home and get some sleep, but I'll be back tomorrow. Call me if you change your mind."

"I won't change my mind," I assured him, as I walked him to the door.

"I hope we're doing the right thing," he said, and he surprised me by leaning over and kissing me on the cheek just before he stepped out into the night.

I spent a restless night, tossing and turning. When I finally did sleep, I slept fitfully. I had dreams about my father, a man I couldn't remember at all. All I could remember was seeing his shoes in the closet. I had another dream: I was running down a flight of stairs in the fog.

I packed a small suitcase to go with me. I debated whether or not I should call Grant, but I talked myself out of it. I told myself that I didn't want to interrupt the shoot, but I was probably afraid that he would try to talk me out of it more forcefully than Gary did. Jealousy wouldn't be a problem, however, since Grant knew all about Gary's personal preferences.

I was so curious and excited that I could hardly stand it. After what seemed to be an eternity, Gary pulled up in the driveway. He helped me load my suitcase into the car, and we were on our way. We had just started down the highway when his cell phone rang.

"Hello," Gary answered. "Alan?" he asked. "Alan, what's wrong?"

I felt my heart sink. Something was wrong, and now I would have to wait to see my father.

Gary patiently listened on the phone and then turned to me and asked, "Do you have a cell phone on you?"

I nodded, not knowing exactly what was going on, and pulled out my phone.

"Alan," Gary was saying, "stay on the line and don't hang up. I'm going to call Zachary on another phone, so just hang on- do you understand?"

Gary took the phone from my hand and dialed a number.

"Frank?" he asked. "Frank, will you please pull Zachary off of the bathroom door and bring him to the phone?" After a brief pause, I heard him say, "Thanks."

After another longer pause, he said, "Zachary? What in the world is going on down there?"

He listened at length, and his coloring seemed to pale.

"I'm only five minutes away. I'm on my way home right now, and I'll take care of it... I understand Zachary, and I agree with you, and I'll personally put blisters on his behind when I get there... No, Zachary, and you know why. That boy lives in a household full of adults. We agreed long ago that the discipline must come from one source. *I* am the one closest to him, and *I* will do it. It has to come from me."

After a few moments, he asked to speak to Frank again.

"Frank," he said, "keep Zachary off of that bathroom door. I'll be home in less than five minutes, and I'll take care of this mess."

He hung up my phone and spoke back into his.

"Alan? I'll be home in a few minutes. You can stay in the bathroom until I get there, but once I get home, I want to see you. Don't make *me* come in there after you."

He hung up the phone with a huge sigh.

"Is there a problem?" I asked, trying not to let my anxiety show.

"It won't take very long, Joy. I have to go by the house for about twenty minutes or so, and then we can get the show on the road." He patted my hand, and I was aware that he must have read my anxious thoughts. "I'm sorry for the delay, but it won't stop us from going, I promise," he said.

Gary offered a brief, unexpected explanation as we drove to his house.

"Alan has a friend that has been getting into trouble lately. It really hasn't been anything big, but little things here and there are starting to add up, and I've been wondering lately if I should put a stop to their friendship. I guess my mind is made up now. Tommy decided to form a secret club, and in order to join, Alan was told that he had to steal a few items from Mr. Johnson's store as a part of an initiation type thing, and he got caught this morning. Mr. Johnson doesn't want to press charges, but he phoned Zachary, and Zachary was ready to take the law into his own hands since I wasn't around. Alan got scared, grabbed the cell phone, and locked himself into the bathroom to call me. Zachary, in the meantime, is absolutely intent upon breaking the door down. I'm sorry, Joy, I have to intervene, but it won't take very long."

We entered the driveway leading up to the Shawn residence. I hadn't been there in years; in fact, I was only inside his house once or twice late at night. Gary took my arm as we walked to the door. Instead of using a key, he rang the doorbell, which I assumed was to announce his arrival to the scared little boy shut up in the bathroom.

The maid answered the door. "Master Gerald," she said, as she opened the door. We entered the foyer, and Gary motioned for me to sit on an ornate mahogany bench positioned inside the foyer and just outside of the library.

"I didn't know your name was Gerald," I said.

"There's a lot about each other that we don't know," Gary answered.

He said that to me once before, about two years ago. I marveled at the inside of the house. It was ornate in a simplified way, and everything was beautifully decorated. Plush red carpeting ran from the foyer to the spiral staircase, which wound around to the upstairs. Chandeliers twinkled from the ceilings, and antique mahogany furniture was scattered throughout the house.

Zachary walked in. His face was flushed with anger, and he had a thick leather strap in his hand. "You should have let me take care if it," he said to Gary.

"I've already explained to you why that's not possible. Besides, there are other reasons that I can see right now that would make it inappropriate for you to take care of the situation."

"And what might they be?"

"One, you're too angry, and two, you're too eager. You'll hurt him more than you have to." Gary took the strap from his hand and laid it down on a mahogany table positioned right outside of the library. The library was directly across from where I was sitting, and just slightly to the left of me.

"I'm the head of this house now," Zachary said.

"Yes, you have your responsibilities, and I have mine. This one isn't yours."

They glared at each other, and then Zachary stormed out of the room. Gary sat down on the bench beside me and let out a big sigh. The maid brought me a glass of iced tea, and Gary asked her if she would do him a favor and tell Alan that he wanted to see him. A few moments later, a young boy of about ten or eleven years old entered the room. He had the cloudiest face I had ever seen.

Gary reached out to the boy with one hand. "There isn't anything that can't be fixed," he said.

There must have been a magical meaning in those words because the boy's expression brightened somewhat. He quickly ran to meet Gary's outstretched arm and hugged him around the neck. After a few moments, Alan pulled back and looked at Gary's face. "You're going to whip me," he said solemnly. It was more of a statement than a question.

Gary's nod was barely perceptible, but his intent was clear when he answered, "I want you to know exactly why."

"I know why," Alan said miserably. "Stealing is wrong."

"Well, there's more to it than that- stuff that you've probably never thought about." Gary stood up and put his arm around the boy's shoulder. "Let's go into the library, and I'll tell you all about it."

They sat down on a mahogany bench in the library that was identical to the one I was sitting on in the foyer. Gary had left the door partially open, and I could see inside from where I was sitting. Gary seemed not to notice, and he didn't get up to close the door any more. I thought about getting up and moving, but I didn't because this was where I was directed to sit. Maybe I was nosy, too.

"Did you know that Mr. Johnson buys everything that you see in his store out of his own pocket?" asked Gary.

Alan shook his head.

"Well," Gary continued, "he buys things from different places around the country, and then we have the convenience of going into one store to pick up everything we need. He buys things and then he sells them to us for a profit. Every once in a while he has to do what's called a store inventory. He counts everything in the store, and he can tell what he has sold, what he hasn't sold, and he can also tell what has been stolen. He doesn't want to lose money just because people steal from him, so he'll adjust the prices of the other items in the store. He'll raise the price of things here and there, so the consumer, or buyer, which is you and I, will end up paying for the cost of stolen items in the long run. When you stole from that store, you hurt me, yourself, and everyone else who buys things from that store. Do you understand?"

"Yes, sir."

"Mr. Johnson agreed not to press charges," Gary continued. "If he had, a police officer would have taken you downtown to be booked. They would have fingerprinted you, taken your picture, and it would have gone into the record books that they keep on people who commit crimes. After that, a police record could have followed you around for the rest of your life. Some people can't get jobs that they really want when they become adults because they've had a police record in the past. Mr. Johnson did you a favor. What we're going to do later is go down to Mr. Johnson's store and pay him for the things that you took out of your allowance. You will apologize for what you did, and I want you to thank him for giving you a break because he didn't have to do that. I'll go with you, so you won't feel like you're alone, okay?"

Alan nodded. "Okay," he said.

"Now," said Gary, "I'm going to say something that you're not going to like, but I'll expect you to do as I say. I'm putting a stop to your friendship with Thomas Martin. Now, don't look at me like that, Alan. Thomas has been getting into trouble lately, and now he's taking you with him. I know that you'll see him at school, but after school, you will not have any further contact with him. He will not come over to our house, and you will not go to his. You will not have any association with him at all; do I make myself clear? If, at some point, he proves that he's going to be a good citizen again, we can rethink our position. If you disobey me, you'll be worse off than you are today."

"Are you mad at me, Gary?"

"No; I'm not mad at you. Now, Zachary is a different story. He's really angry. But you have to understand that Zachary was raised a little bit differently from the rest of us, and he took on most of the responsibilities of the estate after Dad died. He's afraid that you might have brought some shame upon the Shawn name. People make reputations for themselves. What do they say about the Miller girls?"

"That they're sluts."

I heard Gary clear his throat. "Okay, that's fair enough; that *is* what they say. What about Mr. O'Neill?"

"That he's a drunk."

"Well, Zachary doesn't want people calling the Shawns a bunch of thieves. It could happen, you know. That's why he's so angry. I'm disappointed that you would choose to do something that you know is wrong. But what hurts me most of all, so much that I can barely breathe, is that I have to punish you, and I would give anything not to have to do that."

"Can you give me another chance?"

"What? Another chance to steal? I don't think so."

Alan looked down at the floor, and Gary put his arm around Alan's shoulder.

"Look, Alan," he said gently. "Punishment is not intended to get back at you for what you did. I know that's how some parents use it, but it's supposed to help reinforce the lesson. I want you to remember what we just talked about. If I back it up, you'll never forget it. But there's more to it than that. You see, Alan, punishment is also intended to teach you that there are often unpleasant consequences when you do things that you know are wrong. A young boy might get a whipping from his father if he steals, but a young man would go to jail. If I did what you did, Alan, I would go to jail. Isn't it better to learn this lesson while you're young, and all you might get is a whipping? Wouldn't it be worse to learn the lesson later and go to jail? That's why, in my view, the father who loves his son will not withhold that whipping. Dad didn't withhold it from us, and I can't withhold it from you, no matter how much I'd like to. Do you understand?"

"Yes, sir."

Gary patted Alan on the shoulder. "I also want you to know that you haven't done anything that the rest of us haven't done at one time or other. One transgression doesn't make you a bad person. Many boys lie, cheat, or steal at one time or another. Zachary did. I did. And we got into trouble for it, too. What's important is that you learn never to do this or anything like it ever again. Is there anything else that you'd like to ask me or tell me?"

"Are you going to use that big strap that Zachary had?"

Gary shook his head and pointed to the belt he was wearing. "I think this one will do the job, don't you?"

"Yes, sir."

Gary stood up, unbuckled his belt, and led Alan across the room out of my field of vision. After a short pause, I heard six or seven sharp, rhythmic thwacks of the belt. A few moments later, Gary exited the library and stepped out into the foyer, and Alan, who never shed a tear, followed in step behind him. Gary abruptly stopped, turned around, and stooped down to look into Alan's eyes.

"I love you, Alan. I want you to grow up to be someone that your children will be proud of. If you can do that, then I've done my job. I hope you understand that."

Alan nodded, and Gary stood up straight. Alan suddenly reached up and hugged Gary around the waist. "I love you, Gary."

Gary swallowed hard and rumpled the boy's hair with his fingers.

Just then, Zachary walked into the room. He noticed the thick strap still sitting on the table. "You're too soft on him," he snapped at Gary. Alan released his grip from Gary's waist, and Zachary glared at him. "Don't you ever run from me again," he said, shaking a finger at him.

"I'm sorry, Zachary," said Alan. "I was scared because you were so angry."

"You're right- I'm *very* angry. And Gary should be, too. Do you want the whole town calling us a bunch of thieves?"

"Zachary," Gary said patiently, "we've been over all of this already."

"Well, what are you waiting for?" shouted Zachary. "I thought you had things to do and places to see. And you," he said, pointing a finger at Alan, "you get yourself upstairs to your room. I don't need to be looking at the face of a thief all day long."

Alan started to leave, but Gary held out his hand and stopped him. "No," he said. "I've decided to take him with me."

Alan's eyes got as big as saucers, and Zachary stared at Gary incredulously. "You're going to reward him now with a trip? Are you out of your mind?"

Gary stepped closer to where Zachary was standing and got right up into his face. "I'm not leaving him here for you to mistreat."

Frank entered the room and stepped between them. "Zachary," he said, "you're overstepping your bounds. Gary's right. It's not your place to discipline that boy. It never has been, and you have to deal with it. You remember what Dad said - there's too many of us. Gary did the right thing by the boy. He gave him an old-fashioned licking. Alan paid his dues, and if Gary wants to take him along, then he should."

Gary asked the maid if she would help get a few things ready for Alan to take, and she was back in just a few minutes with a small bag packed for him. Gary reached for my hand and helped me to my feet. We started toward the door when Alan stopped and walked back to Zachary, who was still fuming.

"I want to apologize to you, Zachary. I know that you're the head of the household, and I'm sorry that I might have caused some shame on the family name."

I expected another verbal lashing from Zachary, and from the look on Gary's face, he thought so too, but the anger visibly melted from

Zachary's face. He stooped down to meet Alan's eyes, much the same way that Gary had earlier. "There isn't anything that can't be fixed, son," he said. "You can create a good name as well as a bad name. If you start right now, by the time you're grown, you can make a wonderful name for yourself that the whole family can be proud of." Then he surprised me by giving the boy a hug. "We didn't mean to be hard on you, Alan," he said. "We were just trying to do what's right. Did you learn a lesson?"

"Yes, sir."

"Well, you be good for Gary while you're gone. You know, it really hurt him to teach you that lesson."

"I'll be good!" he exclaimed, as he ran towards the doorway where we were standing.

Finally, we were on our way. We made a quick stop by Mr. Johnson's store, and Gary and Alan got out of the car. I stayed in the car, but I could see what was going on. Alan approached Mr. Johnson, while Gary hung back slightly. I didn't know what words Alan used when he spoke to him, but I saw the glare on Mr. Johnson's face melt, much the same way as Zachary's did. I didn't know exactly what it was, but that child had some sort of magic inside of him.

We drove in silence for most of the morning, and then we stopped at a restaurant to get a bite to eat. Gary excused himself to put some gas in the car while we waited for our food to be served.

"Are you always this quiet?" I asked Alan.

"No, but you didn't plan on me coming along. I thought it would be more polite to be quiet for awhile."

"Oh, I see," I said.

"There's another reason too," he said. "I guess I'm a little embarrassed. Whenever I see you, it seems like I'm getting into trouble for something. You must think I'm a terrible kid, but I really don't get into very much trouble. Gary has spanked me a few times, but he never used a belt on me before today, and neither has Zachary. I'm sure going to try not to let that happen again."

"I think that would make your life and Gary's a lot easier," I agreed.

He nodded, and Gary returned to his seat. The waitress served our burgers and fries. "What have you two been talking about?" asked Gary, as he reached for his fries.

"You sure are nosy," I said.

"I was telling Joy that she must think I'm a terrible kid, but I really don't get into trouble very often," said Alan.

"That's right," agreed Gary. "You never have caused us much trouble, and you always learn from your mistakes. That's a quality of a truly great person."

Alan grinned. I looked at Alan more closely. I had always marveled at how much all of the Shawn boys looked alike. I mentioned this to Gary long ago, and he laughed and said, "Yeah, I guess we do look like we were cut from the same piece of cloth." Zachary and Gary looked the most alike of all of the boys, although Zachary was a few inches taller.

The Sanitarium was located in Maine. I loved the drive through New England. There were rustic farmhouses and covered bridges, and the landscape was so full of evergreen trees that the air smelled of pine. When we arrived, it was about ten o'clock at night. We checked into a large suite on the top floor of the hotel. It was like an apartment.

"It's late," Gary told Alan. "I know you're probably all wound up from the trip, but you need to go to bed and try to get some sleep."

Alan's face looked disappointed.

"Tomorrow, you and I can go swimming in that huge pool down there," said Gary. "How would you like that?"

Alan's face brightened, and he nodded his head vigorously. I wasn't the least bit tired. I kicked off my shoes and plopped down on the couch. Gary sat in a chair beside me. Alan went into one of the bathrooms to brush his teeth, and then he came out to say goodnight. Gary rose from his chair and went into one of the bedrooms with Alan.

"I'm sorry about today," I heard Alan say.

"It's all past history. All that matters to me right now is what you do in the future. All boys do things that they're not proud of."

"I want you to be proud of me."

"I am, Alan. I love you. I'm not proud of what you did, but I'm still proud of you. You took the responsibility for what you did like a man. We fixed everything together, didn't we? Come here; I think we both need a hug. Don't worry about it anymore, okay?"

Gary came out and sat back down in the chair. I decided that I was tired, and that it would be a good idea to go to bed after all. "How long do you think we can keep up this truce?" I asked, as I was about to enter my room.

Gary pulled out a white handkerchief and laid it down on the coffee table. "This will remind us," he said.

I laughed and stepped into my room. I was afraid that I wouldn't be able to fall asleep, even though I felt tired, but I must have fallen asleep and never knew it. I woke up suddenly from a dream. I was running down the stairs in the fog, and this time I could see the last few steps. I wondered where I was going, and it was starting to frustrate me. Even while I was dreaming, I was telling myself to please not wake up yet, but I did.

I got up and walked out into the living room. The clock on the wall said 2:00 A.M. I was surprised to find Gary still up, sitting at the kitchen table in the dark. He was staring out the window, and I assumed that he was looking out at the city lights and the stars. There wasn't anything else that could be seen at this time of the early morning. A cigarette glowed in the dark.

"I didn't know that you smoked," I said.

"I don't, really."

I looked at him strangely because I could definitely see a cigarette between his fingers.

He flicked an ash into the ashtray, and the embers glowed faintly and disappeared. He must have noticed the look on my face. He smiled. "I do, but I don't. Once in a great while, I'll light one up. It kind of calms my nerves. I'm not really hooked- I can go for months without ever lighting up another."

"Wouldn't Xanax be healthier? You could just pop a pill rather than a cigarette."

He shrugged his shoulders and began to look out the window again. He seemed very distracted.

"What's bothering you tonight?" I asked.

He said nothing, but continued to look out the window.

"You don't have to tell me," I said. "I just thought if you needed to talk, you might as well talk to me while we have a truce. That's what friends are for; I mean, if you can call us friends. What *are* we really?"

I was rambling for words, and Gary didn't acknowledge the question. He took another puff on the cigarette, and there was a long pause before he finally spoke. "I think I whipped Alan too hard. He has a red mark on his leg," he said to the window.

"I'm sure Alan knows that you didn't mean to do that. I truly believe that above everything else, he knows that you love him. It's very apparent that you do. You know, you made me feel rather small today."

His eyes momentarily left the window and found my face. "How?" he asked.

"I'm a mother. I've disciplined my child, but I've never before in my life seen such a combination of discipline and love. I think that's what most parents would like to do, but you really accomplish it, and he's your brother, not your child."

Gary stared out the window again. He took another long drag on the cigarette and said more to the window than to me, "Have you ever been in love with someone you cannot have?"

"I suppose you can count Brandon DeLorrier in that question. I loved him, and I certainly can't have him."

"I'm sorry. I wasn't thinking about that."

"Are you in love with someone that you can't have? If you are, shouldn't you tell that person?"

"It wouldn't be considered an appropriate relationship."

I didn't know what to say.

"Do you think it's wrong to keep a secret from a friend?" he asked.

Since I knew his secret, I had to be careful, so I said, "If that person is truly a friend, they'll understand and accept your secret."

"No matter how long it takes to tell them?"

"No matter how long it takes to tell them." I pulled out a chair and sat down next to him. "You know, you sure do have a lot on your mind. No wonder you can't sleep."

I shouldn't have sat down. There was a large void of silence. It was evident that he had no intention of saying more, and I began to feel as if I had trespassed into his space.

"Well," I said, getting up from the table, "I need to try to go back to sleep. I want you to know that I appreciate you bringing me here, no matter what the outcome will be tomorrow."

On an impulse, I leaned over and kissed him on the cheek. He sat there like a stone, but as I turned to walk away, he reached for my hand, gave it one quick squeeze, and then let it go. Then he turned his attention to the window again.

I slept longer than I meant to. It was almost nine when I finally rolled out of bed. I went into the living room, and both Alan and Gary were up. I wondered if Gary had gotten any sleep, but he certainly looked refreshed. He didn't look tired at all. He was in a light, cheerful mood, which was so different from his demeanor during the night.

"Good morning," said Gary. He poured some orange juice into a glass and handed it to Alan. "We thought we were going to have to wake you up."

"I usually don't sleep this long into the morning," I said, apparently feeling the need to explain my unusual length of slumber. "I was awake off and on during the night, and then I finally slept like a log."

"I talked to the doctor this morning. He said that we can come down today and confidentiality will be maintained. The only thing that worries him is your father's behavior. He has multiple personalities, and some of them can be quite violent, so someone will have to be with you at all times. He said that Victor will know you, but the other three may not. Victor is a dominant personality, and so is George, but sometimes the other ones come out if he feels threatened. Your father doesn't get many visitors, so he might feel threatened."

As I put on my jacket, I felt anxiety building inside of me. "I'm ready," I said to Gary. "I've waited almost twenty-five years for this."

"Okay. Alan, you stay here and watch television. Don't answer the door or go outside of our room. I'll take you swimming when we get back." Gary kissed Alan on the forehead as we left, and he took me by the arm.

The Sanitarium, the private mental hospital, was a tall, three-story brick building. It was off of the main road, and we had to travel down a dirt road to get there. The grounds were lovely, and there were elm trees and evergreens all over. The elm trees were starting to change colors, and it was only late September.

The doctor was younger than I had expected. He was about thirty years old. He recognized me at once and assured me of confidentiality. It seemed to take forever to walk down the corridor to my father's room. His door was locked, and I could see him sitting in his room from a window that was placed in the door so that he could be observed by the staff from the corridor. The doctor unlocked the door and asked me to wait outside for a moment.

"Victor?" said the doctor to my father, "I need to talk to Victor."

"This is Victor."

"I have a visitor who'd like to see you. She said her name is Joyce. She's your daughter."

"My daughter, Joyce?"

"Would you like to see Joyce? I'll let you see her, but you must keep George away. Can you do that?"

"I'll try, but you know how he is."

The doctor motioned for me to come in. I entered the room with a surreal feeling, as though I were stepping into a dream. I wanted to lay my eyes on this man for as long as I could remember, and here he was. He had black hair with flecks of gray and steel blue eyes. I realized that Carolyn and I did look very much like him, only our eyes were brown.

"Hello, Father," I said.

"Hello. You grew from the last time I saw you."

"I've always wanted to meet you, but I never knew where you were."

"Your mother thought it was best. I understand that you've become quite famous. You certainly are beautiful."

"I look like you," I said.

He smiled and stretched out his hand. I looked at the doctor, who nodded his head, so I reached out and put my hand in his. His face looked so serene and kind, and I wondered if they had exaggerated his condition to keep him in here. His grip tightened on my hand. "You bitch," he said.

I withdrew my hand quickly and jumped back. Gary put his arm out to steady me.

"George," said the doctor, "that wasn't necessary. You tell Victor to come back."

"Victor can come back tomorrow. I want a chance to look at this little dish. You have great tits," he said, even though I was wearing a jacket.

The doctor stood up and escorted us outside. I leaned against the wall for support.

"That was George," explained the doctor. "He can be very vile, and sometimes quite violent. He is one of the dominant personalities, and he probably won't let you see Victor again today. If you wish, we can try tomorrow. I can also attempt to answer any questions that you might have."

"How long has he been here?" I asked.

"Almost twenty-five years."

"I guess I was hoping that he really wasn't so bad, and that he was just being kept here because my mother wanted him here."

"We've made some progress with multiple personalities, but we haven't been real successful with him. The personality, Victor, is the one who married your mother. He didn't exhibit any unusual behavior until about three years after they were married, and then George exerted his presence. He broke your mother's arm once. She was afraid for you children, although to my knowledge, George never hurt either one of you."

"Who are the others? I understand there's more than two."

"We've seen four. One is a small child, and the other is a female personality. George is aware of all of the personalities, and Victor is aware of George and the child."

"So, is my father considered a schizophrenic since he has a problem with multiple personalities?"

The doctor shook his head. "Most people from a non-psychiatric background make that mistake. The term schizophrenia comes from two Greek words, meaning 'split mind,' and that's often mistaken to mean a split personality in which there are two or more distinct personalities living within the same person. Schizophrenia is characterized by disturbances of thought, but it all occurs within the same mind.

"A person with multiple personalities, such as your father, has what's known as a dissociative identity disorder, and that's considered the correct terminology for this form of mental illness. It's a very rare disorder, characterized by more than one dominant personality living within the same person, and they often include other weaker personalities of different ages and gender. They all have their own memories, likes, and dislikes, just like any other individual."

"This is all so very strange," I said, shaking my head in wonder.
"You've been very kind, taking your time to spend with me, and I really do appreciate it. I only have one more question. Now that my mother and aunt have died, who takes care of him? Is he a ward of the state?"

"No, his durable power of attorney is a niece. I believe her name is Leisel Weingartner."

"Leisel!" I gasped. I involuntarily put my hand over my heart for a moment because it felt like it skipped a beat. Leisel not only knew about my father, but she was his guardian.

The doctor nodded. "Your mother was very adamant that her children not know the truth. She was afraid of the emotional trauma involved, and the fact that this could have adversely affected your career."

I suddenly realized that I was leaning up against Gary, who still had his arm around me. I shook hands with the doctor and thanked him for all of his help. "I guess we'll come back tomorrow and see if he'll visit with me one more time," I said.

We walked out to the car, and all of my emotions exploded.

"How could she do this to me! I'm so mad! So mad!" I yelled out. I balled up my fists and stomped around in the middle of the parking lot. It was a good thing that no cars were coming. "All of the times I told her how I would give anything to know, and she knew all of the time!"

"Well, you don't know that for sure. She might not have known until your mother got sick."

"She still should have told me! She knew how I felt."

My blazing anger turned into hot tears, and soon I was sobbing. Gary put his arms around me and hugged me. I must have cried for ten or fifteen minutes, but Gary just stood there quietly in the middle of the parking lot and comforted me by patting me on the back and stroking my hair, much the same way as I had seen him do for Alan.

"Come on," I heard him say, "let's go back to the hotel."

We went back to the hotel, and I sat on the deck of the pool under an umbrella while Gary and Alan went swimming. They played and splashed like two children, and my mood lightened up just by watching them. A few hours later, when we were back in our room, we sat around the kitchen table drinking iced tea. I was starting to relax and feel better.

"I don't understand why you two sometimes argue and fight," said Alan. "You seem like good friends to me. Why do you fight?"

"I don't know what went wrong," I answered. "I guess I disagreed with Gary's choice of a career. I don't like gossip columnists. They write things about me that hurt."

Alan looked at Gary. "So, she had a point," he said to him.

"I guess you could say that," answered Gary, "but I wanted to work for a paper that would give me a good future. It was a good job, and an interesting one, too. I needed to accept whatever job they gave me in the hopes of working my way up the ladder for one that would interest me even more."

Alan looked at me. "So, he had a point," he said.

"I guess you could say that," I said.

Alan took a sip of his iced tea and looked at Gary reflectively. I could almost see the wheels turning in his head. "Do you remember when John and I weren't getting along very well?" he asked Gary.

"Yeah, I remember. It didn't last very long."

"That's because you made us sit down at the table and say one thing that we liked about each other. I think you two should do that."

"Well, I don't know," said Gary, with great hesitation in his voice.

"You always do the things you tell me to do. Why should it be different this time?"

Gary sighed loudly and set his glass down on the table with a thud. "Okay," he said, looking at me. "You're a beautiful woman, Joy. There's something about you that sparkles. I like that."

"Thank you."

"You're welcome." He looked back at Alan and said, "There. I said it."

"Good," said Alan, who then directed his undivided attention towards me. "Now it's your turn."

I found myself groping for the right words.

Gary grinned. "It is hard, isn't it?" he asked. Then he turned to Alan and said, "Remind me not to ask you to do this again."

Alan smiled at him.

"You have a wonderful way with children," I said. "You're able to draw Alan to you by using pointed, direct questions. It's a skill, you know, and one that's not learned overnight."

Gary seemed slightly embarrassed. "Sometimes Zachary forgets to use it, but he knows how. We had a good father. He was like that with us, and we try to do the same for Alan."

"Now that I've seen it done, I'm going to have to develop that same skill with Jo Dell. I'm impressed."

"Thank you."

"You're welcome."

I moved into the living room and plopped down on the couch. I opened the paper and turned to the celebrity pages. There was another negative comment in it about me from a columnist named Bennie Martin. She said when I put my hair up in a pony tail, and walk up and down the streets of New York, that I could easily be mistaken for a horse's ass. I threw the paper down in disgust, and sat there, smoldering in anger. Gary picked up the paper and looked at it, and he came across what made me angry. I saw him fighting to hold back a smile, and then he regained his composure. I'm sure that I would have thought it was funny too, especially if she had been talking about someone else, but she was talking about me! What she said was mild compared to some of the things that Gary wrote, but I was in a particularly vulnerable mood that day.

Gary looked at me, and his expression changed. He actually had a very concerned look on his face. "Do you always take these things so seriously?" he asked.

"No, not always, but sometimes I get so mad!"

Gary folded up the paper and sat beside me. "If I give you a piece of information about her that she wouldn't want anyone to know, will it make you feel better?"

I nodded.

"Her real name is Brunhilda."

I burst out with peels of laughter.

Evening fell, and Gary asked if I would join him for dinner downstairs in the lounge. Alan was going to have pizza in the room and watch movies on the VCR.

We enjoyed a quiet dinner. Soft music played in the background, and several couples were dancing. I believed that some people recognized me, and it crossed my mind that they were most likely wondering about Gary because he certainly wasn't Grant. I had forgotten what wonderful company Gary could be. He was so bright, and he had a wonderful, dry sense of humor fueled by an air of cynicism. He asked me to dance, and he held me close to him as we swayed to the music. Someone snapped a photograph, and Gary flinched.

"I didn't think about fans looking at us," he said. "I'm sorry."

"It doesn't matter. Let's finish the dance."

We finished that dance, and then a few more. Then we went upstairs to see how Alan was doing. We found him asleep on the couch. It had been a long day for all of us. Gary picked him up and carried him into his room. "He sleeps like a stone," he said. When he came out, he sat down at the kitchen table by the window. I wondered if he got quiet and introspective every night before he went to bed. Some journalists do their best work in the morning, but maybe he did his thinking at night.

I stood up and stretched. "Goodnight," I said. "Thank you for the wonderful company at dinner and for helping me take my mind off of my troubles. Maybe tomorrow will be a better day to see my father."

"I hope so," Gary said to the window.

I thought I awakened early, but Gary and Alan were still up before me. I took a shower and got dressed for the day. I hoped that I would be able to visit with my father just a little. As soon as I came out into the living room, someone knocked at the door. I was standing closest to the door, so I peered through the peek hole. I almost toppled over in surprise when I saw who was standing there. I opened the door and flew into his arms.

"Grant! Oh, Grant!"

Grant hugged me tightly, and then he kissed me on the lips. "I missed you," he said.

How had Grant known that we were here? I released my grip from around his neck and looked questioningly at Gary, who was standing a few feet back from the open doorway.

"I called Grant last night, after you went to bed," he explained.

I was astounded. "Oh, Grant!" I said. "I never thought you would have been able to come." I reached up and hugged him again.

"Well," said Grant, as we walked into the suite and closed the door, "Gary called last night, and there were only a few more song and dance sequences to be done. The director filmed my last one early. I missed being in the finale, but that's no big deal. I took the next plane here."

Grant hugged me and kissed me on the cheek again. He was clearly pleased to see me, and it made my heart sing. Grant had that sort of effect upon people. Gary walked across the room and picked up his bags. I noticed then, and only then, that he and Alan had already packed and were ready to leave. He motioned for Alan to come with him, and Alan quickly jumped off of the couch and stood beside Gary. I was in shock that this had happened so quickly. Gary had given me no inkling the night before that he was going to call Grant.

"Grant is better trained in this area than I am, and he can help you more," said Gary. "Keep the suite as long as you need to." He slung a bag over his shoulder and shook hands with Grant. Then, almost as an afterthought, he walked over to the coffee table and picked up the handkerchief. "The truce is over," he said brusquely, as he brushed past my shoulder on his way out of the room. He stuffed the handkerchief into his pocket, and he and Alan exited the suite.

I walked out into the hallway and stared after him for a few seconds, wondering what that was all about. Up until bedtime, everything was fine between us, and the truce seemed to be working. I entertained the hope that we would set a common ground of peace and have a new understanding after this was all over, but apparently, that was very naïve of me. I wondered what I might have done to upset him and make him decide to leave and take his white flag with him.

I turned around and faced Grant. "I can't believe you're here!" I said. I threw my arms around his neck and kissed him again. We went to the couch and sat down together. I put my head on his shoulder, and he stroked my hair.

"Don't you think you should have told me what you were doing?" asked Grant.

"I was afraid that you'd try to talk me out of it."

"Maybe I would have, but don't you think you could have given me the benefit of the doubt? I still think that I had a right to know where you were. What if something had happened to you? I wouldn't have known where you were. I think it's only common courtesy to let me know if you're not where I think you're going to be." He was still stroking my hair, and his voice wasn't angry.

"I'm sorry, Grant. All I could think about was that I'd finally get a chance to see my father."

"I know. There's no real harm done. I'm surprised that Gary brought you here."

"I am, too. I thought he would plaster it all over the papers, but I guess he has no intentions of doing that."

"Well, that just confirms what I've felt about him all along."

"And what's that?"

"That he likes to irritate you and get under your skin, but way down deep, he really cares about you."

"Maybe so, but I don't think I've seen the last of his poisoned pen. He has probably dreamed up something else to say about me by now."

Grant accompanied me to the Sanitarium, and we tried one more time to visit with my father.

"Victor?" asked the doctor, "Joyce has come back to see you."

"Joyce?"

"I'm right here," I said. "I brought my husband to see you, too."

My father held out his hand to Grant, and Grant stepped forward to shake his hand.

"I hope you're taking good care of my daughter."

"Oh, yes, sir. I love her more than anything else in the world."

My father smiled. His expression changed, and he said to Grant in a very small, childlike voice, "Do you like little boys?"

"Why, yes, I do," said Grant. "What's your name?"

"Charlie."

"How old are you, Charlie?"

"Six."

"Charlie, are you afraid of something?"

"George."

"Are you hiding from George?"

"Yes."

"Who protects you from George?"

"Victor, but I never see him. I just know he's there."

"Can you ask Victor to come out and guard you?"

"I guess so."

A few moments later, the expression on my father's face changed, and Victor returned. I felt very strange witnessing this. It was like something out of a movie.

"I think I know why you came," Victor said to me. "You want some reassurance from me that I haven't forgotten you. I never have, and I never will. You kind of remember people as being the same as they were the last time you saw them, and well, the last time I saw you, you were a baby. That's how I always pictured you. Now I have to get used to a new picture."

"Would you like me to send you pictures?"

"Yes, I'd like that very much."

I leaned over and kissed him, and Grant held my hand as we exited the room.

On the plane ride back to New York, I asked Grant what made people have multiple personalities.

"Several studies have proven that people who have multiple personalities usually have experienced a major emotional trauma in their lives, and very often it was some form of repeated physical or sexual abuse. They need to escape, so they create another personality to take their place. The other personality has to live through this emotional experience, not them. I don't know this case, of course, but it's possible that the little boy, Charlie, was created by one of the other personalities when he was six years old. He's nervous and afraid."

I shook my head. "This mental torment must be anguish to live with. The doctor said that they haven't had much success treating him. How do they go about treating something like this? It seems so impossible."

"The main objective is to reduce the degree of the dissociation, where they go from one personality to another. They have to try to create a co-consciousness between all of the personalities living in the same body, and the goal is to ultimately merge them all into one system where they'll have the same thoughts and memories. If they cooperate and work together, it can be done, but the problem seems to be that the two dominant personalities are fighting for their own control."

"You mean Victor and George."

Grant nodded. "It's a rare but very debilitating disease."

"I found out that Leisel has known about my father and never told me."

"She was probably asked by your mother to keep a secret."

"My mother isn't alive. She wouldn't have had to adhere to that secret."

"She must have felt that she had to."

We landed in New York. As we stepped off the plane, photographers spotted us and began taking pictures. Grant waved to the cameras and thrust me in front of him so that they could get pictures of both of us. Sometimes I thought he was too accommodating for these rude photographers, but he maintained a philosophy that publicity was the key to continued success. I had to admit that it was working. He was seldom without a job to do.

When I got home, I decided to go over to Leisel's house and confront her. It was in the middle of the day, but she looked tired and worn out. She invited me in, and we sat down on the sofa in the living room.

"I'm not planning on staying long," I told her. "This isn't exactly a social call."

"I didn't think so," she said defensively. "You never pay me any social calls."

"You never come around me anymore, either. Have I ever done anything to offend you?"

"No, not that I can think of right now."

"Well, *you* have offended me. You've known about my father for years, and you kept this to yourself all of this time." I saw her face flinch, but her eyes stayed steady with mine as she looked at me. "Why didn't you ever tell me that my father was alive?"

"I made a promise to your mother and my mother years ago."

"How many years ago?"

"Does that matter?"

"Yes, it does."

"Why?"

"Because I'd like to know just how long you've been deceiving me, and because I used to tell you my secrets and dreams."

"I know that you shared secrets with me, and I treasured and saved them all. But I made a promise, which I had to keep. I also agreed that it might have hurt your career."

"I shared dreams with you, too. I had all of those dreams that he would see me on television and come walking into the house one day to see his famous daughter. You knew each time I told you this that it would never come true."

"I'm sorry, Joy."

"Does Carolyn know?"

"No. I kept my word."

Carolyn entered the room. "Does Carolyn know what?" she asked.

"I was asking if you knew what happened to our father."

She shook her head and sat in the chair that was closest to the sofa. "No, do you?"

"Yes, I do, and so does Leisel. She has known for years and years and years!" My voice was rising.

"What happened?" asked Carolyn, very calmly.

"He's in a mental hospital up in Maine," I said. "He has been there twenty-five years."

"What?" Her face turned pale.

"Yes. It was felt that we should be spared the knowledge that our father has been suffering from mental illness all of these years. He has a problem with multiple personalities."

"Have you seen him?"

"Yes. Gary took me to see him."

Leisel's head jerked up in surprise. "Gary!" she gasped.

"Yes, Gary. He found out somehow, and then out of some unexplained goodness of his heart, he told me about it and even took me up there. I went with Gary and his little brother, Alan."

Leisel still had a surprised look on her face.

"I suppose you want to see him?" I asked Carolyn.

She shook her head. "No. I don't think it would be a good idea. We don't need unnecessary publicity."

I was surprised at her reaction, and I thought she took the news remarkably well. I might have told her just as easily that our father had a common cold. "Well, I took the risk," I said. "The doctor arranged for us to come at a special time, and he was the only one who saw us. He'd probably be willing to do that for you, if you want."

"No. I think it's still a risk. It's enough for me to know the truth." She turned and looked at Leisel. "You know," she said, in a very calm manner, "sometimes you really stink." And she stood up and walked out of the room.

"I guess that about sums it up," I said.

-38-

I watched the telecast of the variety show that Grant had worked on in Los Angeles. I thought he stole the show. Other people must have shared my opinion because we were approached by a network producer about doing a pilot for a weekly variety show of our own. Grant was enthusiastic, but I was more reserved. I was concerned because they wanted to do the filming in Los Angeles, so we would have to move there at least while the show was being taped. We could possibly spend half of our time in Los Angeles and the other half in New York.

The offer was very lucrative, and it would give us exposure to other people and prove that we could do other things besides a weekly dramatic series. It would be a combination of songs, dances, and skits, as well as showcasing other acting talents and interviewing other stars. I finally agreed to do it. I hated to fly, but I knew that commuting from coast to coast was going to become part of our lives, so I decided that I might as well start getting used to it. I didn't like the idea of splitting up schools for Jo Dell, but she didn't seem to mind.

Our show was an instant hit. One of my favorite parts was when we took hits from Broadway shows and performed them for the audience. We had a small cast of "regulars" who helped us do the skits, but we were the major stars. The very first year, we were nominated for an Emmy award. We didn't win, but in our third season we were nominated again, and this time we won.

Grant was so happy and enthusiastic that I thought all of his buttons would pop off of his shirt when we went up to accept the award. He held my hand tightly and stepped up to the microphone. "In view of the competition, it's a real honor to stand here on this stage to receive this award. I want to thank all of our loyal fans for their support and for providing the inspiration that we need to give good performances every week. I'm only one half of this team, so most of all, I want to thank my wife, Joy Bryant, for helping me become the person I am today. I can think of no one else that I'd rather share this honor with tonight. Honey, I love you."

He kissed me and shook his award in the air with jubilation. Then he turned to exit the stage, half-running, half walking, and dragging me with him every step of the way.

Shortly after winning the Emmy award, the media dubbed us "Hollywood's Happiest Couple." We did countless interviews, and our faces were plastered all over every magazine cover available. I was very surprised when Paramount approached Grant for a starring role in a movie. He was in the process of looking at the script and making a decision. He said that his first role needed to be a good one; otherwise, it would be better not to do it at all. If his first role bombed, he might not get another chance. He later decided to turn it down and hope for a better one.

I hoped with Grant's meteoric rise and popularity that he would become more popular at home with Jo Dell, but that wasn't the case. One day, when she was eleven years old, she had to do a short essay in her English class about her parents. This was the paper that I read:

My mother's name is Joy Bryant. She is a famous actress, and everyone loves her. She is so beautiful, and I have always wanted to look like her, even though I know it is impossible because she is not my real mother. She adopted me when I was born because my real mother, who was her best friend, was dying.

My father's name was Brandon DeLorrier. I have pictures of him, and I look quite a bit like him. He died when I was almost a year old, so I do not remember him, but I wish that I did. Sometimes when we are alone together my mom and I watch his movies, and then we get a chance to see him. Sometimes I wish that I could see him and talk to him, just once. I would tell him how much I love him, and how I wish that he could have been a part of my life. No one will ever take his place in my heart, not even Grant.

I was appalled when I read it. It was almost as though she had read my own heart and applied it to herself. I would *not* have shown this to Grant. I would have thrown it away if I had seen it first, but it was Grant who found it first. It had fallen out of her notebook, and he picked it up. Apparently, it caught his eye and he read it. He didn't say anything, but I could tell by his eyes that he was very hurt. I even wondered if he drew any similar conclusions from this essay.

That night, I spoke to Jo Dell about it. "I saw the essay that you wrote about Brandon and me."

"Did you like it?"

"Well, yes, and no."

Jo Dell frowned. "How can you like it and not like it?"

"I liked the nice things you had to say about me, but I'm curious as to why you wrote about Brandon and not about Grant."

"Brandon is my real father; Grant isn't."

"I suppose that I could understand that line of reasoning, except that I'm not your real mother; Marilyn was. Don't you think if you were going to write about Brandon, that you should have written about both of your real parents?"

"But you're the only mother I've ever known."

"You don't really remember Brandon, do you? Isn't Grant the only father you've ever known? Grant saw this, and I think it hurt his feelings."

Jo Dell just tossed her head and made a face at me.

"You don't care that you hurt his feelings, do you?" I asked.

She shrugged her shoulders.

"What is love, Jo Dell? What does love mean to you?"

"Sharing and caring, I guess."

"Okay. That's fair enough. Love means something different to everyone. People are always trying to define love in philosophy, literature, and movies, and it's a very difficult thing to do. I've decided to define love in a different way. I think that love is a *name.* When two people agree to marry each other, the man usually offers the woman his name, and the woman usually accepts the name. My legal name is Joyce Lynn Carlton. Grant loved me and wanted to marry me, and he wanted to give me his name. I loved him, so I agreed to take his name. It also works in other matters. I loved you and your mother, and I wanted to give you my name, so you became Jo Dell Bryant. And later, Grant loved you and wanted to give you his name. He didn't have to do that. He could have kept your name as Jo Dell Bryant, but he loved you and wanted to give you his name too, and we could all be a family. It was his way of sharing and caring, as you like to define it."

Jo Dell was looking down at the floor and fidgeting on the bed. I decided that I had said enough, and that I had to let the pieces fall where they wanted to. At first, I didn't think anything I said would have an effect, but later I began to realize that Jo Dell was making an effort to include Grant in her conversations.

-39-

Grant's friend, Thor, visited us briefly every year. I never disliked him, but I never liked him, either. I never felt quite comfortable around him. There was something odd about him that I could never put my finger on, but Grant used to tell me that I was nuts and that I never gave myself a chance to get to know him. Once, a few years back, I asked Thor what attracted him to psychology and acting because they were so dissimilar.

"They're similar if you really think about it," he told me.

"Similar? In what way?"

"All people are strange in their own little ways. Acting just gives them an outlet for their strangeness. I think that strangeness in people is the most intriguing part of being a psychologist. Some people are just so good at hiding it, that an untrained eye may never see it. Those make the most interesting of cases."

"Why?"

"Well, the next-door neighbor may be a mass murderer, and everyone who ever knew him is in shock when they find out because they never saw it coming. That was the case with Ted Bundy. He was called "the deliberate stranger" because he purposely killed strangers. That way, no motive could ever be pinned upon him. Around people that he knew, he was gentle and kind. The other type interests me the most, though. The kind that is clever enough to plan to kill people that they do know and get away with it. This takes more planning, more cunning, and more skill. These types of people make wonderful case studies." He leaned forward, and his eyes were shining.

I excused myself from him because he was making me feel creepy. How could Grant not think that he was creepy?

This year, Thor was going to stay in New York all summer. He accepted a position as a psychology professor, so he would be teaching during the regular school year and taking the summers off. I wasn't sure how I would feel about Thor being around all summer. It's strange how you can change your mind when confronted with a different perspective. The reality of the situation was that he came for the summer and ended up staying forever. There's a big difference between a summer and forever. Somehow when faced with forever, a summer didn't seem so bad.

He was married briefly in Ohio, and he had been divorced for about three years when he came to visit us for the summer. When it was time for him to return to Ohio, he resigned his position and accepted another one in New York because he had fallen in love- with Carolyn. He and Carolyn had met before, but no sparks flew. Maybe they just needed to spend more time together. He used to come for just one week at a time, and they probably met each other only in passing. This time, they had more opportunity to get to know each other.

Grant was thrilled, but I couldn't get past the fact that Thor might become my brother-in-law. I had to admit, though, that he seemed less creepy. Maybe I was getting used to him. Once, I decided to take the liberty of asking him about my recurring dream. It was so frustrating that I wanted to scream every time I woke up from having it.

He told me that my subconscious part of my brain was controlling the dream, and it probably did have some significance, but he cast doubts as to whether it was a preview of an actual event that might take place.

"What are you wearing?"

"I have on a dress, and it swishes in the wind."

"What color is the dress?"

"I don't know."

"The next time you have the dream, try to pay attention to things like colors, shapes, and sounds. You might see if you have that dress or those shoes in your closet. You might hear a sound that tells you where you are. Do you remember hearing anything?"

"I don't know. I'm calling out, but I don't know what I'm saying."

"Do you think that you're afraid?"

"No, I get the distinct feeling that I'm running to something or someone, and that I'm not running away. If I'm running to someone, who do you think it could be?"

"It could be just about anyone."

"I think I'm running to someone I love."

"Maybe."

"Do you think I'll ever get there?"

"It's possible- especially since you get a little bit closer each time. Do you have an idea who it might be?"

"I've wondered if it's Brandon. That's why I never asked Grant. If that's the case, then it's definitely not a preview of an actual event, unless I happen to be dead, too, when it happens, and that's a spooky thought."

"Since you're trying to tell yourself to stay asleep and finish the dream, a part of your consciousness is attempting to exert its power over the dream. Try to channel your consciousness into paying attention to finer details. See if you can hear sounds, smell aromas, see colors, and determine other shapes that might come out of the fog. I wish I could be more help, but that's about all I can suggest at this point."

I could see it coming, but I was still surprised when Thor and Carolyn announced their engagement. We threw an engagement party for them. I invited Leisel, but she declined to attend. Carolyn told me that Leisel was drinking more and more, and that she seemed generally unhappy. She said sometimes at night, she could hear her crying. She kept a trunk locked in her room and took the key wherever she went. Carolyn said that she knew it was none of her business what was in the trunk, but she had become so curious that she would have broken into it if she thought it were possible to look inside without Leisel ever knowing. I felt bad when I heard this because when we were younger, Leisel embraced life with zest.

I still thought that Thor was a strange bird, and I had my doubts that he could love Carolyn in the way that she needed to be loved. Carolyn had romantic notions and ideas, probably from a lifetime of books, and I just didn't see Thor as being able to fill that role. Also, Carolyn never liked to leave the house very much. She was never very sociable, and Thor liked going out on the town.

The night before they were married, I came by her house to try on my dress. I was the matron of honor. She seemed filled with anxiety.

"You look so beautiful in your dress," she told me. "I'm afraid you might be more beautiful than the bride, and maybe Thor will notice."

"That's not possible. We look too much alike, and you'll be glowing because it's your day. Besides, Thor loves you, not me."

"I know! Isn't it wonderful?"

"Yes, it's wonderful. So, why do you look so sad?"

"I don't know. He loves me. This is the first time in my life that someone really seems to love me, but I keep thinking that he's analyzing me all of the time, and that he knows what I'm thinking."

"That's because he's a psychologist. It's only natural."

"Grant's a psychologist, too. He went back to school and finished his semester. Do you ever think that he's analyzing your thoughts in his own head?"

I thought that was an odd way to put the question to me, but I tried to answer it as best I could. "Sometimes. I know he's a trained psychologist, but I guess I don't think about it very much. Maybe I would if he actually worked in that field like Thor, but I think that feeling is all in our own heads."

Carolyn shook her head. "I think they know," she said, almost in a whisper.

She said it very seriously, and I couldn't tell if she was joking or not. It had to have been a joke; however, Carolyn was never able to successfully jest well about anything. Her jokes usually fell flat, and I figured that was one reason she never tried very hard at having a sense of humor.

Carolyn slipped into her wedding dress, and I helped button her into it. I walked around in front of her and stepped slightly back to get a good look at her with the dress on. She really did look beautiful. Still, her face looked troubled.

"If you have doubts, now's the time to back out if you want to," I said.

"I never said that I wanted to."

"But if you don't think you'll be happy-"

"I don't think happiness has anything to do with it."

"Happiness has *everything* to do with it!"

"Oh really? Did it mean anything for you?"

"Of course it did."

"Oh, come on, Joy! You're talking to *me*," she said, pointing to herself in an agitated manner. "You married Grant so that he would sign his contract and not leave town. Hollywood's Happiest Couple is Hollywood's best-kept secret. No one knows the truth; not even Grant."

I was so taken aback at this outburst that I had no energy to respond. I stood there for a few moments trying to recover from her shocking words, when I saw her eyes look past my face to somewhere behind me. I turned around and saw Grant standing there.

"I waited for you to answer her," he said. His voice was cracking with pain. "Why didn't you answer her, Joy?"

He didn't wait for an answer to his question. He just turned around and walked out of the door. I heard the screen door slam. I turned back and faced Carolyn.

"Oh, my God," she said. "I didn't know he was there."

When I returned home, I was afraid that Grant wouldn't be there, but he was. I had never seen him look at me that way, as he stood in the doorway of Carolyn's home, and I was afraid to talk to him. I found him standing in the living room staring out of the window. He didn't turn to face me as I walked into the room.

"I'm sorry that you felt that way, Grant," I said to his back, "but you have to let me explain." I stood behind him and put my arms around his broad shoulders. He didn't move at all, so I continued to try to explain. "I was shocked at her outburst, and I didn't know how to respond. She was upset and out of sorts, and I thought it was just the night before the wedding jitters. It still might have been, I don't know. I was torn between defending myself and not wanting to upset her any more than she was."

Grant was still staring out of the window. It was dark, and nothing could be seen except reflections from inside of the house. Then he said a strange thing. "If you found out that Brandon were alive today, you would divorce me tomorrow."

"I guess this is my night for not knowing how to respond to other people's statements, Grant, because I sure don't know how to respond to that one. Brandon's dead, and there's no way that I'll find out today that he's alive. You're playing a game of 'what if,' and it's very unfair."

Grant slowly turned around and faced me. "I love you, Joy," he said, sadly. I put my arms around his neck and buried my face in his chest, and he held me for a long time.

-40-

One of the regulars on our show quit, so we were in the process of replacing her. We were also assistant producers of our own show, so we had a say in who was hired to work with us. We were looking for a fairly attractive person who could play the stereotypical role of a dumb blonde. As unflattering as it sounds to call someone that, it's still a crowd-pleasing comedic role. One day, I went into my office and found a blonde woman of about twenty-five sitting at my desk. She had her hair pulled into a ponytail.

A horse's ass, I thought. I had never been able to look at a ponytail in the same way since Bennie Martin's article. Maybe I was ashamed of my thoughts because instead of asking her to leave, I asked her to stay.

She was bright and funny, and I found myself laughing at almost everything we talked about. I was sure that she had some natural ability, so I asked the casting director to look at her. We liked her screen tests, so we hired her to be a regular on our show. Tiffany Andrews and I became fast friends, and we began going places and doing things together. Carolyn had been married for two years, and I didn't get a chance to see her very often. Leisel had been distant for years, so I missed female companionship. I couldn't remember when I enjoyed another woman's company so much. I probably hadn't felt that way since Marilyn. I tended to shy away from making friends because I never knew what people wanted from me. I was always afraid that they wanted to be my friend because of my celebrity status. It occurred to me that I might have cheated myself over the years from having a few genuine friends, but I couldn't let myself take a chance. It was nice having Tiffany around. She always kept my spirits up, and I was able to discuss some of my most personal problems with her.

One was Jo Dell. She was growing up, and she would be going into high school the following year. She had been begging me to send her to an exclusive private school in Hollywood or to a boarding school in Europe. I avoided doing this because I didn't want to raise a rich Hollywood brat. I also wanted her to have what I missed, and to have as normal of a life as possible, given our circumstances. She got mad and threw tantrums at times. Tiffany thought it was just a stage that she was going through.

"When I was growing up, I hated everything at that age. I hated my looks; I hated my teachers and my school, and I hated my parents because I felt that they didn't understand me. They used to tell me that they were young once too, but it never helped much. As far as I was concerned, they must have been born old."

"What did help?"

"Nothing, really. It was just a stage I had to outgrow."

One day I told Tiffany that Jo Dell always had problems with the fact that she wasn't exactly what one would call pretty, and she was jealous of me because I was. It didn't help to tell her that she was beautiful to me, or to voice my opinion that she would grow into an attractive adult, because those things didn't help the way she felt now.

"Teach her to make the most of what she has," said Tiffany. "Haven't you noticed that the clothes and makeup she wears isn't flattering for her coloring?"

"No," I said with a start. "I can't say that I have."

"She chooses clothes and makeup which would be more suitable on a person with a darker complexion, like you. She might be jealous of you, but she admires you, too. She associates the colors you wear with beauty. Help her find her own beauty."

When Jo Dell came home from school that afternoon, I was waiting for her. "I bought you some new makeup that you might like to try," I said. "You seem to wear mine, but mine is for darker skin. Let's try this, and I think you might like what you see."

We tried it on, and the results were startling. Then we went shopping for clothes that had colors that would look good on her. After that, I noticed her confidence had undergone a big boost. She was even more popular in school. I silently thanked God for bringing Tiffany into my life.

One day, an event occurred that I had lived in silent fear of happening ever since Jo Dell was born. She found out that I wanted Marilyn to abort her. She wouldn't tell me how she found out, but there were only a handful of people who knew: Grant, Leisel, Carolyn, and myself. One afternoon, I found her in tears.

"I thought you loved me," she said in a very accusing voice.

"I do love you," I insisted.

"Then how could you have wished that I were never born?"

I knew then that someone had told her. "Honey, you don't know all of the circumstances."

"Well, I hate you. I wish you weren't my mother!"

She stormed out of the room and locked herself in her bedroom upstairs. She refused to come out for me or for Grant.

"You need to know the whole truth," I said through the door. "If you still want to hate me, then go ahead and hate me, but you should at least hear the truth first. You owe that much to yourself."

She opened her door and agreed to let me come in and sit on the bed beside her.

"You have a good friend- a best friend- don't you?" I asked.

"Sure."

"What if you found out that she was dying and there was something that might save her? Would you want her to do it?"

"Sure."

"Well, that's exactly what happened. Your mother was sick and needed treatment, but she couldn't have chemotherapy while she was pregnant. The doctor wanted her to sacrifice her pregnancy so that she could get started on it right away. That's what I encouraged her to do. I didn't know you; I only knew her, and I wanted to keep her around because I loved her so much. But I loved you right after you were born. You need to know that. I've always been happy being your mother."

Jo Dell said nothing, but I could tell that she was listening.

"Once some nut was threatening to kill me, and I thought he was in the house. I tried to save you first before saving myself."

"What happened?"

"Your father came over to the house, and it must have frightened him away. I never heard from him again."

"Now that I know the whole story, I don't hate you," she said, and she gave me a hug.

-41-

Leisel was in a minor car accident, but it was determined that she had been drinking and driving, so her license was revoked for a period of six months. She usually called Carolyn to take her places, but every once in a while she called me if Carolyn happened to be in a particularly antisocial mood. One day, she had a strange request. She wanted to attend the high school graduation. I thought it was strange at the time, but considering the source, maybe it wasn't. Maybe she attended them every year. She always did volunteer work for the schools, and she even supported their baseball and football games.

It occurred to me as I watched the students in their caps and gowns that Jo Dell would be graduating in just a few more years. I gripped the program in my hand, and I tried to listen to the commencement, but I was extremely bored. I found that I wasn't exactly listening, and I didn't know anyone there. I couldn't wait for this to be over, and I couldn't wait for Leisel to get her driver's license back. Tiffany once told me in jest that I thought the world revolved around me, and I supposed that she was right.

As we got ready to leave, I finally did see someone that I recognized. I saw Gary Shawn, and then I realized that all of his brothers were standing beside him. I saw Zachary, Frank, and Patrick. I looked about for Alan, and then I saw him on the other side of the room. Dressed in a cap and gown, he walked over to where his brothers were standing. When he reached them, Gary stepped forward and hugged him, and so did Zachary. Then his other brothers shook his hand. I couldn't believe how much he had grown. I had to speak to him, so I weaved my way through the crowd.

"Alan! I can't believe it! You're all grown up. You're taller than Gary."

He smiled at me. "I missed you for a long time after we went on that trip," he said. "I would have come over to see you, but I wasn't sure if I should because you and Gary began feuding again right afterwards."

"I'd love to see you any time, whether Gary and I are feuding or not. I've thought about you so often over the years. Are you going to college?"

"I was accepted at NYU. I start this fall."

"You'll have to come and visit me when I'm in Manhattan. The apartment isn't too far from Washington Square."

Alan smiled. "I'll take you up on that," he said.

Gary walked over to us.

"Hello," I said to him.

"Hello, yourself. What brings you here?"

"Leisel insisted on coming, for some reason, so here we are."

Gary looked around. "Where is Leisel?"

I looked over my shoulder and saw that she was gone. "I don't know. I guess I better go look for her. Congratulations, Alan."

"Thanks."

I finally caught up with Leisel. She was extraordinarily quiet and hardly spoke at all on the drive back home. I wished I could break through whatever barrier she had set up between us, but I didn't know how.

-42-

Not everyone was as taken with Tiffany as I was. I had a friend named Sharon that worked in the wardrobe department. She was about ten years older than I was. We weren't the type of friends to socialize after work, but we took breaks together, and we enjoyed spending time together at work. I used to go down to the wardrobe department between takes just to talk to her. I valued her opinion, and we shared the same views on most things, except Tiffany.

"You need to watch her," she told me, as she sewed a tear in a costume. "I don't think she's as true blue as she seems."

"She helped me in a few critical situations. Isn't that what friends do for each other?"

"Sure, but I still think that you need to watch her."

"About what?"

"She's aggressive and ruthless. I know it in my bones. She wants more out of life than being a second banana in a variety show. I also think that she's attracted to Grant."

"Grant?"

"Yes."

"I certainly haven't seen it."

"She'd be stupid if she let you see it, wouldn't she?"

"Look," I said, waving my hand at her, "I don't want to argue about this. You don't like her, and I do. Besides, it takes two to tango, and one thing I know beyond all doubt: Grant loves me."

"That he does," she agreed. "I've never seen a man love a woman so much, but happily married men have been known to stray."

I shook my head. "Not Grant," I said, and Sharon never brought the subject up again.

Gary Shawn started hanging around and bothering Tiffany for a scoop on me to use in his column. I honestly believed that when I was in Los Angeles, I would be free from the venom that Gary would spit in my eye every chance he got, but I was wrong. He ran a celebrity column, which meant that he had to travel to Los Angeles and Hollywood at times. I must have assumed that he stayed in New York exclusively and threw stones at me. Gary would have been the first one to tell me that this fallacy was yet even more proof of my egocentricity. Tiffany was extraordinarily bright, and she always had an artful way of dodging him. But Gary was bright too, and he was the type of person who always got everything that he wanted in the end. One day he got more than he bargained for, and so did I.

About six months after my conversation with Sharon about Tiffany, I was in Tiffany's dressing room closet filtering through her costumes. I wanted a certain type of look for our next skit. I heard the door open.

"Oh, it's you again," I heard Tiffany say.

"I've come for my story," said Gary, standing in the doorway.

"How many times do I have to tell you that I don't have a story to give you?"

"Oh, I think you will this time."

"What makes you so certain?"

"A little bit of blackmail."

"Blackmail?" Tiffany's voice suddenly seemed hoarse.

"How would you like me to tell Joy about your little rendezvous with Grant last night?"

I felt myself stiffen. I put my hand over my mouth to prevent any involuntary gasps from escaping.

"You don't know what you're talking about. Get out of my room, or I'll call security!" She attempted to shut the door in his face.

He put his hand out to keep her from closing the door. "I don't know what I'm talking about? Let's see. Your apartment is located in a building directly across from the one that I use when I come here. Really, Tiff, you should close your blinds when you have a clandestine meeting with someone. I saw what I saw. I'll tell you something else, too. No matter what anyone thinks, Joy is my friend. I should probably tell her anyway, although I don't quite know how."

"You just did," said Tiffany.

I removed my hand from my mouth, and I somehow managed to walk out of her closet with some dignity. Gary's eyes were as big as saucers, and his face turned ashen when he saw me.

"Are you in love with my husband?" I asked, in a very calm manner.

"No, Joy- it was nothing like that."

"Well, don't you think that it would have been better if you had been?" I snapped.

I walked out of the room without waiting for a reply. I felt like I couldn't breathe. Grant? Tiffany and Grant- together- like that? Oh, my God, how could that be possible? I walked to the end of one corridor. I still needed to make one more turn to head down to my room, but my legs didn't want to carry me any further. There was a chair at the end of the long corridor. I needed to catch my breath, so I sat down in the chair. I kept thinking about last night. Grant did come home later than usual. He seemed distracted and upset about something, but I never asked what was wrong. I just assumed that he would tell me when he felt like it, as he always did. I was so lost in thought that I didn't realize someone was next to me.

"Joy?"

I looked up. It was Gary. He knelt down in front of me.

"I didn't know you were there; honest, I didn't. I would never have hurt you like that for anything in the world. Please, you must believe me."

"You're a liar. You hurt me all of the time, and you enjoy every minute of it."

Gary took my hands in his. "I'm so sorry; please forgive me. Please." He kissed my hand, and I didn't have the strength to pull away.

"You have a great story now, don't you?" I asked.

"No, I don't." He shook his head vigorously.

"Why not? You might as well be the very first one to break this story. You don't think it'll just go away, do you?"

"Yes, I do." He squeezed my hands and looked at me. His eyes were pleading with mine. "Look, there are only four people in the world who know: you, me, Grant and Tiffany. It doesn't need to go elsewhere."

"But it will. I can't continue to work with her, and she'll blab the story all over once she's fired. We'll probably have to buy out the rest of her contract."

"No, she won't go blabbing. I already told her that she should walk away with her mouth shut and try to get another job because if she doesn't, I'll destroy her. I set out to bother you, but not destroy you. I *will* destroy her, and she knows it. She doesn't have the name that you did, and people won't be as sympathetic to her. Let her go, right now, and never mention this again."

"That solves one problem, but the next one can't be as easily fixed. Gary, Grant loves me. I know he loves me. How could he do this to me? How could he do this to *us?*"

I was too stunned to cry earlier, but now the shock was wearing off, and I was in unbearable pain. Tears were burning my eyes, and it wouldn't be long before I would have to open the floodgates. Gary must have intuitively known this.

"Come on, Joy," he said, tugging at my arm. "Don't fall apart here in the hallway. At least let me help you get to your room." He pulled me to my feet, and I allowed him to lead me to my room. I sat down heavily in the nearest chair. "Are you going to be okay?" I heard him ask. His voice sounded far away.

I nodded, staring off into space.

"Is there anything I can do?"

I interrupted my trance-like stare with some effort and focused on his face. "You've done enough already," I said.

My voice was cold and detached. It didn't sound like me, not even to my own ears. I saw a genuine look of pain in Gary's eyes. *Good,* I thought. *I hit my mark.* I wanted to hurt somebody; it might as well be him. He turned and opened the door.

"Gary?" I asked, feeling ashamed of myself. In spite of everything, I was able to realize that he didn't do this on purpose.

"Yeah?" he said, turning around.

"Thanks."

He nodded and quietly exited the room.

I don't know if hours had passed, or if it had only been a few minutes. There was a knock at the door, and I forced myself to get up and answer it. Tiffany was standing there.

"What are you doing here?" I asked, coldly.

"I didn't want to leave it this way between us."

I leaned up against the door. I had no intentions of inviting her in. "And you think that you can come in here and talk it over, like we only had a small disagreement, and then forget all about it? You must be more naïve than I ever was. You didn't just steal candy from my drawer, you know."

"I know, and I'm so terribly sorry."

"And that makes it all right? I let you into my life. Do you know how rare it is for me to do that? I don't know why I liked you and trusted you, but I did."

"I did care about you, Joy," she said, wringing her hands.

"All you cared about was getting your hands on Grant. It isn't like

I wasn't warned. People told me not to trust you, but I paid no heed. You spent time with me so you could be around Grant."

She began to get defensive, and her whole attitude changed. "Okay, I lied when I said I didn't love Grant. I do. I think he's the nicest, most handsome man I've ever met. He worships the ground you walk on, and sometimes you push him aside - he told me so. I don't think you know what a treasure you have. Grant deserves better."

"Better?" I shouted. "What's better? *You?*"

"Maybe," she retorted.

"Well, maybe," I said, with a nod. "And then again, maybe not. Look, I don't know what happened between the two of you, and I don't know why Grant did what he did. He never does anything without a reason, but *this I do know,*" I said, enunciating my words distinctly and clearly, "Grant loves me, and there isn't anything that you can do that will ever change that fact."

I knew from the look on her face that she was beaten. I could glean at least some satisfaction from that. I told her that my lawyers would be in touch with her to see what could be done about what was remaining on her contract, and then I shut the door. There was no more to say.

Grant took one look at my face, and he knew. I sat down on our bed, and he sat beside me. "I don't know what to say," he said.

"I do. How could you do this?" I turned my head away from him. I couldn't even meet his eyes.

"I don't blame you for being angry. I'm angry with myself. If I could take it back, I would."

"I thought you loved me." I felt hot tears rolling down my face.

"I do, Joy," he said gently. "I love you." He tried to wipe the tears off my face with his hand, but I jerked my head away and wiped them off myself with my sleeve.

"I believed in you. I believed in you so much until today. I never, not once, ever considered that this was possible from you." I felt another tear roll down my face, and I quickly wiped it away. "Now, all I believe in is lies. You loved me, and you lied. Tiffany loved me, and she lied. Liesel and Carolyn haven't always been honest with me, and even Brandon loved me, and he lied."

"Brandon!" Grant shouted, and he jumped off the bed. "It's always Brandon! I'm so sick of Brandon that I could die! I know that I did something that's unforgivable, but so have you."

"Me!"

"Yes, you! How do you think I feel when you eat, sleep, and drink the name of Brandon DeLorrier? He's in every breath that you take! He has been dead over twelve years, and we've been married for ten, but he still sleeps between us every night!"

"So, now this is my fault?"

"Yes, and no."

"How did I possibly push you into bed with Tiffany?"

"I know that I'm responsible for that. You didn't make me go to bed with her. But you do play a role in this, even though you probably don't realize it."

"Pray, tell me how I could have forced you to walk upstairs to her apartment, enter her bedroom, take off all of your clothes, and hers, and stick yourself inside of her?"

"Just let me tell you without being interrupted, and then I'll do whatever you want me to. I'll go, or I'll stay. The choice will be yours, but please let me tell you my side."

I folded my arms across my chest. "Okay, I'm listening. Go ahead."

"It's been hard living all of these years competing with a dead man. I've been made to feel second best. You don't think that I know whenever I make love to you that you wonder what Brandon would have felt like? You've blamed me for the night that we spent in the storm cellar, even though there were extraordinary circumstances."

I snorted. "It seems as though that's your excuse now- extraordinary circumstances."

"Are you going to let me finish or not?" he snapped.

"I'm sorry- go ahead."

"I've just been living in a shadow. Every year you go into some kind of funk in October. You shut down around the tenth of the month when he died; you always end up being sick around Jo Dell's birthday, and then Carolyn has to come to the rescue. You stay this way until a few days after the sixteenth - the day you would have been married- and then you decide to snap out of it. You want nothing to do with Rogers and Hammerstein's musicals, and you won't even eat strawberry cheesecake, for God's sake. I know that you have a stash of his movies, and I know you sit and watch them whenever I'm not around. The hardest thing for me is that you pretend at times when we're making love that he's with you. Sometimes when we're making love, you call out his name. I'll bet you never knew that. I truly believe that if Brandon were alive, you'd leave in a minute, even after ten good years of marriage."

I sat there like a stone. I didn't know what to say. Brandon told me so many years ago that affairs were not about love. They were about what one was not getting from the other.

"I don't know what happened with Tiffany," continued Grant. "I've known for a long time that she's in love with me- really in love with me. I don't know how I've known; I could just feel it, I guess. And I think that for once in my life, I wanted to experience being with a woman who loved me completely, as completely as I loved you. I wanted to *feel* for once, Joy. Can you ever understand all of this?"

I didn't answer his question. Instead, I said, "I want you to tell me what you did. I want to know every kiss, every lick, and every touch. I don't want to go through the rest of my life having questions. You tell me everything, and then maybe we can discuss a future together."

I knew that I was being cruel, but I couldn't help it. With tears rolling down his face, he told me everything I wanted to know.

I had a big choice to make. I could separate from Grant, or I could go on. I weighed the pros and cons, but I had to acknowledge my own role in all of this. Every word Grant said was true. Besides, if we separated, our show would be cancelled. It was better in the long run to forgive.

About a week later, I received a peace offering from Gary Shawn. A package arrived in the mail. "It's probably a bomb," I told Grant as I opened it, but when I pulled it out, I gasped in surprise. It was a picture taken many years ago. Gary must have had it enlarged for me. It was Brandon and I sitting in the restaurant when he proposed to me. He had grasped my wrist with one hand and was slipping the ring on my finger with the other. The photograph captured the happiness and surprise on my face. It was a beautiful photograph, and it would have been worth a lot of money if he had sold it back then. He had saved it all of these years and then gave it to me. I knew that I couldn't hang it up in our house, so I put it away where I had other old photos stored, but I cherished it. Grant said nothing about it at all.

-43-

Tiffany moved on, and Grant and I tried very hard to forgive each other. I made a conscious effort not to fan the flames of Brandon DeLorrier in Grant's face. I put the movie reels away and didn't look at them anymore, and when October came around, I made a great effort not to go into a funk.

At first, it was difficult for me to be held by Grant without thinking of him being with Tiffany, but he was very patient and kind. He knew that the hurt wouldn't go away overnight, and he tried hard to make up for it. For our eleventh anniversary, he surprised me with a trip to Hawaii. I had always wanted to go, but it seemed like we never had time.

We decided to go to Kawai, the smallest of the Hawaiian Islands. It was known as the garden island because of the lush, green, tropical land. We stayed in a condominium that was only about 150 feet from the beach. We could look out of the window and watch the tide rolling in. We sat on the beach and watched the waves as they crashed over the coral reefs and washed up over the sand.

"This is so peaceful," I told Grant. "I don't know why we never did this before."

"We've been so busy the past few years. We just needed to stop the revolving door and take time for ourselves."

We had dinner at a fish and chowder house, which was about a mile's walk from the condo, but it was so beautiful out that we felt like walking. As we sat there, I noticed a small lizard on the wall near the ceiling, and I pointed it out to Grant.

"It's a gecko," said Grant. "He won't hurt anything."

"I think he's kind of cute," I said.

Grant lifted his wine glass and clicked it against mine. "May our love last a lifetime," he said.

I smiled and reached for his hand. I had always heard that Hawaii was one of the most romantic places in the world, and I decided it must be true. All I wanted was to be alone with him. I could forgive and forget anything painful in our past and go on. I couldn't wait to get back to our condo, and I prickled all over in anticipation.

We walked back toward our condo hand in hand, eventually drifting toward the ocean. We waded in it, splashed each other playfully, and soon we were up to our waists in the water. Grant pulled me to him and kissed me, and I felt the same magnetic attraction that I used to feel when he touched me prior to his affair. The wetness of his skin against my lips was very stimulating as I kissed him, and soon we were pulling off each other's clothes in the water and tossing them up on the beach. It was beginning to get dark outside, and I hoped we weren't giving someone an eyeful, but I was so caught up in the moment that I didn't care. We made love in the water, and also on the beach as the waves washed over the top of us. We lay in each other's arms for a long time because we had no strength to move. Finally, I got up and began to put my clothes back on.

"I lost my shirt," I said. Everything else seemed miraculously within reach.

"Here," he said, handing me his. "No one will look twice at me without a shirt, but with you, it'll be an entirely different story."

The next day we took a drive through the island. We rented a car and drove up into the mountains. The road circled around and around the mountains, and we went higher and higher. The turns were short and quick, and I almost felt like I had motion sickness. The view from above was breathtaking, and I soon forgot about my queasy stomach. The mountains were totally green with deep canyons and valleys below. We came across a cascading waterfall, flowing gracefully into the valley below, and eventually draining out into the ocean.

"No wonder they call this place paradise," I said.

That night we attended a luau. We were met with the Hawaiian greeting of "Aloha." A young man handed me a lei and kissed me on the cheek, and a young woman did the same with Grant. We sat at the table, shared a few Mai-tai's, and waited for them to serve the food. The main course was a suckling pig. It was cooked in the ground surrounded by hot rocks and covered with palm leaves. There were all kinds of seafood available, as well as some nasty white stuff called poi.

"Everyone hates it," said Grant, after he fed me a scoop off of his spoon and I promptly spit it out.

The highlight of the evening was the dance. The girls wore colorful grass skirts; the dances were tasteful, and they told touching stories. It was absolutely beautiful.

They later tried to involve the audience, and they picked out a few of us to come up and dance. Someone pointed to me to come up on the stage. Grant laughed himself silly as I tried to go through the moves. Kate showed me a little bit of almost every dance, but she never taught me how to do this one. I didn't mind making a fool out of myself. There would always be a four-year-old child named Jenny Johnson who lived in my heart.

All too soon, it was time to return home. As soon as we got home, Hawaii seemed so very far away. It was as though it had only been a distant dream.

-44-

I n the spring of 1996, we were notified that the network was not going to pick up our show for the fall season. It had run its course, and in show business, all good things must come to an end. I was relieved, anyway. I was tired of cross-country commuting. I thought our lives might settle down, but I was wrong. Grant jumped right into a role on Broadway, and he received rave reviews from the critics. He even won a Tony award that same year. We went to movie premieres, benefits, and parties for networking purposes, and there always seemed like there was something to do.

The editor of a national fashion magazine approached me to do a photo-op for the magazine's cover and an interview for a feature story. I didn't want to do it, but Grant maintained that it could be good publicity for me. I was always afraid of them twisting my words. It was just amazing to me that people could actually think that my life was made from the same material that dreams were made of. My best friend died, the love of my life was killed in an automobile accident; I never had any biological children of my own- though God knows we tried, and I had a stagnated career that never reached the heights I always envisioned it would. What was there to envy? But once they were done polishing the story and dressing me in pretty clothes for pretty pictures, my life would look like a fairy tale come true as Hollywood's Happiest couple rides off together in the sunset every night in a torrid blaze of glory and glamour.

I also hated doing guest appearances and television interviews, but I did consent to doing one on a major network's prime time slot in the late Fall. Everything seemed to be going well until the interviewer asked me about Brandon.

"I've never forgotten Brandon," I told him truthfully. "He died fifteen years ago, but sometimes it just seems like yesterday."

"Do you ever think about how things might have been?"

"Sure, but I had a friend who explained to me once how dangerous it is to play a game of 'what ifs.' It puts me in a bad situation. You see, if I say that I'm sorry that Brandon died, then it's almost the same as saying that I'm sorry that I'm married to Grant, and I'm not. Yet if I say that I'm not sorry that I'm married to Grant, then it sounds like I'm glad that Brandon died, because if he hadn't died, I surely wouldn't be married to Grant." It seemed like a complicated, roundabout way to explain it, but he seemed to be following what I was saying. I suddenly stopped talking, smiled, and shrugged my shoulders. He went on to the next subject.

I received a visit from Brandon's brother, Reginald, who happened to be in New York City on business. I almost fainted when I saw him. I knew that Brandon had a brother, but I didn't know they were identical twins. Brandon never told me that. As soon as I recovered enough to find my tongue, I invited him in.

"I saw your interview," he said to me. "I never knew that you loved my brother that much."

"Yes, I did. I've never gotten over it completely. Can you tell me where he's buried?"

"It's in our family plot. It's overlooking green meadows, blue skies, and chalk downs, which are undulating, rolling hills that cut across the entire Island. It's not a bad place to spend eternity."

"As I recall, you were very dead-set against our marriage."

"The whole family was, actually. We missed him in England, and of course, we wanted him to come home. If he married you, chances were that he would never have come home."

"He might have. He might have brought me with him. You know that Brandon has a daughter, don't you?"

"I have heard as much."

"Would you like to meet her?"

"Why, yes, I would."

I invited him to stay for dinner. Grant turned pale as soon as he saw him. It was as though he thought he had seen a ghost. Reginald said that he planned to stay for three days, and then he would be returning to England.

Jo Dell was unusually quiet at the table. I thought she would be overjoyed to see Brandon's brother, especially since he was a blood relative, but she seemed unimpressed. I noticed that she kept stealing looks at Grant.

I found myself watching his every move. He even threw his head back and laughed the same as Brandon. Sometimes I had difficulty believing that this man wasn't Brandon. On the last full day of his visit here in New York, I asked him what I considered to be a stupid question, yet I couldn't help myself. "You're not playing with me, are you?" I asked, as we took a walk through Central Park. He wanted to see the sights, like the Brooklyn Bridge, Central Park, the Statue of Liberty, and the Empire State Building.

"In what way?"

"I haven't seen Brandon in more than fifteen years, but it seems as though he has come back to life. Are you Brandon? Did you somehow fake your death so you didn't have to marry me? Did you see my interview and understand that I still love you, and that I would accept you back into my life?"

He shook his head and laughed. "I'm Reginald; I swear; however, I do see how my brother would have found you most captivating. I've seen pictures of you, but they don't do you justice. You're the most interesting and unusual woman I've ever met." He stopped walking, reached over, and touched my hand. "I know that this is terribly inappropriate, and I'm usually not given to whimsy, but would you care to go to England with me? I know it's incredibly selfish of me, but I'd like to know you just a little while longer, even if it were meant to be only a day, a week, or a year. I could show you where Brandon grew up, where he lived, what he liked to do, and where he now lies."

"When are you leaving?" I heard my voice ask.

"Tomorrow evening." He studied my face closely. "Are you really thinking about this?"

"Yes, I am."

"What would your husband say?"

"Grant and I understand each other," I said without thinking, yet I knew it was true. Grant always maintained that I would leave if I ever had the opportunity to see Brandon again. Grant, of all people, would understand why. Besides, there was no mention of starting a physical relationship, although I supposed one could read between the lines.

"I see. Well, I'll see you tomorrow, unless you change your mind."

My mind was reeling. I knew that he wasn't Brandon, but I was still fascinated by him. He looked exactly like Brandon. He sounded like him, and they even had the same laugh. I spent the last three days in his company, and if I hadn't known for a fact that Brandon was dead, I would have believed that Brandon had come back to me. It was like getting a second chance.

It never occurred to me to ask Grant what he thought. I instinctively knew that he wouldn't approve in any way of a relationship between Brandon's brother, who was the spitting image of him, and myself, yet I continued to spend almost all of my time with him over the past three days. Oddly enough, Grant said very little about it. That night, as Grant held me in his arms, he whispered, "I love you so much, Joy. Please don't let anything happen to us."

The next afternoon, Reginald was at my doorstep. I had already packed my bags. I knew it was insane, but I had to go. I left a note for Grant, who wasn't there at the time, and just left. I wasn't thinking about anything else. I wasn't thinking about Grant and the past twelve and a half years, or of Jo Dell, who was sixteen years old and still needed her mother. All I could see was a man who shared Brandon's face, and who laughed and sounded just like him.

We drove to the airport, but we had a twelve-hour layover because our flight was canceled. When it was time to board the plane, I had the strangest feeling wash over me like waves. "I can't go with you," I told him.

"Why not?"

"Because I've been living in a crazy dream. You're not Brandon; you're his brother. Brandon is dead, and even if you look and walk and talk like him, Brandon is still dead."

I left him while he boarded the plane, and I came back home. The reception that I got from Grant was iced cold. I tried to plead temporary insanity. I told him that I came to my senses and that nothing had happened, but it didn't matter. He maintained that if Reginald had been Brandon, I would have left. I couldn't argue because I knew it was true.

"I told you all along that you'd leave if Brandon were alive. I guess I was right," he said.

"But nothing happened. Don't you believe me?"

"I believe you," he said over his shoulder, as he threw some of his belongings into a suitcase.

"If you believe me, why are you leaving?"

"Because you left me."

"I didn't leave you. I came back."

"You still left. How do you think I felt when I read your letter? I had to give you up in my heart last night."

"Please don't do this, Grant."

"You made your choice."

"Yes, and I chose you."

"I don't think so. You chose Brandon, but you realized it was Reginald. I'm still second best; just as I always said I'd be."

I watched helplessly as he walked out of the door and out of my life.

-45-

I searched for Grant for days. Every place I went, I thought I saw his face. I even walked up to complete strangers and touched them on their sleeves, only to apologize because I had made a mistake. I felt sick inside. I just knew that if I could find Grant and talk to him, he would be able to forgive me. Jo Dell was terribly irate that I had done such a thing, and she moved out of the house with him. It seemed strange that she had disliked Grant for so many years, and then she ended up taking his side in the matter.

I talked to Carolyn and Thor to see if they knew where he might have gone, but they didn't know, either. Carolyn was in absolute shock that something like this could even happen. "He's going away forever," she said accusingly, "and this is all your fault."

"I know I'm to blame," I said defensively. "I didn't say that I wasn't."

I couldn't understand why she was so upset over it, but I was too upset myself to try to analyze it. When I got home, there was a message on my telephone answering machine from Jo Dell. She said that she needed to speak to me as soon as possible, and left a phone number where I could reach her. I checked the time of the phone call on the machine and realized that she called only a few minutes ago. I dialed the number immediately.

"Mom! Oh, Mom! I'm so glad you called me back!"

"What's wrong?"

"It's Grant. I'm so scared."

"Is he hurt?" I asked. I could feel fear rising in my chest.

"No, it's nothing like that, but I've never seen him this way. He was drinking something- some kind of alcohol; I don't know what it was, and then he took one of your wedding pictures and smashed it. Glass went flying everywhere. Then he sat down on the couch. He's crying, and I can't get him to stop."

"Tell me where you are."

"Grant will be mad if I tell you."

"You *must* tell me where you are."

She finally told me, and I drove there as quickly as I could. When I walked in, I found Grant sitting on the couch. I had seen him have too much to drink before, but not like this. Usually alcohol made him happy and even more entertaining, if that could ever be possible.

I slowly approached the couch. "Grant?" I asked.

He didn't even look up. "What do you want?"

"I want to see you."

"Well, I don't want to see you."

"Jo Dell was scared, and she called me." He wasn't crying anymore, but I could tell by looking at him that he had been.

"She didn't need to be scared."

He wasn't in any condition to reason with, or to have any serious conversation with, so I said, "I just want to sit with you, okay?"

"Suit yourself," he said, moving over so I could sit beside him.

A few minutes later, he laid his head on my lap and went to sleep. He slept almost all night long. I dozed on and off, but I didn't bother to try to get up. I just sat there and held Grant's head in my lap. I stroked his dark hair and studied his handsome face. I pulled an afghan off the back of the couch and covered us with it. The sky was starting to glow with a faint orange light when Grant finally awoke and sat upright.

"I'm sorry about last night," he said.

"I'm sorry about a lot of things. Can't we try to work this out?"

Grant shook his head. "I always knew this would happen."

"How would you know?"

"When Brandon died, you were in the hospital. I assisted his family in retrieving his things. I met Reginald at that time. I lived in silent fear that one day you'd meet, and if you did, I always knew that you might want to go with him."

"You never told me this, and you lived with this all of these years? Oh, Grant! You should have told me!"

"I told you that if Brandon were alive, you would leave the next day. I know the attraction of someone who looks like the person you love. You tend to project your feelings into that person."

I supposed that he was talking about his fleeting attraction to Carolyn, who did look a great deal like me.

"Besides," he added, "I wasn't wrong, was I? You still went with him."

"I chose to come back home."

"You chose not to go to England. What would have happened if he had stayed here?"

I was getting desperate. "Grant, I know that we promised each other never to bring this up, but I forgave you once, and you did more with Tiffany than I ever did with Reginald. I drove to the airport with him; I didn't go to bed with him."

"No, but Brandon still sleeps between us, and he has for almost thirteen years. Look, Joy, I just need a little more time. I'm not ready to go home with you. I need to see if I can find some happiness on my own because I'm just so tired of trying to make someone else happy who won't bury her past."

I had no choice but to return home. It was very lonely rattling around in that big house all by myself. Carolyn and Leisel came over to break the monotony. I couldn't remember the last time that Leisel had come to see me. We didn't talk much, but her presence was a way of telling me that she was sorry for what I was going through and that she would support me. There was another message on my answering machine.

"Mrs. Carlton," a woman's voice said, "I would like to talk to you sometime this week concerning Jo Dell."

"Oh, one more bother," I said.

"Who was that?" asked Leisel.

"Jo Dell's English teacher. She always calls me Mrs. Carlton. I'll have to call her, but I just don't feel like it today."

"How about the three of us getting out of the house tomorrow and going out for lunch or something?" Carolyn asked. "It can be like old times."

"I guess so." I wasn't thrilled with the idea, but it was probably a good idea to get me out of the house.

-46-

The doorbell rang. I went to answer the door, and that was the very last thing I remembered. I felt like I was drifting. I was peacefully asleep, and I felt safe and warm. Then I heard a woman's voice. "You've been here for three days," she said. "Don't you think that you should go home and get some rest?"

I heard a man's voice say, "No. Not until she wakes up."

"It could be a very long time," said the woman.

"That's fine," I heard the man say.

I continued to drift. Sometimes I felt someone holding my hand. I still heard a man's voice at times, but I didn't recognize it; things weren't very clear. Voices seemed very far away, almost like an echo. I had absolutely no desire to open my eyes. I just wanted to drift. I heard his voice again begging me to open my eyes. I thought it was Grant. I tried to call out his name, but I didn't hear anything come out. I might have tried harder to open my eyes if I had known for certain that he was Grant.

After an undeterminable amount of time, I wanted to open my eyes. I had to fight just a little bit, but they finally fluttered open. I could tell by looking around the room that I was in a hospital bed. It was rather frightening not to know why. I flexed my arms and legs and looked down at my body. Everything seemed intact. I looked up and saw Gary bending over me with a worried expression on his face. He had a beard, which was something I had never seen on him before, and he had large, dark circles under his eyes.

"You look terrible," I said.

"You don't look so well, yourself," he retorted.

I looked around the room. "What are you doing here?"

He didn't answer. Instead he said, "I called Grant. You were asking for him."

"How long have I been here?"

"About four days."

"Four days!" I exclaimed. "I was asleep for four days?"

"Just like Rip Van Winkle. I was afraid you'd never wake up."

"What happened?"

"Apparently you fell and bumped your head. Don't you remember?"

I shook my head. "I don't remember a thing. I just remember going to the door."

Gary walked over to the door. "I should let the nurse know that you're awake now. The doctor will probably want to know. I'll be back in a few minutes."

The doctor came in and examined me. He looked in my eyes with a light and tested my hand grasps and reflexes. Everything seemed fine. He questioned me about my fall, but I didn't remember any of it, not even opening the door. I asked if this was anything to worry about.

"It isn't uncommon for someone to receive a blow to the head and not remember things. It's called retroactive amnesia. The only thing that still puzzles me is that the blow didn't seem severe enough to have caused a loss of consciousness for any extended period of time. The CT Scan and the MRI were normal, and there was no evidence of intracranial bleeding or hematoma."

I touched my forehead, but I felt no bump. The doctor pointed to an area on the back of my head, near the base of my skull, and just slightly to the right side. "It wasn't very pronounced," he said, "and now it's just barely palpable."

I reached back and touched the area he was referring to with my fingertips. It was just a little bit tender, like I was touching a bruised area. I wondered how I could have bumped the back of my head when I was walking forward to answer the door. The doctor told me that they were going to keep me another day or two for observation, but after that I should be able to go home.

After the doctor left, Gary came in and sat in the chair beside me.

"The doctor said the bump on my head wasn't really that bad, and I shouldn't have been unconscious for so long," I told him. "I wonder why I don't remember anything."

"I fell off my bike once when I was a teenager," he said. "I still don't remember falling off. All I know is one minute I was riding down the street, and the next minute I was waking up on the ground with my bike lying next to me. This sort of thing can happen."

"I did something like this once before- when Brandon died. I slept for two days. The doctor said that it was hysteria."

"Your body must react that way to shocking things, whether it's emotional or traumatic. I think it was a melodramatic way to do it, but considering the source, I guess I shouldn't be surprised."

"You should put that into your column."

"I did," he said.

"No, you didn't, but you probably will."

Gary shook his head. "No, I won't."

"Well, if you don't print it, somebody else will."

"We've been pretty successful keeping it out of the media, and now that you're awake, even if it does leak out, it won't be too much of a problem to handle. You can tell them you had pneumonia or something."

"How did you know?"

"I was driving by your house and I noticed the ambulance, so I stopped. Carolyn and Leisel said that they went to your house for lunch and they found you on the floor."

"You said that you called Grant?"

Gary nodded. "He was very difficult to find, but I finally found him."

"We're separated. That's why you had trouble locating him."

Gary had a shocked expression on his face. "When did this happen?" he asked.

"A few days ago. It just hasn't had the chance to leak out. I guess you have the first scoop on a really big story. Hollywood's Happiest couple hopelessly bites the dust. It has a good ring to it, don't you think?"

We didn't have time to say more about it because the door opened at that moment, and Grant walked in.

"She's awake," Gary said to him, and he rose from the chair.

Relief flooded across Grant's face. He sat in the chair and held my hand. "What happened?" he asked.

"I don't know. I don't remember anything except answering the door."

"Well," said Gary, who now seemed to be feeling uncomfortable, "I had better be going."

"You need a shave, a bath, and a good night's sleep," I said.

He smiled. "I probably do." He hesitated for a moment, and then he leaned over and kissed me on the forehead before he left the room.

As soon as we were alone, I asked, "Grant, can't we please get back together again?"

He patted my hand. "I don't think we should discuss this right now. You don't need to upset yourself."

"No, I'm all right. I need to know. I still can't believe that I did what I did. It had to have been the most impulsive thing that I've ever done in my whole life."

Grant nodded. "Yes, it was, but it was also the most heartfelt thing that you've ever done, too." He saw the hurt look on my face and tried to explain. "Logic to the mind is what impulse is to the heart. That's why it hurt me so much. You wanted to do this with all of your heart, and only the power of reason brought you back."

"But I did come back. I have no desire to go to him now. You do believe me, don't you?"

Grant nodded and kissed my hand.

I felt a surge of hope rise within my heart. "Can we please try again?" I struggled to sit upright in bed, but I felt incredibly weak.

"I want to; I really do, but I want what's best for you," he said, squeezing my hand.

"For me?"

"Look, Joy, I've had a lot of time to think things through. Ever since I met you, you've had some kind of sadness in you. I never knew what it was. I used to think that it was Brandon, but then I realized that I recognized this about you when we first met, even before Brandon died. You act as though you're searching for something or someone you lost."

"I don't know what you're talking about," I said, sinking down into the bed.

"I'm sure you don't."

"Do you know what it is that I've been searching for?"

"I think so."

"Then why don't you tell me?"

"Because you'd never believe me in a million years. You need to find out for yourself. I think that you need time to be by yourself and to find whatever it is that prevents you from really being happy. Maybe when you find it, you won't want it after all. Maybe when you find it, you'll still want me. I'm willing to wait for you for as long as I can, but I need to set you free."

"Please, Grant-"

He stroked my hair. "You must be free," he said.

-47-

I was released from the hospital a few days later. The day before I was released, Grant, Leisel, and Carolyn came by to visit me.

"Do you think it's possible that she'll eventually remember?" Leisel asked Grant.

"It's possible, but often a person with retroactive amnesia related to a traumatic event permanently loses the memory of the actual event, and sometimes they even lose the memory of some of the events leading up to and immediately preceding the accident. It can be minutes, hours, days, or in extreme cases, it can be weeks or years. In Joy's case, though, she remembers going to answer the door, so it looks like she didn't lose many of the preceding events. There are no other holes in her memory."

"I'm not going to worry about it," I said. "Falling and bashing my skull would be an unpleasant memory. I don't need to remember the actual event."

"Is it dangerous to tell people that have amnesia what happened if they don't remember?" asked Leisel.

I thought that it was a strange question, but then, Leisel was known to be strange at times. "Why?" I asked her. "Do you know something that I don't?"

"I've always heard that you don't tell someone who can't remember something what happened because it can be traumatic, you know, like when you don't want to wake up a sleepwalker."

"There are different types of amnesia," said Grant. "The kind you're thinking about is a hysterical type, where a person wants to block out something horribly unpleasant. In that case, a therapist would have to tread carefully. This is an injury, so it isn't the same thing. If you saw Joy fall it wouldn't hurt to tell her, but it probably wouldn't help her, either. She has a physical reason for not remembering, not an emotional or mental one."

"We didn't see her fall," said Carolyn, who had been unusually quiet, even for her.

"How did you two get into the house?" I asked.

"When you didn't come to the door, I used my key," said Carolyn. "I haven't used it in years, but part of the house still belongs to me. I still have a key."

I hoped that Grant would reconsider, but he didn't. I was served divorce papers a few months later. I thought that we might have a legal separation, but never a divorce. I felt incredibly sad inside as I signed my name to dissolve a union that had lasted nearly thirteen years. Tabloids soon picked up on the story, and all kinds of rumors and innuendos began circling. Someone sniffed out the story about Brandon's brother, and they made it sound as if we had a sordid relationship together. The tabloids, and even reputable magazines, were having a hey-day with this story.

One day an article surfaced about Grant's affair with Tiffany. I was incensed. Only four people in the whole world knew about it. I sure never said a word, and I was positive that Grant never did. That just left two people. I decided to take the lesser of the other two evils, and I called Gary.

"This isn't a good time," he told me, when I said I wanted to see him.

"I don't want to hear that today, please. I need to see you tonight. I don't know if *you* are the cause of the latest gossip, but I have to find out." The hurt and desperation must have showed in my voice because he agreed to come, but only after dark.

"Look, I really shouldn't be here," he told me, when he showed up. He seemed very nervous as he stepped inside my house. "Can you speak your mind, and then we can be done with it quickly? I might have been followed, or my phone might have been tapped, and I don't want you mixed up with this mess."

"What mess?" I asked, as I led him to my sitting room.

"It's complicated, really; although you might find some humor with my present situation."

"What situation?"

"Well, if you must know, I was printing small pieces on some illegal activities going on in New York City. In this business, though, you have to tread lightly around certain subjects if you don't want to get mixed up in things that might be unhealthy for you to know. Some investigative reporters will lay everything on the line for the recognition of unearthing a good story, but I never felt that way. I've seen too many come up dead. A co-worker of mine, an overzealous junior reporter, unearthed some pretty damaging pieces of evidence against one of the major crime families. I would never have printed that piece without more evidence, and I told him this when I read it. He submitted it to another editor under my name, and the editor, who has learned over the years that I always have the evidence to back up my stories, printed it.

"The crime family is certain that I have all the pieces to the puzzle, which I don't, and I've been subpoenaed to testify in an upcoming trial. They know about the subpoena, and if I show up and testify, it will bring down the whole family, and they know it. What they don't know is that I'm not the author of that piece and, in reality, I know very little. My lawyer has told the D.A. this, but apparently he feels that he can wring something out of me. I have to live long enough to be able to swear in court that I wasn't the author; I have no sources to reveal, and that I'm no threat to them."

"Shouldn't you be in protective custody?"

"I don't trust that system. I'd rather try to take care of myself."

"When's the trial?"

"Not for another three months."

"Three months! You have to keep a low profile for another three months!"

"It looks that way."

There was a knock at the door. I looked out the window and saw some strange men standing on my porch. I froze. I had forgotten to reset the security system after I let Gary in, and that's how they were able to make it to my front porch.

"We can either talk, or we'll break the door down," I heard a voice say.

I was terrified. I pushed Gary toward the basement and went to open the door. I had to remind myself that I was prone to hysteria, so I better not faint. I opened the door, and three men pushed their way inside.

"You're trespassing," I said.

"We're looking for an acquaintance of yours: Gary Shawn. We have reason to believe that he came here tonight."

"Gary and I have never been on good terms. I asked him to come here so I could give him a piece of my mind, but he has been here and gone already."

The one who acted like he was the boss spoke up. "We're not looking in the usual places that he might be. We're looking at the unusual. We might as well have a look around while we're here. And we better not find him. It would be a shame to mess up such a pretty face."

He held out a switchblade in a very threatening manner. His smile was cruel, and I could tell that he thoroughly enjoyed frightening me. I was somewhat vain; I couldn't help it, and I thought it would be a shame to mess up my pretty face, too. One man, who had red hair, went upstairs, and another one went down into the basement. The man with the knife stood next to me the whole time. I could do nothing but stand there helplessly and try not to act unusually nervous. The redheaded man who went upstairs finally came down. "He's not up there," he said.

The one down in the basement was taking longer. I was so scared, and it was getting worse by the second, but I tried not to show it. Finally he emerged from the basement. "Let's get out of here," he said.

"If you know what's good for you, you'll keep your mouth shut about our little visit. We wish you no ill will," said the man who enjoyed showing off his knife.

They got in their car and drove off. It took me a few moments to even be able to move. Then I realized that there was no sound coming from the basement. I opened the door and flew down the stairs.

"Gary!" I screamed. "Gary! Oh, my God!"

I just knew I would find a dead body in my basement, and then I would be blamed. I could see it now. My motive would be that I wanted to silence his poisoned pen, and then I would go to jail forever. Then I noticed some movement in the laundry chute, and some clothes tumbled out of it. I watched in amazement as he emerged from the chute, and he was still in one piece.

"I sure am glad that this chute is wider than usual, and I'm sure glad I haven't put on a lot of weight."

He had climbed up into the chute and trailed some of the clothes inside it with him. That way, if they looked into the chute, it would just look like there were clothes up there.

"Do you think they'll come back?" I asked. My knees felt weak.

"No, but they're still looking. I'm sorry that I put you in danger. I should go."

"Are you crazy?"

"Well, I can't stay here. I'll have to think of something else," he said, as we trudged up the basement stairs.

"They've already checked out my house. They don't think you're here. You need to stay here at least for the night. If you do, however, we'll need to set up a truce."

He pulled out a white handkerchief with a grin and waved it in the air. "Why did you want to see me?" he asked.

"My troubles seem mild compared to yours. I feel bad even bringing this up now."

Gary sat down on the couch while I reset the security system and ran around the house closing all of the blinds. I picked up the latest article and showed him the one about Grant and Tiffany. "Did this come from you?"

I knew from the look on his face that it hadn't. "I'll kill her," he said under his breath. He looked up at me over the paper. "I guess she thought that this story was fair game now. She'll find out differently."

I looked at his face, and I knew with the utmost certainty that he would try his best to destroy her. I felt a strange satisfaction with that knowledge.

I slept with one eye open, but when I went to bed that night, I thought about the fact that I had flown down a flight of stairs and was calling out. This wasn't the dream though, I decided. I wasn't wearing a dress that swished in the wind, and no one was standing at the bottom of the stairs. At the time I was flying down the stairs, Gary was wedged inside my laundry chute.

I was glad for the company; it certainly took my mind off of my troubles. The next day, I received a phone call from Jo Dell's teacher.

"Mrs. Carlton?"

"Yes."

"I'm Mrs. Winters, Jo Dell's English teacher. I have a touch of laryngitis, so please bear with me," she said in a raspy whisper. "I need to talk to you about Jo Dell."

"Jo Dell?"

"She seems to be having problems in school, and her grades aren't what they used to be. Have you noticed anything different?"

"Grant and I divorced over six months ago, and she's living with him, so I really wouldn't know. Maybe you should speak to Grant."

"Her problems are probably directly related to the divorce. I'd still like to talk to you about her, but I'd rather not do it on the phone. I think we should speak face to face."

It was after eight o'clock at night when I drove up to the school. As I entered the front door, I realized how big and formidable this building was. I had been there once before - at Leisel and Carolyn's graduation from junior high school. A new junior high had been built several years ago, but in recent years, the high school was overflowing with students, so they reopened this building to use as a high school. It was sort of spooky being in there without a bunch of other people. I put my hand on the banister and ascended the stairs. "Still slick as snot," I heard Leisel say from way back in my memory.

I was still smiling to myself about this when I reached the top of the stairs. All of the rooms were dark, and only the hall lights burned, except for one light way down the hall. *That must be the one,* I thought, and suddenly all of the lights went out. I was startled right out of my skin.

"Mrs. Winters?" I called out, but there was no answer.

I was standing in the middle of the corridor when the lights went out, so I moved over to the wall. A handrail ran against the length of the wall, so I used this to guide me as I took a few halting steps forward. I considered making my way down to the room, but a little voice inside my head told me not to. I could see street lights outside, so there was no power failure from anywhere but inside of this building. I backed away, just slightly at first, and then I began moving faster. I heard footsteps coming toward me. I turned around and broke into a run. As I neared the end of the corridor, I heard the sound of a shotgun, and I believed that a bullet had just missed my head.

Someone was trying to kill me! I was in this big building; in the dark; all by myself, and someone was trying to kill me! It had to be one of those men who were after Gary. They must have found out that I had protected him.

The light of a full moon appeared in the window of the last classroom, and I was able to see the outline of the stairs. I was aware that if I could see the stairs from the moonlight shining in, whoever was behind me would be able to see me, too. As far as I could tell, I had two choices. I could get shot in the head trying to run down those stairs, as this person was only a few steps behind me, or I could break my neck. I opted for the broken neck. I climbed up on the banister and slid down to the ground in a matter of a few split seconds.

I ran as fast as I could to the main entrance, but the door was locked from the inside, and I couldn't open it. A terrible fear gripped my chest as I realized that I was locked in. I ran inside one of the classrooms, shut the door, and quickly pushed the teacher's big desk up against it. I ran to the window, but I wasn't strong enough to open it. The big yellow moon was high in the sky, and I could see my car parked in front of the school. My means of escape was just outside this window. Whoever was after me was only a few seconds behind, probably checking each classroom. I picked up a desk and heaved it as hard as I could through the window and climbed out. I ran as fast as I could to my car and fumbled with the keys. I must have watched too many movies because I had a momentary fear that my car might not start. It did, of course, and I took off down the road as fast as I could go. I was halfway home before I realized that I was crying out of a strange combination of terror and relief.

When I got home, Gary took one look at me and knew that something terrible had happened. I threw my arms around his neck, and he held me until I stopped shaking. I noticed then that I had a fairly long, superficial cut on my leg. It wasn't bad enough to need stitches, and it probably wouldn't scar, but it needed to be cleaned up. Gary went into the bathroom with me to help clean the cut.

"Do you think it was the same people who were after you?" I asked, as he wrapped a bandage around my leg.

"I don't know. It could be, but if they believed that I was here, they would never have left in the first place. You haven't been bothered by that stalker again, have you?"

"No, it's been over sixteen years. Do you think it's a new one?"

"I don't know, but we just can't stay here waiting for someone to blow us away. We have to go somewhere else." He finished wrapping my leg, and we went back into the living room.

"We can't just disappear, can we?"

"Why not?"

"Where will we go?"

"I've been thinking all day, and I know what to do," he said, pacing back and forth. I couldn't tell if he was agitated or excited. Maybe it was a little bit of both. "I hadn't planned on taking you with me, but you can't stay here by yourself. I know some good places. We'll be safe, I promise."

"Should we tell anyone? I know that Grant and I are divorced, but he'd be worried sick if I suddenly came up missing. He'd have the whole world looking for me."

"Look, you don't know who was after you, and at this point, you don't know who you can trust. Tell your caretaker to tell Grant that you're going to take a trip for about three or four months and not to worry. Just tell them that, and nothing more."

"Three or four months!"

"Do you have anything better to do for the next three or four months?"

"I guess not. My marriage fell apart; my show was cancelled; my daughter turned against me in favor of Grant; Carolyn is married to someone I'm not comfortable with, and Leisel doesn't like being around me anymore. My friends became my enemies, and my enemies became my friends. What else do I have to look forward to?"

"A longer life, I hope."

Gary didn't tell me where we were going, but we drove for two days. We were on Interstate-70 for a long time, and then we crossed the Mississippi river, which ran between Illinois and Missouri. The river was massive, and I experienced an eerie feeling as we crossed the bridge. The power of the river was evident; the current was extremely fast, and I had no doubt that it would be difficult to swim across it. No wonder the "mighty" Mississippi had been the subject of books and movies. It was so beautiful, yet so deadly. People were swept away in those powerful currents every year. I saw the tall golden arch in Saint Louis as we drove by.

"This is the tornado belt," I told Gary. "Flatlands and tornados."

"At least it's a beautiful day. You won't have to worry about tornados today." I looked out the window. Farmlands, corn and beans, cows and pigs were stretched as far as the eye could see.

"We're almost there," he said.

"Here in Missouri?"

"I know a cabin about fifty miles from the Ozarks. No one will be there this time of year."

"Why not?"

"Because this is October, and they're in the middle of the harvesting season. They'll be gathering the crops together."

"Are we trespassing?"

"Not really. This land belongs to poor, distant relatives on my mother's side of the family. Will O'Malley is the owner of this property, and he, and only he, is aware of our situation."

"Do you trust him?"

"Oh, yes; I would trust him with my life."

"How well do you know him?"

"When I was a young boy, my father used to send us here in the summers to work. He said that our poor relations could use the help. He also said that we needed to learn what it was like to work hard for our money and see how other people struggled to live. My father worked hard for his money too, and my job isn't exactly a piece of cake, but we never struggled, wondering if we'd be able to keep the roof over our heads every year. It was an invaluable experience. I sent Alan here for a couple of summers, too."

"Why didn't you offer them money if they're poor?"

"They're proud people. They want to make it themselves. They'd never turn down an extra hand to plow the fields, but they'd also never accept money in return for any favor."

We drove down several dirt roads, until finally I saw a small, rustic looking cabin up ahead.

"This will be our home for the next three or four months," said Gary.

I walked inside. It was somewhat chilly, and the cabin was dusty and dirty inside. I took a broom and started sweeping. At least, I thought I was sweeping. I sort of put the broom down, dragged it across the floor, and tried to accumulate dust into a little pile.

"You don't know how to hold a broom right," said Gary, as he snatched the broom out of my hands. "You have to *sweep* the floor. It's not a mop." He demonstrated how to do sweeping motions.

"I guess you can tell that I haven't done this very often."

"This might be an eye opening experience for you."

I made a face at him, snatched the broom back, and made an attempt to properly sweep the floor.

Gary opened up the cabinets. They were filled with cups, saucers, and dishes. "You might get dishpan hands," he said. "There's no dishwasher."

"If you think that I'm going to be the chief dish and bottle washer, you have another think coming. We are going to share the responsibilities."

"Okay, I'll help you wash dishes, and you can help me chop down trees for firewood."

I walked through the rest of the cabin, surveying what would be my home for the next three or four months. A stuffed moose head and a few old portraits hung on the wall of the large living room. The fireplace had a hearth that expanded across an entire wall, and a bearskin rug was in front of the fireplace. The sofa and chairs looked worn, but they were made out of sturdy fabric and looked comfortable to sit on. The table in the kitchen looked like an old picnic table with benches. I was glad to see that there was running water and plumbing for the sink and the bathroom. I envisioned having to use an outhouse, which truly would have been a new experience for me. There were no bedrooms, so to speak. There were a few roll away cots that could be set up to sleep on at night and then picked up out of the way during the day. With no electricity, we would have to keep warm by the fire at night and cook outside on the spit. Oil lamps and candles were scattered throughout the cabin. There was a radio that ran by battery, and I was pleased to find that it was working.

The first night, my fear of the dark returned. I was afraid that Gary would laugh at me, but he didn't.

"Push your cot over here by me; I won't bite you," he said.

I was hesitant to do so, since that was how Grant and I got caught up in an unplanned one-night stand, but I just wouldn't ask him to hold me. Besides, Gary didn't like girls. I found myself watching him for some kind of clue because I just didn't see it. I grew up in show business, which was full of gay men and women. I was used to being around them, and many were my friends. I couldn't always tell who was or wasn't, but most of the time I thought that I could. Gary never exhibited any of the mannerisms that would ever make me think that he was. If I hadn't overhead his conversation in the restaurant so many years ago, I would never have believed it. But, I had to admit that I had known Gary for almost nineteen years, and I had yet to see him in the company of women.

I pushed my cot next to his. It was far enough away so they didn't exactly touch, but close enough to where I could reach out and touch his shoulder if I wanted to.

One day was pretty much the same as the next. Will came over once a week with a sack of groceries and Gary reimbursed him. We got up early and walked through the woods. I boiled eggs in a kettle under a fire, and cooked bacon, sausage, or beans in a cast iron skillet, and sometimes we barbequed on an open spit. We spent our time reading, listening to the radio, and putting puzzles together. Gary also continued to work on his daily column for his newspaper, and he mailed out a week's worth of columns at a time to his editor through Will O'Malley. The senior editor of the newspaper was a personal friend of Gary's, and he was also a free thinker who believed that an honest day's work didn't have to be spent at the office. The end product was all that mattered to him, and it didn't matter if the work was written at a New York City desk or on a farm in Missouri. Gary also did freelance writing under a pseudonym.

I never had so much free time on my hands in all my life, but the days seemed to go by quickly. We talked about everything under the sun. One day, while we were putting puzzles together, we got on the subject of names.

"Why do they call you Gary if your name is Gerald?" I asked. "Shouldn't they call you Gerry instead of Gary?"

"I certainly hope not," said Gary, as he sifted though the box to find a piece. "I hate the name Gerry." He set the box down and looked at me for a moment. "Actually, I was named after my father. His name was Gerald Alan Shawn. I guess they wanted a way to tell us apart, and ever since I can remember, everyone has called me Gary." He picked up the box and sifted through it again, looking for his piece. "I know it's common for the first born son to be named after the father, but my mother loved the name Zachary."

I looked at some of the pieces that were already spread out on the table. I found a piece that fit the puzzle, popped it in, and grinned triumphantly at Gary. He had been searching for this one little piece for quite some time. "That isn't even an Irish name, is it?" I asked.

Gary shook his head. "I don't believe so, but she loved the name. My father spent his entire life trying to make her happy, so he let her give Zachary that name. Maybe he always knew he'd have more sons; I don't know." His face became very reflective, as though he could see the past in his mind's eye. "He was never the same after she died. I think if it's possible to die of a broken heart, he did, although it took him about six years to do it." Then his face changed and he came back to the present and returned to the original subject. "The rest of us were given Irish names, though."

"All except for Alan."

"Well, that came from my father's middle name." Then he directed the subject back at me. "You know, your daughter certainly has an unusual name."

I rolled my eyes. "That was Marilyn's doing, not mine. She wanted to name her, so I agreed. She gave up her life to have her. The very least she should have been allowed to do was name her." I found another piece to the puzzle while he was still digging through the box. "You know," I said, "I used to think the name "Jo Dell" was sort of stupid, but it kind of grew on me after a while. It suits her, I think. Some people have tried to call her Jody, but she hates it. She really wants to be called Jo Dell. I guess I don't blame her for not wanting to be called by anything but her given name."

"Does it bother you that they changed your name?"

"At first it did. I had a hard time getting used to it. The first few times they called me Joy, I didn't answer. It wasn't that I was ignoring them, but my brain just wasn't used to being called that. It took some time for me to realize that people were actually talking to me. But no," I said, shaking my head, "it doesn't bother me anymore. What does a name mean, anyway?"

"Everything, according to some writers," said Gary.

"And nothing, according to Shakespeare. 'A rose…is still a rose,' even if you happen to call it by a different name. It still doesn't change what it is. Even if I'm called by a different name, I'm still me."

"Before you start believing everything that Shakespeare ever wrote, and don't get me wrong, because I think Shakespeare was brilliant, I want to ask you one thing." He leaned toward me, looked directly in my face, and asked, "Would you ever consider going to a dentist named Dr. Payne?"

I burst into laughter. "He might find it hard to be in that particular business. He'd probably have to change his name or get a different line of work."

"Exactly. When it comes to a person, a name might not change the physical you, but it still might change the person you become." Without any warning, he jumped up and shouted, "I found it!"

He startled me. "Found what?" I asked, stupidly.

"That blasted piece I've been looking for."

I got into dark moods at times because I missed Grant. He was my best friend. I might not have loved him in the same way as I had Brandon, but I did love him. I just never knew how much until we separated. Sometimes something would happen, and the first thing that popped into my mind was that I needed to tell Grant, and then I would be sad because he was no longer there. I was finding out that I couldn't erase a twelve-and-a-half year marriage and a sixteen-year friendship just like that.

I was also finding out that Gary, underneath his cynical nature, was a very sensitive person, and he could easily pick up on my dark moods. One night, it was getting dark outside, and he had just started a fire. I was sitting on the couch, staring out the window at the beautiful sunset. Gary sat down cross-legged on the bearskin rug in front of the fire. He took a poker and jabbed at one of the logs. "Tell me about Grant," he said.

"What do you want to know?"

He shrugged his shoulders. "Anything you want to tell me."

"Grant is someone who wears his heart on his sleeve. He laughs hard, plays hard, works hard, and he can pour his soul out into a performance in a way that I have seldom seen in other actors. And he loved me; he loved me with his whole soul. I know he did, and he just walked away."

Gary nodded his head, encouraging me to go on.

"I know what you're probably thinking. How could Grant love me that much and then cheat on me?" Gary shrugged his shoulders, and I continued, "But, I shared a large part of the blame, and that's why I never divorced him for it. I never made him feel like I loved him, and he was extremely jealous over Brandon. I was very hurt when he wanted to divorce me when I had done nothing compared to what he had done." Gary still said nothing, so I went on, "He said that I had to find myself; that ever since he knew me I acted like I had lost something or someone, and I had to find out what it was. He told me that he hoped I'd still want him when I found it."

"And have you found it?"

"I don't even know what he was talking about. Once though, he told me that walking away from someone and letting them find their own happiness is the ultimate form of love."

Gary nodded in agreement. "He was right. Love is like a butterfly."

"Excuse me?"

"Well, I don't know who said this, but I heard once that love is like a butterfly or a bird. You can keep it in a cage, but it never really belongs to you because you're forcing it to stay. If you let it go free, and then it comes back to you, then it's yours."

"Well, I wouldn't do it. I'd make sure that I was their ultimate happiness."

"So you'd keep them in a cage and try to force yourself on them as their ultimate happiness?"

"I guess that doesn't sound very good, especially when you put it like that."

"Don't you think that Grant tried to do that first before walking away?"

"Probably, but the biggest problem we had was that he accused me of being in love with Brandon and wishing that I were with him instead."

"Well, did you?"

"That is the six-million dollar question that has been posed to me for the past sixteen years, and it's a no-win situation."

Gary took the poker and jabbed one of the logs again. Sparks shot out from around the logs, and then they fell and glowed as embers at the bottom of the fireplace. "What's wrong with saying that you're sorry that Brandon died, but that you haven't been unhappy with the life that you made for yourself with Grant after he died?"

I shrugged my shoulders. "I guess I don't have a way with words like you do."

I got up and switched on the radio. To my great surprise, I learned that Grant had just finished a major motion picture with Paramount. He had probably been in Los Angeles, and I wondered if he would move there permanently.

Gary noticed the melancholy look on my face. "He's still moving up in the world of show business," he said.

That night, I had my dream again. I was running down the stairs, and I reached the bottom step. But this time, I thought I saw the outline of a man standing in the fog. He looked like he was wearing an overcoat. I awoke with a start.

"No!" I yelled aloud. "Not yet!"

Gary sat straight up in bed. "Joy, what's wrong?"

"It was just a dream. I'm sorry. Try to go back to sleep." Gary did go back to sleep right away, but I stayed awake for a long time. I noticed something else that was new. The dress I had on was blue. It was foggy and hard to see, but the dress was definitely blue.

In the morning, I decided to tell Gary about the dream while I was making breakfast. "I'm running down the stairs, and I'm calling out to someone that I can't see in the fog, but I always wake up before I get there." I divided the eggs onto two plates and set one down in front of Gary. "Do you think it's a real person? Someone I know?"

"It could be, I guess, or maybe it's a fantasy person."

That was a new twist that I had never thought of before. "Why would I do that?"

"Why does anybody dream anything?" He scooped up a forkful of eggs. "Everyone has fantasies. Cinderella is probably the most misunderstood fantasy in the world."

"So now you're going to pick on my favorite fantasy?"

"No, you're probably not ready for my theories on Cinderella. Look, I'm a firm believer that there's someone out there for everybody; you just have to find them. But the belief that there's just one person in the whole world that's meant for you is a huge fallacy. If you're going through life with the idea that Brandon was the only person in the world that was meant for you, and that's what I believe you have been doing, you'll never be able to get on with your life. It's possible to love more than one person in your lifetime."

"Do you think it's possible to love two people at the same time?"

"If one is dead, it's not very realistic. There really isn't a choice. The choice was made for you."

"No, I'm not talking about Brandon and Grant. I'm just asking a general question. Is it possible to love two people at the same time?"

"Yes, but it would certainly make it more complicated. I must stress, however, that it's always possible to make a choice in the end."

Three months passed, then four. I was beginning to think that the trial would never start. Then we received word that the trial would begin in mid-March. We were ready to come back, but it would be the most dangerous time of all.

"I won't be safe until I get inside that courthouse," said Gary, as he loaded our bags into the trunk of the car. "There might be someone out there waiting for me to walk in. I wish there were a way I could get in there without being detected."

"There is, but you might not like it."

"What do you have in mind?"

"I have a warehouse of costumes. You could wear one and waltz in there undetected."

"And do I just walk inside the courtroom, costume and all?"

"You could go inside the restroom and change."

"And what if they're waiting in the restroom for me?"

"Go into the ladies room and change. They won't be waiting for you there. Actually, I thought I might dress you in a nun's habit. There's no way anyone will know it's you."

"You live in a world of fantasy. You've been in show business way too long."

"I guess so, but I think it would work, if you had the guts to do it."

Gary laughed. "I don't think that I do. What we need to do is contact the police. We can be given police protection for one night and then escorted to the courtroom."

Will O'Malley came over to say goodbye. Gary and Will shook hands.

"Thanks for all of your help," Gary said to Will. "When I'm done with this mess, I might come back and repay you by helping with this year's planting and harvesting. Then you and the rest of the family can meet Joy."

I listened with surprise. Gary wanted to bring me back here after he testified at the trial, but what surprised me even more was that I wanted him to.

-49-

I wasn't able to breathe easy until we were safely inside the courtroom. It was as though I were waiting for a stray bullet to come zinging out of nowhere at any moment. Gary testified under oath that he wasn't the author of those articles, and the real author, a junior reporter, no longer worked for the newspaper. He was fired after putting Gary's name to his own story and for not having the necessary information to back it up.

"Do you think that your troubles are over now?" I asked, as we left the courtroom.

Gary shook his head. "I don't think that the defendant believed my entire story. I think he's relieved that I didn't have the necessary evidence to convict him, but I studied his face. I think he's afraid I'll try to dig up the rest of the story, and he probably doesn't believe there ever was a junior reporter."

"What'll we do now?"

"What we talked about earlier. We'll go back to Missouri and let this story cool down."

I had a chance to talk to Grant and Jo Dell on the phone. Grant was in the process of doing a second motion picture, and he was very excited about it. Jo Dell was attending a private school in Los Angeles, so she finally got her wish to go to some bratty, rich-kid private school. She was somewhat cold to me, so I knew that she still had some anger towards me that she would have to work through. I told them that I was going to take another trip to Missouri, and that I would let them know how I could be reached. Grant never once told me that he loved me or wanted to get back together with me in any way. He was very busy with his career, so he probably didn't have much chance to think about anything else. Work could be a healer, as I had learned long ago.

Gary and I returned to Missouri. This time we stayed on property belonging to Will O'Malley's brother, Tom. Tom had a wife and seven children; their ages ranged from three years to twenty-one. His father and mother lived in the house with them, so they were part of an extended family. Tom and Will had three other brothers, and they all lived less than a mile from each other.

Tom's two-story farmhouse was very large. It sat on a small hill, which sloped down into a vacant field of grass. This vacant field of grass had no trees, and it extended out about eight or nine hundred feet to a much smaller farmhouse which they gave to us to use. Painted yellow and white, it was one of the cutest little houses I had ever seen. My favorite part about it was that it had a large, wooden front porch that extended across the entire front. Four steps led up to the porch, and there were several chairs and a porch swing on it. I loved to sit on the swing and watch the sunset. I got hooked on sunsets after being in the country. Maybe New York didn't have them.

I wondered if they had moved someone out of the house, but Gary assured me that this was not the case. It was strictly a guesthouse. They believed in hospitality, and the best that they could possibly offer anyone was in that house. I had gone nearly six months without a television, so I thought I died and went to heaven when I found one there.

Gary explained to Tom that he wasn't sure if there might be some trouble from that crime family, so it would be better if no one knew that I was Joy Bryant, unless they happened to figure it out for themselves. He introduced me as Joyce Carlton. One of the farmers' wives made a comment that I had a remarkable resemblance to a television actress, and I assured her that people made that mistake all of the time.

I certainly did get a new perspective on life. Gary explained that I was a city girl, so I couldn't be expected to keep up with their robust farm girls. I decided that I would try to do my part, so I got up at four every morning to help feed the chickens, gather the eggs, and milk the cows.

The first time I milked the cow, Gary laughed at me.

"I don't want to hurt the cow," I said.

"That cow wants to be relieved, Joy. She doesn't care about tenderness."

"I'd care about tenderness if someone were pulling on me."

"Then be glad you're not a cow," he said, as he sat down beside me to show me how.

Gary worked on his newspaper column and helped out in the fields. His skin turned a golden bronze from being out in the sun. His light brown hair even turned a touch of blonde. One day, we were invited to a barn dance.

"It's not a Hollywood ball," said Gary, "but you'll have a lot of fun."

I was amazed at the size of the barn. Tom's wife gave me a dress to wear because I certainly never owned anything that looked like their dresses. The fiddle played, and the men whooped and hollered. The couples danced all around the room with great gusto in what I would call a clumsy polka with an exaggerated stomp to it, and beer flowed from kegs.

"May I have this dance?" Gary said in my ear, and he took off with me with a whoop and a holler of his own in the same polka step. I was out of breath when the music stopped. Gary smiled at me.

"I think I need a drink," I said.

Gary left to get me a beer as I stood against the wall trying to catch my breath. I used to be able to dance all night. I decided that I must be getting older.

"Ya'll dance real purty together," said a girl, who was standing by my elbow. Actually, she wasn't a girl; she was almost a woman. She had long brown hair, green eyes, pale skin with freckles, and a nice smile. "My name's Molly."

"Pleased to meet you, Molly," I said.

We chatted briefly, and she told me that she was nineteen years old and engaged to be married after the fall harvest, which would be in about seven or eight more months.

Gary handed me a beer. "I see you've met Molly. She's Tom's eldest daughter."

I nodded. "She seems very nice."

The person who was the "caller" of the square dance announced, "Step right forward to the Virginia Reel."

"What's that?" I asked.

"Haven't you done a reel before?"

"No."

"It isn't hard. Think of *Gone With the Wind*. That's the dance that Rhett and Scarlett were dancing in a line when she was wearing black and should have been in mourning."

"Oh, yeah - *that* dance."

I was trying to picture the dance in my head for just a few seconds more, when Gary grabbed my arm. "Come on! It's fun!"

I took a few quick swigs out of my beer and joined the line. I loved the sashay down the line, the skipping of feet, and the swift swing of the reel. I enjoyed the square dancing just as much. I had a smile on my face the entire time.

Soon spring was over and the crops were planted. As summer approached, the fruitage of their labor was starting to show. "Knee high by the fourth of July," I had heard someone say in regards to the corn. Actually, it was waist high by this time, so it looked like it was going to be a good crop. They were beginning to worry, though, because there hadn't been very much rain.

"We lost over half of our crop last year because of a draught, and I'm afraid it might happen this year too, if it doesn't rain soon," said Tom. He looked at the sky as though he could make it rain by sheer force of will.

I saw all of the hard work that went into the planting of this field. The very thought that they could lose their crop was extremely disheartening.

"That's how it is," Gary said to me that night, as I got ready for bed. "You're getting to see a good slice of American pie, and sometimes the taste can be bitter."

I put my robe on and sat beside him on the couch. "It must make you angry to see that all of your hard work can go down the drain."

"Yes, it does. I hate wasting my time, but my situation isn't the same as theirs. I'm going to return home to New York one day, go back to my big house, and lead what many think is a privileged life. They'll remain here, cut their losses, and hope for a better year next year."

I turned the television on. Grant's movie was a huge success. It grossed more money the first week than any other movie had before this time, and he was busy working on another one. I watched his interviews and read about him in the papers. It was strange that I should resort to reading about him in the papers and tabloids, but that was the only way I could get any information. Gary watched my face closely as I watched the interview with Grant.

"How are you doing in your personal life, now that you and Joy Bryant have been divorced for well over a year?" the interviewer asked Grant.

Grant smiled. I noticed long ago that a whole room would become more pleasant just in the presence of his smile. "Most of my days are filled with work, and time is a wonderful healer. I'll always love her, but I've also learned that it's possible to go on living. I don't think I would have been able to say that to you a year ago, but I still think about her every day."

"Is there anyone else special in your life?"

"Just my daughter. We try to take care of each other."

"This would be Brandon DeLorrier's daughter."

I saw Grant's face flinch. "No, this would be my daughter. She's his biological child, but she's *my* daughter."

"Of course," said the interviewer, and he went onto the next subject. He interviewed the actress who was Grant's co-star in the movie. She was probably about twenty-five, tall, and blonde. She was very pretty, and she gushed on about how wonderful Grant was to work with. Disgusted, I turned off the television.

Gary stood up and stretched. "Goodnight. Four o'clock comes around early."

"Goodnight," I said. I continued to sit on the couch by myself, fuming. I comforted myself with the thought that this girl had her hair pulled into a ponytail.

-50-

It was almost harvest time. The time they all spent out in the fields increased again. It was Sunday, and they tossed all work aside for the afternoon. There was going to be a family picnic, and then there would be a hayride once it got dark. We had been waiting for the full moon so it would be nice and bright for the ride.

I sat on the back of the wagon with Gary. The smell of hay filled my nostrils, and I decided that it wasn't an unpleasant smell. I'll never smell hay again without thinking of this night. The wagon rolled slowly, and some of the family members sang folksongs, while teenagers tossed hay in each other's faces. It was a night of love, laughter, and fun.

Tom and Kelly had been married for twenty-three years, and it was evident that they were still in love with each other. They held hands, and I loved the way that they looked at each other. I was a hopeless romantic at heart. The whole family was close, and I realized that this was the first time I saw a family interact together in peace and harmony and love. I can't say that it was always peaceful, but I thought that Tom and Kelly did a good job maintaining the peace. I came from a sort of dysfunctional family, and I certainly never learned any family values at home.

Tom was strict with his children, especially the boys, and he tended to discipline them much the same way that Gary had with Alan. He was patient and understanding, but at the same time, he was firm. Kelly was always cooking, sewing, or doing something special for the children. I had never seen the role of a common housewife, but I realized that her role was not at all common, living out here on a farm. She had a wonderful relationship with her children, and I realized that my relationship with Jo Dell had been lacking in that rare, special form of intimacy. Sure, we told stories, baked cookies, and did all of the things that I criticized my mother for not doing, but I was almost always working, and when I wasn't, I was making plans to be working. Kelly's latest project was helping her daughter to plan her wedding.

The air was only slightly cool, and a gentle breeze caressed my hair. Kelly handed me a shawl to put over my shoulders. The wagon went over a bump in the road, and I nearly fell off. Gary used his arms to steady me, and I continued to gaze at the full moon.

One of Tom's younger boys looked at us and said, "Are ya'll in love?"

Gary smiled at me. "We're just good friends," he said.

"Have you ever been in love with a girl before?" the boy asked Gary.

"Sure, but it was a long time ago."

"Who-"

Kelly turned around and said, "Kevin, you mind your own business."

I was disappointed when the hayride was over. I mentioned this to Gary, and he said, "It doesn't have to be over. You and I can take the horses and the wagon and go out on our own private ride."

I thought it was a wonderful idea. It was so peaceful, and I wanted to feel this way for just a little while longer. I sat next to Gary in the wagon as he took the reins.

"So, you've been in love before," I said, trying to bait him.

"A long, long time ago."

"Oh," I said. After all this time, he still wouldn't confide in me.

He looked at me. We could see each other clearly in the moonlight. "You have an amused look on your face, Joy. Is it so funny that I should be in love?"

"Well, you never seemed like much of a womanizer to me."

He laughed. "A womanizer? No, I don't think I ever was that. Let's just say that I learned at a very early age that a man has to take responsibility for the things that he does. Running around having sex with a bunch of women never seemed like a very responsible thing to do."

"I wasn't talking about a bunch of women; I was talking about *any* women. I haven't seen you with anyone."

"Well, what are you? A dog? A cat?"

"We aren't exactly lovers."

"If you're asking me if I'm a virgin, the answer is no, I'm not."

We rode for about two more hours, and then Gary thought that we should let the horses rest. We unhooked the horses from the wagon, fed them, and got them settled into their stalls. As we walked out of the barn, Gary said, "It smells like rain."

I heard rain falling on the roof when I awoke.

"Hello, lazybones," said Gary. He was sitting at his typewriter.

I looked at the clock. It was after six, and I missed helping out with the morning chores. It wasn't expected of me, but I always thought that it was the right thing to do. "You said that you smelled rain," I said, reaching for the coffee pot.

"We need rain, but I hope it doesn't rain too hard. Not enough rain and you ruin your crops; too much rain, and you ruin your crops. It's almost time to harvest, though."

I sat down at the table to enjoy my coffee. I wondered what I was going to do today. I wanted to take a walk, but that idea was out. It was raining now, and it would be too muddy later. As I watched Gary working on his article, a thought came over me. I just realized that Gary and I had spent the better part of a year together, and we had not, even once, had a big argument. Actually, Grant and I seldom argued. I would have expected that; Grant and I were best friends, but Gary and I had so many past disagreements that it was rather surprising that no major arguments had occurred. I assumed once we returned to New York that things would return to normal, and Gary would pick up his white flag. I was reflecting on all of this when Molly came by. She wanted to know if we wanted to go with her and her fiancé to the movies. They didn't get a chance to go very often, so they saved their money only for the very best movies. I agreed to go, and after Molly left, Gary turned around from his chair.

"Do you realize that you just agreed to go and see Grant's new film?"

I hadn't realized it, but I didn't want to make a big deal out of it, so I said, "Oh, that's okay. I guess I'm a little curious."

Once I got to the theater, I was more than a little curious. I couldn't wait for the opening curtain. I sat through those maddening previews with growing impatience. I found out through those previews that Grant was in another movie, scheduled to open in December.

I felt detached from everything as I watched this movie. Grant gave a wonderful performance, and I was very proud of him. It seemed strange to watch him up on the big screen. He achieved something that I was never able to do- a starring role in a major motion picture. It was getting easier for television stars to break into the movies, but it was still difficult to do.

I sat in silence on the way back, but Molly chatted endlessly about the movie. She especially went on and on about Grant, although I really couldn't blame her. I thought he was wonderful, too.

"Well," said Gary, when we were back inside the farmhouse, "how did it feel to be looking at Grant up there on that screen?"

"Very strange, and I'm ashamed to say that I'm very jealous. He made the big time; something that I've never been able to do. But I'm proud of him and glad for him, all at the same time."

Gary walked over to the refrigerator to get a can of soda. "I think you're ready to hear about Cinderella."

"Cinderella?"

"Yes, one of the biggest fallacies concerning love in the whole world." He popped the lid of the can and took a sip out of it.

I sat down in a chair across from him at the kitchen table. "How is it a fallacy?" I asked.

"It doesn't portray real life."

"Most fantasies don't."

"But most people don't think of it as a fantasy. They try to picture themselves in that kind of a situation. Do you remember that I once said that there's someone out there for everybody, and not just one person who was meant to be THE one?"

"Yes, I remember."

"People want to chose people that are just as good, if not better than themselves. Cinderella was beautiful, but do you think she would have wanted to marry that prince if he were buck-toothed and bowlegged? No, he would have to be somewhat esthetically pleasing, or it would have ruined the whole story. The prince was handsome. Beauty, not money, was what he wanted. He wanted someone who looked just as good as he did, and so did she, and that has become the epitome of romance. Look at you; look at whom you chose."

"Grant?"

"No, let's back up a moment. Let's start with Brandon. You wanted someone who was just as good if not better than you were. And what was important to you? Looks? Certainly. But, *stature* - that's what you wanted. Would you have wanted him if he were the prop man or the courier?" He shook his head. "I don't think so."

"You're being unfair," I said. I got up from the table and switched on the television. Grant was being interviewed. I threw my hands up in the air. I couldn't turn on the television anymore without seeing him.

"Am I?" he persisted. He followed me over to the couch. "When you were single, and not involved with anyone, did you have any criteria for choosing a mate?"

I remembered with a start that I had told Marilyn that I wanted someone that just not anyone can have. That certainly would have included Brandon.

He knew by looking at my face that he had struck gold. "You did, didn't you?" he insisted.

"I guess so."

"Look, Grant still loves you. I know for certain that a man cannot love someone with his whole heart and then stop. It just doesn't happen that way." He leaned forward towards me and said earnestly, "Tell Grant that you buried Brandon. Tell him that you chose him. That's all that he wants. He'll know if you're telling the truth, and that's all he ever wanted."

"It's not that easy-" I started to say, but he interrupted me.

"Of course not, because you're still hanging on to Brandon. I knew Brandon a little. He was charming, yes, but he could be cold hearted and selfish, too. Do you think that you would have had as good of a marriage with him as you had with Grant? I know that Grant had one little slip, but do you think that Brandon would have been a good and faithful husband to you? Don't you think it's possible that he would have had more than one little slip?"

"I don't know." I was almost in tears.

"I have one more thing to say, and then I'll shut up. Brandon was a good actor, and he had a lot of fans, but I want you to look at Grant just for a minute." He turned and pointed at Grant's face on the screen. "Grant's not just a good actor- he's a STAR! He'll be bigger than Brandon ever was. Yes, you gave him his start, and you taught him things along the way, but there comes a time when the pupil can surpass the teacher, and that's what happened. You never realized it because you were looking at him every day through those rose colored glasses you like to wear." He took me by the shoulders and said softly, "Joy, Grant is a star."

"It's just too late for us, Gary," I said.

-51-

It rained off and on for two days. The skies were gray and dreary, and it was extremely depressing. The crops were getting a good rain, and it would be okay as long as it didn't rain hard for too long. I went to the window and looked at the sky in the hopes of seeing a few streaks of blue, but there were none. Then I noticed the color of the sky. It was greenish black, and with a start, I realized that I had seen the same color once before. Grant had called it a tornado sky. I said something to Gary, and he said not to worry; there was a storm cellar outside, and the O'Malley's had a basement. He seemed like he wasn't worried at all, but he was probably trying to keep me calm. After I pointed out the color of the sky, he kept walking over to the window, and later he switched on the radio.

Rain was falling harder, and then it changed to hail. I found that I was more than worried; I was downright scared. I remembered that it hailed just before the tornado touched down. "There's a tornado out there, Gary. I just know it."

Gary looked up from his typewriter. "It's possible, I suppose, but not all tornados touch down. Ask the O'Malley's. They're used to this kind of weather."

I nervously looked out the window again, and I noticed that the hail had stopped. "I think I *will* ask the O'Malley's," I said. "Besides, I think I'd rather be in a basement than in a storm cellar. I saw that storm cellar. I might get claustrophobia down there." There was a break in the rain, so I ran between the sprinkles over to the O'Malley's house.

"Oh, yes," said Kelly. "We get this kind of weather every year. We just watch the sky and do what the television and radio says to do."

"I couldn't go through this every year," I said.

I heard the screen door open, and Gary walked in. The television announced that there was a severe thunderstorm warning to be in effect until 5:00 pm.

"That's good news," said Kelly.

"A severe thunderstorm warning is good news?" I asked.

"Sure," said Gary. "At least it's not a tornado watch or warning." Kelly nodded her head in agreement, so I felt a little bit better.

"At the risk of being stupid," I asked, "what's the difference between a watch and a warning?"

"A watch is when conditions are right for a tornado, but none have been sighted, and a warning is that one has been sighted in the area," explained Gary.

I was starting to relax some more, when the radio announced that there was a tornado warning for certain counties. I didn't know which county we were in, but Tom said, "That's us. We better go down in the basement for a while." He picked up a radio and gathered up all of his children, his parents, and the dogs, and we all went downstairs.

Kelly pointed to the southwest corner of the basement. "This is supposed to be the safest corner."

"Why's that, Momma?" asked one of the children.

"I think it has to do with the direction that tornados usually travel in the wind, but the safest place is where you can be free from flying glass and stuff."

I thought we would be safe in the basement, and then I realized that there was no guarantee. We would be safer, but we could still get pushed around down there, and I supposed it was possible to get sucked into the winds. I knew that my imagination was running wild and I was playing out the worst-case scenarios in my mind, but I couldn't help it. I looked at everyone else's face, and no one looked even half as worried as I was. They probably weren't scaring themselves silly.

Gary put his arm around me. "She was in a tornado once," he explained, "and she got stuck for several hours in a storm cellar."

"They should never be taken lightly," said Tom. "We get these warnings every year, but it has been a while since one has touched down in this county. I'm worried about my crops right now, but if one came plowing through here, I'd certainly give 'em all up in exchange for the lives of my family."

I heard a loud siren go off, and it made me jump.

"A tornado has been sighted in town," said Tom. "I hope to God it doesn't touch down."

This was the first sound of real worry that I had heard from anyone else. I held onto Gary a little tighter, and Kelly held onto some of the smaller children. "It'll be okay," said Gary, but he also looked worried.

I kept waiting to hear the roaring power of a tornado tearing through at any moment. The radio then announced that there had been a sighting, but nothing had touched down. About thirty minutes later, the warning was downgraded to a watch. I climbed out of the basement, grateful that nothing had touched down, but I was aware that they were still on the lookout for more. The tornado watch was lifted at four o'clock. The thunderstorm warning remained in effect for another hour, and then it was also lifted. I felt as though a big burden had been removed from my shoulders. We had dinner with the O'Malley's that night because it was still raining heavily, and we didn't want to walk across the open field in the pouring rain.

"You can keep the Midwest," I announced, as someone passed a bowl of potatoes to me. "I've decided that I don't like flatlands and tornados."

Tom sank his fork into a piece of meat on a platter and put it on his plate. "That's the price we pay for living in this area. It's fertile farmland, and a wonderful place to raise children, away from the hustle and bustle of big cities, but this is the tornado belt. We have to take the good with the bad in whatever choices we make, including where we live."

We finished eating, and I helped Kelly and Molly clear the table. Molly was excited about her upcoming wedding. She talked about how wonderful her fiancé was, and how he promised to take her to Hawaii one day, even if he had to save up for the next ten years.

"Have you seen Hawaii?" she asked me.

"I saw it a few years ago, and you'll love it. Some of my warmest memories are from there." Warm was an understatement, I thought. I smiled when I thought about losing my shirt in the ocean. I wondered how often Grant thought about those things. Gary and I waited for a break in the rain, and then we tried to run between the raindrops back to the guesthouse.

Molly came over one day and showed me some pictures out of a catalog of wedding dresses and bridesmaids gowns. "Mamma will have to make the dresses because we really can't afford to buy 'em. But if I could, I'd buy these ones right here," she said, tapping the picture in the catalog with her finger. "These are the purtiest dresses I ever did see."

I looked at the pictures. I thought they were awful, but I didn't want to hurt her feelings. "When is she going to start making the dresses?" I asked.

"In October, after the harvest of the corn. I heard Gary say that you'd stay through the harvest, but I hope you'll stay till I get married.

It won't be very long after the harvest. That's what I came by to ask you. Can you please not go until then?"

I saw tears in her eyes, and my heart went out to her. "I'm sure something can be arranged," I said.

Gary was standing in the doorway, and I looked at him. He nodded his head, so I knew we would at least stay until the wedding. I wondered if we would be safe when we returned home, but Gary seemed to think so.

After Molly went home, I realized that she had left the catalogs on the table. I picked them up. "Oh, Gary, these are hideous, and I sure wouldn't be caught dead in one of them, but she thinks they're the most beautiful dresses in the world. Do you think we can buy them for her?"

"I can talk to Tom, and if he agrees, then we will. I don't want to offend them with the fact that we have money. He's a proud man, and he's proud of what he can provide for his children."

"Kelly will be making the dresses soon, so we have to ask him before she gets started."

It rained again during the night, but the sun was shining brightly the next morning. Everyone thought it would be a good idea to go fishing and have a fish boil that evening. It would be like having an evening picnic.

We took our fishing poles down to the brook that morning and tried to catch a few fish. It was muddy because of the rain, but it didn't bother me very much. It would all come off in the wash. I knew that Gary was watching to see if I would be squeamish about putting a worm on the hook, so I decided not to give him any pleasure. I grabbed the wiggling worm and stuck a hook right through its head, just as I saw one of the boys do.

Some of the children were swimming a little further down. I watched as they jumped in and splashed around. A rope was attached to a nearby tree, and some of the bigger boys swung across to the other side, or let out Tarzan calls and jumped in. I shook my head with wonder. I never had a chance to experience any of this. I was too busy working, and I never had the time just to be a little kid.

My train of thought was broken when Tom yelled at the boys because they were scaring the fish away. He told them to let us catch the fish we needed, and then they could splash and play all they wanted.

The fish was delicious, and it was even better because we caught them ourselves. Actually, I didn't catch a single fish, but I had fun trying. I was beginning to regret having to go home, but I knew that this wasn't reality for me. It was an escape, just like Gary said it would be. If I had some place to go like this when I was young, I might have had a different perspective on the world. I would have known how other people lived, worked, and loved. I saw Gary talking to Tom, and I hoped they were discussing the possibility of us buying the dresses.

"It's okay. We can buy the dresses," Gary told me that night.

I picked up the catalog and frowned. "These dresses are so ugly. I wonder if we should get her something else, like this." I pointed to another dress, which was probably five times more expensive.

Gary shook his head. "You can't make a silk purse out of a sow's ear."

"That's rude!"

"I don't intend to be rude, just realistic. Look, would Tom look good dressed in a top hat and tails at a fancy Hollywood ball? Don't you think he'd just look like an overdressed turkey?"

I laughed, but I could understand.

"That's how this would be. You have to give people the respect of being who they are. Her dreams aren't as big or fancy as yours, and because of that, what she considers pretty, you don't. On the other hand, the things that you think are pretty Princess Diana would probably have gagged on. Wasn't her wedding dress just a little bit over the top for you?"

"I have to admit that I wouldn't have looked good in it," I said.

He tapped the magazine with his finger. "This dress is her dream, so buy this one for her, and she'll feel like a princess."

I knew he was right. "Okay," I said.

A few days later, we received a surprise visit from Alan. I was sitting on the porch that morning, enjoying the breeze and listening to the birds sing, when he drove up into the yard. I had to look twice to make sure I wasn't dreaming. Gary was inside the house, but he must have heard the car and looked out the window. He was out of the house and down the steps in a flash. They embraced and began talking excitedly. It dawned upon me that Gary hadn't seen him for several months. Alan looked toward the porch where I was sitting, and I waved and stood up. He ran up the porch steps two at a time and hugged me.

"What a surprise!" I said. "What brings you here?"

"Oh, I guess I just wanted to see Gary, and I haven't seen any of the family here for many years. I spent a few summers here when I was a kid."

"Yes, Gary told me." I had the impression that there was more to it than that, so I excused myself to go inside the house. Maybe then, Alan would come out and tell Gary why he came.

They sat on the porch swing together. I could hear bits and pieces of their conversation, but I wasn't trying to eavesdrop. The walls were just thin. At least, that's what I told myself. They talked about college and how things were in general. I heard Gary say, "You came up here to talk to me about something." It was more of a statement than a question. I didn't hear Alan's response, and then I heard Gary ask, "Is it serious?" There was another pause, and then he said, "You know you can tell me anything, don't you? Why don't we go for a walk down by the brook, and you can tell me all about it."

I walked to the window and looked out, so I was being nosy after all. I saw them down by the brook, and they looked like they were having a very serious conversation. Then their demeanor changed, and they seemed more relaxed. Soon they were wading in the brook and skipping stones across the widest part of the water. After several minutes, I saw them walking back to the house. As they came within earshot, I heard Gary say to Alan, "No, we're just friends. She needs to clear her head, and she needs a friend."

I thought about that statement for a long time. That I needed to clear my head certainly was true. While Alan and Gary were visiting with each other on the porch, I wandered down by the brook. I sat down on a large stone and stuck my bare feet in the water. I finally got a chance to see everyday people doing everyday things. I asked myself if I would have wanted to live that way, especially since I had led a different life. I always wondered if my kind of life was worth it. Tom would say "no," but I had to admit that I would finally be able to say "yes" for myself.

Money and fame certainly had its advantages. I liked pearl studded organza wedding dresses, satin ballroom gowns, and silk pajamas, and not frilly party dresses with elastic puffy sleeves and veils that looked like mosquito netting. I tried to balance the pros and the cons, and I decided that there were definite advantages and disadvantages, as there were in all things. The problem always was that I wanted to have my cake and eat it, too. I could see that plainly now. I waded out of the water and walked back towards the house. Alan wasn't staying very long, and I didn't want to miss a chance to be able to visit with him.

That night when I went to bed, I overheard part of a conversation between Gary and Alan. They were sitting on the couch when I excused myself to go to bed. I wasn't exactly tired, but I thought that they should be able to visit with each other in private since Alan was leaving in the morning.

"You've never told her, have you?" asked Alan.

"No."

"Why not?"

"It just never came up."

"Things are different today, Gary. It's almost a new millennium. The stigma that it once was is gone."

I didn't hear Gary give an answer to that statement. Then I heard Alan ask, "If you could go back and change anything at this point, would you?"

"Not on your life," Gary said.

Gary didn't tell me about the problem that made Alan drive all the way out there to talk to him about, but I assumed that it was resolved because Alan left the next day in good spirits.

-52-

The dresses arrived two weeks later. Kelly was thrilled. "I was running out of excuses to tell her as to why I hadn't started making 'em." Kelly had given me the correct sizes to order for all of the dresses.

"Shall we call Molly to come down?" I asked.

Kelly walked over to the stairway. "Molly!" she yelled. "Come on down here. Joyce has something to show you."

I'll never forget the expression on her face when she opened the boxes. Her eyes opened wide, and she put her hand over her mouth. "Oh, Momma, Joyce, have you ever seen anything so beautiful in all of your born days?" Her eyes filled with tears, and she hugged my neck. "Oh, thank you, thank you; there can't be a greater friend than you," and she went off to try the gown on.

She came down the stairs moments later looking radiant in her dress. She handed me one of the bridesmaid's dresses. "This one's for you," she said. "I asked Momma to make one in your size."

I successfully made the smile freeze on my face. "Thank you," I said. Out of the corner of my eye, I could see Gary smiling.

As the wedding approached, I went over to the big farmhouse to help Kelly as much as I could. We peeled potatoes and carrots, pared apples, and baked bread. She made several pies, and she was even going to make the wedding cake. I marveled at what a whiz she was in the kitchen. I felt silly trying to help out because I never learned to cook very well. She handed me a tomato to slice, and I didn't know how. I wasn't sure if I should slice it in horizontal rows, or if I should try to make wedges out of it. I decided that wedges were harder, so I began to slice them in rows. If I had two left feet in Bordeaux's studio, I had two left hands in Kelly's kitchen, and I told her so.

"Gary told me you were a city girl," she said. "We can't make a farm girl out of you any more than you can make city folk out of us, although you sure have been wonderful at trying. I sure am going to miss you when you leave."

"I'll miss you, too," I said, and I meant every word.

"I hope it isn't going to bother you watching a wedding. Gary told me when you first got here that you were trying to mend a broken heart. He thought we'd be good medicine for you."

"I've been trying, and it's been over two years. I stopped crying a long time ago, but it's difficult to forget about so many years."

"You don't want to forget, honey. All you need is to be able to remember without pain."

"I haven't quite gotten to that place. I haven't loved that many people in my life. Once I love someone, it's hard to stop."

"You'll be able to let go one day, and then you'll know that it's time to start livin' and lovin' again."

Those were wise and truthful words. I had been able to remember Brandon without awful pain after the first two years or so, yet I still hung onto him, and I caused myself and Grant unnecessary pain. There were times when I realized that I would have been perfectly happy married to Grant if I hadn't known Brandon. I was still thinking about this as I walked back to our little yellow farmhouse. Tomorrow was the wedding, and then Gary and I would be returning to New York.

The wedding was in the backyard of Will O'Malley's home. He had the most beautiful yard. Green hedges lined the entire area, and fresh flowers had been planted. Honeysuckle was still in bloom, and bouquets of roses were scattered throughout the yard. A homemade gazebo was draped with green ivy, and roses were weaved throughout the trellises. Several straight-backed chairs were set up on the lawn.

I examined my reflection in the mirror and saw Gary watching me out of the corner of his eye. "I'm glad you're so amused," I said.

"It's not you, but I guess that dress will have to make the most out of having you wear it."

I stuck my tongue out at him. "Save your sarcasm for your column."

"I did," said Gary.

I pulled at the puffy elastic sleeves that pinched my upper arms and smoothed the ruffles that were on the front of my dress. The whole dress was layered in ruffles. I looked like I was attending a square dance rather than a wedding. Oh, well, I told myself; at least the color wasn't orange.

The whole family had come together. They were all laughing and talking, and the children were running and playing. Instead of a stuffy, formal event, it was an informal and joyous occasion. The music began to play, and people took their seats.

"At least it's not going to rain," I heard Tom say, as he and Molly joined arms together.

"What would you have done if it had rained?" I asked another bridesmaid.

She looked at me as though I had just asked the stupidest question in the whole world. "We'd a had it in the barn," she said.

The music was turned up louder, and we were given our cue to walk from the house down a piece of red carpet that was rolled out to the gazebo. I marched out with my head held high and tried to forget about the dress. As I took my place near the gazebo, the music switched to *The Wedding March.* I turned around and watched, as Tom and Molly began their walk down the red carpet. She positively glowed, and Tom was so proud, he could have burst his buttons. Kelly dabbed her eyes with a handkerchief, and the groom nervously awaited the arrival of his bride.

I watched with a lump in my throat as they exchanged rings and vowed their love. I remembered my own wedding, and how Grant and I vowed to love each other that way. I remembered the look on Grant's face as he repeated his vows, and how his voice faltered just for a moment. I felt a sudden, deep regret for the loss of promised love.

The reception lifted my spirits. We danced the Virginia Reel, and then everyone broke out into their spirited polka step. This wasn't an atmosphere in which someone could stay sad for very long.

"Gary tells me you'll be leaving tomorrow," Kelly said to me.

"As much as I've enjoyed my stay, I do have another life."

Kelly nodded. "Tom recently told me. I thought you looked familiar, but I couldn't quite place you. I haven't told anyone else though, although you never know; we're not all backward; some may have figured it all out. I read all about your divorce after it happened. You always seemed a little sad."

"I've been doing all right. Maybe when I get back home, I'll try to patch things up with Grant. Gary has been telling me to."

"Gary? Really?" She had a very surprised expression on her face.

"Why are you so surprised?"

"Oh, surely you must know."

"What?"

"Gary is in love with you."

"Oh, I don't think so. It's not possible."

"Why not? Why don't you ask him? Or ask him the question that my son did at the hayride. Do you remember the question?"

I nodded and smiled.

She pressed my arm. "I saw the look on Gary's face when my son asked him that question, so I made him keep still. Ask him if he's ever been in love before, and then watch his face. He's head over heels in love with you."

After the wedding was over, we all helped clean up while Molly and her new husband rode off into the sunset in their horse and buggy. It was going to be a beautiful evening. I sat on the porch swing of our farmhouse and listened to the crickets while fireflies danced in the dusk. Gary came out and sat on the steps.

"Gary, Kelly told me to ask you a question."

"What's that?"

"It's the one Kevin asked you at the hayride. Remember? He asked if you've ever been in love."

Gary stared at the orange sunset, and without taking his eyes off of the sky, he replied, "And I believe my answer was, 'a long time ago.'" After a few moments, Gary got up from the porch and sat beside me in the swing. "Why does it seem strange to you? It might have been a long time ago, but I still remember what it feels like to be in love. I remember what it's like to love someone so much that you want to breathe in the same air that they breathe and touch all the things they've touched. It's enough just to be near them. You're afraid to ask for more, just in case you might spoil it, and it blows away in the wind."

"Wow. Did you ever tell this person that you felt this way?"

"I didn't use those very words, but, yes, I told this person."

"Well, I can't imagine anyone not wanting to be with you. What happened?"

"I asked her to marry me."

My heart skipped a beat. Did he say *her?*

"And what did she say?" I asked. My voice sounded hoarse.

"She turned me down. She said that I was a social climber and an opportunist."

My own words from long ago came flooding back to me from across an ocean of years. I gasped and put my hand over my mouth. "Oh, my God," I said softly. "Me?"

He nodded sadly, and I laid my head on his shoulder. We swung quietly back and forth as we watched the orange in the sky turn light gray, and finally it was dark. We walked back inside the farmhouse.

The next morning, Gary informed me that he wanted to make one more stop before returning to New York.

"Where do you want to go?"

"England," he said.

I was incredulous. "England? What in the world will we do there?"

"I have business there. I agreed to do a piece on mad cow disease, and I'd like to take you with me."

"Mad cow disease?"

"Yeah, it's making national headlines again. They think there's a possibility it could enter the blood supply."

I sat my coffee cup down on the table with a thud. "But, England! Are you serious?"

"Oh, yes," he nodded. "I'm very serious."

53

We loaded our bags in the car, and Tom and Kelly came over to say goodbye. Gary and Tom shook hands, and I hugged Kelly.

"Ya'll can come back to visit us anytime," said Kelly.

"Yes," agreed Tom. "We can always use an extra pair of hands, even if they do belong to city folk."

Gary and I drove to the airport in Saint Louis, and from there we took an international flight to London. The sky was blanketed with a thick fog as we stepped off the plane in London. It was hard to see the sidewalk. "This is like my dream," I remarked.

"Are you still having that dream?"

"I've been getting it more and more frequently."

The last time I had the dream, I got down to the pavement, and I could see the outline of a man wearing an overcoat, trousers, and a pair of shoes. I tried to make an effort to notice the surroundings, and I noticed that it looked like a London Fog type of coat, but they were so common that everyone was wearing one. Even Gary had one.

We spent several days in London, and once we passed the Royal Academy of Dramatic Art. I remembered that Brandon had won a scholarship there when he was sixteen years old. It was a very prestigious dramatic art school, and very unusual for anyone to be accepted under the age of eighteen. Brandon was also a stage actor with the Royal Shakespeare Company, and that was how he was discovered and given an opportunity to perform on Broadway. Talent scouts noticed his potential and enticed him to try his hand at Hollywood. It seemed very strange to be standing on the same ground that he walked on and to see buildings that had stages in which he had played.

We also spent several days visiting farms and dairies, and talking with different health and government officials while Gary gathered information for his piece on mad cow disease. I was unaware of how much work went into an investigation of a small article that would run in the paper.

Gary told me that the next place we would go was called Cowes. At first I misunderstood him. I thought he was taking me to see a place with more cows, but this was not the case. Cowes was located on the Isle of Wright, an island just off of the southern coast of England, and the significance of this place to me was that it was the birthplace and final resting place of Brandon DeLorrier.

My breath was coming in short gasps as I neared the grave, and my legs felt weak. Gary let go of my hand and encouraged me to step forward on my own and walk up to the graves. "Take all of the time you need," he said.

I furtively approached the tombstones, and I caught sight of the grave that bore his name. Brandon DeLorrier: January 29, 1955–October 10, 1981. Full memory of that awful day came back so vividly that I could feel the sharpness of the pain. I knelt down on the ground in front of the grave and looked at it for a long time. Then I slowly reached out with my hand and traced the letters of his name that were etched in the stone with the tips of my fingers.

"I loved you so much," I said. "I used to think that it was all a bad dream and that I'd wake up and you'd be here with me. You would hold my hand and smile, and we'd laugh because dreams can be so silly and seem so real. When I realized it wasn't a dream, a part of me died, too. But lately, I have begun to think that it didn't die; perhaps it was only sleeping, and that maybe one day I can wake up and feel whole again. It has been so long since I've felt whole." I looked out at the green rolling hills and contrasting blue sky. "This is a beautiful place to spend eternity," I said, stroking the stone. "You're really at peace; I know that now, but I need peace, too. I believe that you loved me enough to want that for me." I kissed my fingers and touched his name with them. "Goodbye, my love."

I walked back to where Gary was standing. He reached out with both hands and wiped the tears that were on my face with his fingers. They had rolled out without any effort, and I was unaware of them until he brushed them away. He put his arm around me, and I laid my head on his shoulder and leaned against him as we exited the cemetery.

We didn't speak very much to each other that night. I was lost in thought, and Gary let me work though this without any distraction. I was remembering Brandon, how handsome he was, and how he made me feel as if I were the most important person in the world. He said that we could have a love that few people would ever see. But it was one that we would never see ourselves. I buried Brandon DeLorrier in my heart that night at long last.

We stayed in England for one more week while Gary put his piece together on mad cow disease. The very last night before we went home, we shared a wonderful dinner in London, and then we went to the theater. I saw Big Ben, and I was pleased that we took just this moment to drive by it because I heard the great clock strike midnight.

"I've wanted to ask you a question for a couple of weeks now," said Gary.

"Why haven't you?"

He shrugged his shoulders. "I don't know. I guess I was waiting for just the right time. Why did you think that I was an opportunist? I honestly didn't want you because you were famous. I have to admit that your celebrity did make you what you were; we're all the sum of our experiences. I couldn't have one without the other, but I had no ulterior motive. I was so hurt that I took out revenge against you in the only way that I knew how."

"Your poisoned pen," I said.

"Yes."

"I thought you were gay."

"What?" he exclaimed in genuine surprise. "What made you think that?"

"You never tried to make out with me at all, for one."

"I was afraid to."

"Why?"

"I didn't want to get you pregnant. Those things were known to happen. One kiss almost always leads to another." He was silent for a moment, and then he said, "Look, there had to have been another reason other than the fact that I wouldn't make out with you. What made you believe this?"

"Well," I hesitated, but then I blurted out the rest of it. "Leisel told me."

"Leisel told you that I was gay?" He looked up toward the sky and said, "Why in the name of God am I not surprised?" He turned back to me and said, "How did she convince you of this?"

I told Gary about being in the restaurant and hearing his friend talk about how he hadn't told me his "little secret," and how marrying me wouldn't have hurt his career. "I got up and ran out. I forgot all about Leisel, who was supposed to join me."

He became very quiet and said nothing to me for the rest of the ride home.

We had adjoining rooms at the hotel, but we left the door between them open so we could come and go as we pleased. I was used to sharing a farmhouse with Gary, so it seemed silly to have my own separate room completely shut off from his. I had my nightgown on, and Gary was sitting in a chair next to my bed, when he suddenly said, "I have it all figured out now. I might be missing a few stray pieces that Leisel will have to help you with, but now I understand the whole diabolical plot."

"Diabolical plot?"

"Yes," he said, as he got up from the chair. "It was brilliant." There was a complementary bottle of champagne in a small refrigerator in my room. I never opened it because it was too much to drink by myself, and I had still never seen Gary drink alcohol. He took the bottle from the refrigerator and began to remove the cork. Champagne bottles always made me nervous until they were opened because I always envisioned the cork flying across the room and striking me in the face. There was a loud popping sound as it was released, and he poured two bubbling glasses.

"Are you ready for a very long, very overdue story?" he asked, as he handed me my glass and sat beside me on the bed.

I nodded my head and listened intently as he took my hand in his and poured out a very sinister story, indeed.

"First of all," he said, "let's start with Alan."

"Alan? Your brother?"

"No. You're the one that assumed Alan was my brother, and I didn't correct you. Alan is not my brother. Alan is my son."

"What?" I exclaimed in extreme surprise. I took a large sip out of the champagne glass. Gary probably opened the bottle because he knew that I was going to need it.

"Alan is my son. *And* Leisel's son."

My mind raced. Leisel's son! I gasped and put my hand over my mouth. Leisel's son! I sat in stunned silence for a few moments. "So it was a boy," I said, more to myself than to him. When I recovered from the shock, I said, "I never knew if it was a boy or a girl. It was a boy. I assumed the father was Bill, her boyfriend. She acted strangely the whole time, and she even refused to acknowledge the fact that she was pregnant."

"She got pregnant on purpose. I talked to her about it, and she didn't deny it. I had a girlfriend at the time. Her name was Anne. We were in love when we were in high school, and we talked about having a future together after college. Leisel and I were very good friends, ever since grade school. We ran with the same crowd, and we saw each other quite a bit. I knew that she was attracted to me, but I didn't feel the same way. I loved Anne. Once I went to a party and got very drunk. After the party, I let my guard down and had sex with Anne. I wasn't aware of what I was doing at the time. I knew that I did it, but I wasn't in control of the situation, and things got out of hand. Alcohol seems to affect me that way, and that's why I seldom drink anything at all. I promised my father never to do this again, and I really intended to keep my promise. One night, Leisel planned a party a few days after our high school junior prom. I thought Anne would be there, but she never showed up. I found out later that she wasn't invited, which was strange because she was always invited to the same things that I was.

"Leisel handed me a glass of iced tea, and I drank it. I thought it tasted funny, but she said it was just brewed differently. I found out later that it was called a Long Island Iced Tea, made out of seven different kinds of liquor. One or two of those can sink a battleship, and I probably had two or three. Before I knew it, I woke up with Leisel. She admitted that she tried to get me drunk because she was aware that I had let my guard down once before. But the real kicker was that she also admitted to trying to get pregnant on purpose. She went so far as to read a book on how to tell when the best time is to get pregnant, and she made her move. I know this all sounds strange, but it's the truth."

I shook my head. Yes, I believed Leisel would do that.

"I talked to my father about it, and he advised me not to marry her if I didn't love her. I would have married her if he had told me to. He tried his best to teach us to take responsibility for things we did, but he also believed in love. He said I would give up every dream I ever had."

"He was very wise."

"Yes, he was," agreed Gary. "I felt very relieved after I talked to him. He always maintained a philosophy that there wasn't anything that couldn't be fixed. I told Leisel that I'd support whatever decision she made, but I wouldn't marry her. It might have been different if she hadn't used deception. She did consider abortion, but she went through a whole lot of trouble to hatch this plan. Just to get me drunk enough was one miracle, and getting pregnant was another. Then she told me that she had decided upon adoption. I couldn't let that happen. I had another talk with my father and told him that I wanted to raise the baby myself."

"Did he try to talk you out of it?"

"No, but he wanted me to understand all it would entail. He told me it's a huge responsibility to be a father. It's more than being a biological father, or even giving a child a name. I'd have to give my time and my love, and it would take a whole chunk out of my life. He pointed out that babies cry at night, and I'd have to get up to feed and change it. And then I'd have to go to school. All of my friends would be able to go to parties, and I'd be home every night. He reminded me that my mother wasn't well. She had raised four sons; she wouldn't be able to take care of another. He made it perfectly clear that I would raise my own child."

"Was he angry like Leisel's mother was?"

"No, he only said that he was disappointed because I had done things which would make my life more difficult. He was very supportive. He told the rest of the family that Alan would be raised in a household of adults and it would be unfair to have six bosses running around telling him what to do. He told them that all decisions, especially in matters of discipline, must be deferred to me."

"How did you ever talk Leisel into going along with this?"

"Well, I remember her asking me, 'Are you crazy? What do you know about babies?' I said I knew as much as any new parent. I told her that I couldn't bear the thought of her giving my child to a complete stranger. I would wonder for the rest of my life whatever became of my son or daughter. I said if she cared anything about me at all, she wouldn't do this. I was prepared to go to court and fight for my own child, but that never became necessary."

Leisel gave up all the rights to her child and promised that she wouldn't try to wrangle custody from him at a later time. She said that she wouldn't interfere with how he was raised, and she did keep her promise. Leisel knew how to keep secrets, and evidently she also knew how to keep a promise.

"I took care of him myself from the day he was born," Gary told me. "I never left the house unless he was fast asleep in bed, and then someone in the family- usually Zachary- would agree to watch him for me while I went out. That's why I seldom showed up until 8:30 or 9:00."

"I still don't understand why she set me up with you."

"That's the part that I had to piece together in my head, but it's the easiest part to explain. She never stopped hoping that we'd get together. We might have, except that I was still with Anne. Anne accepted the fact that I had a son, and she was willing to become his mother. Then one day, Leisel came to my door asking me how I'd feel about taking her famous cousin out. I couldn't turn that down. There wasn't one red-blooded American young man who wouldn't have given his eyeteeth and right nut for a date with you."

I felt myself blush.

"I didn't know how it would go, or how we'd get along, but I liked you from the start. This hurt Anne, of course, who considered it a second betrayal, and she broke it off with me."

I remembered a young, pretty girl who watched Gary and I at the college dance. So, that was Anne. I asked Leisel who she was, and she pretended not to know.

"Leisel expected me to break up with Anne, but she never expected us to fall in love. She had to devise a way to undo it. She orchestrated that day in the restaurant; I know it. I know it because of something my friend said to me. My friend, Brian, who was also a good friend of Leisel's, was gay. He was very open about it. We used to meet everyday for breakfast. In addition to working for the newspaper, I wrote greeting cards, and he was an artist, so he did my illustrations. That's how I paid for college. My family had money, but I wanted to put myself through college. Brian died several years ago, and when I visited him shortly before he died, he whispered something very strange. He said, 'I'm sorry I set you up. I ruined your life.' I tried to get him to explain, but he was too weak, and he never did. It's all so clear now. Leisel met him and told him what to say for your ears. He said something about my little secret and how it wouldn't hurt my career if I married you. That was all you needed to hear. It was ingenious, but no one has ever disputed the fact that Leisel is ingenious."

I put my head in my hands. It was all so incredible, but at the same time, I knew that every word was true. "That explains why she has been so distant with me. She has been living with that guilt all of these years." I looked up at him. "Why didn't you tell me about Alan?"

"I was an teenaged unwed father. Unwed mothers weren't exactly accepted with open arms back then. A teenaged unwed father raising his own son was almost unheard of. I wanted to make sure that you loved me first. I was going to tell you, but every time I tried, the words got stuck in my throat. I made up my mind that night to tell you, but I never got that far. I'm not sorry that I had Alan. I tried to be a good father to him, as good of a father as mine was to me, and I tried to raise him right. He has been a good son to me."

I had to agree with that. I had witnessed the love they had between them. I assumed that it was an unusual situation between brothers, and now I knew that it was a deep love between a father and his son.

"I've always loved you, Joy. I loved you so much that I told myself I'd never marry anyone unless I felt the same way about someone again. I don't believe in Cinderella. I don't believe that you are the only person that I could ever love, but I just never felt that way again. So, you see, Leisel has tried to ruin my life twice."

I became very angry with Leisel for toying with our lives. I knew that she paid a high price for doing it because she was never truly happy. Some of her zest for life had evaporated in the process.

Gary set his untouched glass of champagne down on the bedside table and looked directly into my eyes. "Joy," he said, "I know it was a long time ago, but would you have married me if Leisel hadn't cast cruel doubts?"

It was a long time ago, but it was as though it had all happened yesterday. "Yes, Gary," I said. "I would have married you." And for the first time in almost twenty years, Gary leaned over and kissed me. His kiss was gentle and sweet, yet full of yearning. I wrapped my arms around his neck and kissed him back. I remember feeling like I was falling with him in slow motion across the bed. He held me against him, and I felt his body pressing into mine. He continued to kiss me with a building passion that had been repressed for almost twenty years. Then he hesitated. "I don't want to complicate your life any more than it already is," he whispered.

"It's okay, Gary," I assured him. "We've waited nearly twenty years."

He touched and kissed my body everywhere. It was as though he couldn't get enough of his skin touching mine. Dawn's morning light was making a subtle appearance across the sky when Gary finally turned to me and whispered, "I have loved you for so long, Joy. I don't want to go through the rest of my life letting you slip through my fingers. Will you marry me when we get back home?"

It would have been very easy at that moment to say, "Yes," but I couldn't. Instead I said, "When we get back home and our lives return to normal, I think we should talk about it again. There are loose threads that need to be cut, and I can't snip them until I get back to New York."

His voice sounded disappointed, but he tried to hide it. "At least you didn't tell me, 'No,'" he said.

"No, I didn't. I'll seriously consider it, I promise." I reached up and kissed him again. "We have tonight. Let's enjoy tonight, and then we'll worry about tomorrow, tomorrow."

Gary wrapped his arms around me tighter and began to kiss me, and once again, we matched each other perfectly in a beautifully choreographed dance of love.

54

After being gone for over a year, it seemed strange to be home. The house was full of memories from Grant, and I decided that I would have no real peace unless I moved out or sold it. We remodeled every room to suit our tastes. It no longer looked like the house that Carolyn and I grew up in. To me, all houses have a personality. When we were children, that house had my mother's cold and unfeeling personality. Later, after Grant and I did a major overhaul, it housed some of Grant's presence, and now I found it difficult to build a new life when I expected Grant to walk out of every room at any time. I spoke to Grant, who told me to go ahead and sell it if I wanted to. After I returned home, I noticed a sense of peace that I never felt before, or had not experienced for a very long time. The visor grip that Brandon's memory held on my heart had been released, and I felt like I could let go of Grant, too.

I went to see Carolyn. She was aloof at first, much the same way as when we were children and I had been away for a long period of time, but then she warmed back up to me. I asked if she was interested in the house, or did she think we should sell it. She was still half owner of the house because, although I lived in it, I never bought out the equity from her. I should have; I didn't know why I hadn't done so.

"No," said Carolyn, "I don't think that Thor would be comfortable there. It's much too big, anyway."

"Maybe I'll put out the word that we're interested in selling. Someone in the neighborhood will probably want it."

There hadn't been a house available in the neighborhood for several years that I was aware of, but nothing was ever formally up for sale, so it was hard to know for sure. Word leaked out, usually informally, and the houses were sold quickly.

I asked her how she and Thor were getting along, and to my surprise, she opened up and talked to me.

"I still get the feeling that he's analyzing me all of the time. Did you feel that way with Grant?"

"Sometimes, but I still think that's a normal feeling when you're around someone who has special training. Are you happy?"

"I guess so. Marriage isn't what I thought it would be. He's not very romantic, you know. He hardly ever wants to make love. Is that normal? Did Grant ever stop wanting to make love to you?"

"No," I said. "Grant and I had a very healthy sex life."

"Oh," she said. She seemed somewhat disappointed. "It hurts, you know. It hurts when you have a husband who doesn't pay much physical attention to you. At first I thought that I was the problem, and that maybe he didn't find me attractive anymore, but I don't think that's the reason. All he ever wants to do is work and study. He writes journals half of the night. Sometimes I wonder why he ever wanted to marry me. To stay close to Grant, I think; you know- to keep it in the family."

"Have you ever thought about leaving?"

"Sure, but then it would just cause other problems. I don't want to make any major changes. I don't want to be like Leisel and bump along from one relationship to another. I like stability, and Thor does offer that, if nothing else."

I could understand that. She never did like very many changes.

"You know," said Carolyn, "if you sell that house, Grant might not come back to New York. Are you sure that you want to break all ties to him completely?"

"I don't want to break all ties. I want to stay on good terms with him, but I have to break some of them. We're divorced. We've been apart now for over two years. His life is going on. I've seen the beautiful company that he keeps. Some of them are ten years younger than I am."

"But he still loves you," Carolyn said.

"I don't know that for sure anymore. I'm a firm believer that absence doesn't always make the heart grow fonder."

"It worked that way with Brandon," she said. She knew that it would irritate me, but she said it anyway.

"Brandon's dead now," I said, and then I made some excuse to leave.

I decided to sell the house and rent another apartment in Manhattan. The suburbs hold a special charm because they're just out of reach of the hustle-bustle of the big city, yet close enough not to be deprived of the benefit of it. I considered looking into nearby New

Rochelle, but then I decided against it. I wanted to surround myself with other members of the performing arts again. I called Andrew to let him know that I was interested in working again.

Gary seemed pleased that I was letting go little by little, and that I was trying to start a new life and be happy. He also had an apartment in Manhattan, which was not very far from mine, and he came over quite often to visit me. He hadn't asked me to marry him again since our return, although I was expecting him to broach the subject at any time. I decided that if he asked me again, I would agree to become his wife.

-55-

I walked over to Leisel's house and rang the doorbell. I wanted to hear in her own words and from her own mouth why she sabotaged my relationship with Gary so many years ago. I was shocked when I saw her. She was forty years old now, but she looked older. I heard that she was an alcoholic, and that's probably why she looked older than she was. She seemed sober enough to me when I showed up at her door. She let me in, and we sat down on the couch together. She knew it wasn't a social call, and instead of relaxing on the couch, she sat on the edge of it as though she could get up suddenly and walk away if the conversation didn't suit her. I, on the other hand, sat back on the couch and got comfortable. I wasn't about to leave until I got satisfactory answers, and with Lesiel, I knew that this could take all night.

"I want to hear this from you," I said, and then I told her the story that I knew.

"It looks like there's not much left to tell," said Leisel.

"But why? Why would you do that?"

She shrugged her shoulders. "I loved Gary. Remember how crazy you were about Brandon? Well, I was just as much in love with Gary as you were with Brandon. I've loved him since I was six years old. I always believed that Gary would have looked at me differently if it weren't for Anne. I was trying to break them up. I never thought you two would fall in love. I expected you to marry some big movie star like Brandon or Grant, but never Gary."

"And why not Gary?"

"Gary was a nineteen or twenty year old college boy. He hadn't made a name for himself at that time. You used to say that you wanted somebody that just not anyone could have. He almost married Anne, and as far as I was concerned, she was anyone, the same as everybody else. Look, you got together with Brandon after you and Gary broke up.

Do you honestly think that you would have stayed with Gary while Brandon was standing there, holding his arms out to you?"

"I can't say I would have, and I can't say that I wouldn't have. I might not have met Brandon again if I had stayed with Gary. I took that Broadway job to keep myself busy right after Gary and I broke up, thanks to you, it seems. If I hadn't, I might not have run into Brandon again, and I might have been spared the biggest heartache in my life, so you can't go back and re-write history according to what we might or might not have done." I noticed that she was finally starting to relax because she was no longer sitting on the edge of the couch. She seemed relieved to discuss this.

"I didn't realize the extent of what I did until after it was done. Gary was devastated, and it got to the point that I couldn't look you in the eyes anymore."

"I can see why."

"Look," she pleaded, "it hasn't been easy for me, either. I hatched a plan and it blew up in my face. I had a baby that I had to give up, and I never ended up with Gary in the long run. It was all for nothing. Everything that I ever wanted and everything that I ever planned for flew out of the window all at once. I don't think I've had a moment's peace with myself. You can hate me if you want to, but you can't despise me any more than I despise myself."

I thought that I would stay mad, but I found myself feeling very sorry for her. "Why didn't you ever have anything to do with your son?" I asked.

"I wanted to believe that it never happened. It was like if it never happened, then things could go back the way they were before. It doesn't work that way; I know that now."

"Did Gary tell you that you couldn't see him?" I wanted to know this because if that were so, it would have been a very cruel thing to do. He made her give up all right of custody in the adoption, but that wasn't the same thing.

"No, I just thought that it was the right thing to do. By the time I finally realized that I couldn't go back to being the carefree girl that I was, I had to face another hard, cold fact that so many years had gone by." I looked at her skeptically, and she threw her hands up in the air. "Come on, Joy, was I supposed to go up to a ten-year old child and say, 'Hi! I'm your mother. I've lived in this town all of my life, but I never wanted to believe that you had been born. That's why we've never met before?'"

"No, but I think you could have put it in words that might have been more acceptable."

"I think that after ten years, Gary wouldn't have let me see him, anyway. If I were a mother, and the kid's father suddenly showed up after ten years, I don't think I'd be very happy about letting him back into my life. Alan grew up without me. He was used to not having a mother. Gary did a fine job as both parents."

I had to agree wholeheartedly with that. It was also becoming very clear. She tried to forget, and when she couldn't, she stayed away because she didn't want to disrupt the boy's life. Grant would have called it the ultimate form of love.

Leisel got up from the couch. "Gary sent me all kinds of pictures. Come on in here," she said, and I followed her into her bedroom.

She took a key and opened a trunk. She motioned for me to sit down on the floor and look inside. I was amazed. It was filled with carefully pieced together photo albums. It had pictures of Alan for every year of his life. I saw a newborn picture. Gary was cradling him in his arms, and he looked so tiny, but what really amazed me was how young Gary looked. He was not quite seventeen years old.

I went through other photographs. Alan's first birthday, where he had smeared cake all over his face, and Gary, when he kissed him and got cake all over himself, too. Alan was taking his first steps into Gary's outstretched arms. All of his school pictures were there. I saw newspaper clippings of little league games, and also when Alan played baseball and football in high school. This trunk was a living legacy to her son, and it was all that she had of him. I picked up a graduation program and looked at it. This was the graduation that I had taken her to. I opened up the program and read the name, Gerald Alan Shawn III. So, his name was Gerald. I might have known that if I had been paying more attention to the graduation ceremony.

She had put old films that were originally on reels onto discs. She picked one out and popped it into the disc player. I saw films of Alan at about two years old, and Gary was pushing him in a swing. I saw family picnics and outings, and Gary was always right there beside him. There were films of Gary teaching him how to play baseball and football.

Gary told me that he had assumed the responsibility for raising him even though he was very young, and these tapes were a testament to that. Yes, Gary was wonderful with children. He would have made an excellent husband and father for any lucky young woman. It tugged my heart to know that it might have been me.

She reached deep inside the trunk and pulled out an old photograph. "Do you remember this?" she asked.

I looked at the photograph, and my heart jumped. I recognized it immediately. It was taken in the dark with a flash, and it was a picture of me as a teenager, standing by a mailbox without a stitch of clothing on. It had been a dare, and she took this picture to startle me and to get a laugh. I was so irate at the time that I refused to talk to her for two weeks. Her eyes sparkled, and she looked younger and carefree, just as she had before all of her schemes caught up with her. Then her expression sobered.

"Patrick was always an amateur photographer," Leisel said, "and he took most of these pictures and films. Gary always made sure I got copies of everything."

I was in awe of all of the photographs and videos. "It was very nice of him to do this."

Leisel nodded. "This is all I have. I used to think that I'd get married and have other children, but I never did. I wonder how often this happens to other young girls who give their babies away."

"Would you want to see him, if he agreed to see you?"

Leisel's face lit up for a moment, and then the light went out again. "I doubt that he'd want to see me."

"You'll never know unless we ask. He's all grown up now, and he's almost through with college. He can make his own choices now."

"I wouldn't want to make Gary angry."

"You're no threat to Gary now, and he might be willing to set up a meeting between you and Alan. I can ask."

"If only you could," she said. Her voice trailed away before finishing her thought.

56

"**A**bsolutely not," said Gary, when I asked him about Leisel.

"Why not?"

"Because I raised him by myself, without any help from her. She can't waltz back into his life just like that. She never cared enough to be a part of it in the first place."

"You're wrong," I said. "She showed me all of the pictures and videos. She cherished everything she ever had. She probably has a bigger scrapbook than you. She never wanted to interfere with the life you created for him. She sacrificed her feelings for all of these years, and that's what's bothering her now; I'm sure of it."

Gary sighed. "Alan's twenty-two years old. He's serious about a girl, and I believe that he might get married very soon. I suppose he's old enough to make his own decisions about Leisel, but if he says he doesn't want to meet her, then he won't. I'll never try to persuade him. Is that a deal?"

I nodded, and I knew that I had a huge, goofy smile spread across my face. It was good enough for me. If Alan was still anything like the boy that I remembered from long ago, I knew he would agree to meet her.

I went back to Leisel to tell her what Gary's decision was.

"I know Alan," I told her. "He'll agree to see you. You'll meet your son at long last."

Her eyes positively glowed. "How are you getting along with your life?" she asked.

"I'm doing okay. I sold my house, and I'm living in Manhattan right now. I'm still a little fearful of that stalker coming after me again, though."

Leisel leaned forward with great interest. "What stalker?"

"I was threatened in a school building over a year ago. I narrowly escaped from being shot to death in that school."

"My old junior high?"

"Yes," I said, with surprise. "How did you know it was your old junior high?"

"I read about it in the paper. Someone had broken into the school and fired a gun. The police found a bullet in one of the walls. Someone was after *you* in there?"

"Well, I don't know if it was the same people who were after Gary, or if it was the stalker that bothered me before, but one thing I do know: the banister in that school is still as slick as snot. I slid down that banister and got away."

Leisel laughed, but she had a concerned expression on her face. After I left, she placed a call to Grant in Los Angeles.

"Remember when Joy was in the hospital right after you separated?" she asked him.

"Sure."

"There's more to that story than just a bump on the head." She told him a story that curled his hair, and he was on a plane to New York that same day.

57

I was very surprised when Grant and Jo Dell showed up at my door. I hadn't seen Jo Dell for over two years, and I was amazed at how she had grown and how beautiful she looked.

"You missed my graduation," she said.

"You never told me when it would be or where you were," I said. "I knew you were hurt over my divorce from Grant, and I thought that you just needed to work things through yourself. I always hoped that maybe one day you wouldn't hate me."

"I did hate you, and that's why I wanted to stay with Grant. I thought that he was the injured party in all this. But now that I've grown up, I understand that there are two sides to every story. Grant told me that he shared the blame in the divorce, and that he was the one who had the papers drawn up. He said that as much as he loved you, he was standing in the way of you finding out what could make you happy. I'm just sorry that it happened because as I got older, I really thought that you two were made for each other."

"What are your plans now?"

"I've been accepted at Stanford, so I'll be starting next fall. I wanted to take a year off and breathe before subjecting myself to four more years of study. I'm going to visit some of my friends here in New York that I haven't seen for a while, so I'll see you later, okay?" She gave me a hug before waltzing out the door. I stared after her, marveling at what a young lady she had become. I turned and faced Grant. "She looks happy and healthy. She turned into a swan."

"You look better, yourself. How have you been?"

"I've been doing well enough. What brings you here?"

Grant sat on the couch and motioned for me to sit beside him. "I have some information that you need to know," he said. "Have you ever remembered what happened that day you bumped your head?"

I shook my head. "Why? Do you know something?"

"It's considered dangerous to reveal something to someone who's blocking out the truth. The conscious mind wants to shut it out, so it creates a form of amnesia. One school of thought is that if the person is ready to accept it, they'll remember it themselves. It's kind of like when you don't want to awaken a sleepwalker; it's better if they want to wake up themselves. Besides, if I tell you, you probably won't remember it, anyway."

He seemed to be thinking out loud rather than speaking to me, but then I became very confused. Blocking out a memory and being bonked on the head are two entirely different things. Grant had explained that fact to me long ago. "But you said that I had retrograde amnesia, where it's hard to retrieve memories prior to an accident. What you're talking about isn't the same thing, is it?"

He shook his head slowly.

"Do you know what happened?"

Grant nodded. "I received a call from Leisel yesterday."

"Leisel!" I shook my head in frustration. "So, she's keeping yet another secret from me."

"She knew that you should remember it yourself, anyway, because she extracted that piece of information from me in a round-about way. She called to ask if I thought it would be safe to tell you the truth. After what she told me, I knew that you were most likely blocking out an unpleasant memory rather than being affected by a bump on the head. Remember - the doctor said that the bump wasn't enough to have made you become unconscious for an extended period of time."

I remembered. I was becoming fearful, although I didn't know why. Anxiety was creeping in on me. Grant put his arm around me for support and said that he had an unpleasant story to tell, but that I needed to know the truth. He said that the benefits of the truth outweighed the risks of being left in the dark, and events had taken place that would make it impossible to stay in the dark for very long.

"When you broke the window of the school, an alarm was set off and the police showed up on the scene soon after. They found the bullets and saved them as evidence. After speaking to Leisel, I called the police and told them that we thought we knew who possessed the gun. They checked out the lead we gave them, and sure enough, it was a match. I wanted to break the news to you myself because I knew that it would be a shock to you."

"You mean it was somebody I knew?"

Grant nodded his head.

"You mean it wasn't a stalker?"

"No." Grant put his arms around me tighter, as though he could brace me from the shock. "It was Carolyn," he said.

"Carolyn!" I screamed in surprise, and then I shook my head vehemently. "No way," I disagreed.

Grant looked very concerned, but I assured him that I was okay. I pulled away from his grasp, so I could look into his eyes better.

"Tell me why my own sister would want to do anything like that."

"Jealousy."

"Jealousy? That's not possible. Why would she suddenly become jealous? It doesn't make sense."

"She didn't suddenly become jealous. She has been jealous all of her life. Leisel told me that there were several instances that she might have tried to hurt you. Do you remember a horse?"

I reached back into my memory and retrieved Tessie, but I shook my head again. "No, that was just a horse that wanted to get back to her stall and eat."

"Yes, and Carolyn knew that because Leisel rode that horse and it did it to her. Carolyn asked the groom to give her Tessie again, and then she handed the horse to you. Leisel didn't want to make a big issue of it because she knew that you'd be safe going up the path. The horse didn't run until on the way back. She tried to get you to take her horse, but you refused. Before she could insist, or even tell you that the horse might run, you turned the horse around, and it took off. She thought that Carolyn did this to scare you, but not to cause you any real harm. The problem was that it wasn't a harmless prank; people fall off horses all of the time and break their necks, so she was very upset about it. She even refused to come over and visit for a period of time."

I did remember that there seemed to be times that Carolyn and Leisel would have disagreements, and then she wouldn't come around for a while.

"Leisel told me that nothing else happened until a roller coaster ride, and how the amusement park worker said your harness looked like it had been cut. She told me that she thought Carolyn had cut it so that it was hanging by a thread, and the weight of your body tore it more. She said she never saw her do it, so there was no proof, but she told Carolyn in a very subtle way that if people know that others are off balance, maybe they should tell."

I remembered this very episode, and how strange I thought Leisel was to say something like that. It was all making sense, but I didn't want to believe it. I said, "It can still be argued that those were unusual occurrences that could have happened to anyone."

"That's part of the reason that Leisel kept quiet about it. But now she thinks that there wasn't a stalker at all; it was Carolyn, who probably got the idea after John Lennon was killed. The police told her that the phone calls were most likely taped messages that were played into the phone receiver."

With an involuntary shudder, I clearly remembered that this person would say his piece, and how I couldn't deviate him from his message or engage him in a conversation. The voice was high pitched and disguised. "It probably was a recording," I agreed.

"She said after the police questioned everyone, she let out another subtle reminder that maybe a person should tell someone if they suspect that someone else might be mentally ill, and after that, the letters and the phone calls stopped. Carolyn was also questioned by the police, so she was probably scared."

I was starting to believe the story. "She almost succeeded in getting me to kill Brandon," I said. "The voice told me that he was in the house and had decided to kill me, and when the doorknob turned, it was Brandon. I almost shot him. I asked him how he got inside, and he said Carolyn had let him in. She was going shopping, and I knew it, so nothing seemed strange at the time. But, that doesn't explain why I chose not to remember something."

"Leisel said they were supposed to pick you up to go out for lunch. She said nothing had happened for many years, and she thought everything must be okay, but she remembered that sometimes Carolyn seemed to want her as an alibi, so she came early. She watched Carolyn drive up. She said that she didn't notice anything out of the ordinary, but she felt a strange sensation, like an overwhelming sense of intuition. She hid in the bushes and decided to follow Carolyn in. When you opened the door, Carolyn held a gun on you, told you that she hated you, and said that you had taken everything away that she had ever wanted. You backed away from her and fell. Leisel said that she walked in on the whole scene. Carolyn never shot the gun, and you just passed right out. You hit your head on the corner of the wall."

"I've passed out before. Once, when I was ten, Leisel nearly scared me out of my wits, and I keeled right over. And it happened again when you told me that Brandon died." I shook my head with wonder. "I must not have a very strong emotional constitution. But I still don't understand why Leisel would let this go on."

"She loved Carolyn as much as she loved you. She wanted to believe that these things were coincidences as well, especially since these episodes were far and few between. She was lulled into a false sense of security. She loved both of you, and her suspicions were just too horrible to think about. She was also afraid that they'd lock Carolyn up and throw away the key like they did with your father. She went to Thor and told him everything in the hopes that he could either help her himself, or get her the help that she needed. She believed that he did help because there were no more incidences. She was unaware of the school building. After she heard about the school, she called me to see if it was safe to tell you what happened."

"So, they matched the bullets with a gun found in Carolyn's house?"

Grant nodded solemnly.

"What's going to happen now?"

"She's in police custody. They'd like you to go down and fill out a statement and issue a complaint."

"She needs help, not jail."

"Even if you refuse to sign a complaint, the district attorney can press charges, anyway. She shot off a firearm in a public school."

"I don't want her to go to jail," I insisted. "She needs help."

"Maybe we can get her help." He stood up and held his hand out to me. "Come on. I'll take you down there."

I filled out a statement and asked to see Carolyn. When I did see her, she was like a stranger to me.

"I do hate you," she spat at me.

"Why? What have I done?"

"What have you done?" she screamed back at me. "You have taken everything good that should have happened to me. First, you stole my role right out from under me. I should have been Jenny Johnson, not you!"

"They hadn't decided on you. Richard said it was between you and someone else."

"They would have chosen me," she insisted.

I decided not to dispute that point because there was no use arguing with an irrational person.

"You stole every boyfriend I ever had," she said in an accusing voice.

"I never stole anyone from you. I never had a date, myself, until I met Gary."

"No, but after seeing you, they broke up with me. They realized I'd be a poor substitute for you. You were friendly and easy-going, and you learned how because you were an actress. You had special training to respond to situations. I would have had that training myself, if you hadn't stolen my part from me. But what's totally unforgivable is that you stole Grant from me."

"Grant? I was engaged to Brandon when you were going out with Grant."

"But he only went out with me because he couldn't have you. He was in love with you, and when he realized I wasn't like you, he broke it off with me. He might have married me if not for you."

"If you were so angry about Grant, why did you encourage me to marry him?"

"Because he was going to leave. I couldn't stand the thought of him leaving, and then I realized that if he married you, I would at least get the chance to see him. I didn't want to go through my life never seeing him again."

"Did Leisel know that you were in love with Grant?"

"She guessed as much. I was at the reception, and you had just married the man of my dreams. I was crying. Leisel walked in and saw me. She said that she knew what it was like to love someone who really loved someone else. She never got over losing Bill, you know."

It wasn't Bill. It was Gary. Leisel kept that secret buried in her heart for years.

"I couldn't believe that you let yourself be divorced. I was so angry that you let it happen, and the fact that Grant was spending most of his time in California, that I wanted to kill you. When you divorced him, you took away the last shred of anything I ever had." She looked directly at me with narrowed eyes. "I do hate you. I never want to see you again."

"That can be arranged," I retorted, and left.

I saw Grant talking to a police officer. Thor was there too, and Grant had a very angry look on his face. When Grant saw me, he held his hand out to me and said, "I guess we can go. There's nothing more we can do tonight."

"What's going to happen?"

"I'm sure that her lawyer will argue temporary insanity or something."

We left the police station and walked toward our car. Grant was still holding onto my hand.

"Thor is a psychologist," I said. "Shouldn't he have known?"

"He did. He's known for years. The police confiscated his journals, and he had been documenting signs of her mental illness from the time he met her."

"Why would he want to marry her?" I asked, but then I remembered that Thor wasn't interested in her sexually, according to Carolyn. He was interested in analyzing her.

Grant concurred with this. "He wanted to see the whole story play out. He was fascinated by what made a criminal mind tick and what made some seemingly normal people do abnormal things. I always knew this, but I never realized what a sick obsession he had with this."

"After she killed me, he could have had quite a book, couldn't he?" I knew he was creepy.

Grant nodded. "Something like that," he said.

Grant never once mentioned getting back together with me, and I assumed that he had indeed cut me out of his heart with a knife. I asked how he was getting along, and he said that things were going well professionally. He had been nominated for an academy award for his latest film, and he had been given a star on Hollywood's Walk of Fame.

When the doctors had a chance to examine Carolyn, she was diagnosed as having a schizo-affective disorder. She exhibited the four major symptoms all of her life, but they became more pronounced when she reached adulthood. They were never on a grand scale, so they had gone largely unnoticed. Withdrawal, suspicion, dependency, and manipulation were all present. She always had a tendency to withdraw into herself, and she was often aloof when I came home from an extended stay in New York City. She didn't like changes, and she hated anything new. She had no hallucinations, which were common to someone with schizophrenia, but she definitely had delusions. Grant told me that delusions are a fixed false belief, and that she had a fixed false belief that I had taken everything from her.

The D.A. agreed not to prosecute if the court would assign her to be hospitalized in a mental institution. Leisel's worst nightmare concerning Carolyn had become true. It was certainly possible that they might lock her up and throw away the key, but inside, I hoped that she would get the help she needed.

I went home and tried to digest all of what had happened in the last few days. I had been so happy, and I almost had my life put back together again when this came along and knocked all of the wind out of my sails. I found myself sitting in a rocking chair in the den next to the window for hours and hours on end. I stared out the window, and I didn't want to get up. Grant, who decided to stay with me for a few days to make sure that I was going to be okay, became worried, and he brought food and beverages to me while I rocked in the chair.

Sometimes I ate, but most of the time I wouldn't. Sometimes he sat silently next to me, just offering me the support of his presence.

I heard a familiar voice coming from the living room, and I realized it was Gary talking to Grant. Grant was filling him in on all that happened, and I was extremely irritated that they were discussing me behind my back. It was actually a good sign. I hadn't been too concerned about anything. I heard Gary tell Grant that I should go back to work as soon as possible, and that it would help me. I heard him ask Grant if he could see me for a few minutes, and this irritated me, too. This was *my* home, not Grant's. I should have been the one to give permission. I was probably afraid that Grant would tell him that he couldn't see me. I was wrong, because a few moments later, Gary entered the room.

He stooped down beside my chair and took my hand. "This is hard, I know, but you'll get through it," he said.

"I was remembering, you know," I said. "I was remembering all of the good and the bad. I was remembering how she taught me to read, and how she let me sleep in her room because I was afraid of the dark. She was so good to me when Brandon died. She packed all of the things away that might upset me, and she helped me take care of Jo Dell. Then I think about what she tried to do to me over the years. I can't get the image out of my head of how she looked at me with eyes filled with hate. Gary, I feel like someone has died."

For the first time since this whole story unfolded, I began to cry. Gary knelt beside the rocking chair and put his arms around me. I was aware of Grant's presence in the doorway, but when I looked over Gary's shoulder again, he had moved away. When I finally stopped crying, Gary said, "Do you feel better?"

"Whoever said that crying never helps anything was an idiot," I informed him, trying to manage a smile.

"I came over here to tell you some good news. I almost decided to leave it for another time, but I think that after what you've been through, you deserve to have a little good news."

"What kind of news?"

"Alan is getting married, and he'd like you to come to his wedding."

"Alan! Really?" I was suddenly smiling. "I'd love to come to his wedding. When is it going to be?"

"A week from Saturday."

"So soon?"

"Well, I'm about to become a grandfather in about four or five more months. I guess she wants to look reasonably thin in her wedding dress."

Gary told me that Alan came to talk to him about it when he visited us in Missouri. He had been dating this girl for almost two years when she informed him that she was pregnant. Alan was feeling overwhelmed, and he sought out Gary's advice. Since Gary once stood in the same shoes, he was able to empathize with the situation.

Gary stayed a few minutes more, and then he left. So, Alan was getting married! I was in much better spirits. Gary called me two days later to see how I was. Actually, I was doing much better. I finally pried myself out of the chair, and I was taking more of an interest in life. I was eating again, and I was giving more attention to my appearance. I had sat in the same clothes for three days. Grant saw that I was better, and he said that he had to return to Los Angeles because he was about to start filming another picture.

"I'm still a little bit angry with Leisel," I told Gary over the phone. "She knew about this for years, and she did nothing about it. Any one of those things could have caused me great harm. I must be living a charmed life, after all."

"Don't be too upset with her, Joy. She finally had to make a choice in the end, and she chose you."

"You know, I used to think that Leisel was responsible for all of those coincidences. She used to love to get a laugh at someone else's expense. I don't think she has laughed for a very long time now. Have you talked to Alan?"

"Yes, and he's not sure if he wants to make contact with her. He has lived his entire life without her, and he's comfortable with his life the way it is."

"The boy that I knew would have agreed to see her," I said.

"He's not a little boy anymore. He's a young man."

-58-

The days flew by, and soon the day of Alan's wedding was here. He looked so handsome in his tuxedo. I watched the girl walk down the aisle, and I thought that she was very attractive. Small flowers were weaved through her dark brown hair, and she carried a bouquet of red and white roses. I was reminded of my own wedding to Grant because I carried the same colors in mine. Gary held my hand and watched with pride, as his son became a married man.

During the reception, Alan came over and sat beside me at my table. I wasn't sure if it was appropriate to bring this up to Alan on his special day, but I didn't know when I would see him again, so I asked him about Leisel.

He shook his head. "I don't think that I want to meet her. She had absolutely nothing to do with me when I was small. Gary had to be both mother and father to me."

"Maybe you don't know why she did what she did," I said.

I was afraid that I might make him angry, but he patiently sat there and listened to me.

"She was the most fun loving person I ever met. She always liked to laugh, and sometimes she made other people the butt of her jokes. She always had a scheme going on in her head. When she got pregnant, she knew that she had made a mistake, and she wanted what was best for you. She wanted to give you up for adoption, but Gary asked if he could raise you. She thought if she could make herself believe that nothing had changed in her life, then she could go back to being the carefree girl she always was. She tried to think that way for years without success. By the time she realized that it wasn't working, you were old enough to have resented the fact that she wasn't in your life. She decided not to disrupt your life, and in the process, she led a very lonely life full of regrets. She loved you. She went to all of your games and to your graduation, and you never knew it. She never missed any day of yours that would have had any importance to you. Gary sent her pictures, and she has every one of them carefully tucked away in neatly put together albums. She loved you, Alan, but she loved you from afar." I finally paused for a breath.

I saw him nod his head, but I couldn't tell what he was thinking. I saw him sweep the room with his eyes, and then he looked back at me.

"Look," I said. "This is supposed to be a happy day for you. I've said too much as it is. I want you to do what's right for you, and only for you, okay?"

He smiled and asked me to dance.

"You dance very well," I told him. "Who taught you how?"

"My father. He taught me everything I know. If I'm half of the father that he was, I'll be very pleased."

"You'll be a wonderful father. You had a good teacher." I looked over his shoulder, and I saw Leisel making an exit from the room. She had been there. I spoke the truth when I said that she had never missed an activity of any importance, and she certainly wouldn't want to miss her son's wedding.

"Does Alan even know what she looks like?" I asked Gary.

Gary shook his head. "I never had any pictures of her, and I never pointed her out to him. I didn't want to upset him. He was never overly curious about her, and I tried to do things right so that he wouldn't feel the absence of a mother."

"Did you know she was here?"

"I saw her." He decided to change the subject. "Lets dance," he said. "This is my son's wedding."

He took me to dinner that evening at a river café overlooking the Hudson River. The view was breathtaking, and we watched the ships as they passed by in the harbor. "This is beautiful," I said.

He took both of my hands in his. "Joy, you told me to ask when things got back to normal, so I'm asking you once again. Will you marry me? I have loved you for so very long."

"Yes, Gary," I said. "I would be proud to be your wife."

-59-

Andrew called with an offer of a Broadway play. I turned one down before, but he was hoping that I would want to put my troubles behind me and go back to work. He was right; I was more than ready. I was offered the lead as Magnolia in a revival of *Show Boat*. Then he told me my co-star was Grant! He was going to play the role of Gaylord.

"I thought he was going to do a movie."

"He changed his mind. He said he'd rather do this."

"He's probably doing this for me because he thinks that I need to get back to work and stop dwelling on my troubles. I certainly hope that he's not sacrificing a really great role."

"I don't think we have to worry much about Grant's future. It'll only continue to rise, especially after he wins the Academy Award next March."

"Do you think he'll win?"

"Yes, I do. I have a very strong feeling about it."

I called Gary and told him that I was offered a role, and he seemed genuinely happy for me. If he was upset by the fact that Grant was going to be there, he certainly never showed it. We discussed setting a wedding date, and then we decided it would most likely be after the New Year. I had rehearsals and then the actual performances to concentrate on.

I wasn't sure if I was going to feel awkward doing this play with Grant, but he was his usual, friendly self. His celebrity was noticeable, and almost everyone's head turned when he walked into a room, and not just women. He was what one would call a man's man, because he appealed to men as a good, strong actor, and he was a ladies man, because he exuded charm, sexuality, and sensitivity. It was as though a magical air followed him wherever he went. Even the directors and producers treated him differently. Gary had said that Grant would be a star of far greater magnitude than Brandon ever was, and that I never recognized it because I was in such close proximity. Gary was right, I thought, but then, it seems as though Gary was right about most things. One just had to wade through the cynicism to see the truth.

I asked Gary if there were any residual problems with that crime family. He seemed evasive about it, and it frightened me. I didn't know if he was receiving threats, or if he just had invalid jitters.

I had two dreams that night. In the first one, I answered the door. I saw Carolyn, and she was acting strangely. She reached in her purse, pulled out a gun, and held it on me.

"What are you doing?" I asked. "Don't you know it's dangerous to point a gun at someone? It's not loaded, is it?"

"Of course it is, you idiot," she said. "There's no value in pointing an unloaded gun. You are of no use to me. You've taken away everything that ever meant anything to me."

I began to get very scared because I knew that this was no joke. I started to back away. Leisel walked in, and at the expense of her own safety, she yelled, "Carolyn! What on earth are you doing? Put that down now!"

Carolyn was distracted, and I thought for a moment that she might turn that gun on Leisel. I chose that moment to run, but my legs felt like Jell-o. I lost consciousness and fell. Or, maybe I fell and lost consciousness. Either way, I passed out onto the floor.

I woke up and realized that I had just remembered what had happened. I was also told the story, so it might have had some influence over the dream, but I was certain that this was how it had happened.

I also had my recurrent dream. I ran down the stairs and saw an overcoat, trousers, and shoes, but this time I saw something else. The man was extending his arm out towards me, and I was reaching out to touch his hand. I was telling myself to stay asleep and not wake up, but I was also telling myself that, above all else, I must see the expression on this man's face. I woke up anyway, of course, and I was so mad that I started to punch my pillow with both fists. Then I stopped punching. It suddenly dawned upon me that the expression on his face was just as important as his identity. Not only must I know the identity of the man, I must also see the look upon his face.

O pening night was a magical night, just as it was when I performed *Cinderella.* We sang in perfect harmony, and the old chemistry we had on stage was still there. Gary missed opening night because he was busy working on a story, but he promised to be there the next night. He showed me rave reviews in the paper the following day.

"I want to see your review," I told him.

"You will tonight because I plan to be there in the very front row. Don't expect me to go easy on you just because we're engaged," he warned.

Even though we had performed the night before, I still felt like it was the first time. The curtain lifted, and I knew that Gary was somewhere in the audience. Grant was in the opening scene, and I listened with pride as I heard him sing his first song. He always danced better than he sang, and now I wasn't sure which one he did best. I felt the adrenalin rise as I took my cue and walked out onto the stage. Grant and I performed the song, *Make Believe,* and it felt like there was magic in the air. Brandon once said that I had the voice of an angel, and I believed this was the best that I had ever sounded. I felt the familiar electric energy from Grant surging into me, and it made me want to sing out even more. Yes, it was good to be back, and it was wonderful to feel whole.

In one particular scene, the actress playing Julie sang a song about only being able to love one man all of her life. I remembered how Gary said that was a real fallacy, and I ruefully wondered if he would have something cutting to say about it in his column.

At the end of the play, the two once married and now separated lovers were reunited. After the first performance, someone wrote a piece about how good it was to see Bryant and Carlton performing again, and how it would be so wonderful if true love didn't just happen in "make believe."

At the close of the final curtain, we went out to take our bows. Gary stood in the front row giving us a standing ovation along with everyone else. He had a huge smile, but there were tears rolling down his face. Our performance must have affected him, too. I couldn't see very well past the stage, and I thought that I probably imagined the whole thing. It wasn't like Gary to become emotional, especially about something silly like a play. He used to make fun of me for crying at movies.

Gary met me backstage. He hugged me and told me what a wonderful performance I gave. He was going to wait for me to go home with him, but there was a party backstage, and it looked like I was going to be detained for a little while longer.

I finally returned home around two in the morning. I should have been tired, but because of all of the adrenalin flowing through me from the performance, I wasn't at all. I turned on the television set and plopped down in the nearest chair. I thought that I might be able to wind down by watching television. A few moments later there was a "Breaking News" story that flashed upon the screen. The news anchor announced, "A car bomb explosion rocked Manhattan's Upper East side less than an hour ago. Dead is newspaper editor and reporter, Gary Shawn, who gained wide acclaim as a celebrity reporter, and was well known for his public and private conflicts with actress Joy Bryant. The next of kin has been notified, and an investigation is pending."

I gasped as I saw his picture on the screen. All of the blood drained from my face, and my breath was coming in short, shallow gasps. My fingers began to tingle, and I realized that I was hyperventilating. I made an effort to breathe more deeply. I called the police station and they confirmed the news report, but they wouldn't give me more details, other than to say that an investigation was pending.

I couldn't just sit there and do nothing; I had to do something. I jumped into my car and drove over to his apartment. The police were still there, and they had the area sectioned off with yellow tape. I saw the car, and it was ripped to shreds from the blast. I asked a reporter what he knew, and he said that a body had just been removed, and that it was burned beyond recognition. Gary was identified by a piece of jewelry that he always had in his possession, and also from the shoes he had been wearing. His father had given him a gold pocket watch with a chain before he died, and Gary always kept it with him for sentimental reasons. I remembered seeing the watch with him when he came backstage after the play. Amazingly, according to the reporter, there was very little damage to the watch, and absolutely no damage to the shoes, which had apparently been blown off upon impact. I turned away, and I thought for a moment that I was going to be sick right there in the middle of the street.

I returned home and tried to call Gary's home, but there was no answer. I don't know if I expected him to answer the phone and tell me it was all a mistake, or if I thought someone might be there who could give me more details. A few moments later, my telephone rang, but I couldn't bring myself to answer it. I had no desire to talk to any reporter. I just sat there like a statue and stared at the phone while it rang and rang, and then it was finally silent.

I had a very restless night. I paced back and forth in my apartment, and I kept the television on in case any more information became available, but I never did learn any new details. I must have dozed off in the wee hours of the morning because I awoke to the full morning sun. My neck felt stiff from sleeping in the chair. The phone rang again, but I still didn't answer it. I just didn't want to speak to anyone. What kind of statement could I possibly give? That I loved him? That we were engaged, and we were planning to be married? That everyone I ever loved, except for Grant, had died? It wasn't common knowledge, but Gary might have told someone, and even if he hadn't, the news report linked his name with mine. It was only a matter of time before I would be barraged with reporters. I got dressed and left the house.

A few hours later, I found myself walking aimlessly down the streets of Kensington. I no longer lived there, but I wanted to be close to where Gary had been. I later found myself wandering into the graveyard. He wasn't there yet, of course, so I supposed that I was just giving myself a head start on coping with the grief. I remembered how going to the graveyard helped me finally accept the death of Brandon.

The first grave I saw belonged to Kate. I remembered her beautiful red hair, unusual voice, and I thanked her in my heart for helping me find wings on my feet. The grave of Gerald Alan Shawn I was also there, and soon Gerald Alan Shawn II would lie beside him. My heart went out to Alan. This would be a terrible blow to him.

A bench was nearby, and I sat down. Brown leaves swirled around by my feet in the wind, and I absently watched them as they blew by. It was chilly, but I didn't feel it. I didn't feel anything; I was too numb. Memories flooded over me as I began to remember a turbulent and tender relationship that had lasted twenty years. It was as though I could move through the memories like I could thumb through a book, with rapid, vivid pictures appearing on each page. I was aware of someone standing beside me. It was Grant.

"I loved him, you know," I said.

"I know."

"You knew it all along?"

"Yes."

"How did you ever guess?"

He put his hands in his coat pockets and sat on the bench beside me. "I knew that Gary loved you, for one. He protected you from many major things that might have otherwise been reported in a negative way. He called me to come to Maine when you went to the Sanitarium because someone took a picture of you two together, and he thought there might be some negative publicity if I was nowhere to be seen. He also painstakingly tracked me down when you were in the hospital. He told me that you were calling out for me. But the major reason I know that you loved him comes directly from you."

"Me? I used to tell you that I hated him."

"I know, but things didn't add up. Remember I told you that you acted like you had lost something or someone, and that I noticed a kind of sadness about you even when Brandon was alive? Well, you were involved with Gary shortly before your engagement to Brandon. From the things you told me over the years, you broke it off, and you went immediately to work, and then you met Brandon- all in a matter of a few days. You can't love someone one day and stop, just like that," he said, with a snap of his fingers. "You have to work through a period of grief, and you never did. I believe that you truly loved Brandon, but I also believe that you projected all of your feelings for Gary into Brandon, and when Brandon died, you never accepted it all of the way. You couldn't because what you had projected into Brandon from Gary was still alive in Gary. It was only a theory that I had, and maybe I was wrong. You had to find this out for yourself, and it was destroying you. It was destroying *us.* That's why I had to set you free."

So he *had* been analyzing me. He sat there quietly as I continued to watch brown leaves swirling at my feet. Finally I spoke. "Are you here to pick up the pieces again?"

He shook his head. "No. I'm here to let you know that I've received word that Gary isn't dead."

"What?" I gasped. "Gary is *alive!* Are you sure?" I couldn't take any false hope over this one.

"He's alive. I've talked to him."

"Why didn't he call me?"

"He tried to, but he couldn't reach you, and he had to leave rather quickly. These people were trying to kill him, and they thought that they succeeded. The false news report aided him in his escape."

"But, there was a body removed from there. A reporter told me so."

"Yes, there was a body, but it wasn't his. Whoever placed the bomb in the car was most likely the one killed. It probably went off before he was able to get out of the car. Gary was walking up to his car when it happened, and he was the first one on the scene. He knew immediately that someone had deliberately tried to kill him, and what bothered him most was that he planned to take you home in that car, so you might have been blown up too, if the bomb had worked the way it was originally planned. He saw that there was no way to identify the body, so he threw his watch inside the car. He knew it would be identified because he never went anywhere without it. The man's shoes were blown off by the impact, so he removed the man's shoes from the scene and replaced them with his own. He called and asked me to let you know that he was okay."

I finally breathed a sigh of relief. So, he wasn't dead. "What are his plans now?" I asked.

"He said it depends upon you."

"Me?"

"Yes. He was getting warnings to get out of New York City, and he was in the process of making arrangements to move elsewhere, but he must have waited too long."

"He was probably waiting for me to finish the revival run of *Show Boat.*"

Grant nodded in agreement. "He believes that they'll leave him alone, even now, if he'd stay out of New York for a few years. He wants to keep a low profile for now, and he plans to accept a transfer to London. That's where he is right now. If you decide to be with him, you'll have to keep a low profile, too, for an undisclosed period of time. You're an actress; it's in your blood, and he realized last night while watching your performance that it would be unfair to expect you to give everything up. He was going to talk to you about it after you got home from the performance, and then all of this happened. He told me to relay this information to you, and then you can make your own decision."

"I want to go to him," I said.

Grant stood up and held out his hand to me. "I'll take you to him," he said.

I threw a few things into a suitcase and left with Grant. I pulled the first dress out of my closet that I laid my hands on and quickly put it on. I picked out a pair of blue shoes to match the dress, and then I gathered up my luggage. The air was nippy, and I considered wearing a coat, but I didn't want to be encumbered with one. I would send for more of my things once I got settled. Grant made arrangements to have me flown on his own private jet. He handed my luggage to the pilot, and then he walked over to me to say goodbye.

He hugged me tightly, and I realized that he was having a difficult time letting me out of his embrace. His voice was husky. "Take care of yourself," he said. As I stood in his embrace, I felt his strong body heaving as though he were fighting back sobs. I reached up to kiss him, and his face was all wet with tears. I gently pried myself from his grasp and tried to kiss him goodbye, but he rejected me by turning his face away. He looked more angry than sad at this point.

"Goodbye, Grant," I said, softly.

Grant just stood there. He said nothing, and I ascended the stairs to step into the private jet. I was suddenly cold and wishing that I had my coat on. It was insane not to have a coat on in New York right now, even if it was unseasonably warm. I wondered what the weather would be like in London. This time of year, it might be like pea soup.

-61-

I could see that the weather was foggy from the top of the stairs. I paused, and as I did so, the skirt of my dress got caught up in the wind. It billowed out and swished around in front of me, sweeping slightly to the right in the direction of the wind. I could barely see my feet because of the thick fog, and I could only see the outline of my shoes. I was afraid of falling, but I ran down the stairs as fast as I could. I called out, but I knew in my heart he would be at the bottom of the stairs. He always was. I had seen it happen this way so many times before in my dream, and there was no reason to believe it would be any different now.

I flew down the stairs, and I saw the overcoat, trousers, and a pair of shoes. A few steps more, and I saw an outstretched arm. I reached for his hand with mine, and when they finally met, I was pulled into Grant's arms. And he was smiling.

Epilogue

I have thought about this many times over the past few years. I had almost given up the hope of ever knowing the answer to that dream. I never knew if it was just a dream or something that might one day come true. Now I know. I remember calling out in the wind, "Oh, wait! Please! Grant! Oh, my God! Please wait!" I suddenly knew beyond a shadow of a doubt that I wanted to be with Grant. As I ran down the stairs, I hoped that he would still want me. I was terrified that after I finally knew what I wanted, he would reject me in the end. He had done that once before. I was so relieved when I saw his hand reaching for mine, and a smile was spread across his handsome face.

"Oh, Grant!" I said, as he held me tightly. "I love you; I always have, and I just can't go."

"We have things that we need to forgive each other for," he said, when he could finally speak, "and if we can do that, then we'll be all right."

The words of Brandon DeLorrier came flooding back to me. He had said, "We can make our marriage a love so rare; a love that most people never know can exist; one that most people never live to see." Grant and I could have had that kind of love the first time, and now we knew where we went wrong. I couldn't bury the past, and Grant couldn't control the future.

"We can forgive," I said.

"Let's go home," whispered Grant.

"Where's home? Los Angeles?"

He shook his head. "How about Kensington?"

"I sold our home."

"Yes, I know," said Grant, as he removed his coat and draped it across my shoulders. "You sold it to me. I used a proxy, so you didn't know."

I stared at him in extreme surprise.

"I couldn't let you do something that you'd regret later," he explained. "Kensington was the only stable structure you've ever known; the one thing that never changed. That's how I knew where to find you. I knew you would return there." He leaned over and gave me a long, passionate kiss. "Let's go home."

Grant took me home, and we made love as though it were the first time and not the last. This decision wasn't without great pain. I received a letter from Gary a few days later.

Dear Joy,

I understand that you almost had one foot inside the airplane when you changed your mind and ran back down the stairs. I have consoled myself with the knowledge that you didn't reject me, and that you will always love me, but I know in my heart that you love your career more. I believed at first that you would just have to make a choice between Grant and me. I told you long ago that it was possible to love two people at the same time, but one can always make a choice in the end. Well, you made your choice, and whom did you choose? Miracle upon miracles, it was none of the above! You chose yourself. You chose yourself and your career, and you will always make that choice in the end.

I tried to help you piece your life together so things would not look so muddled. I showed you what the real world is like, and I helped you release Brandon from your heart. Grant should be eternally grateful to me. I only hope that the choice you made is going to be worth the price you paid for it. You paid for it with my soul, and with a part of your own.

Love, Gary

Grant did win the Academy Award the following March, and I accepted a few more roles on Broadway. So far, I haven't achieved the heights that I always dreamed I would in terms of my career, but there's always hope.

Grant and I were remarried on April ninth. We decided to keep the same anniversary as though we had never been apart for two-and-a-half years, although in all honesty, I would never go back and change them if I could. I try not to make myself crazy by looking back, but sometimes I do. I still remember this day with great clarity.

Vera Wang created my off-white, pearl studded, satin wedding gown. I had the traditional something old, something new, something borrowed, and something blue. My wedding rings were something old. I wanted to keep the same set that I had. Music was playing, people were dancing, champagne was flowing, and Grant looked like the happiest man in the world. He looked even happier than the first time we were married, if that was at all possible. He was laughing and talking and dancing with everybody. Reporters and paparazzi were milling around everywhere, but I didn't care as long as they didn't get in the way.

Jo Dell was there, and I could tell that she was truly happy for us. She hugged Grant around the neck and said, "Congratulations, Daddy," and then she hugged me.

Leisel also came to our wedding. She still seemed tired, but she looked much better than she had in the past few months. I asked her if she had seen Carolyn, and she said that she had. She still wasn't well enough to be released, but some of the paranoia seemed to be controlled by drugs. She still hated me, so Leisel told me that it would probably be better if I didn't see her for a while. I had no idea how she would take the news of my remarriage to Grant.

As Leisel was sitting at the table, I saw Alan approach her and sit down. Her eyes widened in surprise. They talked for several minutes, and then I saw him motion to his wife. She had a new baby in her arms. He took the baby from her, and then he handed it to Leisel. She cradled the baby in her arms and smiled at him. I had a chance to see Alan later, and I told him that it was a very nice thing for him to do.

He said, "When you and I talked at my wedding, I saw a woman with red hair sitting at a table all alone, and I realized that I had seen her several places before. I never thought anything about it. It was like bumping into the same stranger all of the time and never realizing it. I wonder how often we all do that. I searched the room for a familiar face, and when I saw it, our eyes connected and I knew who she was. I saw her get up and leave immediately, as though she were afraid. When I saw her again just now, I realized that I was hanging on to some unresolved anger, and I had to let it go. She has a granddaughter now, and she should be a part of our lives if she wants to."

He was holding the baby, and I got a good look at her. She was newborn, probably less than two weeks old. She had brown hair, green eyes, and she definitely looked like a Shawn.

"How's your father?"

"He's doing well, under the circumstances. He likes London, and he says he plans to stay there. He's returning to London tonight."

"Returning? Where's he now?"

Alan pointed to a table situated in the corner of the room. "He has never missed a day of any importance regarding you, either."

I walked over to his table, unsure of what reception I would get, but he stood up and smiled at me. He reached for my hand. "I wrote some pretty nasty things in that letter," he said. "I hope you'll forgive me."

"I've forgiven everything else you've written about me with your poisoned pen, so there's no reason why I can't forgive you now."

"Well, you have to understand that it was written by someone with a large wound in his heart. It wasn't fatal, though. I had the same wound once before."

"I hope that we won't become enemies again. I want to remember us like we were in Missouri and London."

"So do I. I'll always hold a special place for London in my heart. Maybe that's why I escaped there."

We stood there, facing each other, and there was a sudden, awkward silence between us. I heard the music playing. "Dance with the bride?" I asked, just as I had fifteen years before.

"I'd love to dance with you," he said.

As Gary and I danced, I looked around the room. Leisel was sitting with Alan again and holding the baby. Grant saw us dancing, and I wondered if he felt any jealousy, and then I realized that he really didn't. I was watching the happiest man alive as he talked with his friends and shook hands with them at our reception. Gary was right long ago. All Grant wanted was for me to choose him. I could have been dancing with Don Juan, Prince Charming, or even Brandon DeLorrier, and it wouldn't have mattered to Grant one little bit. I chose him.

As we danced, Gary said, "I sincerely hope that you'll be very happy, Joy."

I looked up at him. "Since when have you ever been sincere about anything in your life, Gary Shawn?"

"Oh, I don't know," he said. "I've always been sincere about you."

"Oh, Gary," I said softly. I put my head on his shoulder as we danced, and my heart broke for him.

Printed in the United States
66533LVS00002B/202-228

9 781589 394629